Sharon Gosling is the author of multiple middle-grade historical adventure books for children, including *The Diamond Thief*, *The Golden Butterfly*, *The House of Hidden Wonders* and *The Extraordinary Voyage of Katy Willacott*. She is also the author of YA Scandi horror *FIR* as well as adult fiction including *The House Beneath the Cliffs* and *The Lighthouse Bookshop*. Having started her career as an entertainment journalist, she still also occasionally writes non-fiction making-of books about television and film. Titles include *Tomb Raider: The Art and Making of the Film*, *The Art and Making of Penny Dreadful* and *Wonder Woman: The Art and Making of the Film*.

Sharon lives with her husband in a very small village on the side of a fell in the far north of Cumbria.

Also by Sharon Gosling

The House Beneath the Cliffs
The Lighthouse Bookshop
The Forgotten Garden
The Secret Orchard

SHARON GOSLING

The Forest Hideaway

London · New York · Amsterdam/Antwerp · Sydney/Melbourne · Toronto · New Delhi

First published in Great Britain by Simon & Schuster UK Ltd, 2025

1 3 5 7 9 10 8 6 4 2

Simon & Schuster UK Ltd, 1st Floor
222 Gray's Inn Road, London WC1X 8HB

Simon & Schuster Australia, Sydney
Simon & Schuster India, New Delhi

www.simonandschuster.co.uk
www.simonandschuster.com.au
www.simonandschuster.co.in

The authorised representative in the EEA is Simon & Schuster Netherlands BV, Herculesplein 96, 3584 AA Utrecht, Netherlands. info@simonandschuster.nl

A CIP catalogue record for this book is available from the British Library

Paperback ISBN: 978-1-3985-3888-7
eBook ISBN: 978-1-3985-3889-4
Audio ISBN: 978-1-3985-3890-0

Typeset in Bembo by M Rules
Printed and Bound in the UK using 100% Renewable Electricity at CPI Group (UK) Ltd

Between a tree and a
house, choose the tree.

Carlo Scarpa,
Architect, 1906–1978

Turn your cloaks
for fairy folks
are in old oaks.

Traditional saying

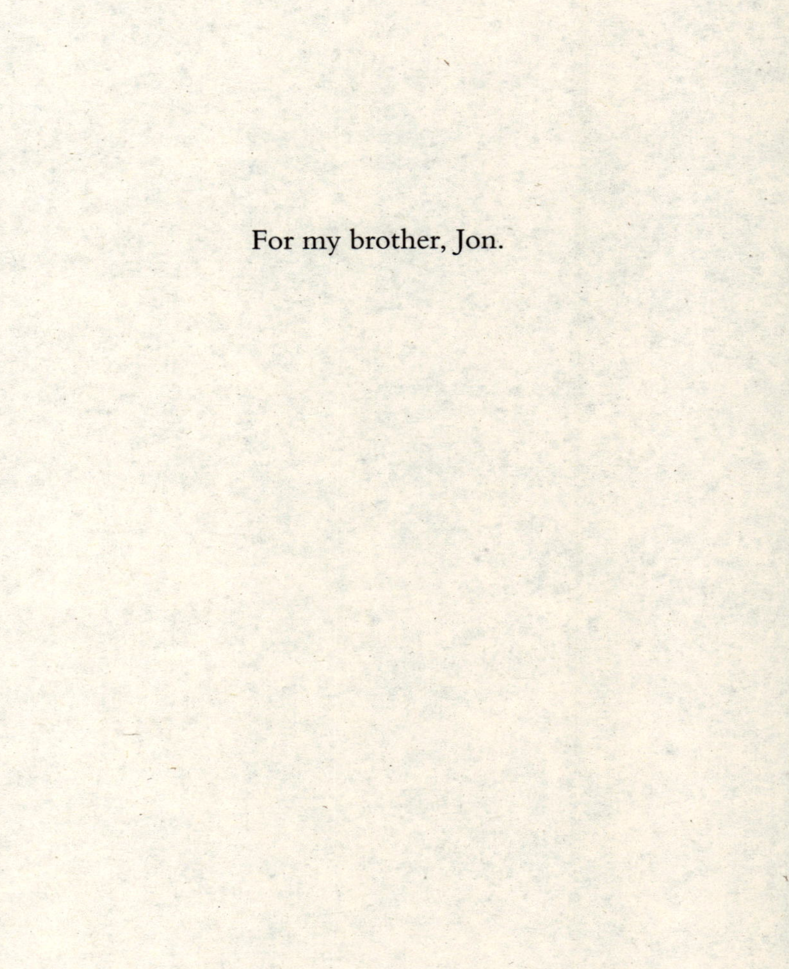

For my brother, Jon.

One

The late-spring day was pleasantly warm. Sunlight glinted through the dense forest leaves to dance in dappled patterns across the tangled understory. Owen Elliot ran one hand through his short dark hair, irritation rising as his patience continued to fray. He was leaning against the bonnet of his silver Hilux, parked beneath the shade of the last line of trees before the cleared grassland sloped towards the overgrown ruins of Gair Castle. He'd been waiting here for the past ninety minutes, having arrived in good time for a meeting that was now running an hour late.

'I *know* I'm going to be late to pick her up. That's why I'm calling. Would you rather I'd left it until she'd got to the school gate before you found out I wasn't going to make it?' he snapped into the iPhone clamped to his ear. On the other end, Tasha continued to berate him.

'No, I can't just leave!' Owen continued. 'You know this is—' He paused to listen as the distant sound of a car engine disrupted the gentle susurration of forest leaves. It drew closer. 'I think she's here. I've got to go. Tell Hannah Daddy's sorry, all right?'

Owen hung up before he heard Tasha's parting shot. He was pretty sure he knew what the gist of it would be, so there was really no point in listening further. He wondered for a moment when the last time was that they'd said goodbye to each other with anything other than bitterness. The answer eluded him, which was depressing enough in itself.

He caught the glint of moving metal through the trees and gritted his teeth. An hour late! Who did that? The woman hadn't even bothered to call to let him know she was still coming. All he'd received was a stark text message that had read, *On my way now. Please wait.* No apology for wasting his time. No explanation. Just six words that sounded like an order rather than a request. To say Owen was annoyed was an understatement, but he also couldn't afford to just blow off this consult. Maybe the woman knew that he didn't have a choice but to put up with her rudeness. On the other hand, perhaps she simply didn't care.

His irritation only grew when he got his first clear glimpse of the car making its way towards him. It was a scarlet BMW M4 convertible, its soft top down to make the most of the sunny day. Owen had already assumed that the woman who had called him – introducing herself, in a cut-glass southern accent, as the intricately named Saskia Tilbury-Martin – had a decent amount of money. She had, after all, bought a castle ruin and its extensive land outright. But the sight of the car made his blood boil. It was easily worth double the tiny flat that he'd struggled to buy for himself and Tasha when he'd got out of the army and that they were still stuck in now.

Some people, he thought, as the car bumped closer, *don't know they're born*.

The car purred to a stop beside him and he saw a woman inside with a long sheen of thick dark hair spread over her shoulders, wearing sunglasses against the glare. Once she was out of the BMW, Owen took in the perfectly tailored navy skirt suit that had probably cost more than he'd ever spent on clothes in his whole life. This outfit was finished by a pair of sleek black heels that he imagined might look at home in a cocktail bar but had no business on a potential building site.

'Owen Elliot?' she asked, coming towards him with her hand outstretched. Owen wondered if he could get away with keeping his where they were, rammed into his pockets.

'Ms Tilbury-Martin?' He grasped her fingers briefly; her skin was cool, her nails cut short.

'It's Saskia. I do hope you haven't been waiting long?'

He returned his hands to his pockets and stepped back. 'Over an hour.'

The woman snatched off her sunglasses, gaping at him. 'What? But why?'

He frowned. 'Our meeting should have been at two o'clock, and I was a little early. Force of habit.'

'Two o'clock?' she said, in horror. 'That's not right! It was 2.30pm that we were supposed to meet. I know I'm half an hour late, but it's no more than that!'

He stared at her. 'No, the meeting should have been at two. Check our emails, you'll see I'm right.' Owen didn't need to check himself – if there was one thing he excelled at, it was timekeeping and sticking to a schedule.

A frown creased the woman's brow as she glanced towards Gair. She looked as glossy as an image on a magazine cover. 'No, I'm sure that's not right, because—' Her eyes widened and flashed up to meet his again. 'Oh, god. I'm so sorry. No, you *are* right!'

I know I am, Owen thought, though he kept his expression impassive.

'I messaged as soon as I got out of the meeting I was stuck in this morning, but I thought I'd only be thirty minutes late at the most.'

Owen nodded. 'Well, I need to get going, so . . .'

'Right, of course. Give me just a second.' She reached into the car's tiny back seat, pulling out a red hard hat and a pair of black wellies, which she swapped for the heels. 'I assume you've done a walk-through?'

Owen grabbed his own hard hat and they set out towards the ancient building. Walking side by side, the top of her head barely came up to his shoulder.

'I have. It's . . . an ambitious project.'

She laughed. 'That's probably the kindest description I've heard yet. Most people just tell me I'm mad and that it's impossible.'

'It's not impossible,' Owen said. 'But it will be . . . tricky.' *Not to mention exorbitantly expensive*, he thought but did not say.

They reached what remained of the outer walls of the castle. It was far more ruin than recognizable building, aside from the single wide tower that was still standing, a twenty-foot-high crenelated structure that looked like something straight out of a fairytale. Time had conspired to separate it from the walls that had once connected it to the rest of the castle, turning it into a monolith. They paused to look through the gap in the three-foot-thick stone. Owen had already done this once before, on his lone walk-through during his long wait for Saskia's arrival, but he was still surprised by how intact it was inside. Ancient stone stairs built into the walls led up to a wooden floor that, though very old, was remarkably solid and therefore must be more modern. It had clearly been maintained more recently than the rest of the place had been inhabited. He knew from his earlier explorations that the steps continued up to further levels, culminating in the roof, from where there was a spectacular view over the forest. Owen thought again of his daughter. Hannah would revel in playing make-believe here.

'My aim isn't to return Gair to how it would have looked when it was first built,' Saskia told him. 'It seems to me that a building like this is able to convey far more about the history of the place as it is now. What I want to do is preserve it with all the decay intact, but made liveable.' She indicated the jagged gap in which they stood. 'This, for example. My idea is to shore up this wall just as it is, make good those edges, and use a glazed passageway to reconnect it to the rest of the structure as a way to recreate how it would have originally existed. The same with the other breaks in the outer walls that are still standing.'

Owen turned and looked over the rest of the ruin, thinking about the scale of what she was suggesting. 'You're thinking open-plan inside, then?' he asked, because one of these fissures was twelve-feet high by his reckoning, beyond the span of a single storey.

'Yes, with a series of mezzanines around a central courtyard,' she said, as they walked on. 'I want to do as little as possible to the existing structure, and what is done will be invisible.' She glanced up at him. 'That's what I told the planning committee.'

Owen nodded. That would have been his next question. 'You do have planning, then?'

She drew in a long breath. 'Yes. It's been a tricky road, but yes. I'm at the stage where I can actually start, but . . .' She hesitated.

'But?' Owen prompted.

She gave a dark little smile. 'Like I said, most people take one look at this place and tell me I need my head examined. Then I explain my ideas and they run a mile without even looking at the plans. That goes for contractors, too. I've lost count of the number of meetings I've had exactly like this.' She raised her eyebrows at him, as if challenging him to have the same reaction as all those other building contractors. 'To tell you the truth, Mr Elliot, you are pretty much my last hope. It's become clear that no one else will take it on.'

Owen looked up into the sunlight cascading over the space

through the non-existent roof. 'You know I haven't had much experience working on projects of this scale?'

'Well,' she said, in the tone of a verbal shrug, 'there aren't really that many contractors who *do* have the experience, are there?'

'How did you get my number?'

'The last contractor I spoke to suggested you.'

'Who was that?'

'Colin Seabrook.'

Owen snorted. 'Can't imagine Seabrook ever doing me a favour.'

'No,' Saskia agreed. 'He wasn't. He told me that if I was really going to do this, I'd need someone either mad or desperate, and that you were both.' She made a face. 'Since I'm apparently both of those things too, I thought it was worth giving you a call. Besides, you're local to the area. You'd be working with local materials and in an environment you know. That's important to me.'

He made no reply to that, looking around the site instead, trying to visualize what she had said she wanted to do with the place from her brief description. He had to admit there was a charm to the idea that went beyond its challenging scope. Gair had a good feel to it, an atmosphere conjured out of the beautiful spot in which it stood, yes, but out of something else, too. It was that peculiar kind of magic that some places had. Owen could imagine this as a complete building, whole again, enclosed against the elements and yet still almost exactly as it was now. He thought he understood where Saskia was coming from, because he wouldn't want to change it either, other than the obvious need to remove the large oak tree that had sprouted in the centre of the crumbling building. But he could also see why all the other contractors had run a mile. It was entirely probable that every step would present some individual difficulty that neither Saskia, Owen nor whichever architect she had employed on the project had considered.

'Have you got the architect's plans with you? I'd like to take a look at them,' Owen said.

Saskia sighed. 'I'm sorry, I haven't. I rushed out this morning and managed to leave them behind. My head was all taken up with the meeting I've just been at. I can bring them to our next meeting.'

Owen had to admit that he felt a certain amount of excitement at the thought of being the one to give this place a new lease of life. But he could already imagine what a nightmare it would be to have to answer to Saskia Tilbury-Martin. Thus far she'd proven herself to be unreliable and disorganized. On a project like this, when she was the one calling the shots, that was a recipe for disaster.

'I need to think about it,' Owen told her.

A flash of disappointment crossed the woman's face. 'All right,' she said. 'But I need to get moving on this project, and if you won't do it, I'll be forced to start looking further afield. Please don't keep me waiting too long for an answer.'

Owen's irritation returned. That was a pretty rich demand given how long he'd been stuck here waiting for her this afternoon. 'I'll be in touch very soon,' he replied and turned back to his car.

'You don't want to do more of a walk-through now? I can tell you what I'm planning, even if you can't look at the physical plans.'

He made a show of looking at his watch. 'Believe me, I've had plenty of time to look around. I need to get on.'

She nodded. 'Well, thank you for coming, at least.'

He nodded a goodbye and made his way back out of the ruins, leaving her there. When Owen reached the outer wall he turned back to see her staring up at the oak tree, a small figure dwarfed by the weight of the history rising around her.

'What's your gut feeling, then?' Stuart asked, wrapping one large hand around the pint that Owen had set down before him. 'Not worth it?'

Owen settled in the seat opposite his best friend with a frown. 'I like the idea of the build. But I have a feeling she's trouble waiting to happen.'

'You don't think she's good for the money?'

'It's not that. She's dripping with cash. The whole thing could tank and it probably wouldn't even make a dent in her bank balance.'

'Jesus.'

'Yeah. But I can see her being a real pain in the arse. She seems like an airhead with a lot of money and what she thinks is a brilliant idea. When has that ever been a good combination?'

'I dunno, man,' Stuart said. 'Works for Elon Musk.'

Owen gave a half-hearted smile and downed a good portion of his pint in one gulp.

'Look at it this way,' Stuart went on. 'It sounds like she's going to do this whether or not you say yes. So if she's going to throw some of her bottomless millions at a project, you might as well stand there with a bucket. Right?'

'Right,' Owen said. 'Except that if it fails – which is more than likely – it'll be my name attached to a massive dud for ever.'

Stuart acknowledged the point with a nod. 'Sure, there is that. But there's the other thing, too.'

'What's that?'

'It's not as if you've got a lot of choice really, is it? Not after—'

'Yeah, yeah,' Owen muttered. 'You don't have to say it.' He tried his best to avoid being reminded of his last disastrous project; he didn't need Stuart to bring it up now.

There was a brief silence, in which both men contemplated their pints.

'Is she hot, then?' Stuart asked after a moment. 'This Saskia Titberg-whatsit?'

'Saskia Tilbury-Martin,' Owen corrected his friend. 'And what kind of a question is that?'

Stuart shrugged. 'Just asking.' He took out his phone. 'I bet she'll come up if I google her. Posh girl who owns a castle, she's probably been on the front of *Hello!* or summat.'

'Don't,' Owen said.

'Why not? You should look her up anyway, see what she's about. Due diligence, innit?' Stuart said, as he tapped away with his thumb, then squinted at the screen. A second later he whistled. 'Well, I can see why you didn't want to answer the question.'

'What do you mean?' Owen asked.

Stuart held up the phone. On it was a photograph of Saskia, her dark hair pulled up and back into a twisted style that had been woven with small white flowers. The shot was of head and shoulders, and so it was possible to see that she was wearing a pale green dress with silky off-the-shoulder sleeves that left her shoulders and neck mostly bare. She was sitting in sunlight, looking at the camera with her chin slightly raised as if in challenge, perfectly made-up, with her high cheekbones looking almost carved out of marble. She was undeniably beautiful, not that Owen had needed photographic evidence to tell him that.

'That photo was taken at her cousin's wedding, apparently,' Stuart said, looking at the screen again. 'Bloody hell, she's married to an actual duke. Rod Stewart was at their wedding!'

'Who, Saskia?'

'No, the cousin.' Stuart studied the phone again for a minute. 'Yeah, they've obviously got money.'

Something else that Owen hadn't needed to be told. 'Put it away,' he told Stuart. 'If she's hanging out with celebs, anything you're going to find about her online is going to be bollocks.'

Stuart shoved his phone back in his pocket and then downed the last of his pint. He grabbed Owen's empty glass, getting up to get them another round without saying a word.

'How's Tasha?' Stuart asked, when he came back.

Owen rubbed a hand over his face. 'Don't even ask.'

'That good, eh?'

'It's just a bad patch, that's all,' Owen said. 'It's the money worries. If we could catch up with our mortgage arrears, it'd all smooth out. All marriages have ups and downs, right?'

'Don't ask me,' Stuart said. 'I've avoided it like the plague for a reason.'

Owen's phone rang, and he pulled it out of his pocket expecting it to be Tasha, as if their mention of her had prompted her into calling to find out where he was. He'd not gone home before meeting Stuart in the pub, wanting to avoid the inevitable row that would be waiting for him when he did. The number, though, wasn't one he recognized.

'Hello?'

'Owen? It's Sas.'

He drew a blank. 'Sorry?'

'Saskia Tilbury-Martin,' the voice clarified.

He glanced up at Stuart. 'Saskia.'

'Look, I just wanted to follow up from earlier,' she said.

Owen glanced at his watch. Almost 9pm, and the woman thought it was perfectly normal to be calling someone about work. Didn't bode well, did it? She was obviously used to having people at her beck and call, no matter the hour.

'I don't mean to press you, but I really do need an answer.'

'Look,' Owen said. 'It's going to take—'

'So I thought I'd offer you something that might make the decision easier,' she went on, as if he hadn't spoken. 'How does ten thousand pounds up front sound?'

'I . . .' Owen's mind went blank for a moment. 'What?'

'I understand that there are difficulties surrounding the project that make it a tricky proposition to throw in with,' Saskia said. 'I'm offering ten thousand pounds as a retainer, up front before any work has commenced, in the hope that this act of good faith will encourage you to overlook any worries you might have.'

'I . . . right,' Owen said, thinking about the mortgage arrears, how that amount of money would wipe them out. He could finally get Hannah a Switch, too. She'd love that. 'I . . .'

'You don't have to say yes right now,' the woman on the phone went on. 'Or no, for that matter. But perhaps you could call me tomorrow? I can have the cash in your account within the day.'

Owen rubbed a hand over his face. Who was he kidding? There was nothing more to think about. Saskia Tilbury-Martin might be a nightmare, but it wasn't as if she'd be on site every day, was it? And when she did visit – well, he could put up with a lot for ten thousand pounds in the bank tomorrow.

'Actually,' he said, dropping his hand, 'I have thought about it. And I'm going to say yes.'

Two

Saskia decided to push the boat out and celebrated the outcome of her call with Owen Elliot by ordering a pizza, directly to her small Carlisle hotel room. When it arrived, she sat cross-legged on the single bed with it, her iPad propped up in front of her so that she could Zoom her best friend with the news.

'Oh, come on, you could have treated yourself,' Vivian scolded her gently. 'Just this once.'

'What's wrong with pizza?'

'It wasn't the pizza I was objecting to,' her friend told her. 'There's woodchip on those miniscule walls, I can see it from here. Is that a single bed? And what on Earth is that *noise*?'

Saskia pushed herself to her feet, picking up the tablet and manoeuvring between the room's curtains to reach the window. The evening was warm, so she'd opened it to let in some air, but doing so had let in the sound of the festivities going on in the street below, too.

'I'm on Botchergate,' Saskia explained, tipping up the screen so that Vivian could see the throng of people milling about beneath her window. 'Friday and Saturday nights, the council closes the road so that none of the drinkers get mown down.'

'Bloody hell,' Vivian said, as Saskia retreated back into the room and snagged another slice of pizza from the box on the bed. 'Looks like they're set in for the night.'

'Yup,' Saskia mumbled, around a mouthful of food. She was starving, having not eaten since very early that morning. She tended to forget basic things like that in the face of anxiety.

'You're okay, though?' Vivian asked, a look of concern crossing her face. 'Not tempted to go down and join them?'

'Not even slightly,' Saskia assured her friend. 'And there isn't even a mini bar in this room, so really, you don't need to worry.'

'I do, though,' Vivian said. 'About you, all the time. You know that.'

Saskia put down her pizza and wiped her mouth on the scrap of napkin that had come with the box. 'I know. And I'm lucky that you do. But I'm fine, I promise.'

'I should think so, what with all that cash in the bank,' Vivian said, pushing the conversation towards sunnier subjects. 'Still not tempted to jump ship and buy an island in the Bahamas or something instead? I could be your house-frau . . .'

'Nope,' Saskia said, 'not going to happen. Even if I end up putting every stone at Gair in place with my own hands, I am staying here until the job is done.'

'I knew that's what you were going to say,' Vivian said. 'Tell me about this guy you've found, then. You really think he's the one?'

'Well, he's the only one who's said yes,' Saskia said, 'and he was pretty much my last resort so from that point of view, definitely.'

Vivian frowned, lifting a glass of wine to her lips. 'You know, that doesn't sound one hundred per cent like a match made in heaven.'

Saskia sighed. 'Well, we got off on the wrong foot because I was an hour late, thanks to the bloody bank and okay, I admit it, *maybe* a touch of my own stupidity,' she said. 'Plus, I turned up looking like I spend all my days sitting in board meetings painting my nails, which probably didn't help. He definitely wasn't impressed.'

'Pfft,' said her friend. 'Even if that were true to begin with, I bet he changed his mind once he'd seen your sketches for the site.'

Saskia pulled a face. 'He hasn't seen them yet.'

'Why not?'

'Because I wanted him to say yes to taking the job, and I was pretty sure that given his mood when I finally turned up, if I'd also told him that *I* am the architect, he probably would have turned tail and ran.'

This had been a ruse that she'd intended to employ at every one of these meetings, but in the end only Owen had been interested enough to ask to see them. Not that Saskia didn't have confidence in her designs for Gair, but she had wanted the contractor to be more invested in the project before revealing her greater involvement. Sure, she'd told Owen that she'd go to someone else, but there really wasn't anyone else. What she hadn't told him was that she'd already contacted a couple of the big nationals and neither of them had been interested. Not enough profit to be made in a single difficult build out in the wilds of Cumbria, compared to a field full of cookie-cutter commuter homes closer to a big city.

'Trickery and subterfuge,' Vivian said, tipping her glass towards the screen in salute. 'I approve.'

'Hmm,' said Saskia. 'Maybe I did learn a thing or two from my mother after all.'

Her phone chimed. Saskia reached across the bed to her bag to get it and saw her mother's name on the screen.

'Speak of the devil . . .'

'Is that her?' Vivian asked.

Saskia deleted the notification and tossed the phone back on the bed. 'It is. She's been emailing me all day. My inbox is full of rants I have absolutely no intention of reading, and even less of answering.'

Vivian hid her little frown behind her wine glass.

'What?' Saskia said.

'Nothing. I just wish you had more support, that's all.'

'We can't all have parents as perfect as yours,' Saskia said, lightly. 'Anyway, we've already established that I've got you.'

'Yes, but I can't be there with you all the time,' Vivian pointed out. 'Which means you're going to have to rely on this . . . what's his name? Owen. You really think he's going to be up to the job?'

Saskia considered. Owen Elliot was a big guy, with the closed-off air of someone who didn't trust easily. If she'd been pressed, she'd have said he was ex-military – he had that air of bodily self-control. He'd annoyed her a little, actually, because she could tell he'd been assessing her as much as the site, and he'd found her wanting as so many others had. But Saskia supposed that she had only herself to blame for that, given the circumstances of their first meeting.

His record also wasn't, as he'd pointed out himself, a particularly auspicious one. But if she was going to judge people on their past and levels of relevant experience, she'd have to discount herself from the job out of hand, so she could hardly dismiss him because of his short and choppy track record. Besides, there had been the way he'd looked at the site. She recalled again, now, his stance as he'd glanced up into the sunlight, in the exact same way Saskia herself did every time she visited Gair when the sun was out. He hadn't interrupted her as she'd talked about her plans, either, the way plenty of the other contractors she'd brought to the site had. He'd actually listened and seemed to be really taking in her words. He'd also impressed her because though he might have needed the job – really *needed* it – he hadn't rushed to an answer, which spoke to the fact that he was a man that gave everything due consideration.

'I think so, yes,' Saskia said. 'I just hope I didn't annoy him even more by calling him so late.'

'Nah,' Vivian told her. 'He's probably out on the town anyway, isn't he? He's probably down there in that street beneath your window right now, chugging back the Stellas with all his builder mates.'

'Don't be a snob, Viv.'

'I'm not saying that in a bad way,' Vivian said, blithely. 'You know I like a bit of rough.'

Saskia shook her head. 'You are a nightmare.'

'I'm not just any nightmare, darling,' her friend declared. 'I'm *your* nightmare. Right, I've got to go. Early start for me tomorrow.'

'Me too. I'll be back with the car mid-afternoon, I should think, assuming the M6 isn't a car park.' Saskia's own knackered Land Rover had given up the ghost days ago and she hadn't been able to fix it in time for this trip. Bless Vivian for lending her the BMW – Saskia hadn't wanted to dip into the castle money to hire a car, but she couldn't get to Gair by any other means.

'No rush. I know you'll take care of it.'

'How's my good boy pup?' Saskia asked.

'An angel, as always. He'll be happy to see you, though.'

They ended the call with Saskia feeling a rush of affection for her friend. They had known each other since childhood. Vivian was one of the few people who had stuck with her through everything, and then some. It was a debt Saskia knew she'd never truly be able to repay, and one that Vivian would not even acknowledge.

*

Saskia woke the next morning with the knowledge that she had secured a contractor and, with the final planning permission agreed and the money she'd been fighting to take possession of for so long in her account, could finally begin the Gair build. She lay still for a moment after opening her eyes, taking it in. There had been many times, some very recently, when she'd thought she would never reach this point. She swung her legs out of bed and stretched, smiling. There was so much to do, and she couldn't wait to get started.

Her first task was to make the drive back to London, return Vivian's car, pick up Brodie and get her own vehicle back on the road. The sun was out, and so Saskia opted to put the BMW's top down again, blasting down the M6 with the wind in her hair and the radio on as loud as it would go. After a little traffic, she reached Vivian's flat in Fulham as the city was heading towards a bright weekend evening. Saskia found London's bustle a strange contrast after the rural quiet of the northern borderlands, Botchergate notwithstanding. She dropped off the car, hugged her friend a swift hello and goodbye, collected an ecstatically happy golden retriever and headed for the Underground to make her way south to her own stomping grounds in Brixton. She was hoping to make it to her trusted local garage before it shut for the night.

Kebba, Saskia's go-to choice when her beloved old Land Rover needed assistance, was still in the shop when she called through the half-open barn doors. Kebba's workshop was in an old railway arch near Brixton market and was one of the few in the area that still dealt with traditionally built mechanical engines. If you wanted an honest-to-God mechanic with grease up to his elbows that could tell what was wrong with your motor just by the kind of knocking sound it made as it revved, this was the place to come. The Land Rover was so old that it didn't even have a digital petrol gauge, let alone an on-board computer.

'Saskia,' the big Gambian greeted her easily, waving her over the threshold as he saw her. 'You nearly missed me, girl. That old heifer of yours playing up again?'

'Pretty sure it's the head gasket,' Saskia told him, as Brodie showed Kebba the same kind of love he'd lavished on his owner. 'Can you give her a total service at the same time, though, just to make sure there's nothing else likely to go any time soon? I'm going north shortly with the trailer and I need to know I'm not going to get stranded on the motorway.'

Kebba nodded, rubbing the affectionate dog's ears. 'Sure, I can do that. How long have I got?'

Saskia considered. There were a few loose ends she had to finish up with locally before she could make the move. But she wanted to get up there as soon as possible. 'How long do you need?'

'Say a week, in case there's something else to fix,' Kebba told her. 'Drop her in tomorrow – I won't be open, but I'll be here. I'll get on her first thing Monday.'

Saskia and Brodie left Kebba and picked up a few supplies in the market before making their way home. Once there, Saskia shut the door behind them with a sigh of relief. She loved the energy of south London, but she wouldn't be sorry to leave it behind in exchange for the leafy quiet of her distant corner of Cumbria. Everything that had happened in her life – and for a long time none of it had been good – had occurred in the south, between the neat lawns of Sevenoaks, Kent, the chichi bars and boutiques of London, and the last hold-out corners of gentrification-resistant Brixton. It was time to start a new chapter, in a new place, so far away that she could perhaps finally put the darkest of those times behind her for ever.

Saskia's phone chimed again. It was her mother.

She ignored it.

Three

If Owen had thought that the injection of Saskia's money would solve all of his problems at home, he was sorely mistaken. It had made the bank happy, but that was about it. If anything, Tasha now seemed even more distant, her temper with him running shorter and shorter. It was almost as if whatever issues there were between them were deeper than a shortage of cash, but Owen didn't want to think about that. His own parents had split when he was small, and thereafter he'd barely seen his dad at all. Owen had no intention of his own marriage and relationship with his daughter going the same route.

He threw himself into preparation for the build, instead. He still hadn't seen the actual architect's plans, though the surveyors who swarmed the site with their equipment had them as digital documents. Saskia had said she would bring the physical blueprints with her when she next visited the site, which was fine by Owen. He'd never really gelled with computers and always preferred looking at properly scaled plans if he could, at least prior to the build starting. Instead the two of them had spent a lot of time talking on the phone, which, if he were honest, Owen wasn't that keen on either, but it was necessary at this stage. Saskia had assured him she'd be at Gair the following week and would bring the architect with her so that the first on-site consultations could begin.

Meanwhile, Owen set about with basic preparations around the site. Gair had been standing open to the elements for centuries, and the vegetation had taken over. It would all need to be cleared, and a better access road provided for the heavy plant machinery. Owen also took Stuart up to Gair to help him mark out the extent of the site. The two men had worked together a lot, and Owen appreciated Stuart's skill. He'd asked Saskia to hire him at a fair day-rate as their first site worker.

'Bloody Nora,' was Stuart's first response as they arrived. 'Mate, this isn't a castle. This is a pile of stones.'

'It's not that bad,' Owen said, as he climbed out of the truck and flipped down the tailgate to get at the equipment stowed in the back. In truth, Gair looked particularly beautiful this morning. They'd arrived early, and though the air was already warm, dew still glinted on the leaves, reflecting the sun's rays. The sky was a piercing blue flecked with ethereal wisps of white cloud, and the view beyond the castle's walls rolled unbroken into the horizon, a patchwork of rising and falling fields and forests tinted many shades of green. There were far worse places to work, and something in Owen rejoiced at the idea that this was where he would be spending the majority of his days for the next year at least.

The two men began by marking the work site's immediate perimeter, which would run in a square ten meters beyond Gair's outer walls. This brought them close to, but not into, the forest on the northern edge. Dense and tangled, it was clear that the trees here had not been planted in the uniform lines of the fir plantation that covered the slope in the opposite direction, and that did not belong to Gair. Branches were tangled with elaborate drifts of moss, the warm air filled with the smell of rich mulch. There was an odd quality of silence that emanated from the densely packed boughs, an aggressive sort of peace of an intensity that didn't bother Owen, but that clearly unsettled Stuart.

'I don't like it,' his friend muttered, as Owen pounded in a stake and Stuart wound the guideline around it. 'Where are the birds?'

Stuart was right: among the thick understory, even the birds were silent. Owen wondered why. Just their presence, perhaps. The wildlife up here wouldn't be used to seeing humans.

'It feels as if something's watching us,' Stuart added, as he fed out the line and Owen counted off the measurement. 'As if something's lurking in there.'

Owen remained unperturbed, but as they tied off the first guideline and began on the second, which required them to feed out the line at right angles in a way that brought them even closer to the treeline, he too got the sense that they were not alone. He paused, looking into the forest, but the shadows were too thick to make out anything more than the haphazard patterns of moving leaves.

'See?' Stuart challenged him. 'Weird. I don't like this place. There's something not right about it.'

Owen turned away, still feeling that sensation on his back, a primordial mammal sense of being stalked.

'Not going to start playing silly beggars with me, are you?' he teased Stuart. His friend possessed the strange dichotomy from which some soldiers suffered: hard as nails in the field, oddly superstitious once away from it. 'Scared the fairies are going to whisk you away?'

'You can laugh all you like,' Stuart retorted, 'but there's some right strange stories about these parts. Got to have come from somewhere, haven't they?'

They continued working, joking with each other, but Owen had half his attention elsewhere. The feeling of being watched hadn't diminished. He'd become convinced that there actually *was* someone watching them work. He and Stuart had been deployed together and could read each other's thoughts in their smallest gestures, and with a slight lift of his chin and a quirked eyebrow, Stuart told Owen he was of the same mind. They continued their banter, lulling their observer into a false sense of security, keeping an eye on their periphery until—

'All right, that's enough,' Owen said, loudly, spinning on his heels.

They caught the slightly paunchy, middle-aged man

crouched behind an elder bush in the act of snapping a photograph of them on his phone. The interloper jumped at their sudden attention, scrambling backwards as he tried to shove his phone in his pocket.

'What are you doing?' Owen demanded, as he and Stuart strode towards him.

The man eventually found his footing and, despite looking as if he wanted to turn tail and run, stood his ground with his hands on his hips.

'I'm gathering evidence,' he spat, angrily. 'You should be ashamed of yourselves.'

'What are you talking about?' Owen asked. 'This is private property. You don't even have any right to be here. You're trespassing.'

'And you're destroying history!' the angry man declared, stabbing a finger at the fractured walls of Gair, rising behind them. 'We won't let you get away with it. You might have paid off the planning committee, but if you think that's the end of it, you're going to get a shock!'

'Get out of here,' Stuart said, 'before we call the police.'

'*You* call the police?' spluttered the man. 'That's rich!' He shook his phone at them. 'I've got evidence!'

'Evidence of what?' Owen asked, mystified and irritated in equal measure. 'Two builders marking out a site with tape? What's that supposed to prove?'

'That you're planning to destroy a site that should be protected,' said the trespasser. 'Well, we won't let it happen. We'll make sure that Gair remains as it is – untouched and available for everyone to enjoy for generations to come, not just the one per cent who think money means they can do anything they want.'

'Gair isn't available to everyone,' Owen pointed out. 'Private property, remember? Anyone coming up here is trespassing.'

'The local community has been walking up here for years,' the man insisted. 'It's not right that suddenly they're not allowed to do that. We want free access to the castle to continue. It's our right.'

'It really isn't,' Owen said. 'Especially not now. This is now an active building site. The next people I catch up here I'll have prosecuted, do you understand?'

The man was fairly apoplectic by this point, a violent red flush rising up his neck from the collar of his sweater. Owen was slightly worried he was about to have a stroke. The man raised the camera again.

'Tell me your name,' he demanded. 'I want to know your name.'

'I am Owen Elliot,' Owen said, as he looked straight at the camera. 'I am the foreman and main contractor at the Gair Castle site. Google me if you want to get in contact, my phone number is online. And just to reiterate, anyone caught trespassing up here from now on will be prosecuted to the full extent of the law.'

The man dropped his hand, still clutching the phone, and looked at Owen with pure loathing. 'You'll regret crossing us,' he spat. 'You might have bought your way to this happening, but we've got friends high up, too. People who actually care about the history around us.'

'Oh yeah?' Stuart asked. 'Go on, get out of here. Some of us have to earn a living.'

The man looked as if he might say something else, but Stuart took a threatening step forward. Owen laid a hand on his friend's arm to warn him back, but it was enough to end the altercation. The man stumbled off through the undergrowth, heading down the hill. Owen watched him go until he disappeared from sight and wondered where he was headed. There was probably a legitimate footpath down there somewhere – this landscape was criss-crossed with them. That was fair enough, but it didn't entitle those who enjoyed using them to stake a claim to every patch of land they took a fancy to exploring. There was plenty of open access fellside and woodland for that.

'Excellent,' Stuart muttered. 'That's all we need – a bunch of nutjobs stirring up trouble. Has Lady Muck mentioned anything about local objections?'

'Nope.'

'What about what he was saying, about paying off the planning committee to get permission to build? That likely, do you think?'

Owen frowned. 'I don't know.'

He didn't want to think he'd committed himself to working on a project that had been given permission to go ahead by nefarious purposes. However annoying the trespasser had been, this *was* a historical site. Maybe it was a little surprising that Saskia Tilbury-Martin had managed to get permission to go ahead with her ideas. What was it she'd said when she'd first showed him around the site? *That's what I told the planning committee.* Something like that. It hadn't struck him as an odd thing to say at the time, but now he wondered if he'd missed the context. Did it mean she'd found a way to circumvent any objections, even if her methods hadn't been legal?

He turned and looked up at Gair. She'd talked him into believing that she wanted to preserve the site as it was as much as possible. Had she been playing him, after all, in the same way she'd played the planning committee? *The one per cent who think money means they can do anything they want.* That's how the trespasser had described Saskia, and hadn't that been Owen's first impression of her, too? And if she had done this – if she had bribed her way into getting to do what she wanted with Gair – where did that leave him? He'd taken her money and used a fair chunk of it already.

'I'll call her later,' he said, his heart sinking in his chest.

'Maybe we should think about barriers to close off the site properly,' Stuart suggested. 'Stop any more like him being able to get in.'

'We'll probably have to,' Owen agreed. 'I didn't think we'd need it, what with the place being so remote. For now, let's finish getting this perimeter marked out.'

Saskia answered the phone out of breath when Owen called her later that day. He imagined that he'd interrupted her at whatever achingly hip gym she and her ladies-who-lunch friends frequented. He tried not to let a mental image of her neat frame in a tight gym outfit settle in his mind. He'd been spending far too much time with Stuart.

'Oh God,' she groaned, when he told her about the run-in he and Stuart had had that morning. 'I thought I'd managed to shut the Historical Society up for good.'

'Apparently not,' Owen told her. 'He made some pretty bald assertions about how you managed to get planning permission on the site.'

'Like what?'

'He accused you of bribing your way to a rubber stamp, basically.'

Saskia gave a brief, bitter laugh that he didn't understand. 'Yeah, right.'

Owen felt he had to ask. 'You didn't . . . grease the wheels at all, then?'

'Of course I didn't,' she said, clearly outraged. 'Owen, what do you take me for? Do you really think I'd risk a build this intricate and extended on a dodgy planning committee pass? I'm not a complete idiot.'

Owen was a little confused by his disappointment. Her outrage wasn't morally based but rested in her not wanting him to think her a fool. On the one hand, her pragmatic reason for not arranging a bribe helped convince him that she definitely hadn't. But her discounting the moral reason for not doing so just made him think badly of her.

'Right,' he said, vaguely.

'I've done everything I can to prove that I don't intend to

cause any damage to the site,' she went on, oblivious to his distaste. 'At this point they don't have any objection to fall back on other than indignation that I'm closing off the site, and they don't like that at all. I'm sorry you had to put up with their bluster.'

'If the guy I met this morning is anything to go by, these people didn't seem the type to give up easily,' Owen said. 'Is it really just bluster? They don't have anything legally solid that could disrupt the build further down the line, do they?'

'They really don't,' she assured him. 'Their first objection, besides me touching the castle remains at all, is that they are absolutely convinced there's a Roman ruin somewhere within the footprint of the castle – that Gair was essentially built right over a fort that has since been lost.'

Owen's heart plummeted. If that was true, and it was proven, it would completely derail the build.

'Why do they think that?'

'Some of the society's members are detectorists, and over the years they've uncovered quite a few finds in the area. Even a couple of gold coins, so I've been told.'

Owen's heart sank even further. 'Around here? That's pretty convincing evidence that there's something down there, isn't it?'

'I guess you could look at it that way – they certainly do.'

Owen rubbed a hand over his face, agitated. 'You can't just ignore something like that,' he told her. 'Certainly the planning committee shouldn't have!'

'They didn't,' Saskia told him. 'Trust me, Owen, there's

nothing down there. Whatever's been found in the past is all there is to find.'

'How can you be so sure?'

'Because when I realized this was going to be an issue, I employed a LiDAR crew to survey the site,' she said. 'The only thing buried within a quarter of a mile around the castle are Gair's foundations and the remains of a couple of outhouses that definitely aren't old enough to be Roman.'

Light Detection and Ranging was a remote sensing method that used a pulsed laser to measure variable distances to an extremely accurate degree. The equipment was usually mounted in a helicopter, aeroplane, or, as was increasingly more likely, a drone, allowing its operators to fly over a site and map it both above and below ground level with pinpoint accuracy. The laser was so penetrating and so accurate that, as long as the land had not been disturbed by later earth works, it could produce digital images of layer upon layer of substance and structure, building an astonishingly accurate computer image of what was below the surface.

Owen was flabbergasted. The technology was phenomenally expensive to access. 'You paid for LiDAR? Seriously?'

'I was lucky,' Saskia told him. 'I had a friend whose partner at the time was working on a film that needed to do a LiDAR scan of Derwent Water so they could model it digitally for their effects department. Since the equipment was going to be in Cumbria already and my site was comparatively small, I managed to do a deal to tack my scans on to the flight. It was still an insane amount of money to spend, but I thought it was worth it to head off the harassment I was getting, and to prove to the planning committee I had no intention of avoiding responsibility.'

'Right,' Owen said, his head spinning. 'And there's nothing there?'

'Nothing at all. I'll bring the scans with me when I come up, you can see for yourself.'

'Then how can these people still be convinced there's something down there? I assume they've seen the scan results?'

'Oh, they have. But since there wasn't a member of the society on the LiDAR flight, they're convinced that the map I showed them is fake, and that I'm hiding the evidence showing that the remains are down there so that I can destroy them without disruption.'

'You're joking.'

'I wish I was. Like I said, at this point, I don't think their objections have anything to do with wanting to preserve archaeological remains. It's become a battle of wills because they don't like that I'm exerting my authority over a site that is legally mine.'

'All right,' Owen said. 'Well, it would have been nice to know this could be a problem.'

'I apologize for not telling you sooner,' Saskia said. 'But I really thought this issue had been laid to rest. I think it has, to be honest. What you saw this morning was bluster with nothing to back it up. We might be in for some annoying protests, but I can't see it being any worse than that.'

'That in itself could be enough to cause delays,' Owen pointed out. 'Maybe it would be better to try to talk to them?'

'I have, repeatedly,' Saskia said, brusquely. 'They don't want to listen. I don't think they've ever even bothered to actually look at the plans in place for Gair, probably because nothing I could propose would make them happy beyond handing over the deeds to them.'

Owen sighed. 'Maybe there's another approach,' he said. 'Let me think about it.'

'Fair enough, but I don't have much patience for them anymore, to be honest,' Saskia said. 'I'll see you in a few days. I'm picking the truck up on Tuesday and plan to be in Cumbria by Wednesday afternoon.'

'All right,' Owen said, envisioning her driving a spanking-new Defender off the forecourt with a stab of envy-driven rage that he tried to swallow away. 'By then we will have started clearing the site.'

Four

Saskia's arrival back at Gair coincided with the delivery of the site office and canteen. She sat behind the wheel of the Land Rover and watched as the cargo containers were winched into position one by one from the back of a flat-bed truck. Gair had changed significantly since she'd last seen it, and she was impressed with how much preparation Owen Elliot and the crew he had assembled had accomplished. It had been two weeks since she'd made the call that had brought him onto the project, and in that time the castle had acquired the look of a real building site, which was thrilling and daunting in equal measure.

Since the run-in with the member of the Historical Society – from Owen's description, Saskia had a hunch this had been Arthur Wheeler, with whom she'd had dealings before – they had agreed to erect an additional perimeter. The first was on the now-cleared access road. Gates and a fence had been positioned where both Owen and Saskia had parked the first time they'd met. The second, inner perimeter had been constructed with a six-foot-high steel fence positioned ten meters from the castle walls to allow room for heavy machinery, with access gates to the north and south. Owen had cleared a pad for the shipping containers outside this fence, not far from where Saskia's Land Rover now sat idling inside the main entrance gates. She could see Owen, dusty hard hat in place, directing the crane operator as they were manoeuvred into position. There were more men on site now, something else that they had discussed over the phone. Owen had taken on ten permanent workers and contracted them for a six-month period to begin with. Each was on a day rate that was paid weekly. The edges of Saskia's pool of money had already begun to evaporate, and there would be more workers needed as the work expanded. Of course this was inevitable, but the sight of that vast figure depleting, however slowly, made anxiety gnaw at her gut. She'd established a separate works bank account and was diligently accounting for every penny. It was what her grandparents – and her father – would have expected.

Saskia watched as the second container was finally put down beside the first, and one of the men stepped forward to cement its steel feet onto the blocks they had erected. They would stay there until the conclusion of the build: one a work room and office for Owen, and the other a break room and shelter for the workers. There were already two Portaloos standing under the trees at the forest's edge.

With the containers in place, Owen turned and saw her waiting. He said something to the man beside him, who nodded, and then he began to stride towards her. He had to come a little closer for her to see the frown set on his face. It deepened as he glanced beyond the car to the trailer she was hauling, on which stood her cabin. She wound down her window and he headed for it.

'Can I help you? This is private property.'

'Owen?'

Saskia saw the tiny double-take he did and realized he hadn't recognized her at all. She remembered how different she'd looked at their first and only meeting and supposed that wasn't surprising.

'Saskia.'

She indicated through the windscreen at the activity before her. 'It's looking good.'

He nodded, hands on his hips. 'We've got most of the clearing done now. There's just the tree we discussed on the phone.'

The oak tree in question had sprouted and grown directly within the castle walls. Owen had relayed to Saskia his plan for how to remove it, but she had told him not to touch it until she got there.

'I'll take a look as soon as I've set this down,' Saskia said, referring to the cabin. 'I'd like to put it as far away from the work site as possible.' She leaned forward, looking around him towards the trees that ran along the eastern edge of the property. There was a semi-circle in the canopy, a small clearing cut into the forest's edge. It was a good distance from the perimeter fence. The office and break room would be out of her sight there, on the other side of Gair's exterior walls. 'That looks perfect,' she said.

Owen stepped back as Saskia pulled around him and slowly headed for the patch of earth she'd identified. She glanced in her rear-view mirror to see one of the other men approach him with a question. Owen shook his head and raised his hands, shoulders lifting in a shrug. A bubble of nerves rose in Saskia's stomach.

This is your site, your build, your project, your land, she told herself. *They might not like it, but they'll have to lump it. Besides, where else are you going to go?*

She parked up, backing the trailer in beneath the shade of the trees, putting the cabin at an angle so that the front door wouldn't be directly visible from the site. Then she climbed out of the Land Rover and checked for stability. It was fine – the ground was firm and level. It was the perfect place to set a tiny home on wheels.

'Come on, boy,' she said, opening the back door of the Land Rover to let Brodie out. He'd been so good on the long journey up. 'Let's face the music, shall we?'

Footsteps sounded on the ground behind her, and she turned to see Owen and with him a man that she assumed to be Stuart Mackey, his friend and the first man he'd employed. Saskia hadn't met him, but Owen had been up front about their relationship when he'd hired Stuart, which she appreciated, and if they worked well together then she was fine with his choice. Now, though, she could tell the guy was looking her up and down as he approached, and she wondered what he saw: wondered what Owen had told him to expect. She raised herself up a little, trying to give herself more height.

'You must be Stuart,' Saskia said, stepping forward and holding out her hand, taking the initiative before Owen had a chance to introduce them. 'I'm Saskia. It's nice to meet you. The site has come on leaps and bounds already, I'm impressed.'

Stuart offered a cocky grin as he shook her hand, just a little too hard. 'Nice to meet you, Miss Tilbury-Martin.'

'Like I told Owen, it's just Saskia. Otherwise every conversation will take twice as long as it needs to, won't it?' She looked at her foreman. 'Shall we do a walk-through? I can look at this tree.'

Owen put his hands on his hips and looked past her at the Land Rover, as if he thought someone else might suddenly materialize from the empty passenger seat. 'I thought the architect was going to be with you today? Is he going to arrive soon? We've reached the point where I can't do more until we discuss the plans.'

Saskia lifted her chin and looked him in the eye. '*She's* here, Owen. *I'm* the architect.'

Owen Elliot's eyes widened slightly in surprise, and then darkened as the muscles in his face went taut. He didn't look happy, but then she hadn't expected him to be.

'You're the architect?'

'I am.'

'This is literally the first time you've mentioned that.'

'I'm aware. Does it make a difference?'

He was furious; she could tell just from looking into his eyes. He stared back at her, and Saskia could see the cogs turning in his head. Presumably he was talking himself out of yelling at her outright.

Someone nearby cleared their throat in the tense silence.

'Well,' Stuart said, 'I'm going to go and check on the break room. The tables and chairs came earlier, the guys can load them in.'

He walked away, back towards the main site, whistling in a studiously nonchalant way.

Owen took a step back and turned away from her. 'You deliberately didn't tell me this until I'd already agreed to take on this project,' he said. 'Why?'

'Because I know I didn't make a good impression on our first meeting and I thought – correctly, by the look of it – that knowing you'd have to work with me throughout the process would put you off.'

'You lied to me to get me to agree to this.'

'I didn't lie. I just left out this detail.'

'This is why I haven't seen the plans yet, isn't it? Because your name is stamped on them. A lie of omission is still a lie!'

'And prejudice is prejudice. I'm not going to apologize for circumventing it to reach the right outcome,' Saskia told him, crisply. 'You've got a chip on your shoulder where I'm concerned. I don't know why and frankly, I don't care. You don't have to like me for us to work together, we just have to respect each other.'

He made a scoffing sound in his throat. 'Respect! You think this is showing respect?'

'I think this is me doing what I had to do to get things done, a skill I have perfected over many years and the reason you have a job right now. So why don't we get on with what we're both here to do?'

'And what if I refuse? What if I say I'm done?'

Saskia shrugged. 'Sure. You can do that. Walk right now, if you like. You can just repay the ten thousand pounds you've already taken from me. Minus fourteen times the day rate for services already rendered, of course. You'll find I always pay my dues, Owen.'

He shook his head, rage clear in the tense set of his shoulders and arms. 'You're a real piece of work.'

'Yes,' she agreed. 'I am. So, what's it going to be?'

'I don't really have a choice, do I?' he said, through gritted teeth.

'There's always a choice,' she told him. 'It's just that some are far easier to make than others. Why don't you send the rest of the men home for the day? It's past three already. I'll pay until close of day. Then you and I can talk and look at the plans.'

Owen Elliot looked as if he wanted to pick her up and hurl her over the Land Rover's roof, and she had absolutely no doubt that he was physically capable of doing just that if he chose, but instead he turned his back and stalked away. Saskia watched him for a minute. Then she took out her keys and walked up the trailer's steps. Once inside, she shut the door carefully behind her and leaned back against it, taking a deep, steadying breath. Brodie sat on her foot, looking up at her with anxious eyes.

She took a few minutes to collect herself and feed Brodie, then gave her faithful companion a pat before leaving him inside the cabin. By then, most of the workers' cars had already left the parking area. Stuart was the last to go. He and Owen appeared to be in animated discussion as she locked the trailer door. Then Stuart got into his car and pulled out in a rush of churned-up dust, beeping his horn loudly as he went.

Owen stood with his back to her, staring at the space where his friend's car had been, as if considering getting into his own and driving away too. Saskia went to the Land Rover and took out the large poster tube that had been resting on the back seat, slamming the door a little harder than usual as she closed it to warn him she had reappeared. Then she began to walk towards him. By the time she reached him, Owen had turned around. There was still tension in his face, but at least the raw anger she'd seen before had lessened. They didn't like each other – that was clear. They just weren't going to gel, that was all. But then, Saskia was used to being at odds with people.

As she drew closer she held up the tube. 'Let's go into your office, shall we? You should at least take a look at these.'

Owen nodded and together they went to the container he'd picked as his own work space. While they had been talking, the men had pushed the sparse furniture into the space, though it hadn't been arranged. Not that there was much to fuss over anyway – a basic desk, a couple of plastic chairs, a narrow set of drawers on castors. There would be no power to the bulb hanging overhead until they connected up the site's generators.

Neither of them sat down. Instead Saskia went to the table and held up the tube, looking at Owen. 'May I?'

He snorted slightly and waved his hand. She opened the tube and pulled out the rolled papers within – sets of her detailed plans for the site and printed scans of the LiDAR imaging, as she'd promised. These she passed over to him.

'There,' she said. 'As you're no doubt asking yourself what else I've *lied* about, take a good look at those.'

Owen barely looked at her as he took the scans and unrolled them, holding them up to take them in. Despite his anger, he seemed fascinated by the contours that had been revealed by the laser pulses. Meanwhile she unfurled her overview of the site and spread it across what was now his desk.

Saskia waited patiently as Owen studied the LiDAR imaging. Eventually he looked over the top of it and met her eye, before dropping his gaze to the table. Silently he rolled up the scans and moved to look at her design for the site. He said nothing, but she could tell that his attention was fully focused. He studied each quadrant of the vaguely square castle in turn. She could tell immediately the moment that he saw the most unique aspect of what she wanted to do with the site. He glanced up at her, then dropped one forefinger to the paper.

'That's the tree we've been talking about.'

'Yes.'

'It's . . . *inside* the building?'

'Yes. Well, inside the courtyard that's inside the building.'

He blinked and frowned, studying the plan again. 'That's insane.'

'Is it?'

Owen looked at her again. 'Of course it is. It's an *oak* tree. It's not even halfway done growing yet.'

She nodded, sliding out another plan, this time an intricate cross-section of part of the roof. 'That's why I've designed a glazed atrium that will specifically allow for the tree's expansion. And it'll be hinged, too, so that it can be opened from the ground floor.'

He took the cross-section that showed her revolutionary design for a roof, shaking his head. 'An entire tree inside a house? It's going to reach through more than one floor.'

'I know. The plans take all of this into account, believe me. I've spent months consulting engineers and looking at other examples. It's possible.'

Owen looked at her. 'It'd be a hell of a lot easier – not to mention cheaper – to just cut the thing down.'

'That would be easier,' she agreed. 'But I told you, I want to preserve Gair as it is now. The oak tree is part of that. I don't have permission to remove it anyway, it's protected.'

He shook his head again, as if not sure what to say. 'It's going to be difficult to accomplish.'

'Yes. But then, I've always liked a challenge.'

He dropped the plan on the desk so that it instantly rolled up on itself again. 'How can you be so flippant?' he asked. 'This project keeps getting crazier. It's like you just came across this place in a photograph online and drew a dream house around it, like a little girl.'

'Take the plans,' Saskia said, refusing to rise to the bait. 'Check my figures, talk to the engineers. I'll show you the 3D rendered model I've built and you can watch the animation of the atrium roof at work. Then tell me how *flippant* I am. This is a good design, Owen, and I'm a good architect. I've put more work into this than you can possibly imagine. I'm not playing around, and the next time you call me a little girl I'll be less inclined to forgive you for it.'

He crossed his arms, jaw set again, but Saskia saw his gaze drawn back to the plans on the table.

'Yes, it's going to be difficult, but you already knew that,' she went on. 'I think you're still interested. I think that you're maybe even a little excited about getting to work on a project like this. Let's face it, it's not as if anyone else is going to give you this chance, is it?'

'You're right,' he said. 'Under other circumstances, I'd be champing at the bit. I *was* champing at the bit, right up until the moment you revealed I'd have to actually work with you on a day-to-day basis to make it happen. Because so far all you've proven is that you're a smooth liar with a lot of money. And I'm honestly not sure I could work with that, however much I wanted to be part of the project.'

'Look,' she said. 'We don't really have to interact that

much. We'll do what we have to together, when we have to, and the rest of the time we'll remain civil and stay out of each other's way. We don't have to like each other to rebuild Gair, Owen. We just have to want the same thing. Take the plans. Look at them overnight. Then come back here tomorrow ready to get stuck back in.'

He stayed silent, and for a long moment Saskia was worried that he would actually turn and walk out. She'd gambled that Owen's own needs and interest in the project would overcome any reticence he felt about working with her, but maybe she'd underestimated just how much he disliked her. Then he leaned forward and picked up the plans, rolling them up to fit them back in the tube.

'Don't take this as a done deal,' he warned her. 'At best you've got a fifty-fifty chance. And if there's anything else you're not being up front with me about . . .'

She held up both hands. 'You know everything now. I promise.'

He eyed her with deep suspicion, as if he didn't believe a word she said. But Saskia supposed she couldn't blame him for that.

Five

'You should see this thing she turned up with,' Owen said to Tasha later that night. They'd had dinner and put Hannah to bed, and now he had spread the Gair plans over their small square dining table. 'Talk about a designer shed. It looks like a mini house on wheels. The square footage probably isn't much different to this place.'

Tasha said nothing in reply, her back turned to him as she moved around the open-plan kitchen, making herself a drink. She had to be careful not to let go of the cupboard doors as she shut them, for fear of them banging too loudly and waking up their daughter.

'I bet it cost about as much as we paid for this place, too,' he went on, shaking his head. 'And all so she doesn't have to mix with the hoi polloi when she's on site. Me and the boys have got to make do with a draughty shipping container and a load of plastic chairs that look as if they came out of a village hall fire sale. Talk about how the other half live.'

Tasha finished making the tea and set a mug down in front

of him before leaning back against the sink. 'Would you want her to share with you and the boys?'

'Not in a month of Sundays.'

His wife shrugged. 'Probably just as well then.'

Owen sighed. 'Although if she did have to hang out with us, she probably wouldn't be around as much. I don't want her there all day, every day. If I'd known she was going to be a permanent fixture, I'd never have said yes to the job in the first place. She's a nightmare.'

'I know,' Tasha said, both hands wrapped around her mug as she stared down at her tea. 'You've said.'

Owen felt a prickle of annoyance. 'Oh, I'm sorry, am I boring you? Excuse me if I want to talk difficult matters over with my wife.'

A silence followed, in which the kitchen tap made its slow, languorous drip to remind Owen of something else he still hadn't fixed. There was something gathering in the air, and he felt the tension knitting together between his shoulder blades. He thought it was another argument until Tasha looked up from her drink and Owen realized that had just been wishful thinking.

'Look,' she said, softly. 'Owen, we need to talk.'

He set his jaw and leaned back in his chair, hands flat against the table, palms pressed against Gair's rough edges.

'Don't worry,' he said, in an effort to head off whatever this was at the pass. 'I'm not going to quit. I can't, I know that. We need the money, and I couldn't pay back what she's already given me even if I wanted to.'

'It's not about that.'

'Then what is it about?'

Tasha took a deep breath. He could see how tight her grip was around the mug – tight enough to turn her knuckles white. 'This isn't working,' she said, still in that soft voice.

'What isn't working?'

She made a sound in her throat, as if it should be obvious to him, when it really wasn't. 'This. Us!'

He crossed his arms and saw her eyes flicker across the gesture, but he didn't uncross them – couldn't now, even though she'd pointed this out before: how defensive he got in every conflict, how he closed down immediately, how difficult it was for her to speak to him without it having to be some sort of full-frontal attack to get him to see what she meant.

'All right,' he said, trying to make amends. 'Then how do we fix it?'

Tasha smiled a little sadly, and she wasn't looking down at her tea this time but directly at him, and Owen realized with a pang that shot straight from his throat to his heart and lodged there, pulsing, that there was nothing left to fix.

'We can't,' she said, still in that tone of voice, as if she were talking to Hannah when she had a fever. 'Owen, we've tried. I know you have, and I really have, but we just keep going around in circles and at some point we both have to admit that it's *just not working*.'

Owen's mouth had run dry. He pushed himself to his feet, leaning heavily on the table, eyes blindly tracing the measured lines on the plans. 'But things are going to be better,' he said. 'We're back up to date with the mortgage. We'll be okay for the next year, at least – however long it's going to take to get Gair up to Lady Muck's standards. I'm going to do a good job on the place, I promise you that, so that when it's done I'll be able to choose what I do next.'

Tasha made an exasperated sound in her throat and turned to put her mug down on the counter beside her. 'It's not about the money, Owen! A relationship – a good one – is about more than whether or not we can pay the bills.'

'I know that,' he snapped back, 'but now that's sorted we can work on everything else, can't we? We can go back to the way we were, when—'

'When what?' Tasha asked, sharply, swinging back around to face him. 'When you were on deployment and I never saw you? Or when you were home and we realized that we really didn't have much in common?'

He stared at her.

'When was the last time that we really spent any time together, Owen?' she asked. 'Just us, enjoying each other's company because we wanted to?'

'We've got Hannah! We do things together with Hannah. Like when we went down to York for the weekend, and—'

'That was three years ago!'

'Because we haven't had the money since! But we do now. We will, from now on—'

Tasha was shaking her head. 'It's not enough,' she said. 'Owen, it's not enough. We love our daughter. You're a great dad. You've done the best you can to provide for us, I know that, and yes, now that's sorted, at least for a while. But it's not enough for me, Owen. We were so young when we got together, and we got married so quickly. I didn't really see you for the first few years we were married. We might as well have still been dating really, because that's what it felt like when you came home. But then you came home permanently and I realized . . .'

'What?' Owen asked thickly. 'You realized *what*?'

She shifted, and he saw tears in her eyes. 'I don't really love you, Owen. Not like that. I'll always love you for giving me Hannah. But I'm not in love with you anymore. And if you were really honest with me, you'd admit you're not in love with me either. And I'm not old enough to settle for that. I'm *not*. And neither are you.'

Silence reigned again. The dripping tap marked time with its slow, sad *plop* against the chrome.

'Is there someone else?' Owen asked, eventually.

'No. Owen, it's not about that—'

There was a sound at the door, and there was Hannah in her pink unicorn pyjamas, seven years old and the best thing he'd ever done. She rubbed her eyes, her blonde hair – so like her mother's – tangled with sleep.

'Daddy?' she said. 'Are you and Mummy fighting?'

Owen blinked and went to pick up his daughter, feeling her weight against his chest and thinking that if anything could hold together the fragments of his heart, it would be this. 'No, sweet pea. You should be asleep or you'll be too tired for school in the morning.'

'I'm thirsty.'

'All right. Mummy will get you a drink of water and then we'd better get you back to bed, eh?'

He managed not to look at Tasha as she passed him the drink in Hannah's favourite pink plastic mug. Owen carried his daughter back to her room and watched as she sipped some water before he tucked her in. He tried to imagine not being there to do this, tried to imagine not being the one to tuck his daughter in every night until she was too old not to want him to. He had to press his fingers to his eyes to stop himself from crying, and then had to lie and say that Daddy was just tired after a long day.

Owen spent the night on the couch in the living room, squeezing his long frame onto the inadequate length of cushion. He didn't sleep much and left early the next morning, though not early enough that Hannah wasn't already up, and Tasha too, so he pushed a few items of clothing into a rucksack and told Hannah he was going to be away for a few days but would be back soon.

It was before 7.30am when he arrived at the site – the rest of the workforce wouldn't start work until eight – but still, Saskia was already there, her Land Rover parked close to where it had been when he'd left last night. He had no idea where she was staying and didn't much care. He was irked that he wouldn't have the place to himself at least for a while, today of all days. Owen had planned to walk through the site with the plans in hand, to get a better feel for how the straight lines and angles on the page would translate to the site itself. Now he'd have to deal with her when he was feeling raw and wrecked.

Owen stayed where he was for a moment after he'd switched off his engine, looking out over the castle's crumbling walls. The morning sun was already bright, the angle of it pulling shadows westwards towards him, long slices of shade as sharp as knife blades. The silence of the place settled into him, and he looked over at that tangle of old forest, dark beneath the massed branches of the trees. There was something almost hypnotic about the way the natural world would not tolerate a right angle. Everywhere he looked was kink and curve as each individual member of that little ecosystem moulded around the other to make a convoluted whole, imperfect by the standards of what a human would design, but perfect in all respects that mattered. He thought of the oak tree that Saskia was so determined to incorporate into the construction; he saw the correlation between what he would have to accomplish there and the interwoven branches of the willow, ash, elder, oak and beech he could see from where he sat. Perhaps that was how to think of this build, he thought. He and Saskia, so obviously such different species, would have to accommodate for each other in the same way to make this work.

A sound drew his attention across to the other side of the site. There he saw Saskia, kicking the door of her trailer shut behind her as she ran down the steps, her golden retriever at her heels. In one hand she held an insulated coffee mug, steam rising from the vent in the closed lid, while in the other was her hard hat. Owen watched as she slapped it on over her hair that had been fastened back into an efficient ponytail at her nape. She was dressed in what she'd been wearing when she arrived yesterday: a heavy-duty pair of old worn work khakis; a well-washed long-sleeved denim shirt over a white tee. It surprised him no less now than it had then. It was such a contrast to the absurd, polished get-up she'd been wearing when they had first met.

She seemed to feel that someone was watching her, because she paused in her stride and turned to look at him. Owen swung out of the driver's door, picked up the tube of architectural plans and went to meet her. She waited for him, sipping her coffee, her face shadowed by the peak of her hard hat.

'I really wasn't sure I'd see you,' she said, once he was near enough.

'Well, here I am,' he said.

'To stay?'

'Yes. You're right, I want to work on this project. So we'll just have to find a way to get around our differences of opinion.'

She smiled, her dark eyes crinkling. 'Good.'

'On the proviso that there isn't anything else that you've left off telling me, obviously,' he warned.

'You know everything important that there is to know,' she assured him, and then glanced at her mug. 'Do you want one of these? There's still some in the pot.'

He said yes, then waited outside while she went back in to fetch him his drink. As he stood there, he studied the outside of the trailer. It was beautifully finished, with a timber-cladding exterior and a shiplap roof, punctuated by four solar panels. A round stained-glass window had been fitted into the gable end closest to him, a tiny landscape featuring an oak tree set against a blue sky, and Owen wondered how much a personal feature like that had cost to add, and how long it had taken. Had Saskia had the foresight to order this months ago, ready for when the Gair project could get underway? It needled at him, this idea, that she had been planning for her own comfort for months ahead of being able to begin, but he'd had to order the bare-box shipping containers for the men who'd actually be doing the work himself.

Saskia reappeared and handed him another insulated mug, and then they set off across the cleared ground.

'Has there been any more sign of our friends from the Historical Society since I've been gone?' Saskia asked.

'No, although Stuart spotted a letter in the local rag, complaining about the perimeter fence,' Owen told her, 'so they've definitely been up here.'

'What were they complaining about?'

'That we were blocking the view deliberately so that no one could see what we were doing inside it. The insinuation was that therefore what we're doing must be criminal.'

'Oh, for goodness' sake,' Saskia muttered. 'These people are unbelievable.'

'Maybe you should invite them up here,' Owen suggested.

'Show them your plans, let them look around for themselves before we get too stuck in to the work to let anyone non-essential on site.'

'I told you, they've already seen the plans. It made no difference.'

'They haven't seen them in situ though, have they?' he pointed out. 'Not as someone's actually taking them around the site.'

'Do you really think that would change their opinion about what I want to do here?'

'Probably not,' Owen said, 'but if you kill them with kindness they'll come across as idiots if they keep trying to push the point.'

'Hmm,' Saskia muttered, over the rim of her mug. 'I've always loathed that term.'

'What?' he asked.

'"Killing with kindness". It's just manipulation. Makes my skin crawl.'

Owen shrugged. He supposed people who went around buying whatever castles they fancied rarely had to worry about being nice. 'Well, it's up to you. Just a suggestion.'

'No, you're probably right,' she sighed. 'It's just galling having to talk to them at all.'

'Well then, let them do the talking. People like that love to educate others. It gives them a chance to hear their own voices.'

She stopped and looked up at him, thoughtful. 'Maybe.'

The sound of a car engine echoed towards them and

Owen looked over her head to see Stuart's car pulling in. He glanced at his watch to see that it was just about eight o'clock. The working day had properly begun, and there was a lot to get done. The site itself had been cleared, but there was other preparation to accomplish. Setting up the generators, for example. Rigging up the site lighting was another.

'I need to get Stuart and the others going,' he told Saskia. 'I'll be right back.'

She nodded and he passed her the poster tube before going to talk to Stuart.

'Morning,' his friend said, as he got out of the car.

'Stu, listen,' Owen said in a rush, as the other cars began to filter in, right on time. 'I need a favour. Can I crash with you for a few nights? It won't be long.'

Stuart frowned. 'Why? What's happened?'

Owen glanced at the other workers climbing out of their cars. He didn't want to talk about this in front of the others. 'I'll explain later.'

Stuart clapped him on the arm with one big paw. 'Sure you can. Be like old times, won't it?'

Owen shuddered. 'I hope not.'

Six

'What I don't get is that it's not even a particularly attractive tree, is it?'

'Beauty is in the eye of the beholder, Owen,' Saskia said, while her foreman snorted.

'Not here, it isn't.'

'It's got a protection order on it,' she reminded him.

He shook his head. 'That doesn't have to be an obstacle, not to development. You must know that. It's supposed to stop people hacking them about without due consideration, which' – he uncrossed his arms to gesture at the oak standing before them – 'clearly hasn't worked in this case, has it?'

Saskia contemplated the tree – *her* tree – and had to admit that Owen was right, on all counts. This argument, about whether it should remain where it was or be removed, had rumbled on ever since he'd seen the plans. He'd explained to her that it wasn't because he had a blanket disregard for natural growth. If it had grown literally anywhere else, he wouldn't have such a problem with it. But–

'I'm not going to be able get the crane in,' he'd pointed out.

The tree in question stood at the centre of the castle ruins. This wasn't mere hyperbole, but a geographically accurate statement. Saskia had mapped and measured everything within the castle's footprint with a care that bordered on obsession and discovered that the oak really was at the exact centre. It was as if the tree had been placed within Gair after careful deliberation, instead of as the result of an acorn accidentally falling or being buried by an errant squirrel at that spot. This could not possibly be the case, although during some of her more whimsical considerations of the site, Saskia had wondered whether the oak was a statement by the forest that surrounded it. *Look at all your human posturing*, it was perhaps saying. *Look at your grand schemes crumbled to dust and ruin, and now look at us. This landscape will always be ours. We will always prevail; we will always take this place back.*

Had anyone asked her about it, Saskia would have said that she found this idea comforting. In all other respects, the oak lacked the essential oakiness that would otherwise, in tree terms, make it classically beautiful. No art director was going to choose it as being representative or aspirational, although there were arguments to say that it could perfectly illustrate some sort of hokey affirmation about survival. It did not reach skyward with an elegant and even crown. Instead, its branches almost resembled a stag's antlers, but that made it sound more noble than it actually looked. Even in full leaf, the brutality of its long life was evident. To begin the catalogue of its tragedies: it had at some point been hit by lightning, an attempted electrocution it had rebuffed despite the attack shearing it almost in half. The trunk had healed over, but the site of the strike was still visible as a blank in the bark, scar tissue in skin that functioned but never looked quite the same. Ever after, no branches had sprouted in the centre of the tree, making any new growth seem strangely bisected, hence its stag-headed aspect.

Further to this natural atrocity had come a distinctly unnatural one. At some point one side of the tree had been topped, although this job had clearly been performed by someone with no clue of what they were doing, nor any sense of aesthetics or care for the longevity and tenacity of the species. Why this had been done neither Saskia nor Charlie Acre, the arborist she had consulted, could work out. Given some of the stone they had found tumbled amid the long grasses at the tree's foot, they had guessed that the butcher had been more worried about the remaining castle walls than the tree. This wanton pruning had slowed the oak down – the arborist had estimated that the mauling had happened around a hundred years ago – but had not killed it or even stopped it from growing. Unlike the lightning, in the wake of this attack the oak had put out new branches. This fresh growth had sprouted in a kind of woody halo from the remaining bark that had survived below the cut. These branches had put out more branches, reaching up and out and over the denuded centre. Now the tree's 'antlers' looked like a balding man of venerable years attempting a comb-over.

Below all of this, the existing trunk had continued to

thicken year after year. One huge, errant buttress of a branch near the ground on its south side stuck out at right angles as if the tree had established an elbow to help hold its weight. The oak was alive, and it continued to grow, but for sure, it was not *pretty*.

Saskia didn't care. She loved the tree perhaps even more for its imperfections; held it as a private symbol and delighted in finding others, like Charlie, who venerated it as much as she did. She would never cut it down, and for more than a decade had been trying to find a way to make sure no one else would, either.

'Well, we need to find a work-around, because it's staying where it is,' she told him. 'A smaller crane, for example.'

She saw his jaw tense and he crossed his arms again, still staring at the tree as if his laser focus would be enough to fell it.

'I'm sorry, but this is non-negotiable,' she pushed on, so that he would be absolutely clear about her priorities. 'The tree stays. If you think it needs pruning, let me know and I'll put a request in with the council for permission. But it's not coming down. That's final.'

That put Owen into a sulk that saw him refusing to speak to her for the rest of the day. He had been, she reflected that night, far moodier and angrier to work with than she'd expected, at least so far. But he did seem to be making an effort to be civil, and the men all respected him without question. Besides, there was no point dwelling on regrets – she knew that of old. They were here now, and they had to make the best of it. She was lucky, she reminded herself, that she had found anyone to help her move this project forward at all.

It probably would have been easier if she hadn't been living on site. Saskia didn't know whether Owen – or any of the other workers, for that matter – had realized that's what she was doing. Owen had made a couple of comments about 'fancy offices', as if he thought that's all the cabin was. She hadn't bothered to correct him: it wasn't his business, after all, and anyway, this was her land. It would be ridiculous either to pay to park it somewhere else or stay in a hotel for the duration of the build. The cabin was her home, and it had been hard-won. She loved it; she had made it as cosy, comfortable and to her own tastes as she could. She wanted to live in it, and so she would.

The first Friday night she'd been on site, Stuart had surprised her – and Owen, she could tell – by asking Saskia if she wanted to come into town with the company for a beer. She'd thanked him but refused, although she'd been touched by the invitation. Saskia had seen Owen's reaction as she'd said no – a sliding away of his gaze, a slight twist at the corner of his lips – and sensed that her refusal had reinforced some image of her that he still held from that first meeting. That she 'wasn't the sort' to like beer, most likely, or that she had said no because their company was not of a quality she could appreciate. Fine, let him think what he wanted, she didn't care. She could have told them the real reason, which was not that she would not enjoy it but that there was a very great risk she would enjoy it too much. This wasn't a truth she was willing to give up to her employees, particularly not since she couldn't yet trust their leader not to find some way to use it against her. Thus a bonding opportunity had been lost, and as the weeks went on the invitation was not repeated. This didn't worry Saskia – she spent the weekends working, meticulously checking and re-checking all her figures and calculations that would be required for the following week's work. It wasn't that she didn't have confidence in herself. She just had to make sure this was right. It had to be right. No, not just right. It had to be perfect.

After the Historical Society's last volley in the local press, things on that score seemed to have died down. Once or twice over the weekends, when Saskia broke from her desk to take Brodie on long, rambling walks through the forests surrounding the castle (he loved the tangle of old growth, disappearing to nose into rabbit holes and the homes of whatever else was living on her patch of land), she had got the sense that she was being watched, but could never pinpoint the source. A couple of times she had smelled smoke, and wondered if these unseen visitors were lighting cigarettes, which as a dry summer began to unfold was of far more concern than the trespassing. On these walks she had located the public footpath that ran outside the north edge of her property line. Owen obviously had too, because he had erected glaringly red 'Trespassers Will Be Prosecuted' signs to warn off intruders on the other side of the fence that marked her boundary. These had at some point been plastered with answering protest posters, expressing the ire of the walkers who had evidently trespassed in order to paste them up. But they were slowly fading in the sun and they had not been replaced. Perhaps, Saskia allowed herself to hope, that particular problem had been laid to rest for good.

By the fourth week they were preparing to sink the first foundation hole for the new internal floor. The plant machinery was in place, the diesel generators – enough to power the build for a whole tower block; Saskia wasn't taking any chances – were hooked up, the huge tanks of water that would have to be refilled often and at great expense were installed. Once this was done, the build would be properly underway, an immense freight train leaving a station and picking up speed. Saskia was excited and nervous in equal measure, because this really was the point of no return. Right now, Gair was still untouched. But once they started building, it would be for ever changed, however much Saskia intended to preserve it as it was. This was, at its heart, both the challenge and the whole point of her taking it on in the first place.

'I'd love to come up there and be with you for the first day,' Vivian told her, as they talked on the phone the Saturday before.

Saskia smiled. 'Worried the stress of the moment will send me overboard?'

'No, not really,' her friend said. 'But it's a momentous occasion and you're up there alone. Thought you might like some company other than that daft pooch of yours.'

'Actually, that'd be really nice,' Saskia admitted.

'When's all this going off, exactly?'

'Monday. That's pretty last minute for you.'

'Nah,' Vivian declared, breezily. 'I'll shove some bits in a bag and drive up tomorrow. It'll be an adventure, I've never been to the wild north.'

Saskia laughed. 'We're really not that wild.'

'No? When was the last time you shaved your legs?'

Saskia refused to answer that question.

Thus it was that Vivian's sleek scarlet BMW slid into view the following evening. Saskia had driven out from the castle to meet her at the nearest trunk road to the M6, not because her friend was incompetent at reading maps, but because trusting GPS in the twilight when Gair wasn't even on an actual road was hit and miss at best. Saskia was leaning against the Land Rover's bonnet as Vivian pulled to a stop in front of her. She was surprised by the visceral burst of joy that exploded in her chest as her friend hopped, fresh as a daisy, from the car. Saskia didn't have many friends, and of them all Vivian, as ridiculous as she could be, was the best. She came towards Saskia in an opulent wave of expensive perfume and Stella McCartney.

'Look at you!' Vivian cried as the two women embraced and held each other tightly. 'You look like an urchin!'

'What?' Saskia laughed, into her shoulder. 'I look like a small, spiny sea creature?'

'No, the other sort,' Vivian said, pulling away and holding Saskia by the shoulders. 'The sort that goes up chimneys in musicals. And you're so tanned! I thought it rained all day every day here?'

'That's because you're an ignorant southerner,' Saskia declared. 'Come on, let me show you my castle.'

'Why don't we go somewhere and eat first?' Vivian suggested. 'My treat. I bet you haven't been out since you've been here, have you? Pizza doesn't count.'

They went to an interesting bistro Saskia had spied during one of her rare trips into town and caught up over sharing plates of finger food as quirky as the décor. Vivian filled Saskia in on the latest in her hectic, celebrity-filled life as a portrait photographer to the stars who was regularly featured in all the glossies. Saskia detailed her dust-filled weeks and the day-to-day struggles of project management and architecture on a site of the size and complexity of Gair.

'I'm so proud of you,' Vivian said unexpectedly at one point, reaching over the table to grip Saskia's hand. 'Look what you've accomplished, it's amazing. I'd never have had the courage or determination to do what you're doing right now.'

Saskia squeezed her friend's hand. 'What I'm trying to do, you mean,' she said. 'I might fail horribly and lose it all. That's the nightmare that keeps waking me up at 3am. Over and over, I'm stuck in this dream where something has gone completely wrong with the castle and I'm in a court room staring at a judge as he tells me I'm a useless failure and belong in jail. The worst thing about that is that, though everything else in the dream might change, the judge is always, always my grandfather. He accuses me of wasting all his money. Then he bangs his gavel – except it's a sledgehammer – and I wake up in a cold sweat.'

A look of concern passed over Vivian's face. 'This is what worries me,' she said. 'You're under so much pressure.'

Saskia gently withdrew her hand and picked up her glass of sparkling water. 'I promise I'm fine. I'm avoiding situations that could cause a problem – this is the first time I've been out to eat, for a start – and I'm coping.'

'I hate that you're up here alone.'

'I've got Brodie,' Saskia reminded her friend, and then, thinking of her dog, glanced at her watch. 'Speaking of whom, we shouldn't be too much longer, really. I took him out for a long walk this afternoon so he's probably just zonked out in his bed, but I don't like to leave him too long.'

'Sure thing,' Vivian said. 'I'm about ready to crash, to tell you the truth.'

As they walked back to where they had parked their cars, Vivian asked if Saskia had spoken to her mother.

'Not since I changed my number. Why? Has she been bothering you?'

Vivian nodded. 'I spoke to her briefly, but wouldn't tell her anything about where you were or what was going on with you, just that I was in contact with you and you're fine. She knows that the money has been released.'

Saskia snorted. 'Of course she does. Why else would she be calling?'

'She was going on about how unstable you are, how worried she is about your well-being and what having access to so much money will do to your mental health.'

Saskia stopped and turned to her friend. They stood in

the twilight that at ten o'clock was finally beginning to blur the edges of the world into night. Vivian was Saskia's closest friend, and more than that, she was her oldest friend. They had grown up together, two girls from privileged families on very different trajectories: Saskia towards heartbreak, hardship and alienation; Vivian towards success and a mother and father who were very much in love, and who loved her in return. They had known each other for ever, but sometimes Saskia feared that Vivian still didn't quite understand how different their backgrounds were.

'Unstable?' Saskia asked, anger rising in her chest. 'She said that? You know that's a smokescreen. You know it's not me she's interested in.'

'Yes,' Vivian said, slowly. 'I know that's how it feels to you. But Saskia – she doesn't need your money. You know how much Richard is worth. And you've changed, haven't you? Maybe she has too? Maybe it's not about the money. I just wonder whether it's worth you giving her the benefit of the doubt. She's the only mother you're ever going to have, after all.'

Saskia locked her jaw. She knew her friend meant well. But Vivian also knew her entire history, and it angered Saskia that Vivian couldn't understand the weight of what she was suggesting.

'No,' Saskia said. 'I don't want her to know where I am. I don't want her to know anything about my life at all. Do you understand?'

Vivian sighed. 'Okay.'

'I mean it, Vivian,' Saskia said. 'Tell me you understand.'

'All right, all right,' Vivian said, holding up both hands. 'I understand.'

There was a moment of silence. 'I'm sorry,' Saskia said. 'But nothing would drive me over the brink quicker than me having to engage with my mother. Don't make me do it. Not now, not ever.'

Vivian made a face and stepped forward to pull her into a tight hug. 'I'm sorry. I do understand. I just – I wish things were different, that's all. For your sake.'

Saskia hugged her back. 'If wishes were horses, beggars would ride,' she quipped, lightly. 'I'm fine with just you, Brodie and this insane project that's going to take over my entire life for years. That's all I need.'

The dark drew in as they drove to Gair. Saskia had become used to navigating the track without the aid of street lights, but she was aware that Vivian would not be used to the absence of city glare so slowed down as her friend followed her towards the castle. When she reached the point where the rough road opened out onto the castle approach, she saw what looked like torch beams inside the compound. For a moment Saskia's mind ran through a gamut of explanations, none of which were good, but as she unlocked the main gates she saw a truck parked in the area reserved for works vehicles and realized it belonged to Owen. She pulled up next to it and Vivian stopped beside her.

'Your men don't work on a Sunday, do they?' Vivian asked, once she'd got out.

'No. That's Owen's car. I've no idea what he's doing here. I'd better find out.' Saskia reached into the back of the Landy and grabbed one of her spare hard hats, holding it out to Vivian, who made a face. 'You've got to if you want to come on site. Sorry. You can leave me to it, if you like. I can give you the key to the house. It's parked over there.' She gestured to the far end of the site and saw Vivian's gaze follow her direction.

'If you think I'm walking past all those creepy trees in the dark on my own, you've got another thing coming, even if Brodie is waiting for me,' Vivian said, taking the hard hat. 'Besides, I want to meet this chap. Sounds like he could do with pulling his socks up around my BFF.'

'Don't say a word,' Saskia warned her, as she slapped her own hat on her head. 'I've got enough to worry about as it is without you trying to "help"!'

Vivian stuck out her tongue, making her look like the five-year-old she had been when they had first met.

The inner site gates were open too, faint voices echoing across the level dust as the two women passed through them. Saskia led Vivian between walls cleaved into pieces by the passage of time until they found Owen with Stuart Mackey.

'Hi,' Saskia said. 'I didn't expect to find anyone here on a Sunday – or this late, for that matter. Is everything all right?'

'Just wanted to do one last check over before tomorrow,' Owen said, coming towards her. 'It's a big day and everything has to be right.'

Saskia was surprised by his diligence and then immediately

wondered why she should be. For all his faults and his complaints about her, Owen Elliot had never been less than one hundred per cent invested in Gair since he'd taken it on.

'That's good of you,' she said, and then looked at his colleague. 'Stuart, you must make sure to log your hours.'

'Nah,' Stuart said, easily, his attention all for Vivian. 'I'm just here as a friend. This one won't sleep otherwise, I know what he's like.'

Saskia looked over at Vivian to find her staring straight at Stuart, with the kind of sparky challenge in her eye she'd developed as a teenager and that she had never quite abandoned.

'Owen, Stuart – this is Vivian, a close friend who's come to show her support tomorrow,' Saskia said. 'I was just going to give her a quick tour of the site in advance.'

The three of them shook hands, Stuart's fingers lingering a little longer on Vivian's than necessary. He was grinning with cocky assuredness, looking straight into Vivian's eyes as she smiled coyly back. Saskia only just managed not to roll her eyes. Really, that was all she needed. Vivian was generally incorrigible when it came to the opposite sex, but *please*, Saskia thought. *Not now. Not on my work site.* She glanced at Owen and saw the same kind of reaction on his face.

'Pleasure to meet you, Vivian,' Stuart said. 'Although you're better off waiting until tomorrow to have a proper look around. It's easier to imagine the place finished by daylight.'

'I don't know,' Vivian said, with her trademark lip, 'I've always enjoyed what goes on at a place in the dark.'

Owen cleared his throat at about the same time that Saskia said, 'Actually, Stuart's probably right. It's got dark quicker than I thought, and besides, it's getting late. Big day tomorrow. We'd better leave it.'

'Yes,' Owen agreed. 'We should get going.'

He began walking back towards his truck and Saskia went with him, Stuart and Vivian following behind as they continued their distinctly loaded chat. Saskia could tell that Owen was as uncomfortable with this as she was, though neither Vivian nor Stuart seemed to have noticed.

'Thanks again for checking the site, Owen,' Saskia said, as they reached the cars.

Owen said nothing in reply, and she glanced at him to see that he was looking at Vivian's scarlet BMW, parked next to her old Land Rover.

'It's Vivian's,' Saskia told him, and smiled slightly as his eyes flashed towards her in surprise. 'Thought it was mine, didn't you?'

'We'll wait for you girls to pull out first, if you like,' Stuart said, from behind, as he reached Owen's truck. 'Ladies first, and all that.'

'Oh, we're not going anywhere,' Vivian said. 'I'm staying at Saskia's place.'

Stuart looked confused. 'Oh? Where's that?'

'The cabin,' Saskia said, and she felt Owen's eyes on her face but didn't look at him. 'It's got space for us both.'

'*That*'s where you're staying during the build?' Stuart asked, looking astonished, and then impressed. 'That's actually really smart. What does one of those set you back? Fifteen, twenty k? Better than pumping money into hotel bills, and you can be on site. Bet that cuts the site insurance too, *and* you can recoup some of the cost by selling it on when you're done with it. Nice.'

Saskia didn't bother to correct him. Owen didn't bother to say anything at all.

'Now that,' Vivian said, as she waved at the departing truck, 'was worth coming north for. Why didn't you tell me the local talent looks like Charlie Hunnam on a particularly good day?'

'Stuart? You're kidding me,' Saskia said over her shoulder, already heading for the trailer. She really needed her bed.

'Both of them!' Vivian shouted, heading after her.

This time Saskia really did roll her eyes.

Seven

The first day of full works on the site went well. They sank ten foundation holes inside the castle wall perimeter, the ancient place reverberating with the massive rattle and hum of heavy machinery for the first time in its long history. Saskia had assured Owen, with the results of an exhaustive survey that had been part of the planning process, that the remaining external structure was still sound enough to withstand the tremors caused by the depth drilling and this indeed seemed to be the case. There would be a two-foot gap between the original wall and the frame of the new 'floating' concrete floor, into which would be constructed further support for the castle's external walls, all part of maintaining what was left of the building in its current state. The castle's internal walls would be incorporated into the envelope Saskia had designed, though none now would be load-bearing. It was, Owen had to admit, a clever design, and it was clear to him that his employer was serious about preserving the castle, even to a degree beyond what was stated on the planning agreement. She wanted everything to stay as it was now. If any loose stones did fall during the foundation drilling, or were discovered during the build, for example, they must be replaced in their original position. This might have been reasonable had it not required him to have an expert on standby who could mix the period-appropriate mortar required to carry out this task. There was only a handful of people in the whole of the UK who could do this, and they were invariably booked solid. Any related mishap would inevitably mean delay, a fact Owen pointed out to Saskia and that she dismissed with the same level of nonchalance that had annoyed him about her from the beginning.

'I know, and I'm prepared for that, Owen,' she'd said. 'There is room in the budget both for the work and to accommodate reasonable delay.'

He was irked by her impatience with him pointing this out, as though there was no need for him to underline facts such as these, when to Owen's mind there was every need given how utterly unprepared she seemed to be. But then, there was the money, wasn't there? Throw money at it and it'll go away, always the fallback of the ultra-rich. Owen thought Saskia very likely had no idea how much of a delay these setbacks could cause.

'What do you care?' Stuart asked him, when Owen had voiced his ire over his employer's attitude in the pub that evening. 'You're on a retainer. The longer it takes, the longer you're employed.'

'It's the principle,' Owen said, a statement at which Stuart scoffed and went off to the bar for another round.

Then there was the tree. Always, the tree. Saskia's obsession with it wasn't merely on the surface, as he'd discovered when they'd discussed where the foundation holes needed to be sunk. She had pulled out the ground-penetrating LiDAR scans, because as far as possible she wanted to avoid damaging the oak's roots and this had dictated where she'd marked out the foundation shafts. It was at this point that Owen realized that the floating floor, which would see the concrete being poured on manufactured-to-order, six-inch-thick, steel sheets raised above the soil, was also for the tree's benefit, in case of any place where the tree's roots broke the surface of the ground. Arguing over it at this point was moot, because in an epiphany that had occurred to Owen as he'd checked the plans one last time on the morning of the drilling, it finally became clear to him that the entire house design had been developed around the question of how to preserve, not just the castle itself, but also the tree. There was no aspect of this build that had not been thought of in deference to it, a realization that staggered him for its absurdity. If the tree was of such intrinsic importance, why do this at all? Let the tree have the castle. It made no sense.

Why couldn't she build her bloody trophy house somewhere else? Somewhere *easier*?

He could have asked her, but he didn't. He didn't want a conversation, only a way to get on with his job with minimum interaction with Saskia Tilbury-bloody-Martin. It wasn't a healthy way to manage a work relationship, but this project was dependent on clear communication, and to Owen's mind, in their case, keeping the flow to a minimum would reduce friction. This wasn't a tactic he was able to employ in his personal life, where copious daily communication with his wife over the management of their daughter's schedule was necessary, and the friction was ever present, a painful reminder of yet another failure. Tasha would probably demand that he think about her as his soon-to-be *ex*-wife, as it seemed that she had no intention of changing her mind about the split. The situation between them was turning ever more sour by the day.

'If you think about it,' Stuart said, over his second beer, 'she's right. You need to move on, mate. Don't dwell on it. This is a new chapter, a new start.'

Owen sipped his own drink, thinking bitterly that Stuart had no idea what he was talking about. He'd never known his oldest friend to have a long relationship. In truth he was in the mood for a fight, and the conversation could have easily turned into one, but given that Owen was still camping out in Stuart's tiny spare room he decided to swallow his retort.

Stuart's phone beeped with an incoming text. He grinned at the screen. 'Going to have to love you and leave you,' he said, typing a quick message back as he lifted his pint and drained it.

'What?' Owen asked, aghast. 'But I've still got a full pint!'

'Not my fault you drink like an old maid, is it?' his friend said, pushing back his chair. 'Don't wait up, eh?'

'What do you mean? Where are you going?'

Stuart waggled his eyebrows. 'Booty call. And since I doubt you'll appreciate being disturbed, I'll make sure we end up back in her hotel room for the night.'

'Her— *what*?' Owen said. Then a terrible thought dawned on him. 'Oh no. Please don't tell me that message was from *Vivian*.'

Stuart grinned again. 'A gent never tells.'

'That's bollocks, for a start,' Owen pointed out. 'You *always* tell.'

'I believe the word I used was "gent",' Stuart said.

'You do understand what a nightmare that would be for me?' Owen asked. 'You two hooking up?'

Stuart shook his head. 'You think too much, mate. Look, drink your pint and then go home and get a good night's sleep. I'll see you at work tomorrow.'

'She doesn't have a hotel room,' Owen pointed out. 'Remember? She told us she's staying with Lady Muck in her Lady Shed.'

'Not so,' Stuart said. 'She's staying an extra night unexpectedly and says she's got a room in Carlisle.' He grinned. 'I like a woman who thinks ahead.'

Owen grimaced. 'So it *is* her. Stuart, seriously, can you please just not—'

'See you tomorrow, mate. Chill!'

He went.

Owen's sleep was fitful that night, tossing and turning on Stuart's ancient, lumpy spare bed, listening to the creak and whistle of the pipes in the old flat. He kept thinking about his friend of almost four decades and his employer's best friend. He couldn't get past the sheer, rank stupidity of Stuart's choice to go ahead with this dalliance despite Vivian's connection to their employer.

For this reason, he was already awake when, at 5.15am, his phone flashed up with a message. He picked it up, saw that it was from Saskia, and read the note with trepidation.

We have a problem, it said. *Can you get here a little early?*

Blearily, he wondered for a moment whether Stuart had been insane enough to follow Vivian back to Saskia's on-site accommodation after all, but then a photograph arrived that had him pushing back the blankets and forcing his way up from the dubious embrace of Stuart's ancient spare duvet.

He flicked on the lamp and peered at the image, trying to work out what he was seeing. It looked out of focus, but he could make out a mass of headlights: it was a group of cars parked in haphazard fashion. He realized eventually that what was distorting the picture was the blurred criss-cross of the site's main gates, outside which the cars were parked in such a way as to block the main access road.

Owen cursed and got to his feet. *I'm on my way*, he sent back, and then, as an afterthought, *Are you there alone?*

Thanks, came the reply, and then, *Yes, but I'm fine.*

Owen continued to curse as he showered and dressed. By the time he was making strong instant coffee in his thermal mug, he had also messaged Stuart. *I don't care where you are or what you're doing, get to Gair. There's trouble.* He didn't check to see if there was a reply as he left the flat.

It took him thirty-five minutes to get to the site. The streets of Carlisle were only just beginning to wake, though the summer sky had already begun shaking off the night even in Saskia's photograph. By the time he reached the turning to the work's access road the morning sun was bright, gleaming through the green of the forest's leaves as if this was just another beautiful day dawning in Cumbria.

There were at least ten cars blocking the entrance into Gair, mostly domestic hatchbacks, although he counted a couple of heavy-duty vehicles, the bulk of which had been strategically placed to cause the most obstruction. The drivers were mostly standing around in the warming air. They watched, stony-faced, as he approached and pulled up. His phone beeped as he turned off the engine: a note from Stuart that simply read, *On my way.*

Before he got out of the car, Owen made a show of turning on the dashcam he'd mounted to his windscreen the year before. In fact it had begun to automatically record the moment he started the engine back in the city, but he wanted to make sure they knew he would have a record of this standoff. He saw a couple of the mob react, leaning over to mutter at each other, presumably about the audacity of his making sure he had video proof of whatever was about to happen. Others lifted their own phones to record him in turn, which was only to be expected. Modern warfare.

On the access road, the post-dawn hush was eerie when

you stopped to consider how many people were gathered in that narrow strip between the trees.

'Morning, folks. I'm going to need you to clear the road,' Owen said, loudly, into the morning quiet.

Evidently the protestors – for Owen had no doubt that's how the group had styled themselves – had been organized enough to appoint a spokesperson ahead of time. It was, perhaps unsurprisingly, the largest guy among them who stepped forward. He was dark and brooding in manner as well as looks; late forties, broad – chunky, but not with muscle. He had a nose that had clearly been broken more than once, a detail that surprised Owen not a bit. He wondered for a moment whether his adversary was also ex-military, but he decided not. His natural size had made him feel as if he didn't need discipline, a mistake no one who had served would make.

'We're not going anywhere,' the man said.

'This is private property,' Owen said, though he knew they were all well aware of the fact.

'We're not leaving,' the spokesman repeated. 'You've already done enough damage. If you think we're letting you do more without the biggest fight you've ever had, you're mistaken. If you want us to move, you're going to have to tow every single car.'

Owen thought about some of the fights he'd been in and smiled. 'Game on, big lad,' he said, quietly. 'Game on.'

They couldn't stop him walking through their little road block to the site entrance, and if they thought he would be intimidated by their angry stares, they were mistaken. Owen wove through the tangle of parked cars until he made it as far as the Gair site's main entrance, glad now that he'd talked Saskia into erecting the large gates and fence that blocked off both the road and six metres either side of it. The forest was dense enough beyond that to do the job itself for any but the most determined walker, but he hadn't wanted just any Tom, Dick or Harry to be able to roll right up to the site's inner perimeter. It looked as if he'd been right to be concerned.

Saskia was on the other side of the fence. She'd driven her own Land Rover up to the wire and parked it smack bang in the middle of the road, with the lights full on so that it stood like a sentry about two metres away from the nearest of the protestors' vehicles. She jumped out of the cab when she saw him, Brodie in her wake. Owen had his own key to the heavy-duty padlock and chain and they didn't speak until he'd opened the gates, stepped through and re-locked them.

'You okay?' he asked, both of them aware of the multiple pairs of eyes watching.

'Fine,' she said. 'They haven't tried to come directly onto the property.'

Owen nodded, noting that she was dressed for the work site, complete with hard hat. 'Have you called the police?'

'Not yet.'

'Well, they're trespassing,' he said. 'Call the police, have them all arrested if they won't leave of their own accord, and have the cars towed. Simple as that.'

Saskia glanced behind him at the gathered mob. 'That's what they want, isn't it?'

Owen rubbed a thumb over his eyebrow. His eyes were gritty and there was a headache forming at the base of his skull. 'Then give them what they want and let's get on with the day.'

From outside the site there came the honking of a car horn, which started and did not stop for at least thirty seconds; then the sound of shouting, growing nearer.

'That'll be Stuart,' Owen said, and went back to the gates to let his friend in. Stuart was alone, he noted. There was no sign of Vivian.

'What's all this silly bollocks?' Stuart demanded, loudly, as he stepped through the gates. 'Do none of these gadgies have jobs?'

The two men walked back towards Saskia, Stuart bending to pet Brodie. Dogs and women, two species who shared an inexplicable and unreserved adoration for his friend that Owen would never be able to fathom.

'Saskia's about to call the police,' he said. 'You didn't key any of their cars on your way through, did you?'

'No, just thought about it,' Stuart grumbled, checking his watch. 'Best get on with it if you want to get rid of that lot before the rest of the boys turn up. The cement truck's got no chance of making it if even one of those cars is still parked out there.'

He was right, and while it was fine that she'd wanted the site foreman present, Owen didn't understand why Saskia hadn't already made the call herself. Was she expecting him to do it? It was when he looked at her next and read the expression on her face that his heart sank.

'Owen,' she began. 'You were the one who talked about killing them with kindness.'

'Yes,' he said, slowly, 'and then you explained the lengths you'd gone to in showing them how you're planning to preserve the site and I realized that was pointless.'

Saskia sighed. 'Maybe not. I mean, I don't think it's surprising that they've shown up here now, the morning after we sunk the foundation holes. We could see what was going on, but it must have sounded horrendous to anyone who couldn't. The ground shook. For all they know we could have demolished the remains of the castle completely.'

Owen turned to look down at the site, which lay below them. He glanced back at the gates. It was true that, even without the hoardings they'd erected directly around the site perimeter, the ruins weren't visible from where the protestors stood. But that didn't mean they hadn't been up here, did it?

'They know it's still standing,' he said. 'All they'd have to do is ignore the No Trespassing signs down by the river, which we all know they've done many times before, and they'd see the top of the tower above the fence. If anything was going to come down, it'd be that. They're just troublemakers, that's all. Reasoning with them isn't going to help.'

Saskia spread her hands. 'How long is it going to take to get those cars towed? Even if they started right now, it'll be hours. In practical terms we've already lost the day. Why not bring them in, let them see the site? What was it you told me before? Maybe they've got stories about the place that'd be interesting to hear. They can tell us those at the same time. If we show them we've got nothing to hide and listen to what they've got to say, maybe this time it'll work.'

Stuart snorted at this. 'Remind me what the definition of madness is, again?'

'Stuart's right,' Owen said.

'Well, I think it's worth a try,' Saskia said. 'If it stops this from happening again, it'll be worth it, don't you think?'

Owen glanced back at the blocked gates. 'Did you know this was going to happen?'

'I hoped it wouldn't,' Saskia said. 'But I feared it would. I've been to sites where they've drilled the foundation holes before and I knew what it was going to be like, but I can imagine how catastrophic it would sound to someone who didn't, can't you? I've also assumed – as you have – that the Historical Society has had someone up here often to see what we've been doing.'

Owen felt the anger bubbling in his gut. 'And you went through this whole thought process and never thought to fill me in?'

'You were pretty busy yesterday,' she pointed out. 'And the protestors aren't your problem. It's not you they've got a problem with. It's this site. It's me. Therefore it's down to me to deal with it.'

'*Everything* on this site is my problem,' Owen said, through gritted teeth. 'How am I supposed to do my job when you're running an entirely different agenda around me?'

'Oh, don't be dramatic, Owen,' Saskia told him. 'If I had told you yesterday you would have complained about the distraction.'

'Come on, family, not in front of the children,' Stuart said, turning his back to the gates and making a face at them both.

Owen looked back. Some of the protestors were still filming. He gritted his teeth again. He'd had to do that so often since taking this job that he was beginning to get a permanent ache in his jaw. 'Fine,' he said. 'What do you want to do?'

'I think we should invite them in,' she said. 'Tell them they're welcome to come and inspect the site for themselves. Then we can all sit and talk.'

Owen glanced at his watch again. 'What about the rest of the squad?'

'I've already messaged them all,' Saskia said. 'I've told them to take the day and be back here bright and early tomorrow. The concrete's been delayed, too.'

He tried to tamp down on his growing anger. 'Fine,' he said. 'Stuart and I will just stand around with our arms crossed like glorified bouncers, shall we? Whatever you say, milady.'

'Owen—'

'No, really,' he said, turning to gesture at the group gathered beyond the gates. 'Let's get on with it. Can't wait to see how this goes.'

There was a moment of silence from Saskia, and then she walked past him, up to the gates.

'Listen,' she called. 'I understand that emotions are running high—'

'Thought you were going to just get away with it, didn't

you?' said one old woman, her voice high and angry. 'Thought you'd be able to just buy your way into doing anything you want up here.'

This was accompanied by jeers as Saskia held up both her hands, aiming to placate the crowd.

'Whatever you think it is I'm trying to do, I promise you, the preservation of the Gair site is my passion too,' she said, to more loud jeers and mutters of dissent. 'And look – I'm inviting you onto the site, right now. You can see for yourselves that we're not destroying the place. We can sit and talk – that's something we've never done, isn't it? Let's actually listen to each other, shall we? Come on – the coffee's on.'

'You think you can buy us off with an hour of your time and some *coffee*?'

Owen squinted through the glare of Saskia's headlamps to see the guy who had tried to block his way standing with his arms crossed on the other side of the fence.

'Do you really think we're that weak-willed?' he asked.

'Hugh,' Saskia said, obviously recognizing the speaker. 'Of course I don't. I just thought—'

'You just *thought*,' he interrupted, with a look of utter contempt on his face, 'that we're a bunch of country bumpkins who can be won over with a few clever words. Well, I've read everything you've ever sent to the planning committee, not to mention all the guff you've bombarded me with personally, and I don't believe a word of it. It's all flannel, meant for pulling over the eyes of the stupid, feckless and/or incompetent. And since none of us here are that, I believe we'll all be staying right here for a good long while.'

This was accompanied by a burst of cheering from the assembled group. Owen saw Saskia's shoulders drop a little as she glanced back towards him.

'Well,' he said to her, after she'd retreated a few steps. 'That went well. Shall I call the police, or do you want to do it? I mean, we've got all day, so there's no rush, but I feel like we should get this show on the road, don't you?'

Eight

Saskia could tell how angry Owen was and knew that on some level he had every right to be. She'd lost them a day's work. Worse than that she'd gone around him, and for what? She'd thought it was worth a try and had been optimistic that perhaps this approach would work. But the minute she'd seen Hugh Carey, the man who had acted as the committee's spokesman, she'd known she was in trouble. He was a charismatic former local government councillor whom she'd run into before. As far as Saskia could tell, he just didn't like outsiders or women, and his dislike of Saskia herself was intense enough to be personal. Despite what he'd said, she didn't think that either he or any of the rest of the group had ever actually paid attention to anything she had said or shown them. In his head she was fixed as an incomer hell-bent on razing the castle ruins for her own benefit. It didn't matter that she had her own history with the place. Not that she had ever attempted to explain what that was to any of them, least of all Carey. She might have tried that today if they had accepted her offer of a tour, although now she understood it would likely not have made any difference at all.

She was merely an outsider and above all, she must be stopped, no matter what. Saskia had given up trying to reason with any of them, but Owen's comment of a few days earlier that what she needed to do was listen to them had stuck with her, as had the realization that perhaps all she could do was wait until she actually had something to show them. She had already anticipated that they would be in a flap over the previous day's drilling. Bringing them inside so that they could see both the foundation bore holes and what they were going to support would have been the clearest illustration she could possibly show of her intentions for the site.

Her plan had completely backfired. Not only that, she'd gone over Owen's head and she wasn't sure he'd ever forgive her for it.

Her phone pinged. It was a text from Vivian. Her friend had already been in touch that morning, shortly after Saskia had messaged Owen, which had told her that he'd already called Stuart. The thought of her friend with one of her workers wasn't the most comfortable idea Saskia had ever had, but Vivian was an adult. She didn't need anyone's permission. Besides, Saskia thought this would most likely be a one-and-done. Vivian didn't do long entanglements.

Are you okay? I'm just getting on the road, but I can be there if you need me.

Saskia sucked in a breath as she sent a quick reply. *All fine*, she said. *Safe drive. I'll call you later.*

At the gates, the police had arrived and were dealing with the protestors. One of the officers was joking with a laughing Hugh Carey. Connections ran old and deep around here. Making new ones, Saskia was beginning to fear, was nigh on impossible.

Once the protestors had been cleared and her disgruntled foreman and his mate had gone home, Saskia took Brodie on a long walk. The forest was a peaceful respite, far away from the bustle of human life. She got back to the site in the mid-afternoon and was walking up the slight incline to her cabin when a car horn sounded from the main gates. She turned to see a small black hatchback parked outside it. A young woman stood beside the car, leaning down through the open window to sound the horn. She waved as Saskia turned.

'Hi,' the woman said, with a somewhat nervous smile, as Saskia went to see what she wanted. She looked to be in her early twenties, with a wispy brunette bob and round pretty face. 'I'm sorry to bother you.'

'Can I help you?'

'My name's Julie,' the young woman said. 'Julie Rhys. I was here this morning? I wanted to apologize. And also . . . maybe to talk to you a bit more? Only, I haven't been part of the Historical Society that long, and I haven't seen any of the material that you mentioned to Hugh.'

Saskia shifted her weight back on her heels, trying to work out if this was some sort of ploy. 'All of the planning submission documents are public record.'

'Well, yes,' the young woman said, blushing as if she might be struggling a little with this exchange. 'I've read all of those, obviously. But it sounded as if there was more? And I keep asking Hugh about it, but he just . . . well, he doesn't really listen to me. I'm training as a journalist, you see, and I thought this would be a great story to focus on for my portfolio. But he always brushes me off and tells me I should already know everything I need to know – but if there's more to the story, I can't just ignore that. Anything I write needs to be properly balanced; that's why I wanted to come here this morning. I didn't realize they were just going to block the road. If I'd had a say, I would have voted to come in and talk to you. But . . . I didn't. That's why I came back.'

Saskia glanced down at Brodie, who looked back up at her and thumped his tail in the dust. She glanced at the woman again. 'What did you say your name was?'

'Julie,' she said.

Saskia pulled her keys out of her pocket and went to open the gates. 'All right, Julie,' she said. 'It's not as if I've got anything else to do today. You'll have to wear a hard hat to go on the site, though.'

'That's okay,' the young woman said, and reached in through her car window to pull an old yellow one from her seat. 'I've brought one with me.'

'You've got your own hard hat?' Saskia asked, as she pulled open the gates.

Julie shrugged, blushing again. 'My dad's a tree surgeon. He wants me to go into the family business.'

'You're not so sure?' Saskia asked, as she pushed the gates shut behind them again.

'Touchy subject. I just want to be my own person, that's all. Find my own way. He doesn't get it.'

Saskia nodded. 'I can sympathize with that. Well, since you're all kitted out, why don't we start with a tour of the site? Were you up here yesterday? Did you hear the drilling?'

'No, but I heard what the others said about it,' Julie said, as they headed for the inner site perimeter gates. 'Hugh said you must have demolished some of the walls.'

'That's just nonsense,' Saskia told her. 'We haven't demolished anything, as you're about to see. We were drilling so we can put in the foundation stanchions for the rest of the build.'

She opened the inner gates and they walked through into the ruins. Saskia noticed that the young woman both seemed to know exactly where they were going and only glanced up at the tower as if to make sure it was still there rather than being fascinated by something she'd never seen before.

'I feel like you might know this place quite well?' Saskia hazarded, as they walked through the great split in the ancient wall.

'We used to come up here for family walks all the time. Dad used to test me on all the trees we came across in Gair Forest. It's one of the most diverse in the country, he always said.'

'Ah,' said Saskia, as they walked into what would become the castle's central courtyard and beheld the great stag-headed oak that stood there. 'Then my guess is you've met this beast more than once.'

They stopped in front of the oak and Julie smiled. 'Oh, yeah. The Gair Oak was probably the first tree I ever climbed.'

Saskia laughed. 'Mine, too. I must have been – what, five, or something?'

Julie looked at her in surprise. 'Really? But Hugh said you hadn't ever seen this place before you bought it.'

Saskia raised her eyebrows. 'Well. Word of advice where Mr Carey is concerned: it might be a good idea to question anything he presents as absolute fact.'

Julie nodded thoughtfully, looking across to the tree. 'He says the tree's probably been here since the signing of the Magna Carta.'

'Since 1215? No, not this oak,' Saskia said. 'It's not old enough for that. In fact, according to the arborist that assessed it after I listed it with the Ancient Tree Inventory, it's likely that this oak is between two hundred and two hundred and fifty years old. Which makes it a baby, really, especially if you think about other ancient oaks nearby. The Dalston Oak is at least a hundred years older than this one.'

Saskia felt Julie's surprised reaction. 'You're the one who listed it with the Inventory?'

'Yes, back in 2013. I was the one who requested the protection order, too. Bet Hugh Carey didn't tell you that, did he?'

'No,' Julie admitted. 'He didn't. He says you're obviously going to get rid of it the first chance you get.'

Saskia almost laughed at the absurdity of this statement.

'That is so very much the opposite of what I am planning to do. You should talk to my foreman, Owen Elliot. He's exasperated at the lengths I am prepared to go to in order to protect this oak.'

Julie stepped closer to one of the foundation boreholes and peered down it. 'What about the roots? These boreholes must have gone straight through them.'

'Nope,' Saskia said. 'The foundation holes have been positioned extremely carefully, using information we got from the LiDAR scans I used to prove there are no Roman ruins in the castle's foundations. The same arborist who helped me get the preservation order on the oak helped me position the holes so they won't do irreparable damage to the tree. I can give you his email address if you want to ask him about it or verify what I'm saying. I'm sure he'd be happy to talk to you about the Gair Oak – or about any tree, for that matter.'

The young woman looked over at her, apparently impressed. 'You've gone to a lot of effort just for this one tree.'

Saskia looked back up at the Gair Oak. 'Maybe,' she said. 'But I think it's worth it. Listen, do you want a coffee? I'd like to hear more about all those times you spent tramping around the forest with your dad.'

They went to the work break room rather than Saskia's trailer, so that Julie could see what Saskia had taken the time to pin up around the walls in the hope that the whole Historical Society would examine them. This included copies of her architect's plans and the ground-penetrating

LiDAR scans that she could use to show both where the foundation holes were and that there was nothing hidden beneath the castle's walls.

'Take pictures if you like,' Saskia said, as she made coffee. 'Or I can email you PDF copies. I can send you the 3D render too.'

'Thanks.'

Saskia handed the young woman a mug and they sat together at one of the tables, Brodie flopping down at Saskia's feet, chin on his paws.

'I'm glad you're not going to destroy the oak,' Julie said, quietly, both hands wrapped around her mug as she stared into her coffee. 'Those times I came up here and climbed it with my dad . . . sometimes I think that's the best our relationship ever got. And the forest . . . I still love it, even though it's been years since I came up here, really.'

Saskia smiled. 'Tell me what you love about it,' she said, imagining that the young woman was going to talk about swimming in the river or collecting chestnuts in autumn.

'I think it's all the folklore, actually,' Julie said, instead. 'It feels so weird up here, doesn't it? I felt that on the very first walk we ever did up here, way back when I was really little. Then, when I was older, Dad told me all the old stories. They were scary, but fascinating too.'

Saskia leaned forward, interested. 'Folklore? I don't think I know any of that,' she said. 'I've read up on as much history as I can, but that's mainly about Gair Castle itself, not the forest.'

'Ah, well!' the young woman said, with an enthusiasm and

confidence that told Saskia she'd hit on a favourite subject. 'It's really intriguing, mainly because even now it's still evolving. But stories about the place go back literally centuries.'

'What sort of stories?'

Julie Rhys shifted in her chair, gathering her thoughts. 'Well, there's the pre-Roman and contemporaneous Roman stuff about a splinter group of the local native tribe, the Carvetti. It was said they were so fierce that none of the three Roman garrisons that tried to establish a post here were successful.'

'Now that I've read about,' Saskia said. 'And I'm guessing that's the main basis for Carey's conviction that there are still ruins under the castle.'

'Yes,' Julie agreed. 'Hugh in particular is convinced that the castle was built over the earlier ruins of at least one of those settlements, using it as a foundation.'

'I know that. But' – Saskia gestured to the scans on the walls around them – 'it is demonstrably not true.'

'Hmm,' Julie said and nodded, looking up at the images as she took a mouthful of her coffee. 'Although you have to admit, the fact that there have been several significant finds here over the decades means there must have been *something* here at some point.'

'You mean the two gold aureus found by Foster and Turner?' Saskia asked. She shook her head. 'They were both found on the old road, more than a mile from the castle site. All that proves is that the route has been a thoroughfare for centuries, not that there was a settlement. This would have been on the route up to Hadrian's Wall, remember? Anyway, this is all stuff I knew before. That's not folklore, that's actual history.'

'Right,' the younger woman said. 'Well, there's a lot of tangled stuff there. It's mainly about the forest, and how old it is. This is one of the few places in the Northern Hemisphere where the remnants of the great boreal forest still persist. It used to cover the landmasses from here right across Russia to Alaska back as far as the last Ice Age. The stories talk about something that has lived in the forest all that time, and is still there, in the oldest, most ancient pockets of the forest.'

Saskia frowned. 'Like what, exactly?'

Julie Rhys shook her head. 'There's no definitive answer to that. One of the themes throughout the stories is the idea of kids being lured into the trees and then finding themselves yanked down into the earth by forest spirits – or by some sort of deity, it varies. It's possible that links in some way to this fabled, unnamed tribe that the Romans apparently encountered here. The story there goes that they kept trying to build a fort in the area but were continually repelled by this particularly hostile tribe. Some say that what was actually holding them back was this deity – often typified as a "she" – and that she has a lair or a palace entwined in the trees' roots. I guess that could go back to some kind of attack tactic by people who made the forest floor and perhaps even under the forest floor their home. Or does it go back further than that? It's impossible to tell. That might account for the smoke, too.'

'The smoke?'

'Over the years, many people have reported seeing smoke up here, rising spontaneously from the ground in the forest. But there's never any fire. Just the smoke.'

Saskia remembered the times she'd caught the scent of what seemed like the drift of a lit cigarette as she'd walked Brodie. 'Really?'

'I saw it myself, when I was a kid. It was really weird and definitely freaked me out. You'll be tramping along through the undergrowth and suddenly out of nowhere there's a wreath of smoke drifting in front of you. It's creepy.' Julie smiled. 'But then, the whole forest is. I think that's one of the reasons it's so compelling – and why these stories have persisted for so long. It's got a definite atmosphere that I don't think I've ever experienced anywhere else. You must have felt it.'

'I have,' Saskia admitted. 'Although I've never found it disturbing.'

The young woman smiled. 'Then I suppose this must really be your home.'

Saskia smiled a little herself at that. 'I'd love to read more about this,' she said. 'Could you suggest some books for me?'

'There aren't many, actually,' Julie said. 'But I've been compiling stories I've come across – accounts written up in tiny local publications, personal memoirs, that sort of thing. I can send you those.'

'Thanks,' Saskia told her. 'That would be great. And look – if you want to write about the build here, I'm happy to co-operate. You could follow our progress.'

Julie looked surprised. 'Really?'

'Yes. I don't have anything to hide,' Saskia said. 'And who knows, maybe it'll convince some people that my intentions really are good, not bad.'

Nine

The Historical Society went quiet in the wake of that visit. They'd probably decided to lay low for a while after the police intervention. Owen, despite his enduring anger at Saskia for what she'd done that day, was glad to get back to work. The first cement pour went ahead without a hitch, several tons of mix sinking into those boreholes around the steel stanchions mounted into their cores. Once set, and after another series of engineering checks, the next major phase would be to position the huge metal plates that were to serve as the floor of the house. They were being specially forged by a shipbuilder in Denmark and would arrive by sea at Newcastle docks in a week. Saskia had shown Owen the purchase order, arranged for an astronomical sum that could have built an entire estate of houses elsewhere.

Still, against all odds the build was more or less on schedule and, much to Owen's relief, there had been no major screw-ups.

Owen wished he could say the same for his personal life.

He was still living at Stuart's place. His friend seemed happy to have him there, but the situation was slowly sinking a well of depression into Owen's chest. He couldn't bear to have his daughter visit him at a place where his room was even smaller than her bedroom at home. Besides, despite his best efforts, the rest of the flat was always a mess. Owen couldn't equate this version of Stuart Mackey with the straight-as-a-die soldier he'd served with, the one whose bunk had always been laced up regulation tight, the one who never put a foot out of line. In his own space, that seemed to have deserted him entirely, and Stuart had resorted to being the worst kind of teenage slob. It drove Owen mad, but the alternative was that he take up a lease on a flat of his own and he didn't want to do that. Not yet. That would be admitting defeat; would be accepting that he'd failed as badly at marriage as he had at everything else since he'd left the service.

He mostly saw Hannah at the weekends, taking her to swimming classes and birthday parties, although two evenings a week Tasha did let him come over to put her to bed and read her a story. These perhaps constituted the most painful periods for him of all, but Owen wasn't going to say no. The worst of it was having to answer when his daughter asked why he wouldn't be there for breakfast. He couldn't tell her the truth. He had told her a half-lie instead, hoping that by the time she was old enough to realize this, she would forgive him for it.

'Daddy's working on a big job at the moment. A really big job. I'm rebuilding a whole castle.'

Her eyes had gone round at that. Owen could almost see the picture forming in her head: a computer-animated confection with peppered grey stone, round turrets and steepled roofs. Maybe a moat with a drawbridge, or else a princess in a tower with hair long enough to climb. There had probably been talking mice and a fairy godmother in there somewhere, too. And a lot of pink.

'A *castle*?'

'Yup,' he said, and then added (and this was where even he could see he'd crossed a line), 'That's why I can't be around much at the moment. I have to stay there until the job is done, and that might be a very long time. Okay? But Daddy loves you very much and will always, always be here if you need him. You know that, don't you?'

Hannah, clearly still playing out fantasies of Disney princesses in her head, nodded. He thought he'd got away with it and went on reading the story she had picked. But then, as he'd kissed his sleepy daughter goodnight, she asked him a question he really should have seen coming.

'Can I come and see the castle, Daddy?'

He'd deflected; mentioned something about 'one day' and 'when it's finished', but after that, it had been their main topic of conversation. Owen had known that he was setting himself up for disaster, but what else could he have done except weave the stories he knew she so desperately wanted? It had taken about a week before Tasha confronted him about it.

'You know she's telling all her friends that her dad lives in a castle now?' she said. 'I keep having the mums at the school gate asking me what's going on. It's embarrassing, Owen. For me right now, and it will be for her in the future, too.'

'You were the one who wanted to split, remember?' he pointed out. 'It's not my choice that I'm not at home.'

'That's not the point,' Tasha said. 'What do you think is going to happen when you finally get somewhere of your own and you can actually have her to stay? What are you going to tell her then?'

They were having this conversation by phone as Owen stood beside his truck, looking down at Gair. Stuart was supervising the tanker that had arrived to refill their water supplies, which dwindled fast in a summer that seemed to grow hotter by the day.

'Come to couples counselling with me,' he said. 'Let me move back in. Let's try again. Tasha, please? Once I'm back home she won't even think about a castle.'

Tasha's angry sigh surfed the line straight into his ear. 'Oh, *now* you're willing to try therapy?' she asked. 'How many times have I asked you for that? For how many years? And how often did you tell me it was a waste of money, that we didn't need it anyway? Every time, Owen, that's how often. And now it's too late.'

'Only because you won't try.'

'I've tried, Owen,' she said. 'God knows I've tried. There's not a person on this planet who would say I haven't – except you.'

'One more chance,' he told her. 'That's all I'm asking for.'

'Owen—' There was a pause, and he somehow knew the

axe that was about to fall before she even said the words. 'I'm seeing someone else.'

And that was that.

'Have you seen this?'

Owen glanced across at Saskia, who was in the passenger seat of his truck, most of her face hidden behind a huge pair of dark glasses. She was holding up a copy of the local newspaper. Owen couldn't remember the last time he'd picked up a national paper, let alone the Westmorland Herald.

'Something in it I should know about?'

She folded back the pages into a more manageable handful. 'Julie Rhys has done a piece on the folk tales associated with Gair Forest, as a pre-cursor to a regular column about the Gair build. It's pretty good.'

Owen snorted. 'Great. That's all we need, a load of cosplayers suddenly being inspired to trespass near the work site.'

There was a brief silence. He could feel her watching him from behind those shades and kept his eyes resolutely on the road ahead. He willed her not to say anything, because he wasn't sure he could trust himself to be civil. His irritation was already dangerously close to the surface. They should have been thwapping along the A69, cutting straight across the county of Northumberland towards Newcastle. Instead, because of an accident snarling the larger road, they'd had to peel off onto the B6318. This was much smaller and slower, built directly on top of the old Roman military road and was habituated mainly by tourists visiting the Roman Army

Museum, the active dig at Vindolanda or Housesteads, to walk along the top of the only section of Hadrian's Wall where that was permitted. The steel floor plates were landing at Tyneside today, and he'd stupidly agreed that they should both be there to supervise the trucks as they crossed the country back to Gair. Now here he was stuck in a car with Saskia Tilbury-Martin. At least she'd agreed that he'd drive, although what he really should have insisted on was separate cars.

She was still looking at him.

'What?'

'Are you okay?'

'*What?*' Despite himself, he glanced at her again. What the hell kind of question was that?

She tucked the folded paper on the floor between her feet. 'You've been even more like a bear with a sore head than usual over the last couple of days,' she said. 'Just wondering if it's anything I can help with.'

Turn back the clock, he thought. *Stop my wife from falling out of love with me and in love with someone else. Have you got enough money for that?*

'I'm fine,' is what he said.

From the corner of his eye he saw her nod, and then she turned away to look out of the window at the landscape. They were moving parallel to Hadrian's Wall, the scant remains of the ancient monument appearing and disappearing on the high ridge of rugged Northumberland fields that ran beside them as they drove. Soon they'd be passing the now-empty dip in the fell where someone, for reasons that would for ever remain utterly incomprehensible to Owen and, he assumed, to anyone else with any decency, had taken a chainsaw to the 150-year-old tree at Sycamore Gap.

'Vivian's coming back up this weekend,' Saskia said, apropos of nothing.

'Okay.' Owen couldn't work out why she had thought he'd want to know this. 'I guess that means a nice girls' weekend for you, then.'

She turned to look at him. He could feel her gaze, piercing through the shade of those glasses. 'Do I really strike you as the type?'

He shrugged. He'd never considered it one way or another. He'd always assumed that over the weekends, Saskia disappeared back down to whatever gentrified bit of London she lived in to party away the time before coming back north again for work. But if Vivian was coming to see her here, did that mean Saskia was staying at Gair even when the site wasn't operational? Why would she do that?

'She's not coming to see me,' his boss added. 'She's coming to see Stuart.'

Owen's fingers tightened on the steering wheel. 'What?'

Saskia snorted a slight laugh. 'Yeah. According to her they've been talking a lot. Well, I say *talking*. From what I can tell they're mainly communicating via text.' She added the next comment after a slight pause that conveyed plenty of meaning. 'And . . . video chat.'

Owen cringed. This was all kinds of awful. What was

Stuart thinking? He'd assumed that his night with their boss's best friend had been both the beginning and the end of the affair. Stuart rarely did second dates anyway, and hadn't Owen made it clear how he felt about the whole idea, just from a professional standpoint? He had no idea what to say to Saskia about it; he definitely had no desire to discuss it with her, if that's what she was angling for by bringing it up.

'I just wanted to give you a heads-up, that's all,' Saskia added, 'because Vivian mentioned that you're living with Stu at the moment.'

Owen gritted his teeth.

'And I know it's none of my business—'

'No, it definitely isn't,' he said, the muscles in his neck so taut that he thought his jaw might be about to pop.

'I'm not trying to pry into your personal life, Owen,' she said, quietly, after a moment. 'But look. If you want to take your daughter to Center Parcs for the weekend or something like that, I'd be happy to cover it.'

For a while he tried to work out what he'd just heard: where it had come from, why on earth she would say such a thing, what it meant about just how much his boss knew about his private life. The silence in the car was thick, suffocating with the strength of his animosity. Why would she bring this up? What made this woman think that he either needed or wanted her help, her *charity*? Why—

'Sorry,' she said, into his silence. 'I didn't— This isn't—' Saskia stopped, sighed, tried again. 'I just . . . thought I might be able to make things a bit easier, at least for a while.'

'My family,' Owen said, bluntly, 'is fine. I'm back home now.'

She nodded, looking down at her hands, folded in her lap. 'Okay. That's good.'

'If you want to do something to *help*,' he said, cutting her off before she could say more, 'you can reconsider your stance on the Gair Oak. Because my life would be considerably improved by not having to find a way to work around it.'

Saskia said nothing, turning instead to look out of the window again. On the high ridge to the north the remains of a wall once designed to cut an entire country in half suddenly fell away. The ridge tilted steeply into a sharp slope that dipped before almost immediately rising again, forming a perfect curve in the landscape. It was almost as if someone had carved a bowl there, made it specifically to hold something. But there was nothing there now. It was empty.

'Without the tree,' Saskia observed, quietly, 'it's just a Gap.'

At the docks, Owen left Saskia to check in with the port authorities before they went to find the trucks hauling the steel. The sun was high and bright, glinting off the choppy waters of the working Tyne. He grabbed a pair of sunglasses from his dash and slid out of his seat, slamming the door shut. Around him Tyneside was in constant movement, frenetic motion that mirrored his tired mind. He tried to fathom how true Saskia's story about Stuart and Vivian was, because why would his friend not have told him if he had (and the term seemed ridiculous for a man fast approaching forty) a girlfriend? For that matter, why wouldn't Stuart have let him know if he was planning to have another guest in his tiny flat this weekend? Sure, Owen had said that he was hoping he'd be out of Stuart's way by the end of this week, and no, he hadn't relayed the content of his last bitter conversation with Tasha to his friend – or to anyone, for that matter – but still. Owen wanted to believe that Saskia was wrong, but he couldn't work out why she would be stirring the pot if what she'd said wasn't true. He took out his phone and was about to call Stuart's number to ask him about it directly when he heard a voice calling his name.

'Owen? Owen Elliot?'

Owen turned to see a figure he hadn't seen for several years snaking his way around the knots of cars towards him.

'Adrian?'

The tall, stocky man grinned as he reached Owen, immediately sticking out his hand to shake. 'Thought I recognized a familiar face,' he said. They were the same height, though in the years since they'd both left the service Adrian Braithwaite seemed to have put on a pound or two, probably not surprising for a man who must now be in his mid-fifties. 'How are you doing, mate? Good to see you. What are you doing on Tyneside? I thought the other side of the country was your stomping ground?'

'It is, I'm just here to check on an arriving shipment. You?' Owen struggled not to finish his question with an added 'sir', because old habits die hard. Back in uniform, Braithwaite had been officer class from the off, a major ranked above Owen's staff sergeant status. They'd got on well though, and Owen had always thought him to be a decent guy, especially for officer class. It helped that they were both from the North, he supposed, though in Braithwaite's case that had meant some family pile in County Durham rather than the ragged wilds of the north-eastern borderlands.

'Something similar,' Braithwaite told him. 'I heard you went into the construction business. That so?'

'It is. I heard the same about you.'

Braithwaite nodded. 'Actually, I'm about to start working over on your patch.' His eyes twinkled as he glanced at his old subordinate. 'Hope I won't be treading on your toes.'

'I doubt it, unless you're planning to construct a line in absurd designer castles for the rich and famous around Carlisle. Because that's what I'm doing for the next year or so.'

His old commander looked blank for a second, and then realization dawned on Braithwaite's face. He raised a hand, pointing a finger at Owen. 'Have you taken on that colossus of a white elephant? What was it called, now . . .' He snapped his fingers, trying to jog his memory. 'Grey Castle?'

'Gair,' Owen corrected him. A frisson of discomfort coasted across his shoulders and he felt himself tensing, though he didn't know why. Saskia had told him herself that she'd gone through a lot of other contractors before reaching Owen. 'You looked at the site yourself?'

'Never got that far,' Braithwaite said, with a grimace.

'Didn't need to when I saw who it was trying to get that project off the ground.'

'What do you mean?'

Braithwaite snorted. 'Saskia Tilbury-Martin? That whole family is a mess, I wouldn't touch any of them with a barge pole, but she's the cherry on the cake. When she called my office, I was tempted to ask her how long she'd been out of rehab. *This* time.'

Owen's blood ran cold. For a moment he thought he'd misheard, but Braithwaite slapped him on the back before sticking his hand in a pocket to pull out a card.

'Look,' he said, passing it to Owen, 'if you ever need a job, call me. I'll be looking for good people in the next few years, and to start with at least it'll be over your way. I'm working with Lawrence Homes on the first stage of these new eco-developments of theirs. If all goes to plan there'll be a lot more coming down the line.'

Owen looked down at the card. 'Thanks,' he said, feeling as if he'd been standing on an ice floe that had just disintegrated beneath his feet. 'I heard about that development. Down in Collaton, right?'

'That's right,' Braithwaite said. 'And look, maybe I'm wrong about the Tilbury-Martin woman. To be honest I would have said no to that job even if I hadn't had prior knowledge, so I'm sorry if I spoke out of turn. Either way, call me. Like I said, I can use good workers, not to mention men who can lead a team. Anyway, I'd better get on. It was good to see you, Owen. You look well.'

Owen felt numb as he watched his old colleague walk away. Had he really thrown in his lot with an addict? The idea made his skin crawl. He thought back to every interaction with Saskia that he'd ever had. He'd never had any inkling that she wasn't stone-cold sober. Now he wondered. She always wore long-sleeved tops, didn't she? He'd never seen her in anything but a shirt, first that tailor-made one and then denim or plaid cotton after that. She hadn't stripped down to a tee shirt or rolled up those sleeves, even on the hottest days at Gair. Was that to hide something she didn't want him to see?

'Owen?'

He turned to see Saskia standing on the walkway above him, waving at him, a sheaf of papers in one hand.

'I've got the loading bay details,' she called. 'You should come and take a look. I want to check everything against the manifest before we start moving. It's this way.'

She pointed ahead of her and began to walk, her boots clanging a distant cacophony on the gangway. He stared after her for a second, and then he slowly began to follow.

Ten

'Oh *God*, Sas,' Vivian said, horrified. 'What on earth possessed you to say anything at all? I'm going to be right up shit creek now. I'm sure Stu told me that in confidence.'

It was Sunday night; Vivian had come to visit after her weekend with Stuart and before her drive back to London. The evening was a warm one, and Saskia had lit the fire pit she'd bought a few weeks earlier, not for the warmth but because the woodsmoke kept away the midges and other bugs that emerged from the forest in the muted shades of dusk. They sat side by side in deckchairs, Gair spread out below them like an eccentric, shadowy lawn ornament, the sort of thing some Victorian industrialist would have built to show off to his friends. Saskia had confessed what she'd offered Owen in the wake of Vivian's revelation that he'd been crashing at Stuart's flat.

'I thought it might help,' Saskia tried to explain, although in truth she'd regretted bringing it up the second the words had come out of her mouth. 'I was thinking about his little girl, that's all. I thought . . .' She trailed off. 'Anyway, it doesn't matter now, does it? He said he was back home and you said he wasn't at Stuart's, so whatever was going on is obviously sorted. I just want this build to work. I'm still waking up at night in a cold sweat, having dreamt that something terrible has happened. Last night it was a bloody great sinkhole. The night before it was a *tornado.* If Owen were to quit, I'd never find a replacement. You know how hard it was to find him in the first place.'

Vivian sighed. 'I do worry about this, you know. Your obsession with this place. I'm not sure it's healthy. It's like . . .'

Saskia's heart clenched a little. 'Don't,' she said. 'Don't say it.'

'I have to, Saskia. It's like an addiction. Like you've swapped one for another. It scares me, what would happen if you had to go cold turkey on this place . . .'

Saskia stood up. She couldn't listen to this. 'You know why this is so important to me,' she said. 'I'm not crazy, Viv. I'm not in danger of a relapse, precisely *because* of this place. And I'm not "unbalanced", whatever my mother is whispering in your ear. That's where this is coming from, isn't it? I told you not to talk to her, why are you—'

'I'm not,' Vivian interrupted, standing up. She reached out to take Saskia's hand, squeezing it firmly. 'I promise. I haven't heard from her for weeks. I've set her ringtone to the Wicked Witch theme so I know it's her before I even look at the screen. And I'd never listen to her over you anyway. You *know* that.'

They remained like that for a moment, looking at the shadows of the barely-there castle. *The only thing that matters in my barely-there life*, Saskia thought, with a bleakness she mostly managed to keep at bay. Maybe everyone else was right. Maybe she *was* mad.

'It must have sounded a bit weird to him though, you can see that, can't you?' Vivian said, gently. 'His boss offering to pay for him to go to Center Parcs for the weekend. What's he supposed to think?'

Saskia frowned. 'I thought it'd mean he could spend time with his daughter, that's all, if that was being a problem,' she said. 'I was thinking about me and Dad, I suppose.'

Vivian squeezed her hand again, laced their fingers together. 'I get it. But I can see why he wouldn't.'

Saskia sighed and rubbed a hand over her face. 'I'll talk to him. Apologize.'

'Maybe don't,' her friend suggested. 'Maybe just leave it. Let the work sort everything out. That's what you're both here for, isn't it?'

Saskia looked down at the site again. The massive metal base sheets formed a shadowy void beside the crane that would lift them into place. A foundation that would help her create something new, from a past too patchworked to separate. For a long time now, the castle had been a metaphor for Saskia's rebuilding of her own life. 'Yeah. You're probably right. At least if he's back with his wife he should be a bit more cheerful. With the men, if not with me.'

Vivian squeezed her hand one last time and then squinted

at her watch in the falling dark. 'I'd better get going. I've got to scout a shoot in Limehouse tomorrow afternoon. Can you walk to my car with me?' She glanced out at the thick shadows gathering beneath the trees surrounding them. 'Honestly, I don't know how you stay here on your own. It's *so* creepy. I feel like something's watching me *all the time* when I'm here.'

Heat shimmered over the site the day the first of the metal sheets was winched into place. The sun roared up overhead as if it had something to prove, setting fire to the sky from the moment it tipped the horizon that morning. Saskia had worked out that to accommodate the tree they would need one large crane standing outside the walls and a smaller 'mini-crane' inside. It meant additional expense in terms of plant hire, labour and time, but it would have to be done. Positioning the first sheet was a fraught process that took hours, but eventually it lay across the foundation settings, the holes cut into the metal sheet jigsawed into place to match the stanchions driven into the foundations below. Saskia had been stressing for days that she had made some miscalculation, that they wouldn't align and the extortionately expensive floor would have to be forged again, at even greater expense because of the delay such a disaster would cause. But no, her calculations were perfect. They should be, she had checked them *ad infinitum*.

They got two of the base plates into position that day, and with every hour that passed the temperature seemed to rise.

All the lads were stripped to their waists, ridiculous in their hard hats, hi-vis vests and naked torsos. Meanwhile, Saskia's shirt stuck to her skin. She longed for a bath, but all she had in the trailer was the smallest possible shower, fed by a very limited water tank.

A couple of times she hitched her shirt up at her waist in an effort to waft air against her torso, and on both occasions she thought she caught Owen watching her, but perhaps she was imagining it. Things between them were still strained. She had taken Vivian's advice and kept her distance, wanting to let him see that she was sorry for the overstep, that she had no intention of making the same mistake twice. He'd listened to her solutions for working around the oak tree with the crane silently, only nodding here and there and giving his assent to the plan once she had finished speaking. They were civil, and wasn't that what she'd told him they needed to be? Civil, and nothing more. She wasn't sure why this felt like a failure.

By the time four o'clock rolled around she was about ready to climb into one of the generator's coolant tanks. Anything to slough off the sweat of the day.

'You want to get yourself down to that river,' Stuart told her, as he left. 'You wouldn't get me out of it if that was running through my back yard.'

It was a good idea – an excellent one, in fact – and Saskia wasn't sure how it hadn't occurred to her before. She'd tramped all over the woods with Brodie, or at least through the parts that were accessible without a machete. As the summer had sweltered on, she'd relished the cool shade that persisted beneath the canopy of leaves as well as the quiet. It was one of the few places she had been in her life where it was possible to stop, breathe in and, notwithstanding the distant roar of the odd airliner passing overhead, hear no human activity at all. And, since she'd begun reading through the strange, unsettling stories Julie had sent her, the forest had taken on a deeper meaning still.

Once the site gates were locked and she and Brodie were alone, Saskia went back to the trailer and stripped herself out of the wet rags of her work gear. Strictly speaking her working day was not yet done – she had orders to make and accounts to input into the endless roll of Excel documents that kept the worst of her night terrors at bay. Today, though, they could wait. She could work later, but for now, the forest and the river called.

Saskia dug out her old one-piece swimsuit and pulled on a fresh pair of jeans and a cropped tee shirt over the top. She filled her drinking bottle with water and packed it along with an old towel and a picnic blanket into an oversized tote bag, pulled on a battered pair of hi-top sneakers and set off.

The cool calm of the forest was a relief as soon as she stepped beneath its tangled canopy. It was as if the trees absorbed all sound. Brodie stayed close, ears pricked as he listened to noises she couldn't hear, made by unseen creatures skittering beneath the ferns and meadowsweet. Beyond the clearing in which Gair stood, the unruly woodland levelled out for a short distance before dipping into a slope that ran all the way down to the river. Saskia picked her way over logs and across fallen branches, careful not to turn an ankle amid the understory. Several times she stopped just to absorb the silence. It was all-encompassing, this quiet, as thick as the smell of loam that drifted around her, layers of scent composed of so many elements it would be impossible to identify them all. The silence felt the same, as if she had been removed from the world and put inside a bottle that contained only this forest. There was no breeze, no bird call, nothing beyond this small, tree-crowded patch of earth.

When she reached the slope the sound of the river drifted up from below her, the glint of it just visible through the trees. She picked her way down to it, bracing herself against trunks, clinging to branches as she tried to keep her footing on the uneven, unseen ground. Everything bent towards the water, reaching for it, so that she had to clamber over an ash that seemed to be growing perpendicular to the earth. After that, Saskia found herself standing once again in sun, let in by the clearing the river had cut for itself through the forest.

She found herself on a section of the river bank she had not come across before. The water gurgled and tripped over itself at her feet, rushing through the channel that was so peculiarly straight compared to the riot of trees around it that she wondered whether it was man-made. The banks were also curiously flat. Saskia realized that she was standing on grey granite covered thickly with moss rather than earth. She had come across a ledge of rock, through which, over the millennia, the water had forged a crevice. Saskia crouched and reached down to trail her fingers in the water. It was cool but not as ice cold as she'd expected, warmed by the sun that had sat above it for most of the day.

She made her way along the stone ledge, moving parallel to the boundary fence that she could just see above her on the far right of the river. It rose away from her and eventually out of sight as she picked her way across the hillocky moss. Brodie, in no mood to delay, jumped straight into the river and bounded along beside her, splashing water into the air in a joyful display of doggy enthusiasm.

Saskia heard the fall of water before she saw it. The river vanished over a small lip in the rock and, reaching the edge, she looked down to see that here the river widened into a pool. It was nowhere near big enough to swim laps, nor deep enough for a human to jump into, but it was a roughly circular cauldron in the stone, hollowed out by eons of water dropping into it from above and then flowing on over another lip of rock. The fast movement of the water kept it clean – she could see the flat, overlapping rocks that formed the pool's bottom, like miniature tectonic plates, their edges worn smooth. The waterfall was shaded by a cracked granite wall that curved around it. Tenacious foliage sprouted from crevices in the stone: tufts of grasses grown long and wispy as they stretched towards the dappled light; tiny twists of rowan trees, the rouge of their berries vibrant against the grey rock; puffs of dwarfed gorse with its bright yellow flowers.

Brodie leapt without hesitation down the naturally stepped, mossy incline that was squeezed between the cliff and the waterfall. Reaching the pool's edge, the dog leapt in, sending a tidal wave of water surging up and out of the pool, high enough for a rainbow of drops to shower Saskia.

'All right, all right, I'm coming,' she laughed, as the dog paddled around, looking up at her as if wondering why she hadn't done the same. Saskia put down her tote and shucked her tee shirt, glancing up towards the boundary line in case anyone was watching from the footpath on the other side, but of course they weren't. The pool wouldn't be visible from there anyway. You'd have to know it was here to make your way to it, or else be following the line of the river, the way she had. She was alone apart from Brodie. A moment later her jeans were off too and then, after carefully negotiating the slope – breaking an ankle here would be a particular nightmare – she was in the water.

It was blissfully cool. Saskia lay back with her ears beneath the surface, floating, the world at a distance as the crash of the waterfall drowned out all other sound. She felt the tensions of the day leaving her shoulders. Far above her was a dappled patchwork of branches, the leaves of the trees atop the cliff and on the other side of the river almost but not quite meeting over her head. She shut her eyes and lay there, breathing in, breathing out, as if she had not a care in the world.

She heard Brodie's muffled barking through the water and lifted her head, bare feet finding the base of the rock pool. Her arms floated beneath the surface, her scars gleaming white against the water.

'Brodie?' Saskia shouted. He'd leapt out of the pool and

disappeared. She listened for him, but the forest was silent. She waded to the edge of the pool and hoisted herself up onto the edge. 'Brodie! Come!'

For a moment she heard nothing, and then there was a sudden eruption of noise and he appeared from the underbrush, panting. There was a leaf stuck beneath the leather of his collar.

'Where did you go?' she demanded. 'Don't run off like that.'

The dog shook himself vigorously, then immediately undid the good that had done by leaping back into the pool and swimming in hectic circles.

'Daft pup,' she muttered, a little unsettled. He'd probably caught the scent of a rabbit and been unable to stop himself from giving chase, but still. It was unlike Brodie to abandon her for anything.

Back in the pool, she remained still for long moments, surveying the forest, waiting for some hint of movement. Was there something out there? Someone, even? She felt as if someone was watching her. Instinctively she looked towards the far bank of the river, searching for the fence that was still out of sight. If anyone was spying on her, surely it would be from there? For a fraction of a second she thought she could smell smoke, but when she turned, it had gone. *You're imagining things*, Saskia told herself. *You've been reading too many of Julie's folk tales, that's all.*

Saskia stayed in the pool for almost an hour and was loath to leave it even when she finally looked at her watch and realized the time. At least now, thanks to her soak, she felt ready to settle down to work again. Getting out of the water she clambered back up above the waterfall, avoiding the lethal stabs of the gorse, and went to the tote. She pulled out her towel, and stopped. Hadn't she also put a blanket in there? Surely she had rolled it up and shoved it in before doing the same with the towel? But it wasn't there. Saskia briefly scanned the ground, as if she might have spread it out beside the pool, but of course she knew she hadn't. She puzzled on this for a second, then decided that she must have left it on the sofa in the trailer after all. It didn't matter – she wasn't going to linger at the river bank, not this evening. She dried herself, pulled on her tee shirt and shorts again, shoved the now-wet towel back into the bag and shouted for the dog.

Back at the trailer she looked for the blanket, but it was nowhere to be seen.

Eleven

It took a week to get all the metal plates in place. The last one was the most difficult, and there was a while where Owen thought Saskia's calculations were wrong, but in the end it slotted in exactly. This was just as well, because the structural engineer was booked in the following day to check their progress and oversee the next phase, which would be to erect the vertical steel beams into the stanchions that ran right down into the foundations. Then the second concrete pour would turn the metal plates into a floor. Once that was complete, they were due a visit from the building inspector and Historic England, after which the second phase – which included the construction of the second floor's skeleton – could begin.

Ever since the Newcastle trip, Owen had been attempting to get Stuart to tell him anything that Vivian had said about Saskia, but his friend flat refused.

'Come on,' Stuart had said, apparently offended by the request. 'I'm not going to do that. Don't put me in that position.'

'What are you talking about?' Owen asked. 'You gab about everything all the time. How is this different?'

'It just is,' was all Stuart would offer. Well, that and, 'Anyway, she hasn't said anything.'

'Then ask her. For me.'

For that one, he just got a look.

Stuart was letting him crash again. It had of course been a complete lie that Owen had been going back home the weekend after he'd driven to Newcastle with Saskia. It was clear now that Tasha was not going to reconcile with him. He'd blown it, completely, and the best he could hope for was that they could find a way to successfully co-parent Hannah and not mess her up in the course of their divorce. Doing that, as Tasha had said bluntly the last time they'd talked about it, meant that he really needed to 'sort himself out', particularly where his living situation was concerned.

'There's no way I'm not going to fight for full custody if you don't have somewhere permanent and *decent* to live,' she'd pointed out. 'Find somewhere that isn't Stuart's hovel, for God's sake. Or move back in with your dad and stepmum. They've got the room, and Hannah loves them. You'd have help with her. I'd be happy with that.'

But the thought of doing that made Owen shudder. As much as he loved them, if he moved back there, he might as well accept that his life was over. Had he really slipped that far? The Gair job was supposed to be a turning point towards a better life, not a worse one. No, he wouldn't move back in with either of his parents.

The problem was finding somewhere else to live, somewhere suitable that he could afford. A house, that was what he wanted. Hadn't he spent enough time building them for other people to have earned one for himself? It wasn't as if he was asking for anything special. A new-build two-up two-down would do, in one of the cookie-cutter estates that were springing up on the outskirts of the city. They were pitched as affordable family homes, and yet even they seemed so far out of reach for Owen as to be laughable. He didn't have even a fraction of the required deposit, and his wage from Gair – while it was the going rate for such a job – meant nothing without the kind of down payment that made him suck in his breath. That was before he even got to the theoretical monthly mortgage payment he'd be expected to keep up with. And this was in *Carlisle.* What was the world coming to? But if he didn't find somewhere soon, he'd be unable to expect any custody at all, and fighting for it would mean punting most of his money at a lawyer instead of into decent housing.

He'd cleared out for the weekend that Vivian visited. He'd gone to a hotel for two nights and tried not to draw equations between himself and Alan Partridge. Not that he could afford to live in a hotel beyond that weekend anyway. He'd considered it for about a second. He'd looked at the idea of an Airbnb too, because a holiday let would at least be clean and nicely done out, but it was the height of summer and it didn't take long for him to realize it was a stupid idea if he wanted to have any chance of putting any money aside.

He'd ended up back at Stuart's as soon as Vivian was gone. His friend had welcomed him in without complaint, and as a lodger who was more grateful for the poky room and the small double bed than he had been just a few days before.

In a way, Owen was obscurely grateful to Saskia for giving him the heads-up about Stuart and Vivian. The whole experience had been a bit of a wake-up call. After his initial outrage that Stuart hadn't told him about this planned dalliance, Owen had realized he'd no right to complain. He'd told Stuart he'd be out of the way and just assumed that it would be no problem if he wasn't. In retrospect he wished his pride hadn't been too great to take Saskia's offer. His immediate outrage had been driven by surprise followed by a strong wave of humiliation. Aside from Stuart, he hadn't told anyone – including his parents – about his split with Tasha and their imminent divorce. Now here was his boss bringing it up as if it were common knowledge. It had stung, and he'd stung back. But it had been a kind offer, he could see that now. What he couldn't work out was how to square it against everything else he knew and now suspected about her.

He'd watched her like a hawk since that day in Newcastle. She never took that shirt off, never rolled the arms up, even when the day was as hot as the inside of Satan's armpit.

'Come on,' he'd said to Stuart, as they caught up in the pub later that week. 'Have you ever thought she might be – you know – out of it?'

His friend had stared at him, mystified. 'Mate, she doesn't even smoke. I've never once seen her drink, have you?'

That was a good point. In recovery, then? But for how long? Adrian had mentioned rehab, and the idea that if Saskia had been in such a place then it wouldn't be for the first time, or probably even the second. And didn't that sort of programme tell you not to make any big decisions for at least a year after getting out? Big decisions such as buying a castle, for example?

'She's an architect,' Stuart pointed out. 'That's not a fake-out, is it? Which means she did that training, and that takes *years*. And she's a good one, as far as I can see. I don't understand what your problem is with her, to be honest. She pays on time, she listens to her guys, she's a grafter. So she has a past. Who doesn't?' There was a pause after this, as Stuart stared at him with an open speculation that made Owen uncomfortable for what he might ask next. 'What's the real problem?'

'What do you mean, the "real" problem?' Owen demanded. 'How about I just don't want to find myself on a sinking ship? Isn't that enough of a problem?'

Stuart shook his head. 'Viv says Saskia's the best person she's ever known. That she'd give someone on the street the shirt off her back if they needed it, and they wouldn't even have to ask.'

Owen snorted at that, an exhalation of disbelief that blew the foam from his pint across the table. But still, he remembered her offer to him and his baby girl, given out of the blue and before he'd even known he needed somewhere to go.

*

'Anyone seen the Hobnobs?'

The distant shout echoed across the work site. Owen wasn't sure of the source; he was concentrating on the lowering of the last vertical load-bearing beam into position.

'We finished the packet, didn't we?'

'No, that was the last one. I opened a new one yesterday afternoon, remember? We can't have finished them already, it's not even eleven o'clock!'

'Dunno,' came the second voice. 'Once Eddie gets going, he's a right Cookie Monster.'

'Oi!' yelled the erstwhile Eddie. 'I resent that! Wasn't me. Swear it. Had my Weetabix this morning, didn't I?'

Owen waved a hand at the crane driver as the beam clanged into position. In an ingenious feat of modern engineering, it would rotate onto the pin already welded into the base stanchion, an innovation in Saskia's design that he begrudgingly had to admire. Half an hour later it was fixed in, the last of a curious forest of upright steel girders in which the genuine oak formed an unlikely centrepiece.

'I can't believe they're all actually in and fixed. It's worked so well! Doesn't it look great?'

It was Saskia's voice, behind him. Owen turned to see her surveying the girders, her face lit with a brilliant smile. He glanced at the completed work, a spark of annoyance flickering in his chest. Had she been worried that it wouldn't work? He'd seen her checking over angles and calculations on the iPad she carried with her everywhere. Had there been some element of uncertainty that she hadn't bothered to tell him about?

'Well,' he said, 'they're up, at least. I'll reserve judgement on anything else until it's been checked and triple-checked by the engineer.'

He walked away, leaving her standing there behind him.

'Do we have a problem?'

Owen looked up from where he'd been leaning over his desk as Saskia walked into his office. She still wore her hard hat, the heat of the day visible in the strands of dark hair sticking against her forehead and curling against her neck. He put down the pen in his hand and stood up.

'Excuse me?'

She glanced out of the door and then pushed it shut before turning back to him with a resolute look on her face.

'Look,' she said. 'I'm sorry that I overstepped the mark with the Center Parcs offer. I was sincerely trying to help. I apologized for it at the time.'

He crossed his arms with a frown. 'I remember.'

She spread her hands. 'I can be sympathetic if you're having a difficult time at the moment—'

'I'm not.'

Saskia looked at him steadily. 'Then I'll ask you again – what's the problem? Before that I thought we'd reached an understanding, Owen. I thought we'd managed to form a decent working relationship after our rocky start. But now it's as if we've gone backwards. You're questioning everything I say. It wouldn't be so bad if you were doing it in private, but you're not. You're doing it in front of the crew.'

'I can't down tools and call a private meeting with you every time I have a question.'

'It's not the fact that you have questions, Owen – it's the nature of those questions and how and when you decide to ask them. As if suddenly you don't trust anything I say.' He saw the set of her jaw and knew she wasn't backing down from this one. 'Something's happened and I want to know what. This isn't good for the project and honestly, I've got enough problems without having to count you among them.'

He stared at her. 'Oh, *you've* got enough problems?'

'That's right,' she said, holding his glare. 'I know you seem to have trouble believing that, but I do. So come on, let's sort this out. What's going on?'

'Oh, I don't have any trouble believing you have *problems*,' he said, pointedly.

'What's that supposed to mean?'

'Are you under the influence of an illegal substance right now?'

The look on her face might have been comical if the stakes of her answer hadn't been so high. Saskia's mouth fell open. 'I . . . What?' she stuttered, clearly shocked.

'You heard me. And if not now, has there been any time you've been under the influence of illegal substances while you've been on the work site? Around me? Around any member of the work team? As we've been using the heavy machinery, or you've been directing the crane, for example, or—'

'No!' Her cheeks, which had turned deathly pale, now took on two livid specks of colour that blazed almost as brightly as the anger in her eyes. 'Of course not. I wouldn't— How could you even *think* that?'

He leaned forward, both hands on the desk. 'You're telling me you've never taken drugs? That you've never been an addict?'

She stared at him, opened her mouth for a moment as if she were about to give an angry retort, but said nothing. Abruptly, she looked away.

'Yeah,' he said, although his heart sank into his stomach at this silent confirmation of his fears. 'That's what I thought. And you didn't think that was relevant information for me to have? You know, before I threw in my entire reputation with this *insane* project?'

'I'm in recovery,' she said, and he could tell she was trying to keep her voice even.

'Oh, really? And how many times have you been "in recovery"?'

Saskia looked at him again then, angry eyes searching his face. She took a step towards the desk, evidently in no mood to back down. Which was fine, because neither was he. 'Where's this coming from? Have you been speaking to my mother?'

'What?' It was his turn to be taken aback. 'Your *mother*? No, of course not. Why would I? Bad news travels, that's all. You should know that.'

'Gossip, you mean?'

'*Is* it gossip?'

She stepped back from the table, turning away from him. There was a moment of absolute silence. He watched her stiffen; could see the taut lines of tension in her neck despite the fall of her bedraggled hair. He heard her inhale, slowly, as if calming herself.

'I . . .' she said, turning to face him and looking him straight in the eye as she said it, '. . . have been officially sober for five years.'

Five years. It was a long time, if that was true. She must have been able to see the doubt on his face, because she shook her head, her mouth twisting into an unhappy grimace.

'You want me to start drug testing every day? Fine. You can check me every day, Owen, if that's what you want. But it'll be a waste of time and money because I'm clean, and I have been for a long time now. I wonder how true that is of every other person working on this site?'

He raised a hand in warning. 'Don't. Don't do that. I run a tight ship. None of my guys—'

'—had a drink or two in the pub last night?' she countered.

'I have a rule,' he said. 'No more than two pints on a work night. They all know it.'

'Admirable,' Saskia said, and he couldn't tell if she were being sarcastic or not. 'Well, you'll find I never have more than zero, so how about that?'

He thought of that offer Stuart had made at the start of the project, when she'd turned down joining them in the pub. She'd been invited several times since, too, but she'd always said no. Worried about temptation, he supposed, and if she still found it that hard to be around drinking after five years clean . . .

'I go to a meeting,' she said. 'Every Friday night. It was the first thing I looked for up here when the work at Gair became a reality. That's why I never come out with the guys after work at the end of the week.'

Owen flicked a glance at her, and she raised her eyebrows at him, defiant and angry, as if she had any right to be either, under the circumstances.

'Anything else you want to know, ask me now,' she said, 'because after today we are done with this. Understand?'

He gave a snort. 'You think you're the one with the right to dictate that?'

'Yes, I do,' she said. 'Because I have never given you any reason to think that I have ever been less than one hundred per cent dedicated to this project since the moment we met. I don't know who's got in your ear, but they're full of bullshit. I've been clean five years. Actually, it's been far longer than that, but that's the point I mark it from because that's the point at which the lawyers started taking official note so that I could prove to all that I was ready to take on Gair and everything that comes with it. I've already proven myself to people with far more to hold over my head than you, Owen Elliot, so come on, have at it. Bring it on. Every question you've got. Let's get it out there, right now.'

He put his hands on his hips, astounded by her audacity, and then wondered why it surprised him. Did she not understand the problem here? This wasn't just about him. His throwing in his lot with her was one thing. But now he had a whole crew of men who were his responsibility. They all had lives, and most had families to support. Gair was a crazy idea whatever way you looked at it and a lot of them had only signed on because they knew him. And to think that they were a relapse away from the whole project sliding into oblivion, because he'd put his faith in an addict . . . He never would have put them in that position, had he known the full facts.

'What was it?' he asked. 'Your poison?'

Her mouth twisted again. 'Anything that I could get my hands on. At the bitter end, anyway.'

His gaze fell to her arms, covered shoulder-to-wrist, as usual. 'Hence the perpetual long sleeves.'

She looked down at herself, hooked her thumbs into her cuffs in a curiously childlike gesture. Saskia said nothing for a moment. 'Sure,' she said. 'If you like. Anything else?'

'Why would you think your mother would call me, of all people?'

'I couldn't think of another reason why you'd suddenly have this rubbish in your head. After all, you're obviously not the sort to trawl the Internet for society gossip, or you'd have asked me this weeks ago.'

This gave him pause. He hadn't considered that the answers he'd wanted about her – or some of them, anyway – might already be readily available online. 'I don't believe everything I read about someone.'

She snorted at that. 'And yet you're willing to believe whatever random crap someone's repeated about me? Why? Because they've done it in person?'

No, was his unvoiced thought. *Because I would trust the man who told me with my life. Have, in fact, on more than one occasion.*

'You should have told me.'

'Why?' she demanded. 'Have I ever given you any indication that I was in danger of a relapse? Would it even have occurred to you to ask me this if not for that meddling little bird twittering in your ear? Tell me, Owen, did you disclose to me every single shameful thing in *your* past before you took my money to do this job?'

He looked away, but she wasn't finished.

'Did I ever even *ask* you about your past?'

He tapped his fingers on the desktop. 'No.'

'No,' she agreed. 'Are we done here?'

She took his silence for assent and turned for the door. Her fingers were on the handle when he spoke again.

'If it had been your mother who had called me, what would she have said?'

Saskia gave a hard snort of laughter at that. 'Every bad thing that you might expect. And none of it would be true.'

'Your own mother? Why would she do that?'

She turned her head to look at him. For a split second there was a pinpoint of sadness in her dark eyes, lurking behind the fatigue of the day. Then it was gone, replaced by a knife edge that glinted like steel.

'Because I would be so much more useful to her if I were

still in that hole. But I'm not going back there. Not for her. Not for anything.'

He believed her. He nodded. A moment later, she was gone.

Twelve

Things quieted between them over the next few days. They avoided each other, and when they did have to interact, they were civil and efficient, but the conversations did not linger. Saskia's fury had subsided almost immediately after their confrontation. She had a tendency to blame herself for any failure anyway – a behaviour learned long before she had fallen into the black hole of her dependency – and she was aware that many would believe she should have indeed disclosed this part of her past to her work colleague. But on the other hand, she hadn't been lying about being clean for years, or the seriousness with which she took the project at Gair. If something were to jeopardize this build ... Well, that's when the danger would strike. In the midst of it, living here at Gair, seeing her plans for the castle slowly inch their way into life ... That wasn't a danger. That was Saskia's reason for still being alive at all.

She was annoyed at herself for letting slip about her mother. Because Owen had been right: why on earth would she call him, of all people? Elsa Cavendish didn't even know he existed, and had she known, she was the kind of person who would treat Owen precisely in the manner he had accused Saskia herself of behaving. This idea that she could be cut from the same cloth as her mother had stung, perhaps even more than his palpable disgust at her addiction.

The rest of the crew could sense the rift. The site had been quiet since their face-off, subdued in a way it had never been since the work had started. It was Stuart who consistently made an active effort to reach out to Saskia, passing friendly comments as they crossed paths during the work day and including her in the coffee round from the break room, even though he knew as well as the rest of them that there was a machine in her cabin. This inclusion is how she first noticed that the mugs were going missing.

'Mick, where's the new one I gave you yesterday?' Stuart yelled from the break room steps, his voice carrying across the work site like a fog horn.

'I left it on the steps,' Mick yelled back, swinging the girder he'd been hefting around on his shoulder. 'There was a whole line of 'em. It must be there somewhere.'

Stuart shook his head, disappeared back inside the break room and reappeared a few minutes later with six mugs, three crammed into each massive hand. He stopped beside Saskia first; passed her one with his brow still knitted into a frown.

'I think we're going to have to order some more, boss,' he said.

'Really?' Saskia was surprised. 'I thought I'd ordered double what we needed.'

Stuart shrugged. 'Maybe this lot are eating them, but they're not here.'

'No bother,' Saskia said, lightly. 'I'll get some more in, or I've got some extras in the trailer if you're desperate.'

'Cheers.' Stuart headed off to deposit the rest of his deliveries. Saskia watched him go as she sipped her drink. She'd spent twenty minutes on the phone to Vivian the night before, so she knew just how well their relationship was progressing. Well enough that her friend was planning yet another weekend trip up to visit, which would be her third in a month. Saskia wondered briefly whether Vivian had talked to Stuart about her past, and whether that was where Owen's information had come from. But no, she couldn't believe that. Vivian was the only one of her friends who had stuck by her through thick and thin. She wouldn't gossip, at least not about Saskia. Besides, if she had, Owen would have known how long her sobriety had lasted. He would have known how determined she was not to let it slip, not this time.

The notification, when it came, appeared from so far out of left field that for a moment there Saskia thought it might actually be a terrible prank.

'Bumper batch for you this morning,' said Ziggy the postie, with his customary cheerfulness, as he hopped out of his van to deliver the wadge of letters and circulars directly into Saskia's hand.

'Ziggy' had been bringing mail to the site since they'd begun work, an arrangement she had put in place with

Royal Mail at great expense and with maximum complication, given that Gair had no post code. Still, once sorted, Ziggy had dutifully appeared almost every day, wending his long way up the access road to the castle in his delivery van, bringing with him high spirits and not a little local gossip. Although, in this case, 'local' was relative. Every time he left, Saskia found herself wondering what Ziggy was taking with him to pass on to others about the works at Gair, and indeed about Saskia herself. The man was himself as much a messenger as the letters and parcels he carried, disseminating information in a currency perhaps even more valuable than the actual letters he delivered. She didn't mind. She liked Ziggy, and she thought perhaps that he liked her a little too, mainly because she hoped his perpetually cheerful persona wasn't an act.

The day was hot, the dust dry. It hadn't rained for at least two weeks now. It was a situation that Saskia was professionally grateful for; the last thing they needed was for the building site to become a mudbath. But still, she'd kill for a little light rainfall, anything to break the breathless, suffocating heat.

She took the offered stack of post and smiled. 'Want a cold one?'

'What I wouldn't give,' Ziggy told her. He was a youngish, energetic man in his mid-forties, not the age she would usually equate with shorts and a tee shirt, but he carried it off with effortless aplomb. Together they headed for the break room and the fridge there, stocked with a variety of soft drinks. She half-listened to the latest update on Mrs Jackson's missing cat – a saga that had been drifting on for a worrying length of time now – as she sifted through the letters. It amazed Saskia how successfully Gair had already been reached by junk post, given that there was no one officially living here. In her hands she held the usual litany of adverts, catalogues and bills, until she reached the last one. It was A5, a tan envelope with a clear window bearing her name and the address she had worked out with the council for Gair. The postage was a stamp indicating it had come from the local planning office. It was the words printed in red that made her stomach turn over. URGENT, they read. OPEN IMMEDIATELY.

'Anyway, better get going,' the postie said, perhaps sensing a sudden change in her demeanour. 'Cheers for the drink, you're a lifesaver. See you tomorrow, no doubt.'

Saskia made a non-committal sound of goodbye, waving him off with an automatic raise of her hand, though her attention was all for the letter. It was just an envelope, blank except for her own name and address, and yet there was something so sinister about it that made her stomach contract as she looked at it. She left the break room with the stack of post still in her hand, the letter that had caused her so much consternation held separately from the others.

'We're about ready to start the pour,' Owen called, as he approached from the site. 'Thought you'd want to be there to see it.'

She stopped on the bottom step and looked up at him.

There must have been something in her face because he faltered in his step for a moment, then picked up his pace until he joined her.

'What?' he asked. 'What's happened?'

Saskia couldn't tell him. She held up the letter. He squinted at it for a moment, the sun glinting against the little, clear, plastic window enough to blind him. He took it from her, saw the postmark and turned it over as if the back might give some more clues.

'Why would you be hearing from the planning office?'

'I don't know.'

He paused, looking at it for another moment before handing it back. 'You've got to open it.'

She nodded, wondering why there was a numbness in her chest. They'd given permission for the works to go ahead. Every one of her plans had been checked, adjusted where necessary, checked again, and then verified and agreed upon. It had taken literally years. The inspection of a week previously had been good. There had been no indication that the two suited men who had come to examine the site and their work to date had any motive beyond genuine interest in the build. There had been no questions she and Owen could not answer, no hint from them to indicate she should worry about anything they'd seen. They had accepted cold drinks from the fridge, removed their jackets and rolled up their shirt sleeves in the sun. Two days later she'd received a call to say that the official report meant they were clear to move forward. This was probably just a follow-up letter, some sort of automatic contact. Except for those red letters, large and angry. A shout, an order. URGENT. OPEN IMMEDIATELY.

'Saskia.' Owen moved closer, hands on his hips. 'Come on. Open it. It's probably nothing.'

She nodded, the numbness spreading. He stood over her, casting shade against the hot beat of the sun. Saskia slid a finger beneath the open end of the flap, tore it open and pulled out the single sheaf of folded paper inside. She opened it and tried to read the text printed there, though she found it difficult to concentrate after the first line, which read:

Notification of Judicial Review into the
Granting of Planning Permission for
Case #2746, Gair Castle, Cumbria

She sucked in a breath, blinked, tried to get her eyes to clear as she read the rest.

'What is it?' Owen prompted. 'What does it say?'

When she said nothing, he moved to look over her shoulder. As he read, she felt him tensing, a storm gathering, right there at her back. She couldn't move; couldn't react; didn't stop him when he reached out and took the letter from her to hold it closer to his face, as if reading it again might change the meaning of the words.

'This is ridiculous,' he said, voice taut with anger. 'This says we have to stop work immediately pending the outcome of the investigation. What investigation? They had the building inspectors here last week. We got the green light!

This is insane – we're about to pour the first floor. The mix is literally there, ready and waiting for me to give the word! They can't *do* this.'

'They can,' Saskia said, finding her voice at last, although it sounded rough even to her own ears. 'They have.'

'No.' Owen thrust the letter back at her and started off towards the site. 'If it was so bloody urgent they would have come here in person. They sent a *letter.* By *Royal Mail.* You didn't even have to sign for it! I say we carry on as normal and tell the bastards it never turned up. Let them prove you've read it. Stuart!' he shouted, raising his voice over the rumble of the cement mixer. 'Spool her up! We're about ready to roll!'

'No! Owen, stop!' Saskia caught up with him and grabbed his arm, pulling him around to face her. 'We can't. If we pour that floor, all that's going to happen is that it'll cause us even more of a delay. They might make us rip it up. At least if the concrete's not down, we've got a chance of reusing the metal plates. If we have to take it all up—'

'Take it up?' Owen repeated. 'You're joking. Why the hell would we have to do that?'

'This has to be about the ruins,' she said. 'Doesn't it? Someone still thinks there are ruins under the castle foundations. They've managed to convince someone at the council,' she added, looking at the letter again, 'or at some higher level, I would think, that there needs to be more investigation.'

'What's going on?' Stuart asked, coming over. 'The mix is ready to go, what's the hold up?'

Owen ignored his friend, focusing instead on Saskia. 'This is bullshit. There's nothing there.'

Saskia spread her hands. 'What do you want me to do?'

Owen set his jaw. 'Someone's messing with you. This is ridiculous. A judicial review? You know how rare they are?'

Saskia looked down at the letter again. 'I know.'

'You need to call them. Find out what's going on. Make them—'

'I *know*, Owen.' She looked up again. The men were all standing around, watching what was going on. The concrete mixer's engine was still rumbling, the driver leaning out of the window, sunning his elbow as he wondered what the hold-up was. Saskia felt a wave of helplessness wash up through her chest. 'I'm going to start making calls. You'd better send everyone home.'

She began to walk back towards her trailer. She'd call from the privacy of her own tiny home office.

'That's it?' Owen shouted after her. 'I just send everyone home?'

She turned mid-stride, raising both arms in a *what-do-you-want-me-to-do?* gesture. 'Don't worry,' she shouted back. 'I'll keep paying the day rate until we know what's happening.'

The site emptied as she spent the next hours on the phone, trying to get someone – anyone – to talk to her. She was passed from pillar to post, playing phone tag with a variety of names, some of which she recognized, some of which she didn't. Eventually Saskia realized that the world outside her cabin had fallen silent. She kept her phone to her ear as she went back outside. The site gates were closed and locked, and the cement truck had gone, as had all the workers. Owen, too. Gair was empty, nothing but a hot, dusty bowl of welded metal and ancient stone.

Brodie followed at her heels as Saskia walked slowly down the slope towards the ruin, crossing the rutted tracks left in the dry dirt by the cranes they had used to manoeuvre the metal base plates into place. It was midday now, and she could feel the heat rising towards her from the steel sheets. Brodie avoided walking on them, not wanting to blister his paws. Saskia skirted the edges, making for the oak. There was no wind, no breeze to skitter the leaves above her head. On the other end of the line, muzak droned. She placed one hand against the tree's grizzled bark. It was warm to the touch.

The line crackled. 'Ms Tilbury-Martin?'

She turned away from the oak and faced her defunct work site. 'Yes. Speaking.'

When Saskia finally managed to talk to someone involved with her case, it was explained to her that the judicial review was an issue for the civil courts. The 'Gair Case' had been added to what Saskia had no doubt was a long list of motions working their way through the system.

'But what am I supposed to do?' she asked, hating how lost she sounded – how unmoored and out of her depth she felt. 'This is an active site. We've already started work, I've employed a crew. The foundation is in! I'm going to lose money very, very quickly. I don't understand this. You *granted* planning permission!'

The voice on the other end of the line – male, nasal – repressed a sigh. 'If I were you, I'd get myself a solicitor and co-operate as much as necessary.'

Saskia rubbed a hand over her face, desolate. 'I thought I'd already done that.'

She spent the rest of the day finding a local solicitor versed in issues of this sort. The offices were down in Keswick, and rather than drive down there, they agreed to meet over Zoom. Saskia explained the ins and outs of the project at Gair and the letter she'd received. The solicitor, a serious-looking woman in her fifties named Beth Gordon, listened carefully before agreeing to take the case.

'Send me everything you've got,' she said. 'I'll make a start. And don't worry – from what you've said this sounds like a spurious claim.'

'Spurious or not,' Saskia said, 'if this goes on too long it's going to make a huge hole in my budget.'

'I understand,' the solicitor said. 'The first thing you should do is release the workforce.'

'I can't do that,' Saskia said, feeling a tight fist of panic grip her heart. 'If I lose the team I may never get the workers back. It was a nightmare finding the right people in the first place.'

'Look,' Beth told her, gently, 'Miss Tilbury-Martin, although the actual court hearing will probably only take a day, you are very likely looking at months before it reaches that point, and longer for an actual ruling. This could take a year in all.'

'A year!' Saskia was shocked beyond belief. 'But . . . it *can't*. That will finish me, even if they rule in my favour.'

'I understand how difficult this must be,' the solicitor said. 'Which is why I am recommending that you cut back as much as you can, straight away. Save money where you can, as soon as you can. If the court rules in your favour – and if everything you've told me is true, I can't see why that wouldn't happen – the LPA responsible for filing the claim will be liable for your damages. But that may be a long way down the line. And you probably know as well as I do that there are expenses you will never be able to recoup.'

Saskia felt her life rapidly spiralling out of control. 'There must be something I can do,' she said. 'There must be a way to speed up the process, or at least be sure that I'm in the best possible position when the hearing date actually happens.'

There was a pause as Beth considered. 'Let me make a couple of calls,' she said. 'I'll get back to you.'

Thirteen

'She's recommended that I let the Local Planning Authority have access to the site.'

Owen frowned, looking out of the window of the truck as he waited for Hannah to come out of school, his phone held to his ear. Saskia was on the line, filling him in on her conversation with the solicitor she'd found.

'Haven't they already had that?'

Her sigh reached him, heavy and unhappy. 'Yes, as part of the planning application. But she's hoping that if we let them do whatever it is they want it won't even reach the hearing.'

He shook his head. 'How is any of this legal?'

'A judicial review can be called up to three months after planning has been granted.' She paused. 'I guess most projects don't forge ahead as quickly as I did with Gair. I was ready to hit the ground running, and I did.'

'What are you going to do?'

'I've told the LPA they can do whatever they need to. They want to send a team of "investigators" in. I tried to push them to get a date for when the team would arrive and what they would want to accomplish once there. They were pretty cagey about it. I get the impression that they're not in a rush at all. The solicitor is going to handle getting them moving and I have confidence in her,' Saskia went on. 'But my gut tells me we're still looking at weeks. Which brings me on to something else.'

'Oh?'

There was a pause, as if she was trying to gather herself for what was coming next. Owen felt a beat of misgiving. 'She's recommended that I release the workforce.'

'Wait. She thinks you should mothball the site completely? But that's just handing these people exactly what they want!'

'This could be a long process, Owen. A really, *really* long process. I don't want to do it, but I can't afford to keep paying for works that aren't happening.'

He rubbed a hand over his face. Out of the window, kids were beginning to stream out of the gates. 'All right. Look, I need to go. Can we talk about this tomorrow?'

'Yes,' she said, and he detected an unhappy note in her voice as she paused before adding, 'I'm not going anywhere.'

He rang off, the image of her standing alone amid her silent work site lodging itself in his mind. It was a Wednesday, and he imagined that by the weekend, she'd be back in London for good, cutting her losses and commiserating with her friends over the failure of this idea that had been nuts to begin with. He, meanwhile, had to find a way to break the news to the guys that the job they'd all thought would keep them going for the next year or more was already dead in the water. He thought immediately of Adrian Braithwaite and The Collaton Project. Perhaps if he got in there quickly, he could sort them all out before they even knew they were out of work.

He spotted Hannah and waved an arm, feeling his heart lift at the wild smile his daughter sent back as she realized her daddy had come to pick her up.

When he found time to call later, Owen was relieved to find that Braithwaite was more than happy to help.

'It's great to hear from you, Owen,' he said, over the phone, his voice raised to compete with the noisy backdrop of industry. 'And yes, we can definitely absorb your workforce. It comes at the perfect time, actually, we're about to step up a gear down here and I was going to put the call out.'

'I hoped that might be the case,' Owen said. 'I remember you talking about going into Phase Three when I saw you in Newcastle.'

'Sounds as if you were paying attention, not that I'd expect any less from you, Elliot,' Braithwaite laughed. 'Sharpest of the sharp, that was always you. I look forward to working with you again. And for my part, it'll be good to have a super I can trust without question.'

'Likewise,' Owen said. 'Okay. I'll let the team know what's going on. How shall we do this?'

They discussed logistics. There were a few aspects of due diligence that needed ironing out, but there was enough for him to be confident that he wouldn't be dropping a bombshell on anyone without also providing a shelter.

He and Saskia agreed to call the men in on Friday afternoon to fully explain the circumstances and, if they wanted it, the transfer of employment from Gair to Collaton. The two of them also talked about the overlap, as the men wouldn't be wanted down on the coast for another week. Without him even suggesting it, Saskia confirmed that she'd continue to pay their day rate until they were signed on with Braithwaite. Over that week they'd close down the site, arranging for the cargo containers to be emptied and for one to be collected. The other would become storage for anything that needed to be out of the elements long-term. The generator and its water tanks needed to go too, as would both cranes. The place would soon look abandoned.

Gair was quiet when he arrived on Friday. Owen stood for a few minutes, listening to the birdsong, to the trees. It always amazed him, how quickly nature returned to a site if work stopped for any length of time. He found Saskia beneath the oak, Brodie at her feet. She was standing with her hand resting against the bark, looking up into the branches with her back to the steel plates and upright girders that would very likely end up being as far as this project ever got.

'Saskia?'

She turned towards him, and he was surprised by how exhausted she seemed. Her eyes were rimmed red by lack of sleep. He felt a flash of unexpected guilt. As much as he had been looking forward to the challenge of this build, he was leaving it behind without much of a wrench. He hadn't considered that the same wouldn't apply to her.

'Hi,' she said, attempting a smile. 'Thanks for coming.'

'No problem. Anything new to report?'

She shut her eyes briefly, her forehead creased in a frown. 'Well, I've just heard that the team the LPA want to send in will be here a week on Monday. It's a group of archaeologists, apparently.'

He shook his head. 'Haven't you already had them in?'

She sighed as they began to walk back towards the break room. 'Yup. The implication seems to be that this will be different because I won't have anything to do with choosing the personnel, and therefore the findings will not be biased.'

'That sounds suspiciously like something one of the Historical Society members would say. Hugh Carey, for example.'

She looked up at him, an ironic smile on her face. 'Doesn't it?'

They stopped on the slope and looked down at Gair. 'I'm sorry,' he said, truthfully. 'I know we haven't always seen eye to eye, but for what it's worth . . . I did enjoy working here.'

She drew in a slow, audible breath. 'That sounds so final, Owen.'

'It's not. I mean, it doesn't have to be,' he said. 'I hope it won't be. Once this review is out of the way, we can talk about a return. The job in Collaton—'

'—will be too good for you to leave once you've taken it,'

she finished for him. 'Which is why I'm going to ask you for a big, *big* favour. Don't go. Not yet.'

He looked out at the site again. 'You want me to stay on the project here? But . . .' He tried to fathom quite what she was asking. 'You've already said this stoppage could be months long.'

'I'm determined that it won't be,' she said. 'I have faith in Beth Gordon, the solicitor. I know there's no case to answer. They're going to find in my favour.'

'Yes, but *when*?' Owen asked, bluntly. 'You've already had a fight just to get them to start the process. And I can't just sit around on my hands.'

'A month,' she pleaded. 'Just give me a month, Owen.'

'I've got to get on with my life,' he said. 'I've got to find somewhere to live, for a start. I can't carry on living with Stuart. It's already been too long. I'm looking at somewhere down the coast, nearer to—'

'I've got somewhere for you to live straight away,' she said, interrupting. 'If you do this for me, if you give me this single month of grace, you can take my cabin and live here, on site. Free accommodation for a month, and all you have to do is keep an eye on the place. If I haven't sorted this out by then, you'll go with my blessing. And either way, I'll pay you for that time, the same as the retainer I gave you when you agreed to take Gair on. *Please.*'

Owen took a step back and put his hands on his hips. How could he turn that down? Another chunk of money, along with what he'd been saving since he'd been crashing at Stuart's and working at Gair? That might just be enough for a deposit. Sure, it would mean living in a trailer in the middle of nowhere, twiddling his thumbs for a month. But he could do that, couldn't he? But was it worth it, to lose the chance of a certain job at Collaton?

'I need to make a call,' he said. 'Can you give me the afternoon?'

She nodded. 'Sure. But if you do decide to take the offer – and I really hope you do – you can move in whenever you like. Tonight, even.'

'Right,' he said. 'I guess you're going back to London once we've spoken to the men?'

'Hmm?' She was distracted by the sound of the first car arriving at the gates – Stuart, right on time as always. Saskia turned back to Owen, flashed him another smile. 'Sure, don't worry, I'd be out of your way. I'll just need to grab a few things. I can do that later. I'd better get the kettle on for the guys.'

Once they'd talked to the team, Owen took the time to call Adrian Braithwaite again. He decided honesty was the best policy; laid it all out on the line. Another month and he'd have what he needed to kickstart his future. Could his old commander wait that long for him to make a decision?

'A month,' Braithwaite said. 'Sure, Owen. I can give you that long. I can tell you now, though, there's zero chance of that issue being sorted in a month. She's throwing her money at you for nothing. Still, I'd probably do the same in your place, to be honest. Take what you can get and we'll see you down here in four weeks.'

Owen privately agreed with Adrian that there was no chance he wouldn't be taking the job in a month. He tried not to feel guilty as he told Saskia that he'd stay. Her relief was palpable, and he felt like the worse kind of mercenary. But a month was what she'd suggested, and she wasn't stupid: she must know how much of a long shot it was that this would be wrapped up in that time. He'd be daft not to take the money and run, wouldn't he? And whatever happened, she could afford it.

Fourteen

Owen stood on the top step of the trailer and looked around, the overnight bag he'd gone back to Stuart's to collect in his hand. He'd heard about these 'tiny homes' but had never been inside one. He'd always thought of them as glorified caravans, and he had very particular memories of awful stays at various parks around the coast of England and Scotland with his parents as a kid. Each of those 'holidays' had, without fail, devolved into a misery of arguments, with Owen staring out of a rain-soaked window while his mum and dad went at each other hammer and tongs behind him. He'd never had the remotest interest in repeating the experience with Tasha and Hannah.

As he looked around now, though, he found himself impressed. Although, he reflected, this was Saskia Tilbury-Martin, so what had he expected? A seventies-patterned fold-out foam sofa and a Teasmade? There was no sign of anything factory-made here. Everything had been created bespoke, fitting perfectly into the limited space.

The door opened onto a seating area with a lift-up bench that he guessed could also be used as a dining table. Behind that, to the left of where he stood, was a comfortable-looking L-shaped sofa arrangement that Owen assumed folded out into the bed that Vivian had used on the nights she had stayed here. So far, so standard, but that was where the similarity with his parents' old Bluebird ended. There was a miniature wood-burner opposite the door for a start, the wrought-iron flue kinking out through a wall that looked more like the inside of a log cabin than a polycarbonate shell. A series of wooden shelves had been built beside the heater, overflowing with books. Owen peered closer, wondering what sort of stories his employer entertained herself with.

'Make yourself at home,' Saskia said, coming up the steps behind him. He stepped aside so she could pass. 'I'll just grab a few things and get out of your way so you can settle in. Kitchen's here,' she said, raising a hand as she passed through a little galley beyond the living area. 'Bathroom's there, opposite the stairs. I sleep upstairs, so it'd be great if you could stay down here.' She indicated the sofa behind him. 'The sofa-bed opens out into a big double, and there are clean sheets and another duvet underneath.'

'Thanks,' he said, as she opened a cupboard beneath the staircase and pulled out a large rucksack. 'I appreciate it.'

She glanced at him, flashing a quick smile as she began to stuff clothes into the bag. 'It's fine. If this is what you need for me to be able to keep you on the project, Owen, I'll do whatever it takes.'

Owen stuck his hands in his pockets, dipped his head in a nod, more guilt adding to his feeling of awkwardness in the small space. He'd expected to walk into a hotel room, blank and barely used, but that's not how this place felt. This felt personal. Homely. It occurred to him for the first time that she hadn't, as he'd assumed, bought this place at the same time as she'd decided he and the guys should have two cargo containers. This felt much older. It felt lived in.

There were a couple of photos on the wall beside the door and he made a show of studying them as she continued to gather her belongings. Saskia was in both of them, although in each she was much younger – a child, a young teen. In the one where she looked about thirteen, she was sitting on a concrete step, her arms around a large golden retriever.

'Hey,' he said, pointing at the picture, thinking that the dog the whole crew had adopted as their mascot must be a lot older than any of them thought. 'Is that Brodie?'

The dog in question, watching from the bed set beside the wood-burner, pricked his ears and gave a soft woof. Saskia made her way back towards Owen, carrying the zipped-up bag in front of her to navigate the limited space. Glancing at the picture, she smiled. 'No, that's Marple. She was a wonder.'

He raised his eyebrows, glancing over at her current pup. 'Marple and Brodie?'

'Before that came Wimsey. What can I say? I was a precocious child with a penchant for reading detective fiction. The tradition kind of stuck.'

Owen found himself laughing. 'Nice.'

She smiled, hefting the bag in both arms and glancing over at her loyal sidekick. 'Come on, Brodie, time to go. Owen will look after your bed.'

'Certainly will,' he said, absently, looking closely at the second photograph. 'Wait – is that *Gair*?'

The photograph featured four people. One Owen guessed was Saskia, because even though she looked barely eight in the photograph her large, dark eyes had not changed. She was standing in front of a man in his late thirties, who, since he was resting his hands on her shoulders, Owen thought was probably her father. Beside them stood an older couple who also shared a family resemblance. They were all standing in front of a tree that, though only partially visible, was without a doubt the distinctive Gair Oak.

'Yes,' she said. 'It is. That's my dad and my grandparents: his mum and dad. Right, I'll get going. I hope you'll be comfortable. Help yourself to whatever you want. Give me a call if there's anything you can't find.' She turned and lugged the bag down the steps.

'Hey, let me carry that to the car for you,' he said.

Saskia turned to look up at him, her face reflecting the soft light pouring out of the trailer, her latest literary detective at her feet. Around them the trees stirred in a warm evening breeze despite the setting of the summer sun. 'It's fine, I can manage. I'll see you Monday?'

'Yeah,' he said, surprised because he hadn't expected her to bother coming back north so soon, not with the site inactive. 'Monday.'

Saskia nodded once and walked away into the darkness, Brodie at her heel.

Owen looked at that photograph again, the one beneath the absurd-looking bulk of the Gair Oak, trying to work out why he felt as if a trapdoor had suddenly opened up beneath his feet.

He spent the rest of the evening finding his way around the trailer, continually surprised by what he discovered. Owen soon became convinced that this wasn't the fancy temporary office he'd always assumed it to be. Most of the fixtures and fittings had been hand-built out of old, sanded-back scaffold boards. This included the well-used kitchen, where everything was placed at the perfect spot for cooking on the tiny, two-ring hob. There was a small convection oven. The multiple pantry shelves, built around the half-sized fridge beneath the miniature sink and around the window, were packed with staples. There were spice jars, canisters of dried pulses and pasta. The knives, lined up along a magnetic strip, were a good make and cared for but old, their blades worn thin from sharpening. The coffee percolator had a cubby of its own that pulled out for use, and the attention to detail over this minor vice made him smile.

He moved on, towards the rear of the cabin, beneath the carved wooden stairs that led up to Saskia's 'bedroom', which could only be big enough for a low-ceilinged chamber beneath the eaves with a futon on the floor. The steps had a utility of their own, with cupboards and shelves built into their undersides, along with what he realized was a full-height wardrobe as soon as he pulled it open. He went to shut it again immediately, instinct warning him against violating a privacy, but still paused for a moment. There wasn't much inside apart from a stack of neatly folded work shirts and jeans, all well worn. What really caught his eye, though, was the transparent plastic dry-cleaning bag that hung above them. Inside was the ridiculously expensive suit she'd been wearing the first day they met, the one that had instantly made him think she belonged anywhere but on a building site. Underneath was a shoe box, presumably for the heels she'd also been wearing that day. Yes, this outfit was expensive, but it was the only one of its type here and she obviously looked after it meticulously, as if it might not be easy to replace.

He shut the door to the wardrobe and stood still for a moment, ruminating before he moved on. Behind him was a narrow door hiding the smallest bathroom he'd ever seen – that was going to be fun for him to use. But it was what he found behind a folding door that closed off the end of the cabin that gave him even more pause. The rear of the trailer was an architect's studio in miniature. There were windows large enough to fill the space with light, but it was essentially a cupboard. Still, into the tiny oblong had been built a desk with its own perfectly proportioned table. There was an angled drawing board with a stool, a crammed bookcase and a filing cabinet hand-built from wood, with exquisitely turned handles. It all felt warm, lived in, loved.

There were technical drawings all over the walls, along with what he assumed were inspirational photographs of buildings she admired. Most of them incorporated trees into their footprints somehow: greenery sprouting in the centre of a marble office entrance hall; a wall of trailing vines; the ghostly white bark of silver birch enclosed by glass and steel; the root-entangled ruins of Angkor Wat; an abandoned cargo ship taken over by mangroves; the immense circumference of a redwood in the centre of a one-storey cabin built around its base. These images looked like something out of a fairytale, as if part of a spontaneous re-wilding of all the world's built-upon places, except that they were real.

There were photographs and illustrations of Gair, too – the ruins from every angle and through every season; and in each image there was the oak, stag-headed and bow-branched, gnarled and bent, seen both verdant and bare-of-leaf, but always, always there. Owen studied these drawings, and realized that they formed a sort of time-machine of sketches that stretched back years, decades. They charted a theme of thought and action that had remained constant through draft after draft of architectural designs, at first tentative and idealized, like a castle drawn by a child, but developing through practice into a consistent, working design. He leaned in, trying to follow the thread back to its beginning and thought he found it pinned up in the centre of this storm of paper, sketched onto a single piece of yellowed paper that seemed to represent the earliest of these images. Two things surprised Owen about it. The first was that, unlike the early sketches that he had identified as being from Saskia's hand, it was as accomplished as any of her later professional plans, confident in its design. The second was that, once he gently peeled back the images that had been pinned to overlap it, he realized it had been torn in half, so that it was incomplete.

Owen stood there for a while, contemplating what he'd found. The feeling that he might have misunderstood something monumental about Saskia – about this entire, crazy project of hers – grew. Maybe he'd ask her about it when he saw her again on Monday.

Maybe not.

A feeling of tiredness suffused him. Owen squeezed himself into the minute square of bathroom and brushed his teeth before crawling into the bed. It was surprisingly comfortable – certainly more so than the old, lumpy mattress he'd been crashing on at Stuart's. He was asleep in minutes, and for the first time in weeks, he slept through the night without waking.

Fifteen

Saskia drove out of Gair feeling lighter than she had since she'd spoken with the solicitor. She really hadn't known whether or not Owen would accept her offer. The relief that he had was so profound that she felt as if a huge weight had been lifted from her shoulders. Rationally, she knew it didn't really change anything – he'd agreed to a month, that was all, and there would need to be some kind of miracle for the judicial review to wrap up in that short a time. But it was a respite, at least. It was hope. And however volatile her relationship with him was, having him there meant she wasn't alone in her quest at Gair.

She checked her mirrors as she drove away from the main gates, but there was no sign that Owen was watching her leave. The next part of her plan would take a little light subterfuge to execute. Saskia drove until she came to the first right turning off the Gair road. It was so narrow that it was easy to miss, a track so overgrown that she doubted many people even noticed it was there as they passed on their way to the castle ruin, and probably assumed it was a footpath or a bridleway if they did. She turned onto it and rattled slowly down the uneven route until she was sure the car wouldn't be visible from the main track, then switched off the engine and took a breath. Brodie woofed in her ear and she reached up to ruffle his ears with a smile.

'Ready for an adventure, Brodie-boy?' she asked. 'It's been a while since we slept under the stars, hasn't it?'

Her phone rang in her pocket. Saskia wrestled it out.

'Hello?'

'Saskia?'

She froze, her shoulder muscles tensing.

'Saskia? Darling? Is that you?'

'Mother?'

'It *is* you!' said Elsa Cavendish. 'I thought for a moment that dear Rebecca was having one of her little turns and she'd managed to give me the wrong number.'

Saskia shut her eyes. *Rebecca.* Vivian's mother. Elsa must have somehow persuaded her to give her Saskia's new number. She gritted her teeth, trying not to let her anger stray towards her friend, nor her friend's mother. After all, she knew first-hand how hard Elsa was willing to work to get what she wanted.

'Now's not a good time,' Saskia said, keeping her voice even despite the angry, anxious thump of her heart.

'Oh now, you can spare your old mama a few minutes, can't you?' the voice on the phone said, just on the edge of wheedling. 'It's *such* a long time since we chatted. Where *are* you?'

Saskia stared out at the dense tangle of trees and undergrowth that surrounded the car. 'Abroad,' she said, shortly. 'I'm on holiday with some friends. It's the middle of the night here, actually, you woke me, so—'

'On holiday with *friends*,' her mother said, with the kind of delighted surprise one might reserve for winning the lottery, or unexpectedly discovering the cure for cancer. It spoke all too well of how unlikely the idea of Saskia having friends seemed. 'Well, how *lovely*. I'm glad you're spending some of your windfall on frivolous pursuits. Where are you, exactly? And which friends are these that have whisked you off so mysteriously? Vivian isn't with you, is she, darling, because Rebecca said she has some big shoot in London this week. She was all a-twitter about it, you know how she gets. They're terribly proud of Viv, both of them. You'd think they'd produced the next Poet Laureate, the way they go on. It's really quite sweet, I suppose.'

Saskia gritted her teeth. 'Why are you calling? Was there something you wanted?'

'Really, Saskia,' her mother said, the pout that Saskia could imagine on her face palpable in her tone. 'Must you always sound so aggressive? Or is it only family that you speak to in that way?'

Saskia passed one hand over her face as she tried to unclench her jaw. Brodie sensed her anxiety and rested his chin on her shoulder. She took a breath, released it slowly. 'I'm not being aggressive,' she said. 'I'm tired and I wasn't expecting you to call, since I didn't give you this number.'

'That's all right, darling, I know how you forget things,' her mother said, breezily. 'I forgive you. And I've got it now, so no harm done.'

Saskia shut her eyes; tipped her head back against the head-rest. 'And . . . *was* there something you wanted?'

'Well, I wanted to see how you are, for a start,' her mother said. 'It's not as if you've been great at checking in ever since you suddenly came into money. You can understand how that might be worrying for the people who really care about you, don't you? What with your history.'

'I'm fine,' Saskia said shortly, wondering how it was possible for her mother to use the word 'suddenly' in the context of an inheritance that should have been hers at least a decade ago. 'And like I said, I have to go, so—'

'Don't rush off,' Elsa said. 'I'm afraid I've got some upsetting news. I've been trying to get hold of you for ages about it.'

Saskia couldn't imagine what news her mother could have that would have any impact on her life whatsoever. They were, to Saskia's mind, as far apart in all respects as two people could get while still remaining on the same planet. 'Oh?'

A heavy sigh gusted from Elsa's end of the ether. 'It's the club.'

Saskia drew a blank. 'The . . . club?'

'The country club,' Elsa clarified. 'I thought I should let you know that after a long and difficult deliberation, Richard and I have decided not to renew our membership this year.'

Saskia stared out of the window, utterly baffled.

'Saskia?' Elsa said, into the silence. 'Have you drifted off, darling?'

'*This* is why you've been trying to get hold of me?' Saskia asked, eventually, not bothering to keep the incredulity from her voice. 'To tell me that you're cancelling a membership to some *country club*?' Saskia herself hadn't set foot on the grounds of the place for almost twenty years.

'There's no need to be so dismissive,' her mother said, sounding wounded. 'I thought you might care, that's all. I wanted to break it to you gently, myself. After all, our family have been members since before you were born. It's where your father taught you to play tennis when you were little, but perhaps you've forgotten that.'

Saskia's heart gave a painful lurch. 'Of course I haven't,' she said. 'I didn't—'

'I always thought that was a special memory for you,' Elsa went on, her voice still tinged with hurt. 'But I must have been mistaken. I'm so sorry for interrupting your holiday with unimportant nonsense. Silly old me.'

'Mum—'

'Anyway, this call is probably costing a fortune, isn't it? I'd better go. I'll say goodbye, Saskia. Enjoy your holiday.'

'Wait—'

But her mother had gone. Saskia stared at the blank screen of her phone, her heart thumping painfully, a familiar knot of discomfort and guilt tangling in her stomach. She contemplated calling her mother back, but she couldn't bear a repeat performance. She typed out three texts that all said variations of the same thing. *I'm sorry.* Saskia hesitated before sending each. In the end she sent nothing at all and was angry at herself for ever having felt the need to anyway. She would *not* get sucked back into the emotional black hole that was the search for her mother's approval.

Saskia sat in the car for another couple of minutes, the brief lightness she'd gained following the agreement she had reached with Owen gone. Then Brodie gave a little whine, which jolted her out of her reverie, and she sighed. The sun was setting, and in the forest the shadows were already lengthening. She didn't want to be tramping around in the dark; it was a sure way to turn an ankle.

'Come on, boy,' she said, opening the car door. 'Let's get on with it.'

She dragged the pack containing her three-man tent from the back of the Land Rover and pulled on the rucksack she'd filled from the trailer. Slamming shut the car's boot, she turned and surveyed the forest. Realistically, there was only one place that it made sense for her to go. The only place, really, that she ever wanted to be. She would let herself into the Gair site via the rear gates and camp there.

Saskia set off into the undergrowth, her thoughts continuing to be maudlin as she cut back towards Gair, circling around and around the all-too-recent conversation with her mother. They had never seen eye to eye, even when Saskia had been a small child. For a long time Saskia had blamed herself for this, even when she'd been too young to realize that's what she was doing. Now, looking back, she was able to see that it had very little to do with Saskia, and everything to do with the fact that Elsa Tilbury should never have married her first husband, Graham Martin, and should absolutely not have had a child with him. To this day, Saskia couldn't really understand why her mother had been with her father in the first place, unless it was her way of spiting her own parents, which was possible. Elsa was from money: the old, serious sort you can't earn or ever be a part of if it's not in your blood. Saskia's father was most definitely not.

From very early on, it had been clear that although Saskia looked the spitting image of her mother, that was as far as the likeness went. In all other respects, Saskia took after her father, in both temperament and interests. The rift between mother and daughter had been established early and only grew as the years went by. When Saskia was five and had been at the local primary school for less than a year, Elsa had declared her intention of putting her in a boarding school for the next term and onwards. Saskia could remember sitting on the stairs of the huge family home – passed down through the Tilbury lineage for years – listening to the ensuing row between her parents.

She hangs off me whenever she's home, Elsa had complained. *She never leaves me alone! I thought I'd get my life back once she started school! Anyway, I went when I was six and I turned out fine.*

Her father had won the argument, but Saskia thought Elsa had probably never forgiven him for it. That had been when their little father–daughter trips had started, presumably so that Elsa wouldn't have to entertain her own daughter over the dull expanse of a weekend. Her father would pick a part of England and find somewhere to stay nearby, and then they would drive around all day Saturday and Sunday, finding interesting buildings to draw. He would buy them each a new sketchbook for every trip, and by the time the weekend was over, they would both be full of drawings. Saskia had learned much about architecture and technical drawing very early from her father.

Once, in the hellish tangle that had been her teenage years following his death, Vivian had gently suggested that maybe Elsa had felt left out. *You and your dad were so close*, she'd said. *All those cool trips you took that your mum didn't get to go on . . .* Saskia tried to explain that, no, that wasn't the case. Elsa had never wanted to come with them. She was never interested in what Saskia had drawn while she was away, or where they had been and what they had seen. Saskia had learned this after the very first trip, when her excited stories about it had been met with indifference at first, and then impatience. Elsa had never suggested doing something else, all together, instead, and if Saskia ever did herself, she'd say she was busy. She had mostly seemed relieved that Saskia and her father weren't around. Vivian had listened, but to this day Saskia wasn't sure she'd ever really fully believed what Saskia had told her. There had been a lot of times back then that Saskia had been jealous of Vivian's family, of the bond they had. It didn't matter what Saskia did, she'd never been what her mother had wanted. That was just the way things were. She was fine with that now; it had taken a long time, but she'd accepted this fact and moved on. At least, she always thought she had. Then there would be the sort of encounter that they'd just shared, and Saskia would be right back on those stairs again, a little girl listening as her own mother argued to send her away.

Later, in her pitched tent, she checked her phone for what must have been the fiftieth time, but her mother had not called or texted since she'd hung up.

That was a good thing, Saskia told herself. It *was.*

Sixteen

When Owen woke the next morning, it took him a moment to recall where he was. He stared up at the tongue-and-groove pine of the cabin's pitched ceiling, feeling properly rested in the first time in too long. Outside, the birds sang among the surrounding woods of Gair and for a while he lay there, listening. Peaceful wasn't a state of mind Owen often associated with himself, but it seemed that here, in Saskia's beautiful trailer, he'd achieved just that.

He got up and pottered about, getting ready for the day. Negotiating the bathroom was trickier when he was trying to do more than brush his teeth. The diminutive size of the shower was a challenge – he supposed that it was easier for its owner, so much smaller than him.

Owen made coffee and was looking thoughtfully out of the kitchen window when something on the wall beside it caught his eye. It was a calendar. There were dates marked in the current month and he looked closer, curious as to what Saskia Tilbury-Martin found it important to note. Most of the entries were about Gair, but there were others, too. *Rebecca's birthday, remember to send flowers*, said one. Something about this struck Owen as odd, although he couldn't put his finger on quite what. He reached out and took the calendar from its hook and flipped back through the previous months. Gair was the dominant subject, but there were plenty of other notes, too. *Dentist, 3.15pm*, one said. *Brodie groomers*, said another. Eventually Owen came across a reference that he realized was about himself. *Owen Elliot, Gair, 2pm.* The strange feeling continued as he went further back in time, looking at arrangements she had made; meetings she had booked in. *Take Landy to Kebba*; *Lunch with Viv in town.* There were numerous mentions of people he hadn't heard of but that he didn't think had anything to do with the Gair project.

Eventually he put the calendar back and returned the open page to the right month. Below it he spotted a small pile of letters leaned against the wall, all opened. Bills, mainly, it seemed. He wouldn't violate her privacy by looking closer, but Owen understood one thing: there was more life here, and in the calendar, than would make sense for this place as a temporary secondary home.

This thought stayed with him throughout the day, even when he was away from Gair. It added to the stack of new questions he had for Saskia that he thought it probable he would never actually ask.

He noticed the light as he prepared to bed down for his second night in the trailer after a day spent looking through his finances and trying to work out a future for himself. Owen was rearranging the sofa cushions when something flickered through the inch gap below the bottom of the window blind. At first he assumed it was moonlight reflecting off something in the work site, but then it moved. Drifted, would be a better description. He turned the cabin's lights off and lifted the blind a little more so that he could see it better. It was wavering and yellow, a small pinprick of illumination against the night-dark expanse of Gair. It wasn't moonlight. Was someone out there? They had decided against floodlights overnight, chiefly because of the power drain but also because Saskia hadn't wanted the noise pollution: twenty-four seven lights meant running the generators twenty-four seven too. The place was noisy enough during the day, she'd said. Owen had seen the logic at the time, and now he knew she hadn't wanted the disturbance, but he wondered whether they had made it easy for someone to sneak in unseen.

There had to be someone out there. The small light was moving methodically through the work site, having apparently found some easy breach in the fence. He'd check that thoroughly in the morning, but right now he was going to have to go out and deal with the intruder. He had a mental image of some intrepid member of the Historical Society tiptoeing around like a cartoon villain, seeding misinformation and planting trouble ahead of the archaeologists' arrival. Whoever had the light was an idiot, too, because it clearly wasn't strong enough. For a moment Owen had the weird conviction that it was a candle. There was something about how it flickered, a flame-quality to the light. Then, as he watched, it winked out.

Owen stood at the window, his gaze roving over the dark landscape. Something prickled at the hairs on his neck. Had it been there at all? There was no sign of it now; there was only the darkness. Then, just as he was about to give it up as some weird aberration – did the UK have fireflies, he wondered, or some kind of moth that gave off a supernatural glow? – it returned. It flickered back into life in almost exactly the same place as he'd seen it last, which made Owen doubly certain that he was watching someone carrying a candle around the castle site and that person had stopped to strike a match and re-light the wick.

Swearing to himself under his breath, Owen shoved his feet into his boots, fished the flashlight he always carried in his coat from his pocket and opened the cabin door. The balmy summer's night air washed over him as he stepped down into the dust. Owen shut the door behind him and flicked on the torch, angling it at his feet. He'd rather do without it and catch whoever the snooper was unawares, but there was no sense in breaking a leg.

From Saskia's trailer the land ran in a gentle slope down towards the castle site. He skirted the edge of the forest, the trees and undergrowth somehow seeming even denser in the night, a lurking mass of the unknown standing right at his shoulder. For the first time since he'd arrived at Gair, despite Stuart's superstitions and the folk tales that floated around the place, he felt uneasy, vulnerable. *Come on*, he told himself. *Get it together. There's nothing here but some daft NIMBY.*

When he reached the castle walls, Owen paused. There was no sign of the light now, but he had the sense that there was something in there, beyond the looming shadows, something more than inanimate machinery. He lifted the torch, but all the light bounced off was hewn granite and the edge of one of those huge metal plates intended to hold up Saskia's brave new world. The oak stood, solid and silent, its grizzled stag head presiding over all. There was no wind to stir its branches, he noticed – in fact, everywhere around him felt unnaturally still.

He lowered the torch again, partly to conceal his progress and partly because the ground ahead of him was rough, barren of the patchy tangles of tough wild grass that grew everywhere else on the Gair site but full of pocked, rutted dust packed hard with the passage of booted feet and heavy equipment. Owen stepped carefully, quietly. There was now no sign of the candle – if that really was what it had been – at all. He doubted himself anew, glancing back to the trailer, distant now at the top of the slope. Could he really have seen anything from up there? It had been such a small light, such a slight glow, and he had been so far away. Now that he was down here, it seemed so improbable. He must have imagined it, Owen decided, or mistaken something else for an actual light.

Still, now that he was inside the castle walls he thought he should do a walk-through, just to make sure. He passed through the first crumbling outer wall and turned left in the direction of the tower, thinking to do a circular pass along the smaller outer 'rooms' before walking back through the centre, past the oak. He was approaching what Saskia had told him had once been a grain store when there came a soft rustling, followed by a woof, followed by a clearer bark and more rustling. He stopped dead, bringing his light up so that it cut sharply against the remains of the wall.

'Who's there?'

There was another short bark, followed by more rustling and the sound of a zip being pulled. He edged forward, wishing he'd brought some sort of protection with him – his tool bag was in his truck, from which he could have retrieved a hammer – when a familiar shaggy mass appeared.

'Brodie?'

The dog woofed again, tail wagging to see a friend.

'Owen? Is that you?'

The voice was thick with sleep. He reached the dog and shined the light into the shadows behind the stone, illuminating a tent that had been pitched in the lee of two intersecting walls. Saskia peered up at him through the opening. She lifted one hand to shield her eyes against his torch and he flicked it away from her.

Owen looked back up the slope to the trailer and then back at his employer. 'What are you doing? I thought you were going back to London for the weekend?'

The tent rustled as she scrambled around until she was sitting. 'London?' she repeated, sleepily. 'For the weekend?'

He paused before he said, slowly, although he had a feeling he already knew the answer that was coming, 'Yes. Don't you go home at the weekends?'

She rubbed one hand over her face. When she dropped it again her expression was steady. 'I do go home. I go home every night after work. But home . . . isn't London.'

He nodded, the pieces he'd been assembling in his mind sliding into place. 'The trailer.'

She yawned. 'I believe the preferred term is "tiny home".'

Feeling awkward standing over her, he crouched, surveying the tent. She was in a decent sleeping bag, her clothes folded neatly inside the door. Brodie woofed in his ear and Owen reached up a hand to rub the dog's soft head. 'What, then? You were planning to camp here and hoped I wouldn't notice that by giving me your place you'd made yourself homeless?'

'I thought I could stay far enough out of your way for you not to notice, yes.' Saskia gave a lopsided smile. 'It's not my first time sleeping in a tent.'

He stared at her. 'But why?'

She raised her eyebrows. 'Have you never heard of camping?'

'Why are you sleeping in a tent *now*?'

Saskia looked down at her hands, folded in her lap. 'I can't waste money on accommodation, not for however long this delay is going to take.'

He tried to fathom what she was saying. He looked around the ruins in which he crouched and then over his shoulder, back towards her tiny home, which turned out to be the only one she had.

'This build. Gair,' he said. 'It really does mean everything to you, doesn't it?'

She gave that smile again. 'It's all I have, Owen.'

He squeezed thumb and forefinger into the bridge of his nose as the enormity of what she was saying sank in. 'You'd rather give me your home than risk losing me from the project.'

'I told you, right at the beginning,' she said. 'You're my last hope. I know that if you go, you won't come back. My plan for Gair will be over. And like I said,' Saskia added, as he looked at her again. 'Not my first time in a tent. I'll be fine. You should go back to bed.'

'Look,' Owen said, after a moment. 'I'm going to ask you something that I should have asked you the first day we met. And I want you to tell me, in detail, right now. The long version.'

She snorted softly at that. 'Okay. Ask me, then. What is it you want to know?'

He looked at what loomed around them. The crumbling castle walls, the tower, the stag-headed oak. 'Why is Gair so important to you?'

Seventeen

They went back to the trailer. Saskia made coffee for them both while Owen folded away the sofa and lit the wood-burner. It wasn't cold, and they didn't need it, but she was of the firm belief that a fire made everything better and Owen agreed.

'I've never seen one so compact,' he said, as he closed the tiny, toughened glass door on the stove and sat back to watch the flames take hold. 'You must have had it made specially?'

'Actually, it was one of the guys in the programme,' Saskia said, passing him a mug of coffee as they both sat down. 'He was an artisanal blacksmith – he had his own forge, creating all sorts of incredible functional artwork.'

'The programme?'

Saskia sipped her coffee and tucked her legs under her, settling more firmly on the sofa as she thought about how to address everything that had led her here.

'This cabin,' she said, indicating around her with a whisk of her finger. 'I built it, as part of a charity programme for recovering addicts that aimed to help them learn new skills. We were apprentices for a company that built house extensions and garden buildings as well as tiny homes. We were paid a reduced wage, and one day a week we were also able to work on building our own, using materials we got at cost and the skills we learned as part of the apprenticeship.'

Owen nodded, clearly impressed. 'That . . . sounds like a really good idea.'

'It was. It worked for me, anyway.'

'And that's what inspired you to become an architect.'

'No,' Saskia said. 'That was something I'd always wanted to be, right from a very early age. Actually, I never wanted to be anything else. My dad was an architect by training, and eventually became a professor at Goldsmith's Centre for Research Architecture. His name was Graham, but everyone called him Gray, even his students. He died when I was fifteen.'

'I'm sorry,' Owen said.

Saskia nodded. 'It was . . . a tough time. Cancer. Anyway, Dad died, and everything fell apart. I went off the rails. Or at least, that's the way my mother tells it. Looking back, I think at that point I was just a normal teenage kid dealing with something terrible. My mother and I had never been close, and we'd fought more and more as I got older. Dad wanted me to have a relationship with her even if they weren't happy as a couple themselves, but after he was gone . . . I just withdrew. Things between us got a lot worse. Maybe me shutting myself away affected her.' Saskia sipped her coffee. 'But I think – and thought even then – that it was mainly because after he died we found out that my dad had set up a trust for me. It was a lot of money. And she wasn't one of the trustees.'

'He'd been squirrelling funds away without her realizing?' Owen asked.

'No,' Saskia said. 'It came from my grandparents. They'd made some good investments back in the late sixties. Apparently Dad hadn't known the full extent of it until they passed. They were never ostentatious people. They lived in a bungalow in Orpington up until they died. Anyway, when Dad realized, he immediately punted it all into a trust for me. The stipulations of the trust were that the trustees would release enough for me to get through university without having to work or take out loans. The rest of it would be held until I graduated and had secured a contracted position. And it . . . was a *lot* of money.'

'And . . . your mum didn't like that?'

'She really didn't.' Saskia gave an unhappy smile. 'I think she felt as if my grandparents' money – which she'd had absolutely no clue they had – meant she'd lost her last chance of making me into the kind of daughter she wanted me to be. But she had no influence over the trustees – they were all university friends of my dad's, who didn't know her, because she'd never shown any interest in getting to know them.'

'I guess that didn't go any way to making for a better relationship between you and your mum?' Owen said.

'No, it did not. I just threw myself into work. It was all I cared about at that point. Like I said, I'd always wanted to be an architect and thanks to Dad I knew exactly what I needed to do to get there. One of the trustees took me on as her intern before I'd even finished my A levels. She told me later that she and Dad had talked about me when he'd first got ill and she was absolutely on board with helping me realize my ambitions. By the time I was applying for my undergrad, I already had a substantial portfolio of work of an impressive standard. And I had a work placement that would see me right through my master's. I was all set.'

Owen put down his mug and leaned forward, his hands clasped between his knees as he listened. 'But?'

Saskia looked into her empty mug. 'Do you want more coffee?'

'Okay. Thanks.'

She got up, picked up his mug and busied herself with making them more drinks as she went on.

'I started taking amphetamines in my second year. I wanted to be able to study more, to stay awake longer. But then I could never sleep, so I started drinking or taking downers to knock myself out. Obviously, things escalated. I think part of me thought that if I only concentrated on my studies, if I didn't do anything but work, I wouldn't have to feel anything. I hadn't ever given myself time to grieve, and the situation with my mother had become so bad that I felt as if I didn't have any family. I didn't do anything other than work, so I hadn't really made any connections at university. The only friends I had were ones I'd had before I went, and we'd already started to drift apart.'

'Except Vivian?' Owen guessed.

Saskia smiled a little at that. 'Yes. Except Vivian. Anyway, of course things went from bad to worse. I didn't eat, didn't look after myself. My work started to suffer and that sent me into an even worse spiral, because I realized I was failing. I should have asked for help, but I thought if I did my mother would have reason to deny me access to the trust fund. I think the crisis point might have been triggered by the anniversary of Dad's death, although it had been building for a while. I OD'd. It wasn't deliberate – or at least, not consciously.'

'How did you survive?'

Saskia looked down at her mug as she scrubbed away an imaginary mark with her nail. 'Vivian. She knew I was in a bad way, and knew the anniversary of Dad's death would make me worse. On the day, she tried to call, couldn't get an answer, and managed to persuade campus welfare to bash the door in. If not for her, I wouldn't be here now. I was in recovery for months, then rehab. I missed out on that year's exams. Lost my place at university. Dad's friend tried to keep my internship at the firm, but eventually I lost that too, so I no longer met the criteria for being given my trust fund. I had no choice but to go to my mother's when I got out of rehab. She'd re-married by then and had my twin stepsisters. I don't like her husband and he doesn't like me. I spiralled again and they tried to get me to talk to the trustees about assigning them conservators of the trust so that it could be released into their care. Their argument was that I couldn't be trusted with it, and besides, they'd paid for the rehab and I was living in their house rent-free. I refused. Said I'd pay them back what I owed them when I was well enough to claim it myself, but they weren't getting the keys to the bank. Her husband's answer was to kick me out.'

Saskia shrugged.

'Vivian and her parents took me in, but by then life didn't really seem to have much point to it. There was barely any reason to be alive, and there definitely wasn't any reason to stay sober. I'd messed up the only thing I had wanted to get right, and it was too late to go back, or at least that's how it seemed at the time. It was a horrible cycle that I couldn't get out of, and at my worst points, I couldn't see the point of even trying. And then Vivian came across the Rebuild Your Life charity. I think we both knew it was my last chance. She went to the ends of the earth to get me a place – her parents, bless them, paid my stake. I went back to rehab again and this time when I came out, I went straight into the programme. That was ten years ago, and I've been in recovery and sober ever since. Eight years ago, Dad's friend and my mentor started her own firm of architects. She called me in and we discussed my trust fund and what I was going to do with my future. She was impressed by the cabin, and when she realized I still wanted to be an architect, she made a suggestion. She was willing to go to the trustees and persuade them to release enough to pay for me to restart my training. With my previous portfolio and a guaranteed work placement, she thought I'd be able to get in as a mature student, provided I was willing to put in the work. I was. The trustees agreed.'

'And here you are,' Owen said, quietly. 'Eight years later.'

'Here I am,' Saskia agreed. 'Five years of training, and three years of employment experience at Tilda's firm later, I am fully accredited and ten years sober. Although for official purposes, it's only been five years.'

'But it's taken until now for the trustees to release your trust fund?'

Saskia gave an ironic smile. 'Actually, they did that a while ago. At the meeting where they agreed to release enough to allow me to study, it was also agreed that I would not only need to prove firm employment but also five years of continuous sobriety – confirmed with regular drugs tests – before they would release it.'

'Five years? Wouldn't that have been five years ago?'

'It would,' Saskia agreed. 'Except for my mother.'

'Ah.'

'She tried her best to argue I was not fit to manage my own affairs. Every time she lodged an "intervention", they were forced to go through a lengthy process, which involved me taking weekly drugs tests at a particular independent clinic. It wasn't as easy as it sounds, because it often meant that to attend the clinic for the test I had to miss partial or sometimes whole work days, and to get my full accreditation there was a low attendance threshold. It took twice as long as it should have, but I got there. Eventually. In the end the trustees had to agree that I'd fulfilled my end of the necessary requirements. My mother's objections were finally overruled and—' Saskia raised one hand, '—the first thing I did was calculate how much I "owed" my mother and her husband, paid them it in a lump sum, and cut ties with them completely. The second thing I did was buy Gair. And then the battle to get planning started.'

She'd spoken for so long that her mouth was dry. Saskia glanced wistfully at the coffee maker, wondering if she dared have another. She looked at Owen, his hands still clasped between his knees, a frown on his face, and wondered what he was thinking. It had been a gamble to be quite as expansive as she had been about her past, she knew. After all, an addict was never recovered, only ever recovering. Perhaps opening up would make him trust her even less, rather than more.

'Which brings me back to my original question really, doesn't it?' Owen said. 'Why Gair?'

Saskia put down her mug and leaned down so that she could see out of the window beneath the blind. Over the castle ruins the sky had started to blush with the colours of dawn. The sun was rising, ribbons of light in vibrant streaks of pink and purple threading the air.

'I'll show you,' she said. 'By the time we get down to the oak, there should be enough light to see.'

'The oak?' Owen asked.

Saskia smiled. 'Yes,' she said. 'It's all about the oak.'

Eighteen

They went out into the chill of the early morning and walked back down the slope towards the ruins. In the rising sunlight the oak seemed majestic despite its odd shape, leaves picked out as shadows edged in gold and crimson faded in the growing light. In the last shreds of darkness its form seemed less tree and more being: as if some vast, ancient creature was kneeling at the centre of the stone ruins with its huge antlered head bent toward the ground. Was it worshipping or waiting to be worshipped? *Surely the latter*, Saskia thought. The Gair Oak was a god of the old times, still surviving.

For a moment they both stood beneath its spreading bulk. The birds that called it home were beginning to stir, a twittering spat breaking out among a family of goldfinches high above, heard but not seen.

'When you're here, you're always working, so you wouldn't have had time to observe this,' Saskia said, 'but the life the oak supports is extraordinary. Whole generations of insects and birds, totally dependent on each other. There's a colony of wild bees in one of the branch knots that has been renewing year after year at least as long as I've been visiting. Part of me thinks it would make a superb documentary to follow it over the course of the season, or perhaps several. A decade-long project to watch one colony of wild bees, how about that?'

Owen said nothing for a while, standing with his hands on his hips and his head tipped back, watching the branches of the oak move gently in the dawn breeze. 'How long is that?' he asked, eventually.

'How long is what?'

He looked at her. 'How long since your first visit?'

Saskia smiled and turned to look at the tree again. 'The first time my grandparents and my dad brought me to Gair I was five years old. My dad climbed *that*' – she pointed to the huge branch that bent out almost at a right-angle, its circumference thick enough to be a tree itself – 'and my grandad helped me clamber up behind him. It was the first time I'd climbed a tree, and I didn't want to get down. I could have lived up there – slept in the crook of that branch, helped myself to honey from the bees, stitched together leaves for a blanket, or clothes. From that moment, it was my fairytale kingdom. We came back every year and I looked forward to those visits as much as I did my birthday. More, probably.'

Owen laughed a little. 'Your grandparents brought you on trespassing raids to Cumbria every year? That's a new one.'

'We weren't trespassing. My grandparents were friends with the farmer who still owned the land at the time. They'd known the family since they were both children themselves.

That's how I managed to buy it – I always kept in touch with the family.'

'Oh?' Owen said, turning to her. 'Were your grandparents from Cumbria, then? I didn't know that.'

'No, they were both from Newcastle originally. But they met here in the war, when they were evacuated. Come on,' she said, 'I told you there was something I wanted to show you.'

Saskia went to the great low branch and stepped up onto it. She had climbed this route up into the oak so many times in her life that she'd probably be able to do it blindfolded. At this level, climbing the oak was like scaling Helvellyn via Striding Edge: just a walk, though you needed to step carefully. Further up, it became more of a technical climb, but if you knew where to look, there were footholds and pinch points. The arborist that had helped Saskia get the protection order had once suggested they put in permanent ropes, but Saskia had refused. There was no way she would pierce the tree's flesh with metal for the rope rings.

'You want me to follow you?' Owen said, doubtfully, from the ground.

She looked back at him. 'Not if you're uncomfortable.'

'I haven't climbed a tree since I was a lad.'

Saskia smiled. 'This is probably about as easy a climb as you can get. And we're not going far.' She looked just ahead of her and nodded to where the hulking great bough joined the main trunk, with another huge branch just above it forming a kind of seat. 'Just there.'

'Okay,' he said, moving closer. 'You go on, and I'll watch where you put your feet.'

It took her just a few minutes before she was sitting in her familiar spot, her back against the branch above. Saskia watched as Owen climbed up after her, cautious but sure-footed.

'Fancy meeting you here,' he said, as he sat on the branch beside her, and she laughed.

The day was awake now, new and fresh. There was dew on the leaves of the canopy around them and the buzz of insects filled the air. Saskia felt the peace of the oak envelop her, as it always did – as it always had. Out of all the places she had visited in her life – physical and mental, joyous and devastating – right here, sitting with her back against the rough bark of a grandfather oak, was still the only place she had ever truly felt herself.

'This is what I really wanted to show you,' she said, and shuffled around a little until she could point out what was carved into the tree's trunk, about a foot above the branch on which they both sat. It was the crude shape of a heart, with an uncertain arrow struck through it, and on either end of the arrow were initials: PM and CD.

'My grandad carved that,' Saskia said. 'When he was twelve. He's the PM – Philip Martin. The CD is my grandmother, Constance. Her maiden name was Darling. They were together from the day he carved this until they both died, within a month of each other. That was decades ago now, and here they both still are, preserved in the oak.'

She leaned forward and laid her hands against the bark so that her fingers framed the heart. How many times had she made the same gesture; imagined the day that Philip and Constance had climbed this old tree and carved this symbol; forged this memory of them both that she had visited so very many times but never tired of seeing? Too many to count.

'I told you my dad was an architect,' she said to Owen. 'Well, for him this place was an important puzzle, and he passed on his fascination with it to me even before I really understood what he was saying.'

'What do you mean?' Owen asked.

Saskia gestured to the ruins they could see below them and through the gaps in the canopy of the spreading oak. 'There are two types of history here. How do we preserve both? The castle ruins, the ancient oak tree. They both hold whole worlds within them, he used to say. The castle will have keys to understanding parts of our human past that we don't even know we don't know. The tree is the same, but for the natural world. As long as it remains healthy, the tree will last longer. The human-built stone walls will crumble long before the branches we're sitting on now rot and fall. He thought that this place was a puzzle box for humanity: how do we preserve both, equally and together? He used to use it as a teaching device for his students. He'd show them pictures of Gair and pose the question – how do you save both the tree and the castle? I think to him it became a symbol. How can humanity live in the natural world in a way that benefits both societies? Because that's what an oak is. It's not just a tree. It's an entire society. It's a microcosm of the world. He spent his life – and mine – trying to come up with a way to use Gair as the perfect example of how humanity and nature can live together, thrive together equally in the same space.'

'And he passed that passion onto you?' Owen asked.

Saskia looked up to find him watching her intently. She smiled. 'Yes. We worked on ideas together, once I was old enough. We tried so many different designs, both separately and together.' She nodded down at the metal plates, raised off the soil and just visible below the tree's lowest leaves. 'The floating floor was a real breakthrough. That happened one Sunday afternoon when I was about twelve. I had a drawing table in his office by then. I sketched something out and he looked over my shoulder and bam! Whatever it was he saw, there was an epiphany. We started again, and by the next week, that floor was in the plans.'

'I saw a sketch I think must have been your dad's,' Owen said. 'On the wall in your office in the cabin? Or half of one, anyway.' He seemed a little embarrassed as she looked at him. 'I'm sorry, I shouldn't have snooped behind closed doors.'

'It's fine,' she said, waving one hand. 'If I'd wanted you to stay out of there, I would have locked it. You mean the torn blueprint on the wall? Yeah, that was one of Dad's. It's all I have left of his plans for Gair.' She paused. 'My mother got rid of most of his papers after he died.'

'Don't tell me,' Owen said, dryly. 'She didn't like you two working together on ideas for Gair?'

'She said we were obsessed and it was all a waste of time,'

Saskia told him. 'And honestly, I can see her point. It was another way of us having something together that she couldn't be a part of, I suppose. I often wonder if I should have tried harder to include her.' She shrugged. 'But the larger part of me knows she wouldn't have wanted to be included.'

They were quiet for a few more minutes. Above them a blackbird sang, a sweet melody in the warm morning light.

'Anyway,' Saskia said, with a long breath out. 'That's why Gair is so important to me. I'm going to accomplish what Dad spent his life wanting to do. I'm going to preserve both the castle and the oak, no matter what. This is all I've got, Owen. This is why it means everything to me. And this is why I am begging you to stay and help me finish it.'

She watched as he laid his hands on the bark either side of where his legs dangled over the huge branch. She wondered if he were doing what she'd done as a child: trying to feel a pulse beneath that thick tree skin. It had always felt as if there should be one.

'This is your family tree,' he said, at length. 'Literally.'

She laughed at the description. 'I'd never thought of it that way. But you're right, it is. This oak is my family. Sometimes I think it's the only family I have left.'

He nodded and then was quiet again. Saskia shut her eyes, tilted her head back and listened to the oak and its inhabitants. When she opened her eyes again, it could have been minutes or hours later – she always found it so easy to lose time up here – she found Owen watching her.

'I'll stay here because I've already said I would, and I am

a man of my word,' he said. 'But I'm not having you live in a tent while I take over the home you built with your own two hands. We can share. Deal?'

She was suddenly more grateful for him than she could possibly express. Saskia held out a hand for him to shake. 'Okay, then,' she said, smiling properly for the first time in days. 'Deal.'

Owen took her hand and squeezed it, one thumb smoothing over her knuckle before he let her go.

Back on the ground, they were making their way towards the trailer for more coffee when Owen paused and stooped to pick something up from the ground.

'Here's your candle,' he said, holding it out to her.

Saskia stared at the cream cylinder of wax with a puzzled frown. 'What candle?'

'The one you were carrying last night,' he said. 'It's how I knew you were out here. I saw the light from the trailer window.'

Saskia took the candle and held it in her palm. 'I was asleep until you appeared outside the tent.'

'What?'

She looked up at him, holding up the candle. 'This isn't mine, Owen. Whoever you saw out here last night, it wasn't me.'

Nineteen

Sleep did not come easily to Owen after that, however comfortable the sofa-bed in Saskia's trailer was and no matter that he was exhausted by the night. *Let's each try to get a couple of hours' rest*, she'd suggested, once they'd reached her front door again. *I don't know about you but I could fall asleep on my feet right now.* But there was too much for him to process in what she had told him. There was the candle, too. He might have been able to dismiss the idea that anyone had been stalking around out there in the wee small hours if not for the candle. He stood it on the bookcase beside the tiny wood-burner and lay back among the many cushions of his temporary bed, staring at it as he heard Saskia settling herself upstairs on her little sleeping platform. Someone had been out there. He hadn't imagined it. But who, and why? Who would come all the way out here to Gair and then use only a candle to light their way around the hazards of a building site?

Saskia reappeared at about eleven that morning, slipping cautiously down the flight of narrow wooden steps, as if worried she might wake him. Owen had already folded away the sofa, having long given up on the idea of sleep. He'd wanted more coffee but had been loath to risk waking her despite her declaration that he should treat the place like home.

'Hey,' she said, when she realized he was both awake and fully dressed. Brodie trotted down the steps from behind her and came over to Owen for a fuss. 'I'm sorry, have you been awake long?'

He smiled, opting for a white lie. 'Not long. I'm due to take Hannah swimming in a couple of hours.'

'Ah,' she said, coming down the rest of the stairs. 'Hannah – that's your daughter?'

He got up and followed as she went to the little kitchenette. 'Yes. She's a bit of a mermaid. Loves the water. Her swimming instructor says she's a natural. Hannah's only six, but Tasha already thinks she's destined for the Olympics.'

Saskia smiled as she filled the kettle and spooned coffee into the machine. 'Sounds like a talented little girl.'

Owen reached out to pick up the mugs they had used last night, intending to rinse them out, but then he realized that there really wasn't space for both of them. 'Sorry,' he said as they bumped against each other and muttered the same thing again almost immediately. Saskia was wearing a pair of soft red-and-blue check flannel pyjamas, her long hair in a thick plait that hung down between her shoulder blades. It struck him that she seemed entirely at home – because she *was* at home. This tiny space was fitted to her perfectly and here he was, looming over her in it like a shadow. He stepped back but didn't really know what to do with himself.

'I'm sorry about the shower,' she said, oblivious to his discomfort. 'It's so small, far from ideal for someone your size.'

Owen contemplated the narrow door of the bathroom and realized how impossible this all was. If he stayed here, he'd have to dry and change in the space in front of the woodburner, in full view of his temporary landlady.

She turned and handed him a mug of coffee. Perhaps she read the dawning of this realization on his face, as Saskia flicked a quick glance around the room and smiled. 'There's not much privacy, is there?' she said. 'You should feel free to use the office whenever you want. There's not a lot of space in there either, but it does have a door.'

He smiled and took the coffee. 'I really think I need to find somewhere else.'

Saskia looked at him over the rim of her coffee mug. 'You don't. If this doesn't work, I'm happy to go back to camping.' A beeping sounded from the phone she'd brought down with her and stood on the window ledge over the sink. She turned and picked it up, checking the notification with a smile. 'Ah,' she said. 'There's my chore for the day. Before I crashed out I ordered a couple of surveillance cameras; that's the shop telling me they're ready for collection.'

'For the site, you mean?' Owen asked. They'd talked about putting up CCTV at the start of the project but decided against it.

'I want to have eyes on when this team turns up on

Monday morning. And I also want to know if we have any more intruders in the middle of the night,' she added, her gaze travelling to the candle that Owen had found. She fell silent for a minute and then looked at him. 'I'm sorry, I probably should have let you know about that before I went ahead and did it.'

He shook his head. 'I think it's a good idea.' She seemed relieved by his reply and Owen felt a flush of guilt. Had he really been so unreasonable that she'd expected his response to be . . . what? Annoyance? Anger? Owen thought back to their recent interactions and realized that yes, this was how he'd reacted to her more than once. He felt more guilt as he thought about how he'd broached the subject of her substance abuse. He hadn't known the full story, but then when did anyone ever know that, really? He should have been kinder, either way.

'I don't know where this is,' she said, holding up her phone, which was displaying a map with the collection address for her order. 'It's a part of the city I don't recognize.'

Owen leaned closer. She smelled faintly of almonds. 'That's the industrial estate. It's easy enough to get there.'

'Great. I'll have some breakfast and then get on with it.' Saskia put her phone down and turned back to the kitchen. 'Can I make you some toast?'

'Thanks,' he said, 'but I think I'm going to head off. I've got a few things to do in town before I pick Hannah up.'

Owen left a few minutes later, stepping into another bright day bathed in warmth. Below him stood Gair and the stag-headed oak, and he stopped for a moment. Something about the place seemed altered this morning, but he couldn't work out what it was. He thought again about the image of Saskia sitting in the mouth of her tent, finally working out what had bothered him so much about it. It wasn't the jarring juxtaposition to the image of her life that he'd always had before, or that finding her there had been so unexpected. Without realizing it, he'd lined this encounter up against that offer she'd made to him a few weeks ago, when even just on the basis of a theory she had being willing to give him a weekend at a holiday resort in peak season. Meanwhile, she'd given up her home to live in a tent in order to save on an expense that could easily be called essential. He hesitated for a moment, still contemplating the castle ruins, and then turned and strode back to the trailer, knocking at the door and waiting on the step.

Saskia opened the door, puzzled. 'Owen?'

'I never thanked you,' he said. 'For that offer you made about Center Parcs. In fact, I know I was pretty rude to you that day, and I'm sorry. It was a generous offer. Hannah would have loved it.'

Her smile this time seemed a little rueful. 'There's no need to apologize. It was intrusive and inappropriate of me. I knew that even as I said it. I was just . . .'

'Trying to help,' he said, finishing for her as she looked for the right words. 'Being kind. That's what you were doing, and I was a dick about it. You just . . . took me by surprise, I suppose. But I should have been more gracious.'

'You know, I was just thinking,' she said. 'You can always bring Hannah here for a weekend visit, if you want. She can sleep upstairs if she likes. I'll go back to the tent. Your wife is welcome to come and check it out first, if that would make her comfortable with the idea.'

Owen snorted. 'Would my daughter like to come and visit the castle she knows her dad has been rebuilding?' he said. 'I think I can probably answer that question for her. Actually, she's been asking to come up here ever since I told her what Daddy was doing up here.'

'Well then, there you go,' Saskia said. 'Hannah would be welcome.'

'I told you,' Owen said. 'I can't turf you out of your home.'

'You won't be,' Saskia said, lightly. 'Gair is my home. All of it. You know that now. As long as I'm here, I'm happy.'

On Sunday Owen helped Saskia put up four small cameras, the feed to which went directly to her laptop and phone. Nathan, the lead archaeologist, was not happy about it when he arrived on Monday morning. To Owen's eyes he was being deliberately uncooperative, as if he were already spoiling for a fight.

'It's a violation of our privacy,' Nathan complained. Owen was already predisposed to dislike him, and this whining didn't help to win him over.

'This is private property,' Owen pointed out. 'You're not the one with a right to privacy, Ms Tilbury-Martin is. What's the problem anyway? Hoping to plant something, were you?'

This exchange soured whatever relationship they might have had, and it got no better from there, especially when Saskia flat refused the team permission to enter the forest.

'You're here to examine the castle ruins, not my property as a whole,' she pointed out. 'I don't have to grant you access to anything beyond the outer perimeter fence.'

'But what we're looking for could be in the forest,' Nathan pointed out.

'It very likely is, yes,' Saskia agreed. 'It's definitely more likely than you finding anything under the castle. Which is what I've been saying for literally years.'

'In which case, you have a duty to let us—'

'No, I really don't. I've no intention of building anywhere else but right here, so why would it matter if there *are* ruins out there?' Saskia asked. 'My planning permission, and therefore the extent of the judicial review, does not cover the whole Gair estate. To go into the forest you'll need a separate permission from the owner. That's me, by the way, in case you'd forgotten. *I'm* the owner.'

Owen was almost amused by Nathan's obvious sulk. 'Is there a chance you'd grant such a permission?'

Saskia's look was icy. 'Not a big chance, no. Concentrate on doing the job you've been employed for and stop wasting my time. And if I catch you nosing about on the rest of my property, I will prosecute for trespassing.'

Nathan muttered darkly about 'having to consult' about this, but he eventually gave up. There was a little additional complaining about not being able to work where the sheet metal had already been laid down. Saskia pointed out that there had already been three separate trenches opened in that area over the period of several years. None of these had yielded any significant archaeological results.

'If you want those removed, you're going to have to get a specific order,' she said, displaying the kind of backbone that filled Owen with admiration. 'I'm not removing a thing without that.'

In the end Nathan finally sucked up his ire and they opened two trenches, one beside the outer wall of the tower and one against the corner where Saskia had pitched her tent.

'Guess what?' Saskia said to Owen later, staring at something on her phone.

'What?'

She looked up at him with an ironic smile on her face. 'Turns out Nathan is Hugh Carey's nephew.'

Owen gave an inelegant snort. 'You don't say. Hugh Carey as in the head of the Historical Society? What a coincidence.'

'Small world, isn't it? No wonder Nathan's such a misery.'

That evening – Monday – was one of Owen's visits for Hannah's bedtime, so he brought up to Tasha the idea of their daughter staying at the castle with him for the weekend. He had coached himself to do this with as much patience as he could muster and not within earshot of Hannah. In fact, he waited until he was leaving before bringing it up, as he shrugged on his jacket at the door.

'You want our daughter to stay with you at a building site?' Tasha asked, blankly.

'Not at the building site. I told you, Saskia's letting me stay in her trailer.'

'A caravan.'

'No, it's—' He stopped, wishing he'd thought to take photographs to show her. 'It's not a caravan. It's a home. You'd like it, Tasha. It's more like a log cabin on wheels. It's amazing. She built it all herself.'

His soon-to-be ex-wife leaned against the open door as he stepped out into the hallway outside, regarding him with a cool eye. 'You've changed your tune.'

'Sorry?'

'It wasn't long ago you were cursing everything this woman did and stood for.'

'Yeah, well,' he said. 'It also wasn't long ago this place was my home, was it?'

Tasha crossed her arms.

'Look,' he said, reeling himself back in. 'She's letting me stay there so I don't have to shell out money for a place. So that I can save up for somewhere decent to have Hannah stay.'

'And now you're living there with her.'

'No, I'm not living *with* her,' he said. 'Well, I suppose technically I am, but it's no different to when I was staying at Stuart's. It's just . . . smaller. And yet also cleaner.'

'And there'll be space for Hannah to have her own bed, will there?'

'Yes, Saskia said she can have her sleeping platform and she'll camp out. Hannah'll love it, it'll be like she's staying in Rapunzel's tower or something.'

'Sleeping platform?' Tasha repeated.

Owen sighed. 'Come and look at it, Tash. Saskia said you could, so that you'd be comfortable with the idea of Hannah staying there.'

'Oh, "Saskia" said that, did she? Not "Lady Muck"?'

Owen looked down at the keys he'd been toying with as they spoke. 'Yeah, well. I might have been wrong about her.'

Tasha shook her head, but she dropped her arms. 'All right. I'll come and have a look. But no promises. And don't say a word about it to Hannah until I say so.'

'Great,' Owen said. 'Fine. Thanks. Give me a call when you want to come over.'

This state visit happened a couple of days later. Owen could tell from Tasha's subtle reaction that the cabin impressed her. Owen asked Saskia to take her up to see the space where their daughter would sleep, including a strategic but subtle mention that he had never been up there, and therefore didn't know where anything was, including the light switch. He stood at the bottom of the wooden steps and listened as Saskia told Tasha that Hannah could either bring her own bedding or she would put a clean set on for her, whichever would be more comfortable for them both.

'Do you want to see around the site?' Owen asked, once he and Tasha stood together outside again.

They each donned a hard hat and Owen led her through the ruins, describing the structure and how it would look when it was finally complete. They finished beneath the oak, where Tasha stood quietly, looking back up the slope towards the cabin. From where they stood it looked for all the world like a chalet built against the backdrop of the woods.

'What do you think?' Owen asked. 'Hannah would love it here, wouldn't she? And I heard what you said when Saskia showed you her bedroom – that Hannah would never want to sleep anywhere else.'

Tasha gave a faint smile. 'She will love it, you're right . . . But, Owen—' She stopped, shaking her head.

'What?'

She looked up at him, and he could read concern in her face. 'I do still care about you, you know,' Tasha said. 'And I want you to be careful.'

'Careful?' Owen repeated. 'About what? What do you mean?'

Tasha sighed. 'Nothing. I'm sorry, I don't want to speak out of turn. But you . . . You seem so comfortable here. And I read the papers, I know about this judicial review thing and how precarious this whole project is. I don't want you to set yourself up for a massive fall.'

'I told you, I've only agreed to stay for a month. Although they're not going to find anything,' Owen said, as they looked over at the team of archaeologists, who were busy in one of their trenches. 'There's nothing there to find, they're just wasting time.'

'That might not make any difference,' Tasha pointed out. 'Everything she did before to get planning permission in the first place didn't, did it? And if someone's out to make as much trouble as they can, it seems to me she won't be able to hold out for ever. She was already willing to camp out to save money. Don't you see how extreme that is? And I know you; I can read you like a book, Owen. You might have agreed to a month, but if she asks you to stay longer, you will. You love this place too, I can tell. Are you really going to pass up a sure job – and any future jobs – with Adrian Braithwaite for something that's more than likely going to leave you with nothing?'

Owen frowned. 'How do you know about Adrian?'

Tasha looked away. 'I saw Stuart the other day. I asked him where he was working and he told me you'd sorted him out. Then he said you'd have it easy down there at Collaton. Certainly compared to this place, anyway. And I get that for whatever reason, you want to be here for Saskia—'

'It's not about Saskia.'

Tasha looked at him. 'Isn't it? You don't have to be honest with me either way. It's not my business anymore. But you should at least be honest with yourself.'

'It's not *about* Saskia,' he insisted, 'other than that I think I understand her better now. More than that, I understand what she wants to do here, and – it's a challenge, Tasha. *That's* what it's about.'

'Well, I just hope you don't want a challenge more than you want a stable income for your child,' Tasha said. 'Because that's what Collaton will give you, but that opportunity might not still be around whenever you're done with this place – or when it's done with you. Braithwaite's being really patient, isn't he? That won't last for ever. Just think about it. I like Saskia. I do, or at least what I've seen of her. But where she's from, what she's used to – it's in a different stratosphere, and—'

'It's not,' Owen said. 'Maybe I thought it was when I first met her, but . . . I was wrong.'

Tasha regarded him silently for another moment. 'Well. I'm fine with Hannah coming to stay, at least once. She misses you and whatever's going on between us, I want her to have her dad around.'

Owen felt the relief pouring through his chest. 'Great. Thanks. When would work best?'

Tasha got out her phone and checked through her calendar. 'Actually, it's going to have to be this weekend. She's got a sleepover birthday party the weekend after and then it's the swimming gala, then it's the competition over in Hexham, so—'

'That's fine,' Owen said. 'This weekend will work.'

'Good idea,' Saskia said, when Owen told her of this plan. 'The weather's finally supposed to turn next week – we might actually get some rain. Better that Hannah's here when it's sunny; she won't want to be cooped up in the cabin all day if it's wet.'

'You're sure you're okay with this?' Owen asked. 'She and I could camp out instead.'

'Nope,' Saskia told him. 'You should tell Hannah to bring her swimming costume, though – if she likes the water, you two should explore the swimming pool while the weather's still good.'

'The swimming pool?' Owen repeated, mystified.

Saskia laughed at the look on his face. 'Haven't I ever mentioned it before? There's a rockpool in the river that's perfect for a dip.'

'Really?'

'Yes, it's beautiful – it's become a favourite place of mine. You have to know how to find it, although I think Brodie and I have probably worn a path to it by now. I can show you.'

Twenty

On the morning that Owen first brought his daughter to Gair, Saskia headed out early, thinking it likely that the little girl would be more comfortable getting to know the place without a strange woman hanging around. She took Brodie and went into town to collect something she'd searched for and ordered as soon as she'd known Hannah was coming and also to do some food shopping. The morning was sultry, the heat of the day to come promised in the early warmth.

She didn't get back until after lunch, pulling her truck in next to Owen's. Brodie's ears pricked up as soon as she opened the door, and a moment later she heard it herself: the high pitch of a child's laughter echoing across the site, followed by the lower tone of an adult's laughing shout. They walked down the slope, Saskia with bags in both hands. She looked across to see two figures chasing each other around the trailer, each armed with a large water pistol. Brodie barked, and the smaller figure turned at the sound, shrieking as her inattention allowed her father to drench her. Saskia called Brodie to heel (she assumed that Owen would have told her if his daughter was afraid of dogs, but still) and went to meet her new visitor.

'Hello,' she said, smiling at the little girl as she got closer. 'You must be Hannah.'

Owen came to stand beside his daughter, one arm around her shoulders as the child leaned against his leg, her eyes guarded but unafraid. 'Hannah,' he said, 'this is Saskia. It's her castle.'

'Hello,' Hannah said. 'Thank you for letting me come to stay. I like your castle. And your dog,' she added, as Brodie sat obediently at Saskia's side, although he was very obviously excited to meet this new small visitor of theirs.

'You're very welcome, Hannah,' Saskia told her. 'This is Brodie. Brodie, say hello to Hannah.'

Saskia nodded to the dog and Brodie huffed, immediately trotting over to the little girl, who laughed as she petted him.

'Have you been up the castle tower yet, Hannah?' Saskia asked.

Hannah shook her head. 'Daddy says I can't this time because he doesn't have a hard hat that will fit me properly. But we can look at it from the outside and maybe I can go up next time if he can find one.'

'Ah, well,' Saskia said, smiling, putting down all the bags she carried but one, which she held out to the little girl. 'Maybe I have something here that will help with that.'

Hannah looked up at her father, uncertain. Owen nodded, and she took the bag with a murmured, 'Thank you.' They watched as she pulled out what was inside: a nondescript brown box. Hannah opened it to reveal a child-sized crash helmet, in bright Barbie pink.

'Wow!' Hannah said, taking it out of its box. She looked up at her father. 'Does this mean I can go into the castle now?'

Owen looked over at Saskia, who nodded. 'It's fully compliant. I just hope it fits.'

The little girl was already pulling the helmet on over her ponytail. 'It does! It's perfect! Isn't it, Daddy?'

'Let me see,' Owen said, crouching in front of his daughter to tighten the chin strap and check the fit. He looked over at Saskia with a smile as he straightened up. 'It's perfect.'

'Come on, Dad!' Hannah shouted, taking off down the slope at a run. 'Let's go!'

'Hannah, wait,' Owen called, going to his truck to grab his own hard hat. He paused as he passed Saskia. 'Thank you.'

'No problem. I'm just going to put some things in the trailer fridge, is that okay?'

'Of course it is. It's your home, we're the guests! We'll see you in a bit.'

Brodie stayed with her, but she could see his ears twitching as Owen hurried after Hannah. He looked up at her and she sighed. 'Go on, then. Go with them, if you like.'

Brodie woofed once and streaked down the hill after father and daughter.

'Daddy says there's a swimming pool,' Hannah said to Saskia, later. She, Owen and Brodie had spent at least an hour exploring the castle ruins together. Saskia had stayed at the trailer, making herself a coffee and pulling out one of the deck chairs that were folded away beneath her little house so that she could enjoy the sun. She'd listened, smiling, to the little girl's shrieks of excitement as she'd scaled the tower; heard her shouting from its crenelated top and waved to them as Owen stood behind his daughter, one hand on her shoulder, just in case. The pink hard hat was hard to miss against the more natural colours of the backdrop of castle and forest.

'There is,' Saskia agreed. 'It's not very big, though. It's for dipping more than swimming, really. It's in the forest.'

'Can we go there now? Please, Daddy?' Hannah asked. 'I brought my swimsuit with me, like you said.'

'What do you think?' Owen asked Saskia, after checking his watch. 'I don't know how far it is a walk to get there . . . Should we leave it until tomorrow?'

'It's not that far,' Saskia said, getting up. 'I'll walk you down and leave Brodie with you; he can show you the way back.'

'But don't you want to swim, too?' Hannah asked. 'I'm going to put my swimsuit on under my dress before I go; you could do that, too.'

'Actually,' Saskia confided, 'I've already got mine on underneath my clothes. I meant to go early this morning but then I got the notification that your helmet had turned up so I thought I'd better go and pick that up first.'

'Well then, there you are,' the little girl said, matter-of-factly. 'Come on, Daddy. You need your swimmers, too.'

They disappeared inside the trailer to get changed. Saskia sat, feeling the warm breeze from the forest and wondering how she was going to get out of this one. She had no intention of stripping down to a swimsuit in front of Owen and his daughter. She glanced down at the long sleeves of the white tee shirt she'd pulled on that morning, wishing she'd thought to order a rashie or two. She'd never expected to be sharing her wild swimming spot with visitors.

'We're ready!' Hannah declared, appearing on the trailer steps. Owen was behind her, carrying a tote, into which he'd stuffed a couple of beach towels. They weren't hers, but she supposed that as the father of a water-loving child, having them around was second nature.

'Okay,' she said. 'Let's go.'

They set off, Saskia ahead, flanked by both dog and child. Owen walked behind, happy to listen to his daughter's excited chatter. She didn't seem at all nervous about heading into the dense forest, its shadows thick despite the brightness of the day. Saskia pointed out wildflowers as they walked, naming them as their bright colours peeked from between the ferns on the forest floor.

'There's a fairy ring here too, you know,' Saskia said.

'What – a real one?' Hannah gasped, looking up at her with wide eyes.

'I think so,' Saskia confirmed. 'It's big, it must have been there a long time. I bet the toadstools always return in the same place.'

'Can we go and see it?'

'Maybe on the way back,' Saskia told her. 'And as long as you promise that you won't touch or step into the circle, okay? We don't want you to vanish into the fairy realm, do we? It looks pretty, but we can only look at it.' She glanced back at Owen. 'The mushrooms are fly agaric – you know, with the classic red cap and white spots? Beautiful, but poisonous.'

'Wow,' Hannah whispered, awed. 'Your forest is magic, Saskia. It's *enchanted*.'

Saskia laughed. 'Maybe!'

At the pool, Brodie scrambled down the slope and leapt straight in, closely followed by Hannah.

'Come on, you two,' she shouted. 'Hurry up!'

Owen smiled and pulled his tee shirt up over his head. Saskia was suddenly confronted by the evidence of his active lifestyle in the form of a well-muscled torso and shoulders. Saskia blinked and was horrified to feel herself beginning to blush. It was a ridiculous reaction which she put down to awkwardness – although some of the men, Stuart included, had stripped down to only their hi-vis vests during the hottest days of work, Owen had not joined them. He'd always kept a tee shirt in place, in the same way that Saskia herself had always worn a long-sleeved shirt – albeit for distinctly different reasons. She turned away as he toed off his trainers and shucked his battered jeans, suddenly wishing that she'd just sent them out here with Brodie instead. She moved away to a fallen tree and sat herself in view of the pool.

'Aren't you coming in?' Owen asked.

'I think I'll stay here,' she said. 'Let you two have the

room. It's really not that big, especially with Brodie splashing about too.'

She couldn't quite look at him, hooking her fingers into her sleeves and pulling her cuffs down over her palms, a habit she'd had since childhood and had never been able to break.

'Saskia?'

She glanced up to see that Owen had moved closer. He was looking at her arms, and she was thrown by the expression on his face. He met her eye, dropping to a crouch in front of her.

'I'm sorry,' he said. 'I didn't think.'

'You didn't . . . what?' she asked, confused.

He went to reach out, but then dropped his hand. 'Your arms,' he said. 'You don't want me to see them. Do you?'

She took a breath. 'They're not pretty.'

He did reach out then. He grasped her forearm, gently. His hand was warm even through the fabric of her top.

'I'm sorry,' he said. 'Do whatever makes you feel comfortable. But I want you to know that you'll get no more judgement from me.'

Saskia tried a smile, but it faltered. 'It's Hannah I'm worried about. It might upset her.'

Owen smiled. 'She probably won't even notice. I mean, listen to her. You'd think she was at Disneyland, the amount of fun she's having.'

Saskia sucked in another breath. 'Owen.'

He frowned. 'What is it?'

'My scars,' she said. 'They aren't exactly what you think.'

Saskia met his eye and in that second, she thought he might already understand. She shifted to pull up her sleeves one by one, and Owen looked down at her wrists as she revealed them. He was very still as the two white scars came into view. Jagged and ghostly, they had torn up her inner forearms, from the base of her thumbs halfway to her elbow. They were very obviously not track marks. After a moment Owen looked up at her again.

'Saskia—' he began, his voice quiet, but then the laughter behind them rose up out of the pool and there was Hannah standing beside them, dripping wet.

'What are you *doing*?' the little girl demanded, impatiently. 'Come *on*. We're supposed to be swimming!'

'You should go in,' Saskia said to Owen, pulling away from him and settling her cuffs back in place. 'I'll stay here.'

'No,' he said. 'Come in with us.'

'You've got to!' Hannah insisted. 'The water will only be magic if you're there too!'

Saskia huffed a shaky laugh. 'Is that right?'

The little girl nodded emphatically. 'The fairies told me. They're everywhere! They like you very much because you are looking after the forest so well. So come *on*!'

Saskia glanced at Owen who was still watching her with a gaze intense enough to make her stomach do a strange backflip in her gut.

'Please,' he said, quietly. 'Wear the top; don't wear the top. Whatever makes you more comfortable, okay? Hannah will be fine.'

He turned away, scooping his daughter up so that she bellowed with laughter, and together they disappeared into the water. Saskia hesitated for another moment. Then she pulled her top up and off over her head.

It was close to five o'clock when they began to head back, Hannah declaring herself to be 'starving'.

'Good,' Saskia said, 'because I've got hotdogs with all the works for a barbecue. Marshmallows, too. Have you ever toasted marshmallows over a campfire, Hannah?'

'No!' the little girl said, skipping on ahead, following Brodie along the path, so much more well-worn than it had been when Saskia had first taken possession of Gair. 'That sounds delicious!'

The girl and the dog ran on ahead, vanishing into the surrounding green.

'Be careful! Stay on the track, and don't go too far!' Owen shouted after his daughter, and was answered by a quick, 'Okay, Daddy!' before she charged off again, chasing Brodie. 'She's got a new friend for life, there,' he observed. 'I should get her a dog.'

'I couldn't have survived the last few years without Brodie,' Saskia admitted. 'He's a great companion. Total devotion, zero judgement. I always think people could learn a lot about friendship from dogs.'

They lapsed into quiet, listening to the commotion of pet and child echoing from the middle distance. The sound didn't seem to disturb the peace of the forest. Around them, the trees absorbed the sound, softening it. Saskia wondered for the first time what the noise from the building site sounded like from here. She hoped they weren't scaring too many of the forest-dwelling creatures away.

'Thank you for today,' Owen said, and she looked over at him to catch a smile on his face. It softened his features, and Saskia realized that he looked younger and less stressed, as if a day with his daughter had taken away some of his cares. 'Hannah loves it here. I hope it'll be a memory she'll keep for a long time.' Then he sighed. 'Maybe it'll help while Tasha and I sort things out.'

'It will,' she told him. 'The memories I have of the trips I took with my dad as a child are some of the happiest – and most potent – of my life. She'll remember this, Owen. I promise.'

They walked on in silence for a few minutes. Overhead the evening chorus was beginning, in spite of them passing beneath. Saskia paused for a moment to take in the sound and Owen stopped beside her. They stood there together, beneath a tree that looked so small compared to the Gair Oak, and yet had probably lived far longer than either of them.

'I get why you love this place so much,' Owen said, quietly. 'I do. And . . .' He stopped, and when she looked at him again the look on his face was uncertain, as if he'd been about to say something but wasn't sure he should.

'What?' she asked.

He raised one hand slightly to touch the backs of his

fingers to her arm, just above her wrist. She was wearing her top again, so her scars were covered, but it wasn't difficult to work out what he was thinking about.

'I'm sorry,' he said. 'I'm so sorry for the assumptions I made. But more than that, I'm sorry things ever got that bad. I hope they never do again.'

She smiled a little. 'It was a long time ago. I don't intend to go back there again.'

He was looking away from her, eyes downcast, his expression troubled again as he thought something through. A shaft of evening sunlight added a soft gleam around his wet hair, turning the curls against his neck dark where they were backlit. She studied his face, the high line of his cheekbone, the strong line of his jaw, the laughter lines thin as spider's silk creasing the tan at the corner of his eyes. Something unexpected stirred in her chest and she took a breath. She wondered how she seemed to him now, now that he knew all her faults and had seen all her most obvious scars. At the sound of her exhale, he turned to her.

'If I—' he began, and then whatever he'd been about to say was cut off by a short, distant scream. It echoed through the forest, followed by a loud bark from Brodie, and then silence.

'Hannah?' Owen shouted, and then he was running, pounding along the uncertain path after his daughter. 'Hannah?'

Saskia followed, shouting too, first for the girl and then for the dog, but there was no answer from either of them.

'Hannah!'

They searched the track but there was no sign. It was as if the pair had vanished into thin air.

'Oh god,' Owen said, white with panic. 'Where is she? I should never have let her run off alone. Where *is* she?'

They'd traversed the narrow well-trodden path right up to where it opened out into the Gair clearing, but there was no sign of either the child or the dog. 'They can't have gone far,' Saskia said. 'And whatever's happened, Brodie's with her.'

They went back the way they had come, Owen forging ahead as Saskia held back, trying to hear something, anything, over his crashing footsteps and frantic shouts for his daughter. This didn't make sense. How could Hannah have vanished? And Brodie, too? Fearful scenarios came to her. But they were in a *forest.* What would an abductor have done? Bundled a screaming child over his shoulder and hiked three miles to the nearest road with a dog trying to stop them?

Involuntarily Saskia thought of those myths and legends, of children disappearing into the roots of trees, never to return, sucked into a fairy realm, an underworld. She stopped. She'd told Hannah about the fairy ring, hadn't she?

'Owen!' she shouted, and that's when she heard Brodie barking. 'Owen! I can hear Brodie!'

He came back towards her, eyes still wide with panic. Saskia forced him to a stop, both hands gripping his arms, holding him still.

'Listen,' she said.

In the quiet they could hear the dog. Brodie sounded impossibly distant, somewhere out there in the forest, away from the path. Owen shook her off and ploughed straight into the undergrowth, Saskia following in his wake, shaking off the tangle of bindweed and celandine, avoiding turning an ankle in the traps of fallen branches.

'Brodie!' Saskia called, and the dog went on barking until they found him sitting atop a slight mound of earth that rose between two large oak trees. He stood when he saw them coming but didn't move, barking, barking, barking.

Owen reached him first and fell to his knees on the mound. 'Hannah? Hannah!'

'Daddy!' The girl's voice was muffled, sobbing and indistinct. Her voice was coming from a hole in the ground. 'I slipped! I can't get out, Daddy, and I'm scared – it's dark!'

Saskia knelt beside Owen and the dog and peered into the hole. It was small, not much larger than a manhole cover. Hannah stared up at them, wide-eyed and tearful, from several feet below.

'It's okay,' Owen said, lying flat on the ground and reaching through the hole for his daughter. 'It's okay, Hannah, Daddy's here now. I'll get you out.'

He couldn't reach her, and neither could Saskia. The little girl tried and tried, but she couldn't climb; couldn't stretch her arms up high enough for either of them to reach her.

'I want to get out,' Hannah sobbed. 'Please, Daddy, please get me out now. I'm scared.'

'I'm coming,' Owen told his daughter.

'There's no way you're going to fit through that hole, Owen,' Saskia told him.

'Then I'll widen it, right now.' He reached down to start tearing at the soft soil, but Saskia grabbed his arms again to stop him.

'Do that and it could all cave in on her,' she said. 'I think I can fit. You'll have to brace me, but it's better than leaving her there until one of us can go and fetch a rope, isn't it? Hannah,' she said, to the little girl sobbing quietly below them, 'stand back. I'm coming down, okay? I'm coming down to get you. We'll have you out in a few minutes, I promise.'

Saskia realized that she was going to have to do this head-first. She lay flat at the edge of the opening in the earth and began to wriggle forward. It would be a tighter fit for her than it had been for Hannah, but it would work. She realized that she would block any light that was getting into the hole and paused to pull her phone from her pocket, thumbing on the flashlight before dropping it down to Hannah.

'Hold on to that, okay?' she told the little girl. 'Try not to shine it straight at my face or I won't be able to see.'

'Saskia . . .' Owen said, doubtfully.

'Don't let me fall, Owen,' she said, glancing at him. 'Or you'll have to fish us both out.'

At first he held onto the waistband of her jeans, but as she edged deeper, he ended up wrapping his arms around both of her legs – first her thighs and then her calves. Saskia tried to stay calm as she found herself dangling with nothing to hold on to. She concentrated on the child below her, holding out both arms.

'Can you reach me now?' she asked, feeling the blood rushing to her head as she dangled upside down from Owen's grip.

Hannah wrapped her arms tightly around Saskia's neck and Saskia hooked one arm around her waist. 'I've got her!' she shouted, and Owen began to wrench them back up. 'Hannah, hide your face in my neck so you don't breathe in the dirt!'

Getting back out was far more traumatic than going in. The soil began to collapse with their weight, crumbling even as Owen dragged them out. Hannah screamed and Saskia thought all three of them were going to end up tumbling back into the hole in the earth. The little girl was holding onto her so tightly that Saskia couldn't breathe. Eventually she felt her hips meet solid ground again, Owen letting go to grab at his daughter, hauling Hannah up and into his arms as Saskia pulled herself out the rest of the way. Hannah was sobbing again by now, holding onto an ashen-faced Owen as if she might never let go.

'It's okay,' he was telling his daughter, over and over again. 'It's okay. Are you hurt? Where does it hurt? It's okay.'

Saskia wiped a hand over her face, dislodging a sheen of dry dust, coughing to clear more from her mouth and nose.

They made it back to the trailer, where it was established that miraculously, the worst injuries Hannah had sustained were a couple of scrapes to her hands and knees. She hadn't hit her head, or even sprained an ankle. Saskia got out the first aid kit and passed it to Owen and then made hot chocolate, which she deemed a necessary nerve-settler. By this point Hannah had calmed significantly, the forest dirt brushed from her hair, and was in a clean set of clothes, but Owen still looked very shaken. Saskia took a clean set of clothes from her cupboard and went outside to change, taking a moment to breathe deeply in the evening air.

'Do you want to go home?' Owen's quiet voice floated to Saskia through the open window of the cabin as he spoke to his daughter. 'We can call Mummy and let her know that you've decided you'd rather sleep in your own bed.'

There was a pause. 'I'm not afraid of the castle or the forest,' Hannah said, matter-of-factly, and with no sign of tears. 'But I am scared of the witch.'

'The witch?' Saskia could hear the puzzlement in Owen's voice. 'What witch?'

'That was a witch's house I fell into,' Hannah said, 'out there, in the forest. I saw her face staring at me when I tried to find a way out. And I broke her roof, so she'll be angry with me.'

Saskia wondered whether she should leave father and daughter to have this conversation alone, but she needed to feed Brodie and retrieve her phone, both of which were still inside.

'It wasn't a witch's house,' Owen was saying, looking up as Saskia slipped back into the trailer. 'Saskia, there aren't any witches at Gair, are there?'

'Definitely not,' Saskia said, reaching for her own hot chocolate.

'There is,' Hannah insisted stoutly, 'because that was her house I fell into. There was a chair, and a kind of bed, like I said. I was lucky she didn't catch me. But maybe she'll come looking for me anyway.'

'Okay,' Owen said, patting his daughter's knee. 'Well, I don't think you need to worry about that. If there was a witch, I think she's long gone.'

'I *saw* her,' the little girl insisted. 'She had a scary face.'

'But Saskia's been living here for ages now and she's never had any trouble from witches,' Owen said, aiming to soothe. 'Have you?' He looked up at Saskia again.

'Nope, not a peep,' Saskia agreed. 'And even if there was a witch here once, I bet she was a nice one, not a scary one. Maybe it was her job to look after Gair before I came along. But now I'm here so she doesn't need to do it anymore.'

'You and Daddy,' Hannah murmured, her small hands wrapped around her mug. 'You're both looking after the castle.'

Saskia glanced at Owen with a smile. 'Yes.'

The little girl looked thoughtful. 'So Saskia is the new witch of Gair?'

Saskia laughed at that. 'I suppose I am. And I promise I am most *definitely* a good witch, not a bad one.'

Hannah seemed satisfied with that. She had finished her hot chocolate by now, and despite the injection of sugar, she yawned. 'I'm tired. Can I go to sleep for a while?'

'Okay,' Owen said, doubtfully. 'You haven't had any tea yet, though. We were going to have a barbecue, remember?'

'I'll have some later,' Hannah decided. 'I just need a little nap. Can Brodie come with me?'

Owen looked at Saskia. 'Sure,' she said. 'He hasn't had his tea either so he'll probably wake you up in a little while.'

'That's okay,' Hannah said, as she got up and headed for the wooden staircase. 'He can be my alarm clock. Come on, Brodie.'

The two adults watched as the girl and the dog made their way up to bed. In a few minutes there was silence. Saskia and Owen took their drinks outside, where the evening summer sun was just beginning to tip towards the horizon. They took seats in the deck chairs and looked down at the great ruined hulk of the castle, the Gair Oak standing at its centre.

'You're bleeding,' Owen said, a moment later, reaching out to touch her arm. Saskia looked down to see that a thin line of blood had soaked through her clean shirt.

She swore under her breath, leaning forward to pull the cloth away from the wound. It stung only slightly. 'I must have scraped myself on something without realizing. Probably a tree root.'

'I'll get the first aid kit,' he said, standing up again. 'Why don't you give me your shirt? If I get it under cold water right now it might not stain.'

'Really, Owen, I can sort it out myself.'

'I'm not saying you can't,' he said, hand still held out to her. 'But you've just saved my daughter from a traumatic experience so I think the least I can do is *this*.'

She smiled a little, unbuttoning her shirt and shrugging

it off. Owen disappeared with it, reappearing a few minutes later with the first aid kit in his hand.

'It doesn't hurt,' Saskia said, of the scratch. 'I'll just put some Savlon on it.' She reached for the first aid kit, but he didn't pass it to her.

'Let me deal with it.'

'Owen, I can—'

He ignored her, kneeling beside her chair and opening the kit, taking out an antiseptic wipe in a packet that he tore open with his teeth. He straightened her arm gently so that her hand rested against his thigh. He held her there, keeping her arm still with one hand, wiping away the blood with the other. His fingers were warm where they closed around her wrist, and Saskia could feel them brush against her scars. He glanced up at her, perhaps thinking the same thing, and as their eyes met she felt the same flicker in her chest she'd felt as they stood beneath that ash tree in the forest, listening to the birds sing, before they'd heard Hannah's distant scream. Saskia swallowed, hoping he couldn't feel the sudden, stuttered, extra beat of her heart through his fingers around her wrist. *What is this?* she asked herself. Nothing sensible, that was for sure.

Owen let her go to retrieve the tube of antiseptic and smoothed a dab of cream along the cut. It stung, but only for a second. She wondered if she was imagining the tension that had spun between them; if it were only her feeling it. Saskia had no intention of finding out. Whatever conclusion she came to would be wrong.

Owen ran his fingers lightly down her arm one last time,

then closed the kit and settled back into his chair. There was a few minutes of silence, and then he let out a long, slow breath, his face bleak.

'I'm going to have to tell Tasha. She'll go ballistic.'

Saskia cleared an unexpectedly dry throat. 'Why? What happened wasn't your fault.'

'I should have been watching Hannah more closely.'

'Kids have accidents, Owen,' Saskia said. 'You *were* watching her.'

'I should never have let her out of my sight. I'm lucky she wasn't more badly hurt.' He made a sharp gesture with his hand, as if castigating himself. 'Maybe I should let her have Hannah full time, if I can't even look after my daughter for a single day without putting her in danger.'

Saskia wanted to reach out to him. To offer a hand, the way he just had to her. She concentrated on the oak, instead. She'd fallen from one of the branches, once. She'd been trying to impress her father by finding a new route up the old trunk, and she'd slipped and hit her head. She hadn't blacked out, but her father had been frantic, and they'd spent hours in Accident and Emergency, only for the doctor to assure them both she was fine. Saskia's mother had barely even registered sympathy for the bruise on her daughter's forehead. 'Perhaps it'll teach you to be less wild,' was all she'd said.

'You can blame it on me,' Saskia said. 'Tell her I was supposed to be watching her for a few minutes and I wasn't paying enough attention. Or tell her I was taking her to see the fairy ring and let her run on ahead.'

Owen said nothing and when Saskia glanced over at him, he was watching her. His expression was unreadable, but she felt that same unexpected judder in her chest again, and she looked away.

'I'm not going to paint you as an idiot just to get out of the consequences of my own actions,' he said. 'Do you really think I'd do that?'

'It's not about you,' Saskia said, more bluntly than she'd intended. 'It's about Hannah. And from what I've seen, you're a wonderful dad. She loves you and she loves spending time with you. But Tasha must know both of those things already, and I'd like to think she would be understanding of what happened today.' The midges were coming out, fine mists of the tiny insects drifting around them in the half-light. She stood, waving her hand in front of her face to bat them away. 'Anyway, let's get the food on.'

Twenty-One

The rest of Hannah's stay at Gair that weekend was uneventful. She woke from her nap starving again, and the evening had passed around the firepit, the three of them – and Brodie – eating sausages and toasted marshmallows as if they might somehow go out of fashion. Owen watched his daughter, anxious for the unexpected, worried that he had somehow missed a head injury or some other grave malaise, but she really did seem fine. Her fear over the 'witch' did not linger, perhaps thanks to Saskia's spinning of the story. Owen watched the two of them together. Saskia was good with Hannah, making her laugh. Little by little, the terror of what had happened when he'd thought he'd lost her loosened its grip and he relaxed, although he would still have to face Tasha as he explained why their daughter had returned with scrapes to her knees and hands.

In the event, though, Saskia was right about that, too. Tasha showed surprising understanding, perhaps because Hannah seemed to have moved far beyond the fearful moment of the fall.

'I fell into a hole in the forest, Mummy, and Daddy couldn't pull me out so Saskia did it instead.' In the flat retelling on a Sunday evening, the event lost some of its power, and Tasha did nothing more than check Hannah's knees and hands. Accidents happen, indeed.

'I'm glad she had fun, Owen,' Tasha told him, as they said goodbye. 'And I can just imagine the stories she's going to be telling at school tomorrow about her weekend staying in a castle.'

And that was that.

'Thank you,' he said to Saskia when he got back to Gair.

Saskia smiled. She had once again plaited her long hair into a thick rope, which hung over her shoulder. He thought that if Hannah saw her now, she might think her not too far removed from one of her Disney princess heroines.

'It was nothing,' Saskia told him, but it had not been nothing. None of it had been nothing. As he settled down to sleep in the home she had built with her own hands, he thought of the scars on her wrists; how she had not hesitated to push herself head-first through that hole to pull his daughter to safety; and how she had trusted him not to let her fall.

On Monday she shut herself in her tiny office at the back of the trailer, citing some research that she needed to do. He didn't know what this entailed, although he did catch a glimpse of her screen and see one of the LiDAR scans, zoomed in to an enormous degree. Owen spent the morning down on the site, watching the progress – or more importantly, the lack thereof – of the archaeologists. They had found nothing new beyond a few broken pieces of pottery that Nathan had begrudgingly admitted were not Roman, but from the heyday of the castle, instead. The day was hot, but the atmosphere was changing. The air had turned humid, dark clouds beginning to gather. The weather was turning, as forecast. He wondered how the teams grubbing about in Gair's dirt would deal with a deluge. What would the ruins look like in the rain? He'd only ever seen them in dry heat and sun. Owen imagined it could be a forbidding place.

Saskia emerged that afternoon, looking thoughtful, coming down the slope and calling to him. 'I want to go back to that hole,' she said, once he'd reached her. 'The one Hannah fell into. Will you come with me? It might not be safe for me to do it alone.'

'You want to go into it again?' he asked. 'Why?'

She shrugged a little, glancing past him towards the people searching through Gair's empty dust. 'Indulge me.'

Saskia had packed a small rucksack and as they set off for the woods, Owen saw several of the team's members pause to watch them go, Nathan included. Her refusal to allow them into the forest still rankled, it seemed, probably because their search within the castle itself had been relatively fruitless.

Owen wasn't sure he'd have been able to find their way back to where Hannah had fallen, but Saskia and Brodie had no problem retracing their steps. He thought again about Hannah's brief fear of the witch she had conjured from her ordeal; how Saskia had put a different spin on it. She strode through the forest with a notable confidence, as if she belonged here, as if she really was the fairytale heroine Hannah had cast her to be. Looking at her sidelong, he thought she could easily fit the part had she swapped the rucksack on her shoulder for something with a little more whimsy. A sword, maybe, or a bow and arrow. First thing this morning her hair had been in a plait, but now it was in a simple ponytail. Owen realized that he had never seen her wear it loose, and wondered what that would look like, especially now, in waves because of the way she had worn it as she'd slept. He flinched uneasily as he realized the turn his thoughts had taken, turning away from her and looking into the forest instead. It was quiet today, almost subdued. He wondered if this was the calm before the storm.

When they reached the hole, Owen looked at it doubtfully. The gap seemed even narrower than it had a day or so before, despite the edge that had crumbled away as a result of the rescue. 'Are you sure you want to go down there again?'

Saskia had dropped the bag from her shoulder and crouched over it on the ground, pulling out a length of thin climber's rope. 'Hannah said she saw a bed and a chair down there,' she reminded him. 'Not to mention the witch.'

'That was just her imagination,' Owen said. 'She was down there in the dark, how could she have seen anything? And anyway, how could those things possibly be down there?'

She looked up at him with a grin and a spark in her eye that unexpectedly made something in Owen's gut twist.

'Don't spoil my fun, Owen,' she said. 'I want to at least check it out. I've searched every millimetre of the LiDAR scans and they didn't reach this far from the castle so they can't tell me what's down there. And' – she pulled something from her pocket as she straightened up – 'there's this.' He took what she held out and realized it was the candle stub he'd found on the ground the first night in the trailer. He looked at her and she shrugged. 'Had to have come from somewhere, right?'

This time her descent was smoother, aided by the rope fastened around a nearby hazel and lit by a portable floodlight. Owen crouched beside the hole as she disappeared into it, a mask across her mouth and nose to prevent inhalation of the dry soil that crumbled as she passed through its crust.

Twenty-Two

The light shone a harsh blue-white ahead of her as Saskia descended into the hole. The journey down seemed longer this time, perhaps because last time she'd been focusing on Hannah's tear-streaked face below her. It was perhaps an eight-foot drop from where Owen waited in the sunlight above her to the floor of the strange, subterranean space. Saskia wondered how on earth Hannah had managed to escape without at least breaking a bone, but as her feet touched down, she realized that the ground beneath her feet was carpeted with a thick bed of dried leaves. She took a step to steady herself at the end of the rope and they crunched beneath her boots.

'Are you all right?' Owen called from above.

'I'm fine.' She untied the rope and took another step, leaving it hanging as she lifted the light to look around. The space wasn't as large as she'd thought the last time she'd been down here. Sinking into darkness, it had seemed like a cavern, but now she could see its cramped contours. The 'roof' was knitted together, a web of tree roots tangled enough to support the soil that had compacted between them. Saskia, with her architect's mind, wondered how the structure had sustained itself for so long. She was standing in a roughly circular space, walls and 'ceiling' meeting in a seamless curve that was mostly lost in shadow. She left the circle of natural light that filtered through the hole above her and reached out a tentative hand. Holding the LED aloft, she parted mosses and the spindle fingers of tangled roots until her fingers brushed against something cold. Saskia paused, holding the light closer, and pulled away more forest debris until she could see grey stone beneath, pitted with age. She stopped, unsure of what she was seeing, and then widened the gap more to reveal an edge, and then another, roughly at a right angle to the first. This was an *actual* wall, very obviously deliberately built from stones that had been hewn into roughly even shapes, not just compacted soil. Could this place really be man-made? If it was, what did that mean? She looked around the underground space, her hand still resting against the old stone.

'Saskia?' Owen called again.

'I'm okay,' she said, stepping back towards the hole so he could see her. 'It's like . . . I don't know, something out of *Lord of the Rings*.'

'No sign of a witch, though, I hope?'

'Not yet, but—'

'But?'

Saskia turned again. This place was certainly worthy of every fairytale she'd read about Gair and its mysterious forest.

'I feel like I've fallen through a crack into an alternate reality,' she said. 'If other children have done the same as Hannah over the years, I'm not surprised the forest has got a reputation. I'm going to move around a bit more,' she added. 'Don't freak out if you can't see me.'

'Just be careful. I can't get down there easily to help you,' he reminded her. 'Don't turn an ankle.'

Saskia held up the light as she circled the space, and then stopped. In one of the alcoves, there was a stack of branches. She moved closer to take a better look. They hadn't fallen at random, they had been arranged deliberately. Knitted together, almost like the tree roots spreading across the roof and walls. They formed a level platform, a little like a make-shift cot. Was this what Hannah had seen and described as a bed? It seemed likely. A whole gamut of historical possibilities lifted the hairs on the back of Saskia's neck as she moved in for a closer look. When had the last person slept here? Two hundred years ago? Five hundred? A thousand? She shivered slightly. Surely not, as even dry branches of that age would have crumbled to meet the mulch beneath her feet eventually. Yet this place was ancient. She could feel it.

Saskia looked around again, suddenly feeling as if there might be someone else there, lurking, watching, but she was alone. Her heart thumped, painfully hard, in her chest.

'Owen?'

'I'm here,' he called back. 'What is it?'

'Nothing.' She breathed out, slowly, settling herself. 'Just checking.'

'Had enough yet?'

If this was the 'bed' that Hannah had seen, where was the chair she'd mentioned? Saskia swept the light around again, but saw nothing that resembled something someone would sit in. But there, what was that? Was that . . . a door? No, not a door, but there, in the shadows between thicker tree roots, was . . . what? A passageway? Certainly a recess.

'Not yet,' she said, her heart still beating an uneven tattoo in her chest. 'But don't go anywhere. There's something here I want to check out.'

There was a pause. 'I'm here. But—'

'I know,' she said. She tightened her grip on the light. 'I'll be careful.'

Beyond the deeper shadow she'd seen was another room, also with a hole in its 'roof', though this one was even smaller, letting in a light so dim it was barely there. Saskia stood on the threshold between the two rooms, scalp prickling. Her heart would not settle, her primordial senses at full alert. She was underground, in the dark and alone with no easy escape. Her ancestors would have already retreated. But she had the light that she held in her hand, heavy enough to double as a weapon. She had Owen, crouched beside the hole up above.

As Saskia flicked her light around, she realized this room was far more put together than the one she'd just left. The dry compacted dirt floor was clear of leaves, as if it had been swept. The was no moss on the walls, showing the grey stone blocks embedded there far more clearly. The roots that hung from the ceiling had been shaped over time, woven into uneven storage spaces. To her left, at eye-level, something shone white in the light of her torch beam. She went closer and reached up to take down one of the mugs that had gone missing from the work site. It was full of bolts that must have come from the same place too. There were more here, too, neatly arranged on the woven shelves, along with other pilfered objects, things she hadn't even realized had gone missing. One of the hard hats. Several pencils. There were small, irregularly shaped candles, too, obviously handmade. These were set in tree-root nooks that seemed to have been formed for the purpose, shaped like little church windows. Some were standing on small shelves whittled from branches. Saskia flicked her torch around the room again, tilting it to look up at the low ceiling. There were bunches of plants hanging from more tree roots, large handfuls of stems tied with string and left to dry. They lent a pleasant scent to the space – herbal and fragrant, not at all damp.

There was furniture, too. A very solid-looking chair, shaped from worked branches that had been stripped of their bark and fixed together with simple but beautiful mortise and tenon joints. A low table made in the same style stood beside it, and on it was a whittled chess set. When she moved the torch beam to the other side of the room, Saskia saw that against the stone wall, beneath another, larger woven bower of tree roots, there was a bed. This was a bigger version of the one she'd seen when she'd first descended the rope, fashioned from branches, again apparently without the need for metal fixings. There was bedding on it, too: a pillow, a camping mattress, a sleeping bag and . . . something else, something soft that Saskia recognized with a jolt. She went over to look closer, picking it up. The thick cloth unfolded with a tumble, and when it did, the thrill against the back of Saskia's neck became an electric chill of shock.

It was the blanket she'd been missing since that first day she'd gone to the river to swim, apparently neatly kept and still clean.

Her heart thumped as she tried to work out quite what she had found; what was going on in this strange, underground place. That first room could have been ancient, but this? This was different. This felt lived in. This felt like a *home*.

She swept the light around the room again, and something gleamed in the darkest part of the room as the beam moved past it, in a hollow in one of the walls. There was something hunched there, and when she turned the light back it illuminated two black eyes and a mouth, wide open in a silent scream, a pale face framed by wild hair. Saskia screamed herself, heart pounding so hard she felt light-headed as fright took her over. She fled back towards the opening in the roof, grabbing the rope.

'Get me out,' she shouted, her voice strange in her throat, high and harsh. 'Pull, Owen, *get me out*!'

He hauled and she climbed, dropping the torch in her haste to escape. Once Saskia had scrambled high enough for her fingers to graze the edge of the hole, he let go of the rope and grabbed her arms instead, dragging her bodily from the earth until they were both above ground. Owen let her go and Saskia stumbled away, falling to her knees on the loam, coughing, sucking in air through her panicked breathing.

'Hey,' Owen said, going to her, hands on her shoulders. 'Hey, it's okay. What happened? What did you see?'

Saskia didn't answer at first, trying to catch her breath, trying to quell the visceral fear that had momentarily overtaken her. Around her the trees were waving green leaves in a breeze that smelled of the change in the weather, despite the sun still shining overhead. Birds were singing; life was going on as normal. But down there, amid the roots, under their feet . . .

'There's someone *living* down there,' she said, hoarsely, once she could form words.

'What?' Owen dropped to a crouch beside her. 'Are you sure?'

Saskia nodded, wiping a shaking hand across her face. She thought again about that moment when two pairs of eyes had met in a place no human belonged. 'It's a man, I think. He must have been down there a while. He looks . . . old. And he's been collecting stuff.'

'Stuff?'

She held out her hand and Owen took it, helping her up. The shock was fading now, bleaching away to leave only a slight sense of dislocation. 'The mugs that were going missing from the work site: they're down there. Things like that.'

Owen looked back to the hole. 'What? That's . . . God. We'd better call the police.'

'The police?' The thought brought Saskia up short. She was still feeling shaken, off-kilter.

'Yes.' He looked at her, a quizzical look on his face. 'Whoever's down there is trespassing. They're obviously a thief, too. We need to report it. I don't want to confront whoever it is on my own.'

He fumbled in his pocket, pulling out his phone, but before he could thumb the screen Saskia reached out and wrapped her hand around Owen's wrist to still him. 'Wait,' she said. 'Just ... wait a minute.' She was thinking about those eyes and the terror she had seen in them. Her own fear had been born of shock, a visceral reaction to coming across something unexpected in a strange place. 'I don't want to call the police. Not yet.'

'What?' Owen frowned. 'Why not?'

Saskia dropped her hand and stepped away from him, facing the hole at their feet with a shake of her head. 'Whoever it is, I don't think they're a threat.'

'You don't know that,' Owen said. 'They scared you, didn't they?'

'That was just because I didn't expect to see anyone, that's all,' Saskia said, faintly embarrassed. 'Whoever it is probably just needs help.'

'Yeah, and the police can give it,' Owen pointed out, his phone still primed in his hand.

Saskia blew out a breath. She was remembering the times she'd had run-ins with the police herself. None of them had ever been particularly helpful, and she understood why, but still. 'No,' she said. 'Owen, don't call them. I'm asking you not to. I'm *telling* you not to.'

He watched her carefully for a moment, his face serious. Then he gave a terse nod and put his phone back in his pocket. 'It's your property.'

'Yes,' she said, faintly relieved. 'It is.'

He raised both hands in an expansive gesture. 'So . . . what? You're just going to leave whoever it is down there? Pretend you didn't see them?'

'No,' Saskia said. 'Of course not. But there must be another way to help them, beyond calling the police. Let me think about it for a bit.'

Owen watched her, his hands on his hips, a slight frown on his face.

'Come on,' she said, before he could say anything else. 'Let's get back. Please don't mention it to anyone else until I say so.'

Saskia started back towards the work site. There was a moment of quiet and then she heard Owen's footsteps crunching through the brush behind her. She was relieved. He obviously wasn't comfortable with her decision, but she appreciated that he was apparently prepared to accept it without further argument.

Now she just had to work out what to do about her unexpected underground tenant – whoever they were.

Twenty-Three

'We've moved one of the cameras from the work site to the forest, which will hopefully capture an image of whoever it is,' Owen said, rubbing a hand over his face. 'But there must be another entrance because so far, no luck. I'm having trouble working out what her reasoning is,' he added. 'She doesn't make irrational decisions, as a rule. But this . . .' He shrugged, picking up his pint.

He and Stuart were catching up over a drink for the first time in a while, mainly because it was also the first time in a few weekends that Vivian wasn't around. She'd gone to Paris for a shoot, and they'd both agreed that wandering the city alone while she worked wasn't something Stuart would particularly enjoy, so he'd opted not to join her.

Owen had been surprised by the good changes he could see in his old friend. He seemed to have lost weight, for a start, though not in a drastic way. It was just that the fuzzy edge lent from years of careless eating had slipped away, leaving the kind of definition Owen hadn't seen on his friend since their army days.

Stuart snorted a little as he picked up his pint; his relationship hadn't dulled his sardonic nature. 'That's not what you were saying about her a few weeks back, when this all started,' he pointed out. 'In fact, I'm pretty sure you thought she was nothing *but* irrational.'

Owen made a face. 'Yeah, but I was wrong. I know her better now. All the stuff with Gair, that all makes sense. Letting some vagrant stay in a secret underground bunker on her property . . . that's something else.'

'Is it?'

Owen frowned. 'Isn't it?

'Well,' Stuart said. 'From where I'm sitting, it sounds like she's being empathetic towards someone whose shoes she's almost been in more than once. And given that you're currently living in her home for the same reason, I'd say it's pretty par for the course.'

Owen stared into his drink, morose. 'I guess you're right,' he said, eventually. 'But still . . .'

'Still what?'

'It's not safe, is it?'

Stuart said nothing, and when Owen looked his way again, he found his friend watching him carefully. 'What?' Owen asked.

'How long did you say you'd give it before moving on from Gair?'

Owen flinched a little at the pointedness of the segue. 'A month.'

'Right,' Stuart said. 'And that's up – when? Week after next?'

Owen shifted in his seat, uncomfortable. The time had gone faster than he'd expected. Too fast. There was no sign of the teams working for the judicial review board even finishing at the site, let alone handing in a report.

'Yeah,' Owen said, not really wanting to think about it.

Stuart nodded. 'Does that mean we're going to see you down in Collaton from the end of the month? Because it stands to reason you've already arranged that by now, especially since that coincides with Phase Three getting underway. Perfect timing, right?'

Owen said nothing, just supped more of his pint. He was getting through it quickly tonight, perhaps because he hadn't had a drink all week. There was no way he'd insult Saskia by having alcohol on the property she was so generously sharing with him, even though he knew without asking she wouldn't object.

'Owen,' Stuart said, in a tone that suggested a verbal shake of the head. 'Mate. What are you doing?'

'You know what I'm doing,' he said. 'I said I'd give her a month. I'm not signing up for anything before that. If I take up a contract somewhere else, Saskia's finished.'

'Saskia?' Stuart asked, with his eyebrows raised. 'Not Gair?'

'You know what I mean.'

'Yeah,' Stuart said, 'I think I do.'

'What's that supposed to mean?'

Stuart sighed. 'Owen. Look. I like her. I'm rooting for her and Gair, I really am. I loved working on that project while it was a goer, and I mean, I'm with her best mate, right? Like, really with her, in a way I didn't think I'd ever want to be, maybe even for the long haul, and—'

'Wait,' Owen said, glass paused halfway to his lips. 'Really? You and Vivian, you're that serious?'

His friend shrugged, but it wasn't quite as nonchalant a gesture as it would usually be. 'Yeah.'

'Wow.'

'Yeah.'

'That's a really big thing for you. I'm glad.'

'Thanks, it's—' Stuart apparently realized that he'd become side-tracked, because he frowned, holding up a hand. 'That's not the point I was trying to make. My point is, I get it if you're falling for her. Why wouldn't you? The two of you, up there, on your own, all cosy like—'

'Hey,' Owen said, interrupting. 'That's not what's happening. And anyway—'

'Anyway what?' Stuart asked.

They looked at each other. Owen opened his mouth to continue his train of thought, but instead an image of Saskia shot through his head: that moment when he'd been kneeling beside her chair, one hand wrapped around her wrist, the fingers of his other smoothing down her warm skin – and it derailed whatever he might have said. Stuart made an *and there it is* expression, and downed the rest of his pint.

'That's not what this is,' Owen tried, again. 'Okay, I'm not going to say that I don't like her, because I do. I know her now, and because of that I know where she's coming from and what she wants and why she wants it and Stuart, she deserves to make Gair work. She deserves that.'

Stuart nodded. 'And you care about her.'

'No, I—'

'You don't care about her?'

Owen was beginning to lose his patience. 'Don't be a dick. I know what you're trying to do.'

'Okay.' His friend stood. 'My round. Just have a think while I'm at the bar, yeah?'

Owen watched Stuart join the throng waiting for drinks and then glanced at his phone. It was getting on for ten o'clock, the latest he'd been away from Gair for a while, certainly since their discovery of whoever it was living in the woods. He'd tried in vain to get Saskia to let him call the police, but she'd refused, and since it could only be called trespassing if the owner of the land said it was, there wasn't anything more he could do. She'd gone back twice, leaving food and blankets for whoever it was, adding notes to the effect that they could ask for whatever help they needed. It was clear that her unexpected lodger had found these offerings, because both parcels had been removed when Saskia had gone back to check. That was when she'd agreed to the camera. Part of him had found the care she had shown for this unknown person more affecting than he'd ever admit. Another part of him had begun to grow more and more anxious about the situation, especially when he wasn't at Gair but Saskia was. Whoever it was couldn't be in their right mind, could they? He knew she could probably look after herself, but still. His mind kept wandering back to those scars on her wrists. She'd dragged herself out of a hellhole and rebuilt herself a life, and she'd done it mostly alone and more than once. He didn't want her to have to defend herself again – that was all. He didn't want some unknown variable threatening a life fought for with such backbone.

And yeah, he cared about . . . that. He tried not to think about the couple of times when he'd thought there had been the flicker of something else between them, something more, because that was a very full can of worms that it would be insane to open.

Owen swallowed the rest of his beer and left that thought where it was.

'So what are you going to do?' his friend asked when he returned, and for a moment Owen wasn't quite sure what he meant. 'The opportunity in Collaton is closing, you know that.'

Owen nodded. 'I know. I *know*. I just . . . It's not that easy. I thought it would be. But it's not.'

Stuart nodded, but he said nothing more about it.

When Owen got back to Gair that night, all the lights were on in the cabin. It still hadn't rained, but stepping out of the car he could smell the ozone in the air and knew that there was a downpour coming in the heavy clouds pressing overhead, and soon.

'Owen?' Saskia called, as he pushed open the door.

'Hey,' he said, peering through the kitchen to find her looking back at him from the small square of space that was her office. 'Everything okay?'

She got up and came towards him carrying her laptop, her eyes bright. 'Look at this.'

Owen shrugged off his coat and hung it on the peg on the back of the door. Then he took the computer, looking at the screen as he went to the sofa and sat down. On it was a frozen colour image. It was surprisingly sharp and had obviously been captured by the camera they'd put up above the forest mound. He glanced up at her. 'It worked.'

Saskia smiled. 'It did.'

She tapped the space bar as she sat down beside him and together they watched the footage. It was brief – less than thirty seconds – but it showed a figure moving through the camera frame. Whoever it was wore a hooded cloak so long that its hem brushed the ground. All that was really visible of the person beneath was part of an arm and one pale hand clutching a long, stripped branch, which it was using as a walking stick. As Owen watched the screen, a prickle skittered across his neck. It felt as if he were watching something out of a folk tale; a character who didn't quite belong to this world. And yet, there they were, as real as Owen himself.

The figure passed out of the camera's view and Saskia reached over and tapped the space bar again, freezing the image. 'That's all there is,' she said. 'They don't come back the same way. It has to be my lodger though, doesn't it? They were probably looking to see if I'd left more food.'

Owen relinquished the laptop, and she closed it. 'What does this mean for you now, then?'

He watched her face as she frowned, knitting her fingers

together. 'I need to talk to them. Find out where they've come from.'

'Sure,' Owen said, 'but you can do that once he – or she – is somewhere safer than a hole in the ground, can't you?' As he spoke, the first spatter of rain dashed itself against the window and he turned to glance at the drops sliding down the glass. 'The weather's changing,' he pointed out. 'It might have been dry down there when you first went in, but if we have the kind of weather they're forecasting, that's bound to change, isn't it?'

'I don't know,' Saskia said. 'You didn't see it down there, Owen. It felt *lived* in. Homely. Things had been perfectly built for the space. That's taken longer than a few days – longer than weeks, even. I think whoever it is has been there for months. Maybe even years. Because they must know the forest better than any of us, mustn't they? Or they wouldn't have been able to stay out of sight for so long. They've been coming in and out of the work site without us seeing them. And whoever it is took a blanket from a bag of mine while I was swimming and I didn't notice, even though they must have been less than ten feet away, so—'

'What?' Owen turned to her sharply. 'I didn't know about that. Why didn't you tell me?'

She looked momentarily thrown. 'It was before you were staying here. I didn't even think about it.'

'Saskia, this is crazy,' Owen said. 'I mean, I don't think it's healthy for whoever that is we've just seen on the screen, obviously, but it's you I'm more worried about.' He gestured around her home. 'What if they decide they want something out of this place?'

'If they wanted to do that they'd have already been up here,' she said. 'And I don't think that's happened. I'd be able to tell.'

'Then what's your plan?' Owen asked, trying to hide his exasperation.

'I'm going to leave a parcel of food with another note. This time it'll say that I'm going to come back and visit to talk face-to-face.'

'What?'

She spread her hands. 'Whoever it is hasn't come to us, and I don't know if that's because they're ignoring the messages or if they can't read. But I'm not going to just go barging in there without warning. I agree that we need to find some way to help, so this is my solution. We'll leave a parcel in view of the camera so we know when it has been collected. It'll say that I'll be in the room where they first saw me at midday on the day after the parcel's collection. And then I'll take it from there.'

'There's no way you're going on your own,' Owen said. 'I'm coming with you.'

She looked faintly frustrated. 'If you insist, you can wait above the hole, the same as before.'

'And what if this person decides to attack you?' he asked. 'How am I supposed to get to you?'

Saskia gazed at him for a moment, as if trying to work something out. He felt momentarily exposed, uncomfortable, as if he'd shown his hand in a game of poker.

'Owen,' she said, eventually. 'If that happens, it won't be the first time I've had to defend myself. But it will be the first time I've had to fight back against a person who's been living in the woods for who knows how long and who is frail enough that they have to use a walking stick made out of an old branch.'

There was a moment of silence.

'All right,' Owen said. 'Point taken. I just—'

'I know,' she said, and to his surprise she reached out and put her hand over his. 'And I appreciate it. But I'll be fine. And,' she added, with a slight smile to soften her next words, 'I'm not asking your permission.'

Twenty-Four

This time, Saskia's descent into her forest underworld was a little less fraught. She took with her a bag of groceries and wore gloves so that her hands didn't chafe against the rope. She could feel Owen's agitation as she disappeared into the hole, but there really was no way he could go with her, at least not through this entrance. Anyway, she had no desire to intimidate whoever was down here.

Saskia wasn't sure whether to be touched or irritated by Owen's obvious concern. She wondered where it had come from; whether he was compensating because at the moment he couldn't watch out for his daughter in the way he wanted.

The room below the entrance point was as empty as the first time she'd climbed down into it, and this time she thought she understood why. The weather had finally broken, and although the rain had for now lessened into a drizzle that was almost non-existent beneath the forest canopy, the night before had been a rough one. The clouds had rolled in over Gair, splitting in a storm that rocked the trailer and lashed hard torrents of rain against her windows. This underground chamber had been bone dry the last time Saskia had set foot in it, but now she could see the bed of leaves underfoot was wet. No wonder this 'room' wasn't used regularly.

'I'll be back,' Saskia called to Owen, who was waiting at the edge of the hole above her.

'Still not happy about this,' he told her.

'I know.' She smiled up at him. 'I promise, I'll use this if I need you.'

She held up the tin coach's whistle he'd presented her with that morning and that Saskia had stowed in her pocket. It wasn't a terrible idea, she had to admit. If anything was going to carry to him through this underground lair, it would be the piercing blast of an old-school whistle.

She shouldered her bag of offerings and lifted the light in her hand as she headed for the second room, the one where she'd found the beautifully carved bed and chair, and where she had first encountered her unexpected tenant.

'Hello?' she called, but there was no answer. Saskia moved deeper into the room, shining the light into its furthest reaches, wondering whether the old man was cowering in the shadows somewhere, as he had been last time. Her light swept across the hollow where he'd been then, and she froze. He was still there, in exactly the same place: still with those round eyes and wide, silently screaming mouth.

'Hello?' Saskia's heart was hammering, but this time she stood her ground. Then realization hit her. It wasn't a *person* looking back at her. It was a statue of some kind. She moved cautiously towards it. It was carved from pale rock, and it looked extremely old. A crude rendition of a head, with wild hair, staring eyes and a wide mouth formed by pits gouged deep in the stone. It was in a crouching position, and now that she looked at it properly, Saskia could see roughly shaped hands, too: fingers outstretched and gripping a larger piece of stone that was about the size of a headstone in a graveyard. Is that what this was? she wondered. A sunken grave? But no – this stone had a bowl-shaped depression at its base. It was more like an altar than a grave. It was free of lichen, as were the rest of the walls in this room, as if someone were looking after it, tending to it.

As Saskia pulled her phone out of her pocket to take a picture, she became aware of a sound drifting to her from some small distance. It was a bubbling, organic-sounding melody, a little like water tripping over itself in the river, and it took her a second to realize that it was the noise of water coming to the boil. It was drifting from another doorway that she hadn't seen during her last visit, when she'd been so badly spooked that she'd made a run for it. The fact that she could see it this time – that, in fact, the entire room in which she stood was faintly illuminated, at least in parts – meant there must be light coming from somewhere other than the one in her hand. She flicked it off and sure enough, there was a warm yellow glow emanating through the door she hadn't seen on her last visit. Just how many of these subterranean rooms were there?

She stopped in this new doorway and looked around, astonished. This room was smaller, and at some point between antiquity and now there must have been a collapse, for one half of the ceiling sloped at an odd angle, its forest roof almost touching the floor at its furthest point. The room was very obviously being used as a kitchen. Here the woven root shelves had been augmented by larger storage cupboards, all shaped and carved from planed wood that in most places still retained the bark of the branches from which it had been cut. It all matched the style of the furniture in the room behind her. The cupboards formed a pantry, holding provisions that definitely hadn't been here long – not even months, let alone years or centuries. Saskia could see tins of baked beans and soup, glass storage jars full of dried pulses and herbs, even a few cans of fizzy drink, alongside large canisters of water and non-edible goods such as batteries. On other shelves there were cooking utensils; folded cloths that looked like well-used tea-towels; glasses; more of the mugs that had gone missing from the building site and all manner of tins that might hold anything from biscuits to flour.

There were two things that really threw Saskia, though, and they were the strings of lights that were giving off the glow she had seen from the other room and the gas-powered camping stove, both entirely too modern for this space. The latter stood on what she could only describe as a 'kitchen island'. It was in the middle of the room, built from wood and topped with a central slab of what she thought might be slate from the mine at Honister. Above it there was a vent in the earthen roof, a hole far smaller than the one through which Saskia had entered. The stove was lit and the bubbling she had heard had come from the tin kettle mounted on it. As she stood there, still trying to process the incongruous domesticity of what she was seeing, it began to emit a piercing whistle.

There came a flurry of movement and suddenly Saskia was not alone. She jumped as a figure bustled into view, appearing as if from out of the wall itself. It was the old man, moving with a speed that seemed at odds with the tentative steps she'd captured him making on camera. *But that was above ground*, she found herself thinking, *in a world that is not his own. He was feeling his way there, uncertain, but here in his subterranean home he knows exactly how to move and where to go.*

He was wearing the same cloak, hood still pulled up so that she couldn't see his face. As he busied himself with the kettle, she wondered if he knew she was there. Was he deaf, perhaps?

'Hello?' she said.

'Well,' he said, his back to her as he took down two mugs, a small earthenware jar and one of the canisters of herbs. 'At least you're punctual.'

Saskia froze. This voice was definitely not what she expected from an old man. It was strident and strong, not weak and wispy. This voice matched the quick, confident movements she'd just observed, not the ones she'd seen on the security camera. He swung around, put down the mugs and then pulled back the cloak hood to reveal himself.

'Morning,' he said. 'Tea? It's a blend I make myself, you'll like it.'

For a moment Saskia was speechless. The man before her definitely wasn't a doddery tramp. He couldn't be more than mid-fifties, his mid-length hair salt-and-pepper grey and his chin stubbled, but with no sign of an unkempt Merlin-style beard. His skin was lined and tanned but clean and healthy. He looked strong, and his blue eyes were bright. He seemed amused by her obvious consternation.

'Pulled off a good act for your little spy camera, didn't I?' he said, as he used a whittled wooden spoon to add herbs to each mug. He poured water from the kettle in on top, before adding something viscous and golden from the earthenware jar. He finished by giving the whole concoction a brisk stir. 'Thanks for the treats, too. I do like a Hobnob, as you probably worked out from my pillaging raids onto your site. Sorry about that, but the squirrels and mice would have had them anyway, you can't leave that sort of thing out overnight.' He turned and waved a hand at his wall of storage containers. 'That's something I'm very careful of down here. It wouldn't take much to be overrun.'

Saskia finally found her voice as he pushed one of the mugs towards her. 'Who *are* you?'

He picked up his own mug and looked at her over its rim. 'I'm Tim.' He glanced around. 'Sorry there's nowhere to sit. I'm not used to having visitors. In fact, you're the first.'

'Tim,' Saskia repeated, trying to regain her equilibrium. 'I'm Saskia.'

He gave her a look. 'Yes,' he said, his voice carrying an edge of disdain. 'I know exactly who you are.'

'What . . .' Saskia didn't even know where to start. She looked around the kitchen, so perfectly appointed, so very out of the ordinary. 'Tim. What are you *doing* here?'

He sipped his tea with a shrug. 'I live here.'

'For how long?'

He leaned against his beautiful, unconventional worktop and thought about it for a minute or two. 'Seven years, give or take.'

'Seven *years*?'

'Yeah. There have been a couple of winters where I've had to decamp as it's been too much even for me. No heating down here apart from naked flame and I won't cut down the hardwoods so I'm only burning the softwood – goes up far too quickly and I can only store so much.'

'Then . . . you've got somewhere else to go?' Saskia asked, trying to sift through what he was saying.

He watched her carefully for a moment before answering. 'I go to my brother's in Glasgow if I really need somewhere. His place is my registered address. Once every couple of months I hike into Carlisle to stock up on supplies, get a haircut, that kind of thing. He comes down to meet me. We get some food and catch up, he gives me any post I need to see.' Tim gave a slightly unsettling smile. 'I've got a bank account and a passport, too. I'm not a neanderthal, *Saskia*, I just don't like living around people.'

Saskia rubbed a hand over her face. 'Okay,' she said, a little overwhelmed by the rapid fire of his words. 'Sorry . . . I'm just trying to take all this in.'

Tim lifted his mug, using it to gesture to hers, still untouched. 'Don't *waste* it.'

She glanced down at her drink. It actually smelled delicious. 'What is it?'

'Wild sage, dried apple and honey.'

Saskia took a tentative sip. 'Mmm,' she said, surprised. 'That's really good.'

He nodded, apparently satisfied. For a few minutes they stood in silence, drinking.

'Look, Tim,' Saskia ventured. 'Can you tell me a bit more about yourself?'

He regarded her with narrowed eyes. 'What do you want to know?'

Again, Saskia wondered where to start. She looked around the room. 'How did you end up living here? Why are you living here? *How* are you living here? Take your pick.'

He smirked a little, and for a few minutes Saskia wondered whether he was going to ignore her questions. Then he put down his mug and crossed his arms. When he spoke, it seemed to be to the air, rather than her, and she wondered when he'd last had a conversation.

'I don't do well with people,' he said, bluntly. 'Never have. Never been good at making friends. I'm better on my own. Even when I was really small, I just wanted to be out in the woods. Wasn't interested in TV. Didn't care about music, either, unless it was a bird singing. Too much noise, too raucous. It was the same with the playground, all chatter and shrieking. That kind of "fun" was never fun for me. Didn't make for a very comfortable time at school.'

'That must have been difficult.'

He looked at her sharply, as if trying to work out whether Saskia was mocking him. 'It was. And then when I was about thirteen they started trying to fit us into their little capitalist boxes, started trying to work out what boring, restrictive office job we'd be good at when we were older so that we could make enough money to buy a boring house in a boring place that we'd never leave, all so we could keep paying into the system. 'Little Boxes', just like the song says. That's when I realized I had to get out.'

'Get out?'

He shrugged, then gave another twisted smile. 'If I'd been born in America, I would have taken off into one of their great wildernesses. Gone up to Alaska, maybe, or the mountains. Built a cabin. Hunted, foraged. No one would have bothered me there. But I wasn't in America, I was here, so I started looking for any corners that were left where I could disappear. Started learning everything I needed to know about how to live where I didn't have to be with *people* all the time.'

'How did you come across Gair?'

'I did a couple of forest management courses up here and then started working at Kielder. At first I thought I could buy a woodland, but there was no way I could afford somewhere big enough to sustain me, and anyway, they have people checking that you're not living on them full-time. Then I thought I could manage somewhere for someone else, but that meant ... *people.* Then I heard the stories about Gair. First time I came up here, it felt like what I'd been looking for my whole life. The ruins, the oak, the river, the woodland.' He looked over at her. 'I know you found my bath.'

'Your ...' It took her a moment to realize what he meant. 'You mean the swimming pool?'

He gave that odd smile again. 'That's what you're calling it, is it?'

'You took my blanket, didn't you?'

He sighed. 'You can have it back. I shouldn't have taken it, it was stupid. I was just ... already angry with you, and there you were, in yet another of my places.' He gave her another look, as if to mean, *Come on, say it. Tell me it's not mine, it's yours.*

'Keep the blanket,' Saskia said, instead. 'And I'm sorry I invaded your space. It wasn't intentional.' She looked down at her mug again. 'This really is delicious. Where did the honey come from?' She looked at the jars of condiments stacked neatly on Tim's shelves. 'Is it local?'

'You could say that. It comes from the Gair Oak bees.'

Saskia was astonished. 'Really?'

'There's a hive up there.'

'I know,' she said, and then she remembered something else. She reached into her pocket and pulled out the candle stub she'd been carrying since her first visit. 'I think this probably belongs to you. Did you make it with wax from the same hive?'

Tim reached out and took the candle, his rough fingers brushing against hers. He held it up and nodded. 'Nearly got caught that night, didn't I? Didn't realize that great bear of yours would be out and about on patrol.'

Saskia smiled a little at this description of Owen. 'He saw the candle light from my cabin.'

Tim didn't return the smile. 'I didn't realize until then that you were living on site. I thought I'd be safe to come out and see how much of Gair you had managed to destroy in a single day.'

The smile fell from Saskia's face. 'I'm not destroying it. I'm preserving it. That's what I'm doing here – preserving the castle and the oak.'

Tim snorted a little at that. 'It's funny, isn't it, how when humans get involved, it's hard to tell which is which. What makes you think they need you?'

Saskia looked around the unconventional room in which they stood. The walls, despite being underground, were clear of moss and undergrowth. She could see the ancient rock, so carefully hewn and placed by hands long gone, stacked one on another. In the corner, against one wall, was propped a slab of stone about the height of her knee. It was carved with symbols – another altar, perhaps.

'It looks to me as if you've been doing some preserving of your own,' she pointed out. 'You must have had to move a few things around to make this place liveable.'

Tim gave an inelegant snort. 'Touché. The difference being that nothing I've done involves disturbing an entire ecosystem or introducing anything permanent to this place that wasn't already here. I built with what had already been discarded by the forest. Everything here is temporary. When I go, it will all fade.'

Saskia contemplated this for a while, eyes still searching out new treasures on his woven root shelves. There were what looked like fragments of other ancient stonework. What could have been broken clay pots, too. She could imagine what Nathan and his team would do with all of this.

'You didn't tell me how you found this place,' she said. 'Did you stumble on it, the way Hannah did?'

'Hannah? You mean the little girl who crashed through my ceiling? Is she all right? I would have helped her if you hadn't found her. But I thought me appearing out of the dark would probably give her even more of a fright. And your dog was there, so I figured you'd find her eventually.'

'She's fine,' Saskia told him. 'That wasn't the first time you'd met Brodie, was it?'

'No, he found me that day I stole your blanket. He's a good boy, but quite easily won over by some fuss and a biscuit.'

Saskia had to laugh at that. 'Yes. It's his only shortcoming.'

'I heard the stories,' Tim said. 'That's how I found this place. I came up here on a guided walk once – it was only along the footpath on the other side of the beck, but the guide pointed into the forest and told us all these folk tales, about a fierce ancient tribe the Romans couldn't conquer, and the smoke that floated up from the ground, the witch with a lair in the roots, all of that. I was fascinated, so I came over by myself to wild camp for a couple of days – that was when I was working as a ranger for the Forestry Commission, over at Kielder. I didn't see any smoke, but I did stumble on the entrance to this place. It was sheer luck. I might have completely missed it and never known it was here. But when I found it . . . I knew I was finally home.' He looked at her with that bitter, unhappy smile again. 'That was ten years ago. It took me three years to properly move in. And now here you are, to evict me.'

Twenty-Five

It started to rain again, falling against the leaves above him, thousands of soft drumbeats as the drops peppered the overgrowth. Owen checked his watch. Saskia had been gone for almost an hour. He'd remained beside the hole, straining to hear the whistle, but aside from the sound of her footsteps growing fainter, before vanishing completely, he'd heard nothing.

The downpour grew heavy, then heavier still. He traded in his post, moving closer to the nearest tree trunk and out of the rain. The scent of petrichor rose around him, the long-dry earth opening itself to the soaking. Owen didn't mind the rain. Two tours in Afghanistan back in the day, both straddling the suffocating heat of a summer out there, had made him appreciate British weather in a way he'd never previously considered.

Still there was no sign of Saskia. He realized now that they should have discussed how long he should leave it before coming in. He also realized that he should have got her to at least sketch out a rough map of what was down there so that he wouldn't be going in blind. *You're getting soft*, he berated himself. *Losing it.*

As the rain fell even harder, he also considered *how* he was going to get down there. He never should have listened to her, he thought. Why did he keep doing that? Something about this woman meant he kept pushing his best instincts to one side. He still hadn't firmed up the job in Collaton and his month of grace would be up in a week. It was madness: the reluctance he felt every time he thought about packing in the pipedream of Gair for a job that was certain and *there*, just waiting for him.

Owen wiped one hand across his face, casting off a sheen of rain from his forehead and cheeks. And then there she was, as if appearing out of thin air between one heavy raindrop and another. Saskia stood in front of him, reaching out to grasp one damp elbow.

'Come on,' she shouted, words muffled and distorted by the rain. 'Let's go!'

They ran through the forest, grasses and leaves dashing themselves wetly against legs and arms. He noted that Saskia didn't even check where she was going; didn't even pause when they came to a break in the narrow track. As if this place was known to her now, as if she were a creature of the forest.

Back at Gair, the archaeologists had abandoned their trenches, covering both furrows in the earth with weighted tarps to fend off the worst of the torrent. Their van had gone, too.

Owen and Saskia stumbled up the steps and through the door of the cabin, Saskia first. She was laughing breathlessly, petting Brodie, who had been left behind and was eager to welcome his damp mistress home.

'I'll get towels!' she said, and she went to one of the drawers set into the stairs, opening it and pulling out armfuls of soft fabric. She came back towards Owen and thrust one at him, still laughing, still breathless. After that there was a moment of quiet as they scrubbed at their wet hair, faces, arms. Saskia was wet through, the white cotton of her shirt plastered against her. She wound her soaked dark hair up in a towel, sweeping it back from her face and neck, her eyes closed, her face lit with a kind of free joy he'd never seen from her before, and with a shock Owen felt the jolt of something like lust. He turned away so that he couldn't see her – not her face, so lit with happiness, not her lithe body through her wet shirt. He made a show of wiping his face with the towel, burying it in a thick softness that smelled of her – almonds, coconut, flowers.

'Have you got a spare pair of jeans?' she asked. Her voice came from further away and he realized she had gone to the wardrobe beneath the stairs.

He risked removing the towel. Saskia had the wardrobe door open, searching for something, and so he could no longer see her. 'Yeah,' he said. 'I can change.'

She shut the wardrobe door, smiling, holding a fresh shirt in front of her. Her cheeks were flushed with the exhilaration of their rush back home. 'I'll use the office. Shout when you're done.'

Saskia vanished into her tiny work room and pulled the folding door shut. Owen stared at it for a moment, shaken.

Ten minutes later, she was making them both coffee. Owen remained at a safe distance beside the sofa, petting Brodie. 'Where did you appear from?' he asked her. 'You didn't come out the same way you went in.'

'No, as we thought, there's another entrance. There are other connecting rooms, too. Can I call them rooms if they're underground? Caves.'

Owen looked up from the dog to glance out of the window. The rain had lessened a little now, but it was still falling. 'How stable are they, do you think?' he asked. 'After a storm like that . . .'

'I didn't even know it was raining until I came back out,' Saskia told him, as she carried their mugs over. 'He moves out of one of them when the weather's bad, but other than that, I think he's pretty secure.'

Owen reached out to take a mug, careful not to let his fingers brush hers. He still couldn't look at her directly. This room was far too small. The only place for her to sit comfortably was beside him, and when she did that they were so close their knees kept brushing together. She didn't seem to notice, but Owen did, hyper aware every time they touched.

'He,' he said, focusing on the topic at hand.

'Yes,' Saskia sighed, and then sat back. 'He says his name is Tim Burney. He's been living down there for seven years.'

'What?' Owen stared at her, coffee mug halfway to his lips. '*How?*'

'He spent years preparing to live wild, and then years getting the place ready once he'd found it,' she said. 'He goes into town regularly, and if the winters are too harsh he moves in with his brother, in Glasgow. He's nowhere near the age we assumed. He's fit and healthy. He trained as a forest ranger.'

'How did he seem?' Owen asked. 'How did he come across?'

Saskia considered. 'Not like a basket case, if that's what you mean. He's spiky, though.'

'How do you mean, "spiky"?' Owen asked.

'He doesn't like people. Hence his choice of dwelling. He's perfectly happy on his own, off grid, with only the forest for company. A modern-day hermit.'

Owen gazed into his drink as he considered what that meant. 'Then what's the next plan of action?' he asked. 'Are you going to call the police? Or do you think it's more of a job for social services?'

Saskia averted her eyes. 'I don't want to involve either.'

'Then what?' he asked. 'You can't seriously be considering leaving him down there?'

'Owen, it's his home,' she said. 'He said that, repeatedly, as well as making it clear he doesn't want to leave.'

'But he can't live there,' he argued. 'No one could, not indefinitely. It's crazy.'

'He *is* living there,' Saskia pointed out. 'He's been living there a long time. He's comfortable. You should see the place, Owen, it's a real home. If it were an Airbnb, there are people who would pay good money to stay in it. He's got a working kitchen – that's where the mysterious smoke in the forest comes from, by the way, vents above his fires. His pantry is better equipped than the one here.'

'I'm sorry,' Owen interrupted, too incredulous to let her finish. 'But you've decided that the best thing to do is let an old man stay in his mud cave that could collapse at any minute instead of—'

'I told you, he's not old. He's probably fitter than I am. He definitely knows more about living at Gair than I do. And it's not made of mud,' Saskia said, cutting him off. 'It has walls built out of stone. Some of the ceilings are the same. It's been there a long time, Owen, and it's going to be there a lot longer still.'

'It has *walls*?'

'Yes.'

'You didn't mention that.'

'Well, it does.'

He stared at her. 'You realize what that means?'

She studied her drink. 'What?'

Owen shifted on the sofa, turning towards her sharply enough that Brodie lifted his head, sensing the sudden tension in the room.

'"What?"' he repeated. 'Don't play ignorant with me. There's been a team of archaeologists digging up our work site looking for exactly what you say is sitting there under the forest floor. It has to be the Roman ruins, doesn't it?'

'There's no proof of that. Actually, I don't think they're

Roman. Neither does Tim. He thinks they might be older.'

He made a sound, astonished. 'Are you kidding me? You knew, didn't you? You've known since the minute you went down there that first time. You *knew*.'

She wouldn't look at him. 'I knew what?'

He stared at her for a long moment. 'You've had me sitting around here on my arse for almost three weeks, letting me spin my wheels while the clock ticks down. While those people out there dicked around in the dirt, knowing that they're not going to find what they're looking for because you already knew exactly where it was.'

'I didn't know,' she protested. 'I *don't* know.'

'Don't give me that,' he scoffed. 'You're not a fool.'

Silence prevailed. In it the sound of the rain pattered a soft beat on the roof of Saskia's tiny home.

'You realize that this is the solution to all our problems?' Owen asked, his voice tense through a dry throat. 'You tell the planning authority and the court where that site is, and they'll have no reason to continue the stoppage at Gair. You always said there were no ruins on the castle site, you backed that up with evidence. Nathan's lot haven't found anything either. Now you can give them an alternative site and it'll all be over for the judicial review.'

'I'm not going to do that,' Saskia said, her voice quiet but resolute. 'It would mean throwing a person out of the only home he has.'

'It's *not* a home,' Owen said, struggling not to raise his

voice. 'A home is what he'll get when they take him out of there!'

'It won't be what he's used to,' she pointed out. 'It won't be where he wants to be.'

'You mean, it won't be a damp, bare hole in the ground?' Owen asked, incredulous that he was actually having this conversation. 'No, it definitely wouldn't be that.'

She reached out and put down her mug, clasping her hands together as if to plead with him. 'I know who he is, now. I know why he's there. I need to think for a while before making any rash decisions about a life that isn't mine.'

Owen stood up, his anger flaring. He'd put everything on the line for this woman, and here she was, more concerned about some total nutter who'd buried himself in her forest than she was about him, about his future. About his *daughter's* future.

'This is insane,' he said. 'I thought you were committed to the Gair project.'

'I am,' she said, standing to face him. 'You *know* I am!'

'Well, so was I,' he said. 'Even though everyone – literally everyone – told me what an idiot I was not to grab the sure job at Collaton with both hands. But here I am, Saskia. I've done everything you wanted me to do. I was actually considering turning down guaranteed work on the off-chance we could get Gair back up and running. Now I find out that you're able to do that, but you won't. As if my time means nothing to you.'

He grabbed his soaked kit. Brodie sat with his ears pricked, whining.

'Owen,' Saskia said. 'Don't go. Not like this. I'm sorry. Look, I want to get this right. I just need a few days, that's all, to work out the right thing to do—'

'Fine,' he said, yanking open the door onto an evening drenched in recent rain. 'You've got until the end of next week. That's what I agreed to, and that's what I'll stick to. But after that, it's over. This is the second time you've kept something back from me, Saskia. And I'm done.'

'Owen—'

He left her there in the doorway of the trailer, the light pouring around her like a halo, her dark hair still wound up in that damn towel. As he stormed towards his truck, Owen wasn't sure why he was quite so angry, except that as he glanced towards the shadows cast by Gair's walls, he realized that he'd been beginning to think of this place – of her – as home.

You really are an idiot, he told himself, as he drove through the Gair gates. *You should never have got caught up in this in the first place.*

He got out of the truck to lock the gates again, and as he went to turn the key, a shout echoed to him across the site. It was Saskia, running towards him through the rain. For a moment his heart gave a lurch, and he waited as she came towards him to hear what she was going to say, wondering if—

'Look,' she said, breathless as she reached him. 'Owen, don't tell anyone about Tim. Please. Just for now.'

He stared at her for a moment. Then he locked the gates and turned away. The last thing he said to her was over his shoulder before he slammed the truck's door. 'Lock your door tonight. I won't be back.'

Twenty-Six

The rain went on and on, sometimes a torrent, other times lessening enough for Saskia to walk down through the woods to check on Tim. Now that she knew where the entrance was, she no longer needed to descend through the vent that Hannah had stumbled across. Which was just as well, since Owen hadn't returned to Gair since the night they had argued. Tim never refused anything she brought him, but he never seemed to need it, either. He was hunkered down in his underground home, cosy and dry, with enough provisions that he didn't need to leave and could wait out the worst of the rain. His underground complex seemed entirely safe.

The Gair site was waterlogged, the archaeologists' trenches flooded, their tarps sunken beneath mud and water. She hadn't seen Nathan and his crew for days. Back at the trailer, her own small and unconventional home was warm and dry, but strangely empty. Saskia sat and puzzled over what to do, thinking a little too much about Owen.

'He's back at Stuart's,' Vivian told her, during a late-night on-screen catch-up.

'Right,' Saskia said, trying not to care and wondering if her friend knew why he'd left Gair.

'What happened between you two?' Vivian asked, from behind a pair of huge sunglasses. She was on a shoot in Cape Town, South Africa. Behind her was the most brilliant blue sky, and Saskia had the momentary wish that she was there too, far away from the sodden, grey backdrop of Gair and the mess that she had made for herself.

'Nothing,' Saskia lied. 'He probably just got tired of sharing this place. You know how small it is with two people in it.'

'Hmm,' Vivian said, as if she didn't believe this for a second. 'Are you okay there, on your own? What's the latest?'

Saskia looked out of the window. Below her the castle was an inky black shape against a miserable sky. It wasn't raining at that moment, but a thin wind had risen, stirring the trees into waving shadows that flickered at the periphery. The oak stood silent and still, impervious as always.

'Nothing's happening. The place is a mudbath.'

'Well, what does that mean for you?' Vivian pressed. 'It's been weeks now. They can't just leave you hanging indefinitely!'

'I've been trying to get through to the planning committee, but no one will take a call, or at least,' Saskia said, 'no one will return one. The solicitor is having the same issue.'

Vivian was quiet for a moment, watching her from thousands of miles away.

'What?'

'It's probably nothing.'

Saskia shifted in her seat, leaning forward. When Vivian said it was nothing, it was always something. 'Tell me.'

Vivian sighed. 'I just heard a murmur, that's all. Through the family grapevine.'

Saskia sat very still. 'About me?'

'About your stepfather, actually. The Prick.'

'Right,' Saskia said. 'Well, what's that got to do with me? I haven't spoken to Richard for years, you know that. Actually, it's at least a decade, at this point.'

'I know,' Vivian said. 'But you know what Mum's like, she thinks I care about the minutiae of who's doing what in their set, when I really couldn't care less, but I let her ramble on. Do you remember Carlson Holt?'

Saskia frowned. 'The MP?'

'He's not a back-bencher anymore,' Vivian said. 'He's the environment secretary. Has been for the last few months, after the last disastrous re-shuffle. God knows why, the closest he's ever been to nature is probably the grass at Ascot. No need for you to have taken notice. I didn't. But the point is, do you remember what *else* he is?'

Vivian raised both eyebrows, as if willing Saskia to answer, but she was mystified.

'I have no idea, Viv. What does any of this have to do with me?'

'Most likely nothing,' Vivian admitted. 'But he was at Harrow with Richard. They're close. He was best man at the wedding – not that I expect you to remember that. And obviously this is just me spouting, but I'd imagine that if someone wanted to trigger a judicial review into a planning consent—'

'—then having the environment secretary on side might help,' Saskia finished, blankly.

'Right,' Vivian agreed. 'And it's not that I want to sling mud and maybe it's just a coincidence and all that. But . . . well. It did make me wonder, that's all. It wouldn't be difficult for your mother to figure out that you'd bought Gair with your grandparents' money. It's not as if she didn't know that was always your dream. And this would be a good way of throwing a spanner in your plans, wouldn't it?'

Saskia frowned. 'Well, I'm sure Richard could be that vindictive if he wanted to be, and he definitely hates me enough, but I can't see why either of them would bother, to be honest. What would be the point? As you've pointed out, he doesn't need my money. He'd rather forget I existed at all. I think he'd probably just tell my mother to leave it alone if she asked him to meddle like that.'

'You're right,' her friend sighed. 'I'm sorry, I should never have brought it up. I just thought it might be a connection, that's all.'

Saskia stared into the shadows beyond her screen. She always thought she was okay with her estrangement from what was left of her family until she was reminded of how twisted that was. Then she always felt very, very alone.

'I spoke to Elsa a couple of weeks ago,' Saskia said finally.

Vivian paused with her glass halfway to her lips. '*What*?'

'Your mum gave her my number.'

Vivian cursed. 'Oh, no. I'm so sorry, Sas. I told her—'

'It's all right,' Saskia said. 'She would have found a way to get it eventually, you know what she's like.'

'What did she want?'

Saskia shrugged. 'She said she mainly just wanted to know how I was doing.'

'Right,' Vivian said, her tone sceptical. 'And how did that conversation end?'

Saskia gave the screen a wry smile. 'How it always does. With me feeling guilty without really knowing why.'

Vivian sighed. 'I wish I was with you,' she said. 'I hate you being all alone. At least when Owen was there I knew you had *someone* with you.'

Saskia thought of Tim, hidden away in his underground burrow, safe from all the different kinds of chaos that existed in the world above. For a moment she was so envious of his successful exit from the human-made world that she could barely breathe. If she had somewhere like that, she wouldn't want to leave it either. The idea of tearing him away from it bit at her insides anew.

'I'm not here on my own,' she said. 'I've always got Brodie.'

After that call with Vivian, Saskia lay awake beneath the trailer's eaves as more rain pattered overhead. Early morning saw her back downstairs, curled on the sofa with her laptop and coffee, re-reading what she'd researched the previous day as she prepared for the meeting she had that afternoon.

Once she'd had a name to search under, Tim Burney was easy to find. As off-grid as he prided himself in being, he'd still left a digital footprint from when he was employed as a ranger for the Forestry Commission, and even from some jobs further back. There were a few photographs of him attached to articles about the management of Kielder Forest. Saskia peered at these images of her curious tenant. In them she saw a healthy middle-aged man with an intense expression that rarely included a smile, even when whoever else had been captured in the photograph with him was laughing. Still, what she found confirmed what Tim had told her.

She had also managed to find his older brother, Christopher Burney, who lived on the outskirts of Glasgow. Saskia had thought long and hard about whether to contact him. Her own fraught relationship with her family meant she knew full well how complicated and delicate such relationships could be. But Tim seemed to have been truthful about everything he'd told her about himself. He'd said his brother let him stay with him when he needed to and that the two met up regularly, so it seemed clear to her that they had a good relationship. That being the case, Saskia thought he'd probably be the best person to talk this over with besides Tim himself.

Rationally she knew Tim couldn't stay where he was indefinitely. For one thing she needed to be able to point the judicial review towards the ruins that he had made his home, which would give even more credence to her argument that there were none beneath the foundations of Gair itself. Besides which, however cosy he had made it, she was very doubtful that it was a safe living situation long-term. But Saskia didn't want to throw him out with nowhere else to go. She wasn't even sure how she'd get him to move on if he didn't go willingly. She hated the thought of bringing the police in or otherwise using strong-arm tactics. Her hope was that Christopher Burney could help her persuade Tim to leave Gair of his own accord, perhaps to live with him more permanently, even if that was only a temporary measure.

It began to rain again as Saskia and Brodie left Gair for the drive north over the border. She watched the gates recede in the rear mirror, slowly subsumed by the trees that crowded in on each side of the road to the castle. By the time she had reached the B-road that would take her back to civilization, it was easy to believe that there was nothing behind her but forest.

For some reason, Saskia had expected the older Burney brother to live in a house. In her head, she'd imagined a large and neatly kept suburban garden, perhaps with a few trees. Instead, the address her GPS led her to was in an achingly modern tower block of apartments in an area of the city obviously undergoing rapid redevelopment. Saskia looked up at the building as she climbed out of the Land Rover, feeling the first probing finger of misgiving. As much of a stranger to her as he still was, she couldn't imagine the Tim she'd met being comfortable here. There were no gardens, only tightly controlled raised beds of pruned foliage – certainly no wild spaces. Everything here was dominated by glass, concrete and steel: pristine and man-made, completely at odds with the natural tangle of Gair's forest.

Christopher Burney came down to meet her once she had told the concierge at the front desk who she was there to see. The lift opened on a neatly turned-out man who looked almost identical in age to his younger brother, dressed in pressed navy chinos and jacket over a crisp white shirt and blue tie.

'Hello there,' he said, with an affable smile, and then indicated the café that was built into the ground floor of the block. 'Thanks for meeting me here, I've got a whole slew of meetings I have to dash around for today and slotting it in this way made by far the most sense. We can have coffee down here, or upstairs at my place, whatever you're more comfortable with.'

Saskia smiled. 'Actually,' she said, 'if it's not too much of an imposition, I'm pretty curious to see what one of these apartments looks like from the inside. I'm an architect, myself, you see, and this block is so impressive. Unless you'd rather not have my dog upstairs?'

The elder Burney brother gave a laugh that made him seem very unlike his grumpy sibling as he bent down to pet Brodie. 'I love dogs. I'd have one myself if my hours weren't so ridiculous. By all means, let's go up. I don't blame you for wanting to have more of a look.'

On the journey to the seventh floor, Saskia searched for a resemblance between the two brothers, finding it only in the piercing blue eyes and square jaw.

'Come in, come in, do,' said Christopher Burney, as he opened his front door and ushered Saskia into a huge open-plan space with a large, spotless modern kitchen and floor-to-ceiling glass windows. 'I'll get the coffee on, and then we'll chat.'

'Thank you.' Saskia looked around as he made their drinks, taking it in with a sinking heart. There was a mezzanine floor on which she could see a bed, but there were no walls apart from around what must be the single bathroom. The living room area did include a large, plush, L-shaped sofa which she assumed was what Tim slept on when he visited, but there would be no privacy. She already knew this couldn't possibly be a long-term solution, and probably not even a short-term one. She was even more convinced that this was not the type of home the Tim that she had met would ever choose for himself.

'Smart place, isn't it?' Burney said, and she turned to see him watching her with a smile. 'One of the advantages of being a lawyer specializing in estate management. I knew this place was coming before the planning had even been approved. I put my name down straight away. Transport into the city centre is a dream; there's a gym in the basement and a top-notch bar and restaurant on the roof. The whole place is wired into a dedicated app: I can make myself a coffee on my ride up in the lift and it'll be waiting for me once I've unlocked the door.' He laughed. 'It's the sort of futuristic place I daydreamed about as a kid. The only thing missing is being able to take my flying car out for a spin, but who knows, maybe that's coming too. I had no idea tech would advance quickly enough for me to see any of this in my lifetime.'

Saskia forced a smile around her anxiety. It wasn't her sort of place at all, but her architect's heart could understand the wonder of it. 'It's amazing. And what a view of the city.'

Burney came around the counter, holding out a coffee mug for her to take. It was a strong blend, served black; he hadn't asked her if she wanted milk.

'You said you were from Gair Castle, isn't that right? I looked it up after I got your email. I imagine this is a little different to what you've got down there.'

She laughed. 'Oh yes, just a bit.'

He smiled. 'Which is why I'm curious as to what I can do for you, Ms Tilbury-Martin. I assume you're interested in my agency expertise, but I can't work out why you've chosen me. Not that I'm shy about my accomplishments, but there must be local lawyers better suited to take on your case? I assume you need help with this judicial review.'

'Oh,' Saskia said, surprised. She hadn't thought to elaborate when she'd told him who she was and where she was based. She'd assumed he'd realize the connection with his younger brother from the estate's name alone. 'Yes, you're right, I already have a solicitor for that, although I would be interested to see what you think of the situation. But what I really wanted to talk to you about today is Tim.'

Burney's eyebrows rose and he paused, regrouping. 'Tim?'

'Yes. Your brother is Tim Burney, isn't he?'

Christopher Burney frowned. 'Yes,' he said, slowly. 'I do have a brother called Tim, that's true. He's a ranger for the Forestry Commission, based in Kielder Forest, so perhaps not far from you, actually.'

'Ah, well—' Saskia started, and then stopped, realizing that things had got off to an unexpected start. 'He . . . works for the Forestry Commission?'

'Yes. He lives in a cabin way out in the wilds – "off-grid", as they say.' The older Burney brother gave a brief laugh. 'He's a bit of a character. You could say we are polar opposites. I love him, but he lives in a way that I absolutely cannot comprehend. He was always an odd one when we were kids, and he never seemed to grow out of it. Nowadays he'd probably be given some sort of neurodivergent label, but that didn't exist to the same extent back then. And he seems happy enough – at least, he is now he's found a way to live that suits him.'

The sinking feeling got worse. 'Right. I see. He told me that he comes here, though, when the winters are too bad for . . . the cabin?'

Christopher Burney looked surprised. 'Well, he's come here for Christmas a couple of times, but he never said that was the reason. He can't stand it here, that's obvious every time he visits, so I assumed it was because even the most curmudgeonly of us needs some creature comforts every now and then. And despite our different outlooks on life, we do get on for the most part. That's why we still meet up every couple of months. His place is so out of the way that he gets all his mail sent here and I pass it on when I see him.' Burney gave an affectionate smile. 'Never does anything easy when he can make it hard for himself, that's Tim. So, do I take it you're neighbours?'

'Sort of,' Saskia said, faintly, trying to work out how to get out of this one. It seemed she'd inadvertently managed to do exactly what she hadn't intended, stepping right into the middle of a complicated family situation. This Burney clearly didn't know the absolute truth of how his brother was living, and she had no idea how he would react if he did.

Apparently though, her silence spoke volumes, because Burney was studying her shrewdly, his eyes narrowed slightly. He put down his mug and leaned against the work-top, crossing his arms in a manner that suddenly reminded Saskia of his younger brother.

'Why do I get the feeling that something I've said has blindsided you?' he asked. 'Is my brother in some kind of trouble?'

'No, he's fine,' Saskia promised, wishing that she'd never had the idea to come here in the first place. 'Actually, I think he's probably healthier than me. But look . . . I don't think he's told you everything about how he's living. Or where.'

Burney frowned. 'What do you mean?'

Saskia considered her options. Realistically, who else was she going to enlist to help her if she wasn't going to go to the authorities? Christopher Burney was it. And he obviously cared about his brother. Despite her miscalculation, the older Burney brother was surely still her best chance of helping Tim in a way that would ultimately be in his interest – and hers.

'What I'm about to tell you might be a bit of a shock,' she began. 'But Tim doesn't work for the Forestry Commission. Or at least, he doesn't anymore – he quit about seven years ago. He's actually living on my land, at Gair, and he has been since before I bought it.'

'I . . . see,' Burney said, slowly. 'Well, that is a surprise, I admit. He didn't tell me he'd quit his job. Then, this cabin he's living in, it belongs to you? It's an old hunting cabin, or something, is it?'

'Not exactly,' Saskia said. 'And really, this is why I wanted to see you. I thought you were aware of Tim's living arrangements.'

'Me too, but it would appear not,' Burney said, with a cautious note to his voice.

Saskia briefly outlined the details of how and where Tim was living. Christopher Burney listened carefully as she spoke, his brow knitting further and further together as he took in what she said.

'And look,' Saskia said, when she'd finished. 'If I could find a way for him to stay that wouldn't impact the Gair build, I would. I don't want his leaving to be unpleasant, and the last thing I want to do is make him homeless. But—'

'—but there's no way he can stay where he is indefinitely,' Burney finished for her. 'No, of course not. I assume he has no sanitation or heating?'

'I haven't seen the entire extent of the ruins,' Saskia admitted. 'But I wouldn't be surprised if he's built himself a bathroom of some sort. He might even have a composting toilet, like the one in my trailer, for all I know. But there's no running water. He has heating in the form of wood fires. It's quite remarkably equipped. Beautiful, really.'

Burney tutted. 'Still, there's no way it would meet habitation codes. Who knows how good the structure is long-term? And apart from all of that, it's your land. You would be legally liable were anything to happen to him if you know he's living there in a place not rated for human habitation and do nothing to rectify the situation.'

Saskia blinked. 'That hadn't actually occurred to me.'

Christopher Burney let out a long breath and looked out of his huge windows, as if contemplating his next move carefully. 'Well, then,' he said. 'What did he say when you confronted him?'

'He's assuming I'll evict him, but he's made no move to leave of his own accord. And truthfully, I can understand why.' Saskia scrubbed a non-existent mark on her mug with her nail. 'I wouldn't want to leave either.'

Burney smiled. 'He's lucky that you're the landowner whose land he decided to trespass on. I can't imagine many others being so patient and understanding. Why don't I come down and talk to him? He was never very good at forms and paperwork, anything like that. Avoided them like the plague. I'll offer to help him find somewhere else suitable and deal with any of the legal stuff. He has savings. From what I can tell he's never spent very much and our parents left him an inheritance. It's small, but it's something.'

The relief Saskia felt was acute. 'Thank you,' she said. 'That would be a great help. I'd far rather find an amicable solution, even if it takes a bit longer.'

'It's no problem,' Christopher told her, glancing at his watch. 'To be honest I'm fascinated to see this home my little brother has made for himself, it sounds extraordinary. Let's have a quick look in the diary and work out when I can make it down there. Then I'm going to be the one turfing *you* out – I've got to go, I'm afraid.'

Twenty-Seven

Owen looked out over the waters of the Solway Firth as he drove the coast road towards Collaton. It was early morning – not even seven o'clock, the sun still rising, casting an unlikely array of dawn colours across the wide expanse of water. He was on his way to talk to Adrian Braithwaite and be given a tour of the first houses that the team had completed as part of The Collaton Project. The estate was a new innovation in affordable eco-housing that incorporated, among other things, solar panels as standard and kitchens with waste units for water recycling. Owen was curious to see how the build had come together, and Braithwaite had made it clear that he was seeing this meeting as an onboarding session for a new foreman.

He hadn't spoken to Saskia for several days. He could have called to see how the situation at Gair had progressed, but he wasn't above holding onto a little pride. Besides, it was probably just as well that he kept his distance. They'd become far too close – he realized that now. And they were just very different people, with different goals, responsibilities and outlooks on life. It was no one's fault; it was just how it was. He had Hannah's and his future to think about. He couldn't afford to get caught up in Saskia Tilbury-Martin's past.

But he was still thinking about her even as Adrian began to give him the tour of the site. It was an impressive project, all the more so for having been started in such an unlikely place. The more Braithwaite showed him, the more Owen could see the importance of what the team behind The Collaton Project was trying to do. He'd seen the news, of course: the burning of the community garden; the battle the locals had had in trying to rebuild it, having fought so hard to make it in the first place; that wonderful, triumphant transportation of a remarkable double-decker bus and all its verdant growth. That The Collaton Project was the brainchild of one very talented and determined teenager from the wrong side of the tracks had always stayed with him – he'd rooted for her, for them, for this place. And yet, now that he was here, he found himself thinking about another underdog. When he'd first met her, Owen never could have imagined that's how he would ever characterize Saskia, but now? Now he found that he was rooting for her just as much. She'd beaten all the odds, time and again. What if she'd reached the final hurdle and the reason she failed to get over it this time was because he'd left her high and dry?

Owen tried to set these thoughts aside. He wasn't wrong to put his own needs and, more importantly, those of his daughter first. The Collaton Project was long-term and stable, two things that with the best will in the world Gair would never be. Though sure, there was an element of the cookie-cutter about this estate, despite all its innovations. But what Saskia wanted to do at Gair and what Harper Dixon was doing in Collaton were two sides of the same coin, weren't they? Trying to live harmoniously with nature. Attempting to preserve the past while constructing a new future.

'Penny for 'em?' a voice said. It was Stuart, appearing beside him, grime-covered from the day. 'You're miles away.'

'Sorry,' Owen said. 'Just thinking a few things through.'

'What do you think of the place, then?' Stuart asked, as the two of them surveyed the busy work site. 'I've got to say, it's been a good job so far. Good set of people, you know?'

'Yeah,' Owen said. 'I know.'

His friend looked at him askance. 'But . . . let me guess. It's not that easy to let go of Gair?'

'Something like that.'

Stuart sighed, finished the can of Coke he was holding. 'I understand.'

Owen looked at him. 'You do?'

His friend crushed the can in one hand and grinned. 'Sure. I mean, come on. You told your kid you were rebuilding a castle. Can't disappoint Hannah, can we? I'm on a monthly rolling contract here but that's up the end of this week. If you want to go back to Gair, I'm with you. Just tell me what you want me to do.'

Owen smiled. For all Stuart's rough edges, he was always the friend he could turn to in a pinch. 'Thanks for the support. Really. I appreciate it. But there's no need for you to burn any bridges. I've still got a couple more days to think things over.'

Stuart gave him a thoughtful look. 'I get it,' he said. 'If it were just the castle, that'd be one thing, right? But you've got to walk away from Saskia, too.'

'It's not that,' Owen said, even though his friend's words caused a strange kind of tremor in his chest. 'It's *not.* I just want to see if I can come up with some other alternative before I quit for good. I don't want to leave her high and dry without at least trying to find someone to take my place if and when it does move forward again, that's all. Adrian's given me a couple of leads.'

Stuart tossed his crushed Coke can into a nearby bin. 'Well, let me know,' he said, with an air of finality, though Owen got the sense that there might have been more he'd thought better of saying. 'I'll be there, either way.'

Twenty-Eight

At Gair, the weather changed again. The rain stopped, and the late-summer sun began to shine through the dissipating clouds. The castle ruins glinted as the old stone began to dry after the constant downpour. Saskia and Brodie went to visit Tim, trailing through the wet forest along paths still thick with mud, and found him safe and well. It was remarkable, how perfectly he seemed to be attuned to his forest way of living, which sparked in her renewed guilt that she could not let him stay. Saskia hadn't told him about his brother's imminent visit, which had been set for the end of the week. They would make the visit as non-confrontational as possible, but neither she nor the elder Burney thought a forewarning would help.

Owen had not returned. Saskia had sent him a message after she got back from Glasgow, to tell him that she was working on a solution to the problem of Tim and hoped to have it sorted soon. *That's good news*, he'd replied. For a moment the 'Typing . . .' legend had hovered at the top of their message stream, as if he'd been about to say something else, but then it vanished, and he'd written no more.

She couldn't blame him for leaving, and yet there was part of her that was angry all the same. Saskia couldn't quite work out what had happened. After their rough start, she'd thought they were doing well together. She'd opened up to him in a way she rarely did to anyone and thought that he'd understood what she was trying to achieve at Gair. He *did* understand – she knew it. Perhaps if he'd met Tim himself, seen his underground home, he would have realized why she couldn't just throw him out and be done with it. Instead Owen had just left, and she thought that if he hadn't already taken the job in Collaton, it was only because his sense of honour dictated that he wait until the grace period he'd agreed to allow her was officially up.

With the change in the weather, Nathan and his team of archaeologists returned, peeling back their drying tarps to see what the downpour had wrought on their empty trenches. Their arrival coincided with the day that Christopher Burney was due to visit, and Saskia went down to see them. It would probably be a good idea to try to get on a better footing with the team. After all, it was likely that soon she'd be handing them exactly what they were looking for, though she was determined to wait until Tim was happy elsewhere and also that any subsequent access to the ruins would be completely on her terms.

'Hi,' she called, to Nathan, who was standing with his

hands on his hips beside the largest of the trenches. 'How's it looking?'

He gave her a morose look. 'Terrible, which I'm sure you'll be very glad about.'

'Not at all,' Saskia said. 'I'm sorry to hear it. I know what it's like to have work you really care about interrupted indefinitely, after all. Would you all like a coffee? There's still a kettle in the break room.'

The archaeologist looked suspicious. 'Sure. That would be great.'

She nodded as the sound of an engine echoed across the site and she turned to see a car she didn't recognize approach the main gates: Christopher Burney, arriving right on time. Saskia began to head towards him. 'I'll put the kettle on, then you can help yourselves. And listen, I'm going to give Julie Rhys a call to let her know you're starting up again. It's been a while since she did a visit.'

First she ran up to the gates and opened it so that Christopher could drive inside. By the time she'd sorted out the kettle, he was standing beside his BMW in a crisp grey suit, the trousers of which were tucked into wellington boots. He grinned somewhat sheepishly as they met.

'Sorry,' he said. 'I've got to go directly from here to another meeting, so you'll have to forgive me looking ridiculous.'

Saskia smiled. 'Not to worry. Good thinking about the boots. The forest is still wet in places.'

They headed along the path that Saskia had been using

regularly since she'd discovered Tim's place. She didn't see Nathan pausing as he reached the top step of the break room cabin to watch their progress with a frown on his face. She was far more focused on the meeting ahead. She got the sense that for all his confidence and self-possession, Christopher was a little nervous, as was Saskia herself. She pointed out the slight mound in the earth which had first given her access to his brother's underground kingdom.

'You'll be relieved to know that we don't have to go in that way, though,' she said. 'After we met properly, Tim started letting me use the main entrance.'

She led him on through the undergrowth, Brodie ahead of her. It looked like a rabbit run or a deer track, they had used it so often in recent weeks. The ground sloped slightly, and they followed it down into a small break in the trees, a cauldron-shaped depression in the ground. The clearing would have looked entirely natural to anyone who didn't know what was hidden between two of the large mossy boulders lying against each other at a lazy angle on the west edge of the slope.

'You'll have to duck a little,' Saskia said, glancing up at Christopher's taller frame, 'and it's narrow to begin with.'

He regarded the rocks, a little perturbed, but nodded. 'Lead the way.'

Saskia didn't call out for Tim until they were inside the narrow passageway that led into the hill. She expected him to be home at this time of day: he avoided being out and about in full daylight, when his 'ghostly old man in a cloak' routine would be easier to see through should anyone spot him roaming about the forest.

'Tim?' she called. 'It's me. And . . . I've brought someone to see you. Will you talk to us?'

Brodie had disappeared ahead into the gloom, entirely at home in the maze of buried rooms. Silence loomed around them, and Saskia could feel the elder Burney brother shifting uncomfortably behind her. She wondered whether he was feeling claustrophobic; it would be easy to be overwhelmed by the weight of earth and rock closing in over their heads. She tried not to think about that when she was down here herself, concentrating instead on the fact that it had remained stable for who knew how many centuries already.

She was about to call out again when a string of lights flicked on at the end of the short passageway. They illuminated a dark figure standing at their centre, with a dog at his side.

'Hi, Tim,' Saskia said. 'Your brother's here, just to talk.'

Christopher stepped forward a little, so that they were standing abreast in the narrow space. 'Tim,' he said, warmly. 'I think we've got a bit of catching up to do beyond the usual, eh?'

There was another beat of silence, and then Tim bent to pet Brodie behind the ears. 'I suppose something like this was inevitable,' he said. 'I hope you brought biscuits. I'm all out.'

They sat and talked, in a far more amicable and productive way than Saskia had dared to hope. Christopher had gone to work for his brother, calling in favours and using his contacts to assemble a series of possible alternative living arrangements for Tim to consider.

'I know you won't want to be in a city,' he said. 'But there are plenty of other options. Kielder might take you back, you know that place as well as anyone. And look, this estate up in the Cairngorms is looking for a ghillie. On paper you're not qualified, but I know the gamekeeper; I've talked to him and he's willing to meet with you. It comes with accommodation: it's not shared, either, there are cabins spread out across the estate. That might suit. I've got feelers out for other places as well, where you'd be more of a ranger or caretaker. There'll be something out there that'll work for you, Tim. But you must understand that you can't stay here indefinitely, especially not now we know you're here.'

It seemed that however resentful he was about the situation, Tim did understand. That was half the battle won, at least.

'I want to make this as easy as possible,' Saskia assured him. 'I'm not going to force you out overnight. But we can't be sure it's safe down here. And the judicial review is draining my resources more every day. These have to be the ruins that the Historical Society are convinced are under Gair itself. They help underline everything else I've done to prove the Society wrong. If I can tell people they're here, show them – you must realize how significant that would be for me? And once that happens, you definitely won't be able to stay here. It'll be out of my hands.'

The look he gave her was a loaded one. 'I suppose knowing

the ruins are here will mean all the focus will be off the castle and the oak,' he said. 'You can carry on "preserving" them just as much as you want.' The inverted commas were audible in his caustic tone.

'Tim,' Christopher said, in warning. 'You do realize how forbearing Saskia is being in this situation? I'm pretty sure anyone else would have had the police drag you out of here as soon as they'd found you.'

'It's all right,' Saskia said. 'I hope, one day in the not-too-distant future, I'll be able to show you that I'm trying to do the right thing, Tim. You can come back and visit when the build is completed to see that I never wanted to destroy anything.'

Tim huffed a short laugh but said nothing, instead turning away to refill the kettle again.

Twenty-Nine

The next day, mid-afternoon, there was a knock at Saskia's door. She opened it to find a smiling young woman standing at the bottom of her steps.

'Julie,' she said, warmly. 'It's good to see you; I'll come down to the site with you.'

'I'm glad to be back,' the trainee journalist said, as Brodie ran down the steps for a pet and Saskia pulled the door shut behind them. 'Since I last saw you, I've been trying to build a story about the judicial review, even though no one really wants to talk about it.'

'Yes,' Saskia agreed dryly, 'I've been having trouble speaking to anyone about it myself. I think the local planning committee have collectively decided not to return my calls.'

'I don't think that's necessarily personal,' Julie said, as they walked down the slope towards Gair. 'I think it's more likely because no one there really understands it either. I've been told off the record that it came as a complete surprise, even for them. You know that it's very unusual to rescind planning or even pause it once it's been granted? There are very few criteria that would meet the bar for doing so, and they all know that you had gone above and beyond them to get Gair to the point of passing all the planning requirements.'

'But surely it was the local planning association that instigated the review?'

The journalist shook her head. 'No. That's the thing. I'm still trying to get to the bottom of it, but it came from elsewhere. It must have been from some official body with the clout to direct it, but my source is being cagey. Still, the words *much higher up* have been used. I'm chasing a few leads now, trying to put the pieces together, but my feeling is that Gair has become some sort of test case to further a wider agenda.'

Saskia thought about what Vivian had told her, about her stepfather's connections. Should she say something? But all she had was gossip, and she didn't really want to put her family issues directly in front of a journalist.

'Right,' she said.

The younger woman flashed her a little smile. 'If I find more out, I'll let you know.'

'Thanks. I'd appreciate that.'

Nathan had seen them coming. By the time they reached him, he'd climbed out of his trench and put down his trowel. The two women peered into the narrow strip of earth.

'Found anything?' Saskia asked.

'A lot of pottery shards, a belt buckle. Lucy thinks she might have found the pommel of a sword but it'll be a while until she can be sure it's not just a fragment.'

'Really?' Julie glanced at Saskia in surprise. 'Then – you've found what you were searching for?'

The archaeologist shifted uncomfortably, looking past the two women in the direction of the main gates. 'No. None of the finds we've made are old enough for that. What we're looking at here are discards from when the castle itself was inhabited.'

'Still fascinating though,' Saskia said, mildly. 'I'd love to see those pieces.'

He looked past her again and then glanced at his watch. Saskia was about to ask him if he was waiting for someone else when she heard the piercing, incongruous blip of a police siren. Saskia would have doubted what she was hearing, but for the fact that Julie and Nathan reacted, too.

'Was that . . . a *siren*?' Julie asked, turning back towards the main gates, hidden by the slope and the surrounding forest.

'I think it probably was,' Nathan said, and Saskia looked at him to see the flash of a tight, unpleasant smile on his face.

'Why would the police be here?' she asked, her heart sinking.

He shrugged. 'Perhaps you should go and find out.'

Saskia stared at him for another second. Then she started walking towards the gates, her heart hammering. What was this, now? Julie caught up with her. Nathan wasn't far behind, the rest of the team downing tools to watch what was going on.

Just inside the gates was a single police patrol car with two uniformed officers standing either side of it. There was another unmarked car parked beside it with a man and a woman still seated inside, although they opened their doors and got out as Saskia approached.

'Hi,' Saskia said, as she reached them. 'Can I help you?'

'Afternoon,' said one of the officers. Saskia thought she might have seen him before, and realized he was the same officer she'd observed laughing with Hugh Carey the day the Historical Society tried to barricade the site. 'Are you Saskia Tilbury-Martin?'

'I am,' Saskia said, glancing at her two plain-clothed visitors. They were both dressed in suits. One of them held a clipboard, on which she could just make out some sort of official-looking form. 'I'm the owner of this property, although I suspect you're already aware of that?'

The police officer gave a pleasant smile. 'Ms Tilbury-Martin, we've received a report of a vulnerable person living in uninhabitable conditions on your property. We're here with our colleagues from Community Services. We'd like to do a welfare check.'

'What?' Saskia turned to look at Nathan. 'I expressly did not give you permission to enter the forest. Have you been following me?'

Nathan shrugged. 'Just doing the right thing.'

'The right thing?' Saskia was incensed. 'This has nothing to do with doing the right thing. This is about you thinking you have the right to do whatever you want on my property.'

'Ms Tilbury-Martin.' The officer called her attention back to him. 'Do you want to tell us what's going on? Is it true that you have a vulnerable person living rough in a building you own?'

'He's not—' Saskia began, and then stopped herself. She'd just lost any chance of keeping Tim's presence secret from the authorities. She regrouped; took a breath. 'He's not vulnerable. He's not exactly living "rough", either. Look, this is my property. He's not trespassing. Are you telling me that the police and social services conduct these kinds of checks on every person sleeping rough in the UK? Because I'm pretty sure that's not the case.'

The officer shifted his weight, his expression hardening further. 'You admit that you do have such a tenant, then?'

'He's not a tenant,' Saskia said. 'He was already living here when I bought the place, I just didn't know it until recently. I'm working with his family to find him more suitable accommodation, but at the moment he doesn't want to leave, and I'm fine with that. It's no different than if he were camping in a tent.'

Nathan snorted. 'Oh really? He's living underground in a ruin that could collapse at any minute.'

'That's not true.'

'Says you,' Nathan shot back. 'Who made you an expert on the structural integrity of ancient buildings?'

'Look,' the police officer said, his voice rising over both of them. 'Now that we've had this report, we can't just ignore it. We need to do a welfare check to make sure that this person – Tim, is it? – is safe and secure and not being held against his will.'

'Held against his will?' Saskia repeated, shocked. 'What?'

'There have been precedents,' said one of the social workers. 'We've had this report, so we need to follow up.'

Saskia shook her head. 'I'm sorry, but this is my land, and this is ridiculous. Unless you have a warrant, I'm going to ask you to leave.'

The second social worker held up the clipboard. 'We do. It's right here.'

She stared at the form numbly for a moment, then took it from his hand and read through the warrant.

'Wow,' she said. 'It really does pay to know people around here, doesn't it?'

The second police officer spoke up for the first time. He was young – not more than twenty-five, Saskia thought – with close-cropped brown hair and a composed but wary expression. 'Is that an accusation?'

Saskia gave a short, bitter laugh. 'No, I'll leave those up to this guy.' She pitched a thumb at Nathan. 'Who *is* trespassing, by the way. He's no longer welcome on my property. Nor are any of his team.'

'You can't make us leave,' Nathan said, indicating the two police officers and the social workers as they moved past Saskia onto Gair land. 'I need to go with them.'

'That's not going to happen,' Saskia said, shortly. 'You're going to leave, and you won't be coming back. The judicial review can assign another team if they like, but you're done.'

'But—'

'Out,' Saskia said, indicating the open gates. 'Right now.'

'But our tools—'

'Get them and then go. If I find you still here beyond that, I'll press charges for trespassing.' She glanced at everyone watching. 'I've got multiple witnesses, so I'll repeat myself, just so we're clear. You're trespassing. You're not welcome here. Get your stuff and go.'

Nathan looked to the police but found no support there. Eventually the archaeologist conceded defeat. Saskia turned her attention back to her other unwelcome visitors.

'I don't know what you're hoping to achieve,' she said, 'but this is only going to do more harm than good.' She turned to Julie, who was watching everything with wide eyes. 'I'd like you to record this, if you have the means.'

The journalist held up a small electronic device. 'Oh, don't worry. I pressed record as soon as we got up here.'

'Good,' Saskia said. 'Then let's go.'

When they reached the clearing, Tim was already waiting for them. He'd heard them coming. He was standing beside the two boulders that marked the doorway to his strange home, a scowl on his face, his arms crossed. It was Saskia that he glared at as she made her way down the slope, the others scrambling behind her.

'What happened to taking this at my own pace?' he demanded.

'This wasn't my idea, Tim,' she told him. 'But it's out of my hands now.'

'They're not coming in,' he said, resolutely.

Saskia rubbed a hand over her face. 'It's probably not a good idea to make this any more difficult than it already is.'

'For you?' he sneered. 'Or for me?'

'Tim.' One of the social workers stepped forward, a bright smile on her face. 'We just want to make sure you're living in safe, secure and appropriate conditions, that's all.'

He looked her up and down with disdain. 'It's Mr Burney to you. How about I turn up on your doorstep unannounced and barge in to see what I think of *your* home? How would you feel about that?'

Saskia tried to reason with him. 'Tim, *please*.'

Nothing got any better from that point, and a short scuffle ensured that he wasn't going anywhere but the police station. Saskia called Christopher as the officers escorted Tim back to their patrol car.

'I'll be there as soon as I can,' his brother said, with a sigh.

'I'm sorry,' Saskia told him.

'It's not your fault, you've already gone above and beyond,' said Christopher Burney. 'My brother's inflexibility has always made him his own worst enemy. I'll let you know how we get on, but I think it's safe to say he's not your problem – or your lodger – anymore.'

Saskia supposed she should feel relieved about that, but instead she only felt guilt.

Thirty

Owen sat on a park bench beneath the sudden, blazing sunshine of late afternoon, listening to the screams and chaos of a dozen children playing. He watched as Hannah scaled the miniature climbing wall that was part of the adventure playground. As always, he found himself amazed that somehow, out of the haphazard and faintly disastrous mess of his life, he had managed to create something so perfect. Hannah reached the top of the frame, cheered on by her friends, and turned to see if he'd been watching. Owen stood, clasping both hands above his head in a gesture of victory as he yelled encouragement. *That's my daughter*, he wanted to say, to whoever was standing within earshot. *The best thing in my life by a country mile.*

As he sat down again to watch her embark on her next adventure, he saw Tasha's small red Fiat pull up and park on the road that edged the recreation ground. He watched as she got out of the car and headed for him. She'd tied her blonde hair back in a sharp ponytail and was wearing a dark-blue pencil skirt and matching jacket that both suited her and surprised him. She was coming straight from work, and it was the first time he'd really seen her in her work gear. When they'd still been together, he'd been the one to leave early and return late. They'd been a couple since their teens, and for some reason that was still the default image he had of her in his head: his cute, cool girlfriend who lived in skinny blue jeans, tee shirt, sweatshirt, Converse. But she was no more still that kid than he was the football-playing boy she'd somehow fallen in love with, despite his cockiness. Now, he wondered if he'd even think about talking to her if they met in a bar, and if he did, how quickly she would brush him off. For the first time since their split, this type of thought didn't fill him with melancholy, but merely acceptance.

'Hey,' Tasha said, with a smile, once she'd reached him. 'Sorry I had to call. Thanks for being here.'

'Don't be daft,' Owen said, lifting Hannah's school backpack from the bench so that she could sit. 'It's not a problem. Any time, I'll make it happen. You know that.'

They sat in silence for a few minutes, watching the children, and Owen was struck by a strange sense of time passing, of the world turning. He could see them doing this next year, and the year after, watching their daughter grow up into the inevitably amazing adult she would become; and then maybe, one day, they'd be sitting here watching their grandchildren play in the exact same way. Life went on. It changed; it adapted; it expanded. Always. He could either build a strong foundation for that future to stand on or watch it crumble because he'd refused to do the one thing he knew how to accomplish.

'How are things?' Tasha asked. 'Any news about the Gair situation?'

Owen wondered whether they'd known each other so long that she could read his mind. 'Nothing new that I've heard.'

Tasha sighed. 'Poor Saskia. I do feel for her.'

'Yeah,' he said, clasping his hands together between his knees. 'I do, too. She's worked so hard to get to where she is.'

He felt Tasha's eyes on him. 'The month you gave her must nearly be up?'

He nodded. 'Tomorrow. I told Adrian I'd let him know what I'm going to do by close of play.'

'Right.' Tasha said nothing more, but he knew she wanted to ask. Of course she did, and as the mother of his child she had every right to know.

'I'm going to take the job,' he told her. 'I know it's the right thing to do. Maybe if there had been some movement on the review, some sense that the project will be able to move forward at some point, it'd be different. But as it is, this is the way it has to be. I've got to think of my future now. Of Hannah's.'

Tasha nodded. 'Okay. That's good. And for what it's worth, Owen, I know how difficult a decision this has been for you. I know you're going to look at this as if you're letting someone down. But you shouldn't, because you're not.'

Owen blew out a breath. That was exactly how he felt,

but he couldn't dwell on that. He had to put Hannah first. If there was a way to help Saskia and do that at the same time, he would, but he just couldn't see how to make both work. 'There's something else,' he added. 'A sweetener from The Collaton Project. Adrian called to let me know about it yesterday. Everyone working full-time on this first estate is going to get a preferential deposit rate on a home.'

'Oh?' He could feel Tasha watching him. 'On one of those houses in Collaton?'

'Yeah,' he said. 'I know it's a little way away, and they won't be ready for a while, but it's going to be a good place. And everything I've looked at any closer just seems so unattainable.'

To his surprise, Tasha reached out and laid a hand on his arm. When he looked at her, she was smiling. 'Hey, it's still the same county, right? It's not the ends of the earth. We'll make it work.'

Owen leaned back and took her hand, squeezing it. 'Thanks. I want things to be good. For Hannah. For all of us. However that shakes out.'

'I know you do,' Tasha said. 'And they will be. Have you broken it to Saskia yet?'

'No,' he said. 'Although I think she's expecting it. Still, I feel as if I need to tell her in person. I've asked if I can come up to talk to her this evening.'

Thirty-One

Saskia checked her email for what must have been the fiftieth time that day, but there was still nothing from the Local Planning Authority. She had drafted an email to them about the ruins. It included the casefile number linked to the police report of Tim's removal and a few photographs that she'd taken to illustrate the find. She'd got Julie to look over the email before she'd sent it, and she'd retained the journalist's permission to include her name as someone the review board could speak to as an independent witness if necessary. Then she'd sent it off into the ether, buzzing with excitement and a naïve certainty that the LPA would read it and immediately withdraw the review.

But that hadn't happened. In fact, *nothing* had happened. She'd had no communication from them at all. A day had turned into two days, and . . . nothing.

In fact, the only person she had heard from was Owen. He'd called to ask if he could come and speak to her that evening. He'd kept his tone light, but she knew what it was about. Tomorrow was the deadline he'd agreed to. After this he didn't owe her anything. He was coming to tell her that he'd signed on with The Collaton Project.

Saskia had hoped that, with Tim's absence and her report of the ruins to the LPA, she'd be able to stay Owen's hand. To say, *Look – Gair can go ahead! We can get started again, won't you stay?* But that hadn't happened, and she was out of time. She could press the issue, but really, would that be fair, when she still had no end date or certainty that Tim's absence would make any difference? Still, she was alarmed by how much it hurt that he was going to leave her. Yet why on earth wouldn't he? What was there here to make him stay? Nothing. But without Owen Elliot, what was she going to do?

She tried not to let herself begin to sink beneath this dark tide of bleak thoughts. It wasn't Owen's fault, and she wouldn't make him think it was. There must be someone else out there who would work on this with her, mustn't there? Somewhere. She just had to find them. Again.

Saskia checked her watch and went up to unlock the main gates so that Owen could get in without having to stop. After expelling Nathan and his team she'd started to keep the gates locked at all times, worried about someone raiding Tim's place if they had easy access. She'd already arranged with Julie that she'd come back with proper photography equipment to capture his underground home for her journalism.

As Saskia neared the gates, she realized there was already a car parked on the other side of it, headlights on in the early dusk. It wasn't Owen's truck. It was a gleaming white Audi Sportback, looking distinctly out of place. For a single hopeful second, she thought that perhaps this was someone from the council, come to answer her email in person, but then the driver's door opened. Someone stepped out, and Saskia felt the blood drain from her face.

'*Darling*,' said her mother. 'It's *so* good to *see* you.'

Saskia shut her eyes briefly, wondering how to get out of this. She didn't have to unlock the gates. She could just leave her mother there until she got bored and left of her own accord. Except that at some point Owen would turn up and she'd find some way to talk him into letting her in. No, she couldn't avoid this confrontation – and she had no doubt that's what it would end up being, a confrontation, since that's what any interaction between them always became.

'Mother,' she said. 'What are you doing here? How did you find me?'

Elsa Cavendish trained her expression into an elaborate mask of hurt that made Saskia grit her teeth. 'How did I *find* you? Really, darling. I'm your *mother.* You make me sound like a *stalker.*'

'I'd still like to know,' Saskia said. 'It wasn't from Vivian, she would have warned me if you knew where I was.'

Her mother's dark gaze slid from her daughter to the ruins looming behind them, darkening now as the sun dropped from the sky. 'It wasn't a great mystery, darling,' she said. 'This place has always been as much of an obsession for you as it was for your father.'

'It's not an obsession,' Saskia said. 'It's a project.'

Elsa looked at her again, the same steady, innocently withering gaze that she remembered from her childhood. 'There doesn't seem to be much work going on at the moment.'

Saskia took a breath. 'Why did you come?' she asked. 'What are you doing here?'

Elsa Cavendish sighed. 'Really, Saskia. I've come a long way to see how you are. It took me hours to get here. It really is the back of beyond. Please, darling. Aren't you even going to ask me in?'

Saskia didn't want Elsa inside her tiny home. She could already imagine the unspoken disdain, the disappointment that a daughter of hers could end up living in something so small, so cheap. It was Saskia's safe space, her nest of her own making. A large part of her wanted to tell her mother to get back into her car and get off her property. But she already knew how that would go. Elsa would not leave until she had got – or at least until she felt she had got – whatever it was she wanted. She knew how to fight when she had to. Saskia's only recourse would be to call the police, and what was she supposed to tell them?

'All right,' Saskia said, against every bit of her better judgement. 'Bring the car inside.'

In the cabin, she tried to ignore her mother's quiet poking around while she silently made coffee. Out of the corner of her eye she saw Elsa survey the bookcase and assess the small wall of photographs in which she did not feature. Eventually her mother settled onto the sofa, making a show of trying

to get comfortable. Saskia handed her a mug of coffee and perched on the bench opposite. She felt no compulsion to sit any closer.

Elsa sipped the coffee. Was that a brief grimace that Saskia saw her trying to hide, as if her eldest daughter couldn't even make a hot drink to her mother's standards? Probably.

'So,' Saskia prompted, when Elsa herself was not forthcoming. 'Why are you here?'

'Is it so hard to believe that I just wanted to see you?'

'Yes, frankly.'

'Saskia,' her mother sighed. 'You always were so *hard* on me.'

This statement took Saskia by surprise. '*I* was hard on *you*?'

'I did always try so when you were little,' her mother went on. 'But I was just never enough for you, no matter what I did. It was as if you only needed – only *wanted* – one parent, and that was your father.'

Saskia snorted. 'That's not even slightly true. You were the one who didn't want me.'

Her mother looked up at her with wide, shocked eyes, one hand pressed over her heart. 'How can you *say* that?'

'Because it's true,' Saskia said. 'Demonstrably so. You wanted me to go to boarding school when I was *six*.'

'You would have got an excellent education there,' Elsa protested. 'And you would have made friends – friends your own age, that would have lasted you your whole life. You were so insular, Saskia. You were such a daddy's girl. You spent all your time in your own head, and he didn't do anything to bring you out of it. He loved having you follow him around like a puppy.'

'I was his daughter,' Saskia said. 'He was being a *parent.* A state seemingly entirely beyond your grasp. I had a father who actually wanted to be around me, and a mother who didn't. He spent all of his time trying to be both of you.'

'That's a terrible thing to say,' Elsa said. 'And it's not fair. You were a difficult baby, Saskia. You cried all the time. You wouldn't sleep. You didn't want me. You never wanted *me.*'

'And you made sure I paid for that when I was older, didn't you, when I did want my mother?' Saskia pointed out. 'By always pushing me away.'

'I don't know why you're making that my fault,' her mother said. 'Your father was always taking you away on your little trips.'

'He only started that because otherwise you'd have sent me to board so you didn't have to put up with me. No,' Saskia said, 'don't deny it. If it wasn't true, you would have come with us. But you never did, not once.'

'I tried to,' Elsa protested. 'There was a weekend when I suggested I came too. I even looked up the best hotel right in the middle of town for where he wanted to go that weekend – Leicester, I think it was – and said I'd book it for us. But he refused.'

Saskia was shocked by this. 'He said you couldn't come with us?'

Elsa looked down at the coffee held between both elegant hands. 'He said that he didn't want to stay in a hotel. That

I could come if I would stay in the tent with the two of you. Three of us! In a *tent*! When there was a good chance it would rain! Where we'd be sharing a shower block with whoever else was staying there.' She wrinkled her nose as if this was beyond comprehension. 'He wouldn't compromise and I wouldn't do it, so that was that.'

'The camping was part of it,' Saskia said. 'It wouldn't have been the same if we'd stayed in a hotel.'

'It was cruel of him,' her mother declared. 'And ridiculous. It was supposed to be about the buildings, wasn't it? Staying somewhere decent wouldn't have changed that. Camping was just to spite me, to make sure I wouldn't come.'

'It was nothing to do with you,' Saskia said, with a spark of annoyance. 'Except for the fact that he was trying to make sure I wasn't as spoiled as you were.'

There was a silence. Outside, it had begun to rain. Saskia focused on the patter of drops against the glass, a soothing counterpoint to the bitter undercurrent in which she was caught.

'After he died, I really thought we'd be able to start again,' said her mother. 'It'd just be you and me. We could get to know each other properly. But that didn't happen either.'

Saskia spat a short laugh. 'Perhaps if you'd spent time with me for a while instead of immediately getting remarried, we might have had a shot at that.'

Elsa looked up. 'Did you expect me to go into mourning, like a good wife? How long for, Saskia? Six months? A year? A decade?'

'You didn't even pause for breath. I'm amazed you waited until after the funeral.'

'Now that's really not fair. It was a year later, Saskia. A *year.* And in those twelve months you barely gave me the time of day. All you wanted was your father. I tried to get through to you. I did. But you just got angrier and angrier. With the world, with me. As if you wished *I* was the one who was gone, instead of him. How long was I supposed to put up with that, without comfort myself?'

Saskia shook her head. 'You wanted a second shot at a perfect family, and that's what you got with Richard and the twins. You didn't need me anymore. You couldn't be bothered to deal with my grief. So you dumped me.'

She'd been expecting another rebuttal to this, but instead her mother looked away. 'I'm sorry,' Elsa said. 'I'm sorry that I didn't get it right for you. I tried. You might not believe that, but I did. But you never gave me a chance, either. And in the end I did have to think about the girls, about my husband.'

'You let him throw me out.' Saskia was shaken by the apology, by the admission, but still, there was more she needed to say. 'You let your husband throw a grieving teenager out and you didn't care if I ended up on the street.'

Her mother looked at her then, and Saskia was beyond shocked to see the gleam of tears beneath Elsa's perfect lashes. 'I didn't know what else to do,' she said. 'And it wasn't supposed to be permanent. When we told you to pack up and get out, it was just supposed to scare you into doing better, that's all. I was at the end of my rope, Saskia. The housekeeper found cocaine in your bathroom, and she told Richard. *Cocaine*. There were *toddlers* in the house! He was furious. Wouldn't you be? You wouldn't see a therapist. You wouldn't admit there was any problem other than the fact that I was your mother.'

Saskia blinked. 'That's a lie. I would never have left drugs out. He lied to you.'

Elsa shook her head. 'Did he? Are you sure?'

'Of course I'm sure! I would never have left anything where the twins could get at it!'

'Not even by accident? It's not as if your room was ever very tidy, was it? Are you sure?'

Saskia tried to remember back to that night. She couldn't. It was so long ago, and she'd been such a mess. 'Neither of you said that was the reason. You just threw me out.'

'You talk about it as if it was out of the blue,' Elsa said. 'But that wasn't the first time. It was constant, Saskia, the trouble we had with you. You never gave Richard a chance, you were always determined to hate him. And you were old enough by then to be responsible for yourself. You can admit that much, can't you?'

'And when I was responsible for myself, when I was clean and trying to get my life back on track, how do you justify what you did then?' Saskia demanded. 'When you continually tried to sabotage my progress – and my future – by forcing me to prove I was clean?'

'That wasn't sabotage,' Elsa said. 'You wouldn't talk to me.

The drugs tests were the only way I knew you were okay and not shooting up in some gutter somewhere! And I was so proud of you every time they came back clean, but how would I have told you that when you would never *speak* to me?'

There was a brief silence. Saskia was so tense her shoulders felt like rusted cogs.

Elsa sighed and put down her empty mug. 'I didn't come here to dredge up the past. But when I heard you were actually planning to go ahead with this . . . *project* of your father's . . .' She shook her head. 'I was worried. Really worried. I mean, buying the land is one thing, but *Saskia*, you do know that your father would never have wanted you to *actually* do this, don't you?'

Saskia stiffened. 'You're wrong. Gair was always his dream build. I'm achieving what he would have himself – what we would have done together – if he hadn't died.'

'No,' Elsa said, passing a hand over her face. 'No, no. I knew you didn't understand that. I told him, even back then, that he should make it clear to you that it was only ever just an exercise.'

Saskia felt something indefinable beneath her tilt. 'What are you talking about?'

Elsa dropped her hand. 'It's a no-win scenario. He gave it to his most promising students, as a way to gauge their promise and determination. As soon as you started showing interest in his work, he gave it to you, too. A puzzle box with no solution but plenty of potential to learn as you tried to work it out.'

'But I have solved it,' Saskia said. 'It wasn't impossible. I've found a way, and I'm doing it.'

Elsa looked sad. 'If he'd lived, he would have told you not to touch this place,' she said. 'He loved it as it was. He would never have actually wanted to change it.'

Saskia felt the tilt become an earthquake. Her heart gave a sick lurch in her chest. 'What would you know?' she whispered. 'You never came here.'

What her mother said next was one of the greatest shocks of all. 'Yes, I did,' she said. 'When we first started courting, he told me he wanted to show me his favourite place in the world. We came up here for a weekend. We hiked out here from Carlisle. Yes, Saskia, I hiked with him, which should tell you how much I loved him back then. He showed me the ruins and the tree, where his grandparents had carved their names.'

Saskia stared at her for what felt like a very long time, until she could find her voice again. 'I didn't know that. He never said. I . . . didn't know.'

'Why don't you come home with me, Saskia?' her mother said, eventually. 'We could start again. You and me. Get to know each other as adults. Be a proper *family*.'

'I have a home,' Saskia said. 'This is my home.'

Elsa gave a brilliant, brittle smile. 'And it's lovely, darling. Just lovely. So why not bring it with you? I've talked with Richard and there's room for you on the estate. You can have your own field. You'd be walking distance from the house. Doesn't that sound like a good idea? And you know, down south I'm sure you'd get far more clients as an architect. I *do* want you to succeed, Saskia, just as much as your father did. Let me help you do that.'

Thirty-Two

Up ahead, the road made a final turn towards Gair. Owen slowed as the main gates came into view. There was a white Audi convertible driving towards him in the opposite direction. He pulled over into one of the passing places on the narrow road and waited. It was dusk by now, the tones of twilight threading the sky above the forest with colours of rust and gold. As the car neared, he thought for a moment that it was Saskia behind the wheel. The woman driving could almost have been her twin. He looked closer as the car passed, but the driver showed no sign that she'd seen him; gave no thank you or acknowledgement for the space he had left her. Once she was abreast of the truck, he could see that it definitely wasn't Saskia, although the woman could have passed for her older sister. Which meant this could be only one person.

Her mother.

Owen pulled back onto the road as the Audi's tail lights continued into the dimming distance behind him. He glanced into the mirror as the car turned a corner and vanished from view. A sense of disquiet suffused him. He remembered what Saskia had told him about their relationship, that night he'd found her camping out in her tent. There's no way Saskia's mother would have been here by invitation, which meant she'd probably appeared unannounced.

The main gates were open. Owen parked and went up to the trailer, knocking on the door instead of walking straight in, even though he still had a key. There was no answer.

'Saskia?' He knocked again and then, when there was still no reply, cautiously pushed open the door. There was no sign of her inside.

He pulled the door to the trailer shut again and turned to survey the Gair site. The castle ruins stood as silent and still as ever, shadows stretching to join the inner perimeter fence as the twilight wore on. The birds were entering their last chorus of the day, singing the sun below the horizon, and he knew exactly where she would be.

The Gair Oak stood over the site, as stalwart as ever. As Owen walked towards it, he realized how his attitude about it had changed since he'd first arrived. He remembered what Saskia had told him when she'd been trying to explain why they couldn't possibly cut it down. That an oak is more than just itself: it's a community, a society made up of numerous different creatures. That the oak is a microcosm of the world, and an indicator of how the world could work: coexisting, peaceful, connected, interdependent. He remembered the two of them climbing up into its boughs – that seemed a million years ago now – and how he'd watched her face as she'd told him her story: how hard she'd fought to get here, in so many different ways. She loved this place and the oak. She *loved* them. And now, at this moment, Owen realized that he did, too. He saw Gair and its strange tree as so much more now – more than the inconvenience he had first thought them.

Brodie was lying beside the tree's thick trunk, his nose on his paws, his big eyes anxious. Owen stopped and crouched to pet the faithful dog, the oak's thick canopy of leaves meshing together above him. They moved gently in the evening breeze that had risen as the sun dropped. The bees had settled for the night and the birds were roosting. There was a quiet descending, a rare peace. A small shape flitted past him, too quick to properly see: a bat, hunting night insects in the crepuscular light.

'Saskia?' he called, softly, as he straightened up, not wanting to disturb the quiet.

For a moment there was no answer. Then he heard her voice, filtering down through the leaves. 'Owen?'

'I'm going to come up.'

Another pause. 'Okay.'

He found her on the 'seat' she'd shown him that same night he'd finally, truly understood the importance of Gair and this project. She leaned against the trunk and watched him as he climbed towards her, then moved along to give him room.

'Hi,' he said, when he was seated beside her. Her face

was full of shadows, and not only from the tree. 'I passed someone as I was coming in. I think it was probably ... your mother?'

Saskia smiled grimly. 'Yes.'

'I didn't think she knew where you were?'

'Neither did I,' she said, heavily. 'But it seems I was wrong about that. I was wrong about a *lot* of things.'

He frowned. 'Oh?'

She looked down at her hands, folded together on her lap. She seemed diminished, somehow, deflated, and Owen had the urge to put his arm around her, though he didn't.

'What am I doing here, Owen?' she said, eventually. 'Here, at Gair? What am I really doing?'

He wasn't sure what to say, except to repeat Saskia's own words back to her. 'You're going to finish what your dad didn't have a chance to himself.'

She gave a derisory snort. 'I'm such an idiot. So many people have told me that, but I didn't listen. I knew best, I knew what could be done and how to do it. But it turns out I've pegged my entire life on a lie.'

Owen did reach out to her then, wrapping one hand around both of hers. 'I don't understand what you mean,' he said. 'What's happened?'

She said nothing for a moment, and her eyes were still dry, but when she did speak there was a tremble there, a deep one. 'Dad never intended anyone to actually do this,' she said. 'He loved Gair as it was. The idea of rebuilding was just an exercise – a test. For his students, for me. To see how far we'd go with the planning and what ideas we would develop along the way.'

Owen watched her for another moment, seeing the painful emotions play out across her face as he held onto her hands. 'Your mother told you this?'

'Among other things,' she said. 'Like the fact that he brought her here when they first got together.'

'I don't believe her,' Owen said. 'Not about the idea of this place. I've seen that sketch of his. He was working on this too. You worked on it together.'

She shook her head, and now there were tears in her eyes. '"Working together",' she said, her voice full of a scorn that was directed at herself. 'I was so young. I was a child! What did I know? He was encouraging me, pushing me on to this great future. I learned so much, working on the idea of Gair with him. But I believe my mother when she says he wouldn't have actually wanted to change this place. That makes so much more sense than . . . *this*. Doesn't it? I've just been a total fool. I've wasted my grandparents' money. And . . . most of my life. And I've ruined this place.'

Owen squeezed her fingers, leaning forward so that she looked him in the face. 'You haven't ruined or wasted anything,' he said. 'Of course you haven't. What you've achieved – in your life, here at Gair . . . it's huge. It *is*. Don't let someone who hasn't been around to see that get inside your head and tell you otherwise.'

Saskia squeezed his hand but said nothing. Owen waited her out, trying to work out what was going through her head. He wished Vivian were here, her oldest friend, who had stuck with her through everything. She'd know what to say, what to do. He was out of his depth.

'What my mother really came here to tell me,' she said, quietly, 'is that she wants to try again. With me, I mean. She thinks we can rebuild our relationship. She's offered me a place down on the estate for the cabin. She's pointed out that if I want to build an actual architecture practice, I'd be better off down south, where she and her husband have got contacts that can help. And she's not wrong, is she? All I've got up here is a reputation for one hare-brained scheme that antagonized the locals and did nothing but waste a ton of money and that I never even finished.'

'Saskia,' Owen said, 'you're not thinking of giving up?'

'Giving up what?' she asked, dryly. 'Gair's dead in the water either way, isn't it?'

'It's not,' he insisted. 'Of course it's not. Once the Tim situation is sorted and the LPA know you've found the real site of the ruins, then—'

'They know, Owen. Tim's gone, and the LPA know all about the ruins. It hasn't made any difference. I've heard nothing from them, not a thing.' She did look at him then, her dark eyes serious. 'I don't have permission to build. I don't have a work crew. And as of today . . . I don't have a site manager either. Do I?'

He didn't know what to say to that. Because that was

exactly what he'd come to tell her, wasn't it? She smiled, though there was nothing happy about it.

'You've taken the job at Collaton, and that's fine,' she went on. 'Really. Because if you hadn't, I'd just be dragging you down with me, and you of all people don't deserve that.'

Owen took a breath. 'There *must* be a way to make Gair work,' he said. 'After all your work and everything you've done to get it to this point. I *want* you to make Gair work. So you haven't heard from the LPA yet, so what? You know how slow bureaucracy works. It'll happen, and when it does, we'll make sure Gair can get back on track. I've been trying to find a replacement, and I think—'

'It's too late,' she interrupted, tiredly. 'This is just one more thing I've messed up. What was I thinking? If I'd just stayed away, Tim could have continued as he was. The Historical Society would have carried on trundling up here. What harm would any of that have caused? Me coming here: that's what upturned the apple cart. Gair was fine without me, this tree was fine without me, and it all would have continued to be fine without me.' Saskia made a pained face. 'Tim said in preserving the place I was really destroying it. And he's right. My dad would be so ashamed of me. The one person I wanted to—' She broke off, her voice cracking. Owen took his hand from hers, reached out and slid it across her shoulders, pulling her against his chest.

'Ashamed is the last thing he'd be,' he said, into her hair. 'He'd be proud. Any parent would be proud of you.'

She gave a sob, which shocked him and made him wind

both arms around her, holding her tighter. *Her mother has done this*, he thought. *She's been doing this all her life.*

'You can't give up,' he murmured. 'You can't.'

'I have to,' she said. 'I'm so completely alone. My mother's right.'

'She's not. You're *not* alone,' he protested. 'You've got Vivian. And Stuart – and *me*.'

'You've all got your own families,' she said, against his chest. 'And maybe if I'd made an effort to know mine better – all of it – I wouldn't have got myself into any of the messes that I've been causing since I was a teenager.'

He wanted to tell her she was wrong, that she wasn't the one that had caused any of this, that she'd been let down badly by the woman who had now turned up out of the blue, apparently with the sole purpose of dismantling everything Saskia had built – despite all she'd already been through. But he couldn't say that, could he? He'd never even met Saskia's mother.

'I need a drink,' Saskia said. 'A bottle of whisky, that's what I need right now.'

'No,' he told her, tightening his arms around her. 'You don't. Come on. Let's go back to your place. I'll make you a hot chocolate and we can talk about this more.'

She pulled away from him. 'You don't have to do that,' she said. 'I'm just your boss, Owen, and I'm not even that anymore, am I? I can look after myself.'

'No, you're not my boss,' he agreed. 'You're a friend. And I'm staying.'

They walked back to the trailer in silence, an unhappy Brodie trailing alongside Saskia, keeping as close to her as he could get. Owen kept his arm around her, wondering whether he should search the trailer for any hidden bottles of alcohol, but he knew he wouldn't find any. She'd been clean this long. If he could keep her here, with him, and not let her take the truck and go into town to fill this craving, they could weather this. He could get her through it.

As promised, he made them both a hot chocolate and then left her under a blanket on the sofa with Brodie while he stepped out, telling her he needed to lock the gates. Once outside, Owen thumbed through his phone to Stuart's number as he walked.

'Something about this seems really off,' he said, once he'd explained to his friend where he was, what was happening. 'For her mother to turn up right now, when Sas is about to pull a rabbit out of the bag that'll mean the judicial review is bound to be quashed? It's a bit too convenient. And I was thinking, can you ask Vivian if she's heard anything?'

'What kind of thing?' Stuart asked. From the background noise Owen thought he was probably using the hands-free in the car.

'I don't know,' Owen admitted. 'But she knows the family and so does *her* family. Someone must be talking about this somewhere.'

'Okay,' Stuart said. 'I'll talk to her. Where are you now?'

'I'm still here,' he said. 'I don't want to leave her alone.'

'It's that bad?'

Owen gave a shrug that Stuart couldn't see. 'Put it this way, I wish Vivian were here.'

'Leave it with me,' Stuart said.

Thirty-Three

Saskia slept fitfully, dozing here and there until she finally fell properly asleep in the early hours. Owen stayed with her – Brodie, too, the dog watching her from his bed by the wood-burner. Saskia curled up on the sofa and Owen propped himself in the opposite corner. She woke properly at about 6am and he was the first thing she saw. He was asleep, his head had nodded forward so that his chin was on his chest. He had a frown on his face even in sleep, faint lines creasing his forehead. He'd rested one hand on her calf so that he'd know if she moved. She watched him for a few moments; felt an affection in her chest that was almost enough to battle the despair that was lurking in the shadows of her heart. Then she shifted, trying not to wake him but failing. Owen opened his eyes, immediately awake. She supposed that was a military thing, both that he could sleep anywhere and that he could go from asleep to full alert in a split second. She felt guilty that he had felt the need to stay, to keep her from the worst that she could do to herself.

'Hi,' she said, still beneath the blanket he'd spread over her the night before.

'Morning,' he said, quietly. 'How are you feeling?'

How could she answer that? Embarrassed, tired, frustrated and foolish. That was a little of it. 'Fine,' is what she said. She looked at her watch. 'I'd better unlock the gates. Julie's bringing her camera rig back today so that she can photograph Tim's place properly. She'll need to get in.'

Owen shifted, lifting his hand from her calf. She missed the weight of it, the warmth. 'I can do that.'

'It's okay. I need to move.'

He smiled a little ruefully, rubbing one hand at the base of his cricked neck. 'Me too.'

They walked up to the gates together, Brodie with them, breathing in the dew-fresh air of morning. The late-summer sun was already up; the birds were singing in the trees. They didn't talk; just listened to the sounds of Gair waking around them. Saskia didn't know what to say, and it seemed that Owen was content with silence. When they reached the gates, it was to find a car already waiting on the other side of it: a scarlet BMW. Someone was leaning against the bonnet.

'I got here a couple of hours ago, but I thought I might wake you if I called,' Vivian said. 'And from that fabulous bed hair you've got going on, it looks like I was right.'

Saskia unlocked the gates and they hugged. If she'd been less tired, she might have cried to see her friend. 'What are you doing here?' she asked, chin on Vivian's shoulder.

'Owen called Stuart and Stuart called me. I got in the car and started to drive. Damn, you live a bloody long way away!'

Saskia pulled back and glanced at Owen, who had stuffed his hands into his pockets and was looking studiously at the ground as if it might suddenly yield the key to the universe. She felt that tug of affection again, like a sudden flowering of something she hadn't known was in bud. She hugged Vivian again.

'Thank you,' she said. 'But I'm fine, thanks to Owen. You didn't need to come.'

'I wanted to be here,' Vivian assured her. 'I hear you've had an unexpected visitor.'

Before Saskia could answer, there came the purr of another car engine coming up behind them. 'There's Julie now,' she said.

'I'll talk to her,' said Owen. 'I want to go down to the ruins myself, anyway – we can go together. Why don't you two go and chat over a coffee?'

'That's a great idea,' said Vivian. 'I've got quite a bit of news that Sas needs to hear. Hang on and I'll move the car.'

Saskia and Owen stepped away from the gates to let their visitors through. 'Thank you,' she told him. She already felt stronger, better equipped for whatever was coming. 'For Vivian. For everything.'

'No thanks needed,' he said lightly. 'I'm just glad I was here. I'll see you two later.'

He smiled at Vivian as she got out of the car again, and the two women watched as Owen went to speak to Julie.

'He's a good one,' Vivian observed.

'Yeah,' Saskia agreed, with a faint smile. 'He is. He got Stuart to tell you what a mess I was in last night?'

A serious look passed over her friend's face. 'That's one of the reasons I'm here, yeah.'

Alarm bells went off in Saskia's mind. 'Oh? What are the others?'

Vivian threaded her arm through hers. 'Come on,' she said. 'I need caffeine. Then we can talk.'

What Vivian told her shouldn't have been a shock. Not really. And yet it was. As Saskia listened to what her friend had to say, she realized that she had made the mistake of believing that the world – or at least, the part of it that she had come from – had changed in the same way that she had. Despite everything she had known to be the case in all the years she had been her mother's daughter, Saskia had wanted to believe that what Elsa had told her regarding her visit had been the whole truth. She had wanted her mother to be worried for her, to want them to start again, to try to cultivate the relationship they had never had.

How many times and in how many different ways could she be a fool?

'Richard is stone broke,' Vivian told her. 'You know how he was always boasting about being an early adopter in tech, punting money into all sorts? Well, he lost a ton in cryptocurrency investments to that idiot American boy who's gone to jail for, like, ever. He hid it for ages, but rumour has it that part of how he covered it up was by dipping into the twins' trust funds. And now they're empty, too.'

'What?' Saskia asked, shocked. 'But . . . when did this all happen?'

'The big loss was a couple of years ago, but he kept trying to get on top of it with riskier and riskier investments. Hey, his nickname is The Prick for a reason, right?'

'When did my mother find out about this?'

Vivian shrugged. 'Mum's not sure. But probably not until this year. They managed to keep it quiet until it came out that they haven't paid their club fees for two years running. The manager – dear old Lucas, do you remember him? – eventually pulled the plug. The Prick tried to make out that they'd made the decision not to renew because "the quality of service had fallen" or some such bollocks. Of course the real reason came out. You know how our set likes to gossip, especially about their "friends".'

Saskia shook her head, stunned. She could imagine her mother's mortification. 'How has she not left him?'

'Oh, you know what it's like. Desperate to save face, probably. And' – Vivian gave Saskia a significant look – 'I imagine she's thinking that there's no point leaving until the well is completely dry.'

Saskia looked out of the window at the ruins of Gair. 'You think that's why she came here? She wants my grandparents' money?'

Vivian snorted. 'Of course she does. Now more than ever.'

She should be hardened to it by now, but something in Saskia's heart twinged painfully as she thought about this.

'You were the one who kept encouraging me to talk to her,' Saskia pointed out. 'You and your parents.'

Vivian reached out and gripped Saskia's hand, twining her fingers with hers. 'I know. And I'm so sorry for that.'

'But what if you're wrong now?' Saskia asked. 'What if this really is her wanting to make a new start? Maybe what it took is everything falling apart with Richard. Maybe if I walk away now, I'm ruining my last chance of ever having a family.'

Her friend watched her through worried eyes. 'What exactly did she say?'

Saskia outlined their conversation, the offer that Elsa had made for her to move the trailer back to the estate. Vivian's eyes widened as she listened.

'You're not really thinking about it, are you?' she asked. 'You're not really thinking about giving up on Gair? You've barely begun work!'

'And there's no guarantee we'll ever be able to carry on,' Saskia pointed out. 'What am I going to do? Waste my life and what's left of my grandparents' hard-earned money here, when I now know that my dad never intended to actually do this in the first place?'

Vivian shook her head. 'You don't know that. And neither does Elsa.'

'I think she does.'

'And I think she'd say anything to put you somewhere where you feel obligated to help her out of her mess.'

They were quiet for a moment. And then Saskia said, 'You know, I never used to be that bothered. About not having a great relationship with my mother, I mean. I just thought it was one of those things that happens sometimes. But then I saw Owen with his daughter, and it . . . made me wish I had a family. I'm alone, Viv. And the older I get, the more that matters.'

Vivian squeezed her hand again, tears in her eyes. 'You're not alone,' she said. 'You've got me. You've always got me, you know that.'

'I do know that,' Saskia agreed, 'but you've got your own life. This thing with Stuart? It looks serious to me.'

Vivian looked down at their joined hands, tears on her cheeks. 'Yeah. I think it is. But that doesn't mean I won't still be here for you.'

'Of course you will be,' Saskia said, warmly. 'I just don't expect you to put more of your life on hold for me. You've been so supportive for years. But . . . I want what you've got, Viv. What Owen's got, too, or at least the chance at it, and if I'm not careful it's going to be too late, isn't it? I've been just surviving for so long. Everything has been about work, and getting here. And now I'm here, and . . .' She let out a long, slow breath. 'It turns out that maybe this is never where I should have been in the first place.'

'Don't say that.'

'It's true. Look at this ridiculous project. I was so adamant about it. But now? Now it feels like a white elephant. And even if I do manage to get Gair rebuilt, what happens then? I sit in it like Miss Haversham, old and bitter and unable to move on? With no money because the building took every penny I have? Where's the sense in that, especially when there's this alternative to start again with my family, make what I can of that?' She shook her head. 'Some of the things my mother said weren't wrong, you know. I *was* difficult as a teen. You know that better than anyone. And here's the thing: maybe I've been looking at it all wrong all these years. Maybe she did always want me, but I just never made an effort.'

Vivian shook her head. 'You shouldn't have had to make the effort,' she said. 'You were the child, Sas.'

'But there's no point thinking that way now, is there?' Saskia pointed out. 'Someone said something in a group session once that really stayed with me. *The only sure way to ruin your future is to stay stuck in the past.* And look around. Isn't that exactly what I've been doing here? What I've been doing my entire *life*?'

Vivian said nothing for a few minutes, her face serious. 'And what if it is about the money?' she asked eventually. 'What if that *is* all she wants?'

Saskia thought about this. 'Maybe it is,' she acknowledged. 'But maybe the money is just a symbol for something else.'

'What do you mean?'

'I can't believe that she wants to stay with Richard after

everything he's done. If Elsa cares about anything it's about how she looks to her peers, and he's humiliated her,' Saskia said. 'But maybe the only way she can see being able to leave him is if she has something else to fall back on. Like me. Like my grandparents' money.'

Vivian put down her mug and clasped both of Saskia's hands in hers. 'You're still calling it your grandparents' money,' she said. 'It's your money, Sas. *Yours*.'

Saskia nodded. 'But what's the point of having money without having someone to spend it on?' She thought about Owen, how good he was with Hannah. How much he loved his daughter; how much he thought about how he was going to provide for her going forward. 'Right now I don't have anyone. All I've got is a pile of stones and a tree that are perfectly happy being what they are.'

Vivian still looked troubled, and Saskia couldn't blame her. After all, this was a sea change from how she usually spoke about her mother and that side of the family. But Saskia was so tired of being wrong about everything, all the time. She was so tired of struggling, of feeling as if she were always, *always* on the verge of failure. Even if her family wasn't perfect, they were still family, weren't they? If she wanted to have any hope of a future where she was a part of that, something had to change. She thought about the twins, still so young. If Saskia made an effort now, perhaps the three of them could forge some kind of better bond going forward. Even if she would never be interested in knowing their father, even if she would never truly trust her mother, perhaps she could start again with the girls. And anyway, what else was she going to do? Why not just accept the inevitable, and do some good while she was at it?

Thirty-Four

Owen found himself underground, stooping to avoid hitting his hard hat on the tree roots that formed the uneven ceiling of Tim's former home. He was beyond relieved that he hadn't had to lower himself on a rope to get in, the way Saskia had on her first two visits. He'd entered the narrow passageway into the hill from the clearing cautiously, wondering how sensible it was to trust the structure above his head, but it seemed remarkably stable, if dark. Besides her photography kit and their head gear, he and Julie Rhys had equipped themselves with the LED floodlights from Gair's stores before heading for the forest, because the photographer had warned him that there was no natural light in Tim's underground home. Now they were surrounded by a harsh blue-white shine far stronger than the strings of soft battery-powered lights Tim had put in place. The two of them had set up these lamps so that they lit every hidden corner, revealing a peculiar amalgam of natural and artificial. It was clear that Tim Burney had been an avid collector, and he had been trawling this forest and its river for a long time.

'There's so much here,' Julie said, in a hushed, awed voice, as she gingerly picked up a pot that seemed ancient but virtually intact. 'It's going to take for ever to catalogue it all. And that's not including the structure itself.'

They found seven rooms in all, though some were little more than alcoves or cupboards. It wasn't difficult to imagine that the place had been inhabited continually for centuries. Looking at the toolmarks on the hewn stonework, Owen felt as if he were directly connected to the builder who had placed it there back in the mists of who-knew-when. It was a strange feeling, to have such an immediate connection to a past that had otherwise vanished.

'It's funny, isn't it?' Julie said, staring up at one of the vents in the ceiling. 'All those sightings of smoke over the years: at least some of them must have been Tim, living peacefully and out of sight under the loam. And before that, whoever lived in this place before him.'

'Whenever that was,' Owen murmured. He'd found the altar that had scared both his daughter and Saskia when they'd seen it looming out of the dark. It was curiously expressive despite its rough nature – no wonder it had given them both a shock. He turned to look at the journalist. 'Do you think you'll be able to get good photographs of everything?'

'Yes, I've got a decent set-up,' she told him, looking around. 'It's going to take a while, though. It'd be good to take photographs of everything in situ before anything's moved, wouldn't it?'

Owen nodded. 'Definitely. I think we should make sure everything's documented exactly as it is before Saskia even lets anyone else in here,' he said. 'It'd be good to have our own record.' He glanced over to find Julie smiling at him. 'What?'

She shrugged. 'You're making me feel like part of the team. I like it.'

He huffed a laugh. 'I guess you need to stay objective and detached in your line of work.'

'Well, yes. But believe me,' she said, 'I'm rooting for Saskia and Gair.'

Owen put his hands on his hips and nodded. 'Yeah,' he said. 'Yeah, so am I.'

They set to work, Owen acting as the journalist's assistant. He was impressed by her quiet confidence as she decided on angles and light levels. It was easy to see that she knew exactly what she was doing.

It was as he lifted down a large shard of pottery from one of the shelves in the kitchen that Owen saw it. He paused for a second as the light caught on something, then reached out to pick up a glass jam jar. For a moment he couldn't process what he held in his hand.

'Julie?'

'Yes?' She was bent over the tripod she'd set up, concentrating on a shot.

'Look at this.'

Julie finally turned to look at what he held, and then she

froze, her mouth dropping open. 'Are they . . . Those can't be . . . They're not *real*, are they?'

'I think they are,' Owen said, carrying what he held further into the light.

They both stared at what he held between his hands. The jar was packed full of small gold coins, all glinting with an ethereal warmth in the unnatural light.

Everything else they left exactly where it was, but they took the coins back to Gair. Julie cradled the jar and around them the forest seemed to be holding its breath as the riches it had concealed for centuries were carried beneath its boughs. Above them sunlight glinted through leaves the colour of gemstones: emerald and peridot lighting their way. Back at the site, Owen unlocked the empty work cabin for Julie and then went to find Saskia.

'What is it?' she asked, perplexed, as she and Vivian followed him back down the short slope from her trailer to the work site. 'Did you find something?'

'Oh yeah,' he told her, with a laugh. 'It's definitely . . . something. Go up and see, Julie's got them.'

He sent her up the short flight of steps in front of him. Inside the container, stacked with disused equipment, Julie had spread one of the tea towels from the small kitchenette onto what had once been the lunch table. She was gently removing the coins from the jar one by one, laying them with infinite care onto the cloth. She looked up at them with an astonished look on her face when she had finished.

'There are over two hundred coins here,' she said, her voice hushed. '*Two hundred!*'

Saskia looked over her shoulder at Owen, her dark eyes wide. He smiled at her. 'Seems as if Tim didn't spend all of his time trapping rabbits and spooking the locals, eh?'

'Bloody hell,' Vivian said. 'That is a *lot* of bling.'

'But . . . that's insane,' Saskia said, her voice hushed. 'I've never seen anything like that!'

'We're going to have to work out what to do with them,' Owen said. 'And we're going to need to keep the place secure.'

'No one knows about it,' Saskia pointed out. 'No one except us, and I trust everyone here.'

'What about Nathan?' Julie said. 'He must have found his way to Tim's place at least once. And we know the Historical Society have been up here before. What if he shows them how to find the ruins? Or even if he just comes back himself – who knows what else is down there? I've started taking photographs, but—'

There came the sudden sound of footsteps on the stairs behind them. '*Here* you are,' said a brusque voice. 'I thought you'd done another moonlit flit, Saskia, darling.'

Owen felt Saskia tense beside him and turned to see her mother, backlit in the doorway of the cabin.

'Mother,' Saskia said, her voice flat. 'What are you doing here? How did you get into the site?'

'The gates are open. Are they supposed to be shut? You must have forgotten to lock them,' Elsa Cavendish said, with a studied kind of breeziness, wafting into the room as if she'd been invited. Her eyes found Vivian and darkened slightly. 'Well, well. It's a long time since I've seen you, Vivian, dear.'

'And you, Elsa,' said Vivian.

'I should have known you would be here somewhere,' Saskia's mother added, her voice light but with an edge sharp enough to cut. 'You always were a theme in Saskia's more . . . outrageous . . . exploits.'

'Mother,' Saskia said. 'This really isn't a good time.'

'I've got some good news for you, darling. Anyway, we've got a lot to sort out, haven't we? But what's going on? What have you got there?'

Saskia's mother moved until she could see the gold. As her eyes widened, Owen reflected on the striking similarity between mother and daughter. It seemed to him that the only difference was in their age. Elsa's cheekbones were still high and sharp, her lips were still full, but her jawline was softening, and her neck wasn't as smooth as it might once have been. There were creases on her forehead and lines around her eyes. She was a gorgeous woman, Saskia's mother, and she wore the years well. But despite her enduring beauty, age was age. It was also clear to him that although Elsa Cavendish loathed what time was doing to her face and body, what she resented even more was that in her daughter she could see what she was losing, day by day. He could see this woman's jealousy like a green wreath of poison leaching through her every vein, and he wondered how long she'd regarded her daughter as a rival. Long enough that breaking her down had become a habit and more than that, a necessity. Long enough that it had cast a pall over her daughter's life. Saskia couldn't see it, but Owen could. He despised bullies, and here was a prime example of one, a smiling monster hidden beneath a veneer of civility, intent on destroying what he could already see was the only decent thing she'd ever created. And all because she couldn't control her and because Saskia, despite everything, had proven that she didn't need her.

'My goodness,' the woman breathed, pushing her way closer to the table. 'Well, you've really hit the jackpot there, haven't you, darling?'

'We didn't find them. It was Tim.'

Owen watched the expression on Elsa's face. Her eyes had taken on a proprietorial gleam. 'Tim?'

'It's a long story,' Saskia said, 'but essentially these coins – and whatever else is still in the space where he was living – were found by a hermit who'd been living in the forest for years.'

Her mother's nose wrinkled. 'A squatter, then? Well, that makes no difference. It's your land, darling. The Crown will take half of it, but the rest of it is yours. I know about these things because there are always funny little men with metal detectors wanting to root about on the estate. We got the lawyers to draw up papers for them all to sign if they want to set foot on our land. We always make sure one of the staff checks them before they leave every night, too.' She eyed Owen. 'Might be as well to do that here. Make sure that no one has tried to slip anything into their pocket on the sly.'

'This isn't about the money,' Saskia said. 'This is an amazing historical find.'

'Oh, good grief,' her mother said, impatiently. 'You can't *still* be so naïve. It's *always* about the money, and the quicker we make sure we have it sewn up and sealed, the better.'

'"We"?'

It was Owen who had spoken. The single repeated word was followed by a brief but potent silence in which Saskia's mother could have slain him there and then had her eyes held knives.

'Yes,' Elsa Cavendish said, icily. '"We". As in, the family. *Our* family. Saskia's family. Who are *you*?'

'I'm no one,' he said, his tone entirely neutral. 'Just a contractor who's been working on the castle.'

'Ah, I see,' she said, voice like acid. 'I thought someone must have been in her ear up here, egging her on so they could get into the coffers. I suppose with this' – she gestured to the gold scattered across the table – 'you think you can skim even more.'

'Don't speak to him like that,' Saskia said.

'Someone's got to say it,' Elsa Cavendish said. 'Someone's got to make sure you're not taken advantage of any more than you clearly already have been. You're so easily led, Saskia, and with your history of—'

'That's *enough*!'

There was a second of silence in the wake of Saskia's raised voice. Her mother looked at her, shocked.

'You need to leave. Right now.'

'What?' Elsa asked, apparently genuinely stunned. '*Me* leave? But aren't you going to come back with me? I thought we'd decided that was for the best.'

'I'm not going anywhere until I know what's happening with Gair.'

'What's happening with— Oh, for God's sake, Saskia,' her mother snapped. 'Surely you don't still think you can outlast the judicial review? That's not going to happen. This is all so ridiculous, really.'

There was a short silence. When Saskia spoke, her voice was low and cold, full of steel. 'And why would you think that?'

'Why would I think what?'

'You seem very sure that the judicial review is going to drag on,' Saskia said. 'But how can you possibly be so certain? Especially now I have even more proof that the ruins aren't within the castle walls.'

Elsa's gaze slid towards the gold coins again. Owen could almost see the cogs turning in her mind, trying to work out her next move.

'You know because of Richard, don't you?' Saskia pressed. 'Because it was Richard who asked his Harrow buddy Carlson to step in and do whatever he could to delay the build here at Gair. Was that his idea? Or yours? You thought you could push me right up to the edge of losing everything, and then swoop in and "save" me – or, more importantly, the money.'

'That is a very hurtful accusation, Saskia,' Elsa whispered.

'Who's putting this nonsense in your head? You're not thinking sensibly, darling. It's not surprising, really, you've been under so much pressure—'

'Stop,' Saskia said. 'Just *stop*.'

'But really,' her mother insisted. '*Darling*. If you actually take a moment to think about it rationally . . . I mean, who in their right mind would ever allow planning on this place?'

Saskia frowned. 'But they *did* allow planning. The review was called after it had already been agreed. It's so obviously a spurious claim, and it must be equally obvious to everyone involved that sooner or later it's going to fail. But that doesn't matter, does it? Because it was the delay that's important, wasn't it? Because you thought if it dragged on long enough, I'd have to give up.'

'It wouldn't be giving up,' Elsa said. 'It would be doing the sensible thing. I'm your mother, I'm trying to help you. I've done everything I can to get you out of this absurd situation you've got yourself into here. That's my good news, darling. Do you remember Lord Asket? He's been looking for a new hunting estate. I've persuaded him to buy this land from you. Just sell it, Saskia. Get rid of Gair.'

'Sell Gair, and then move back to live on your land in my little off-grid cabin?' Saskia asked. Her voice was very soft now, her gaze still fixed on her mother's face.

'I'm pretty sure that's what you *wanted* to do yesterday,' Elsa said, glancing at Owen, and then Vivian. 'Until someone clearly put other ideas in your head.'

'And what would happen with the money?' Saskia asked.

'The money from the sale of Gair, what's left of my inheritance? And now there's this too, isn't there?' She waved a finger at the gold, glinting from the table. 'I wouldn't use much of it, would I, living in a caravan on a patch of mud, out of sight on a forgotten corner of the estate. Would it just sit in my account? Or . . . would *you* look after it for me?'

'This isn't something to talk about right now, darling, in present company,' Elsa said. 'We'll discuss it all when the time comes.'

Vivian smiled. 'Oh, I just bet you would.'

'You stay out of it,' Elsa snapped, sharply. 'You've always been a terrible influence, Vivian.'

'That's enough,' Saskia said. 'Vivian and her parents have stood beside me through thick and thin. Which is more than I can say for the people who were supposed to be my family.'

'There's no need to take that tone,' Elsa said, feigning more hurt. 'You've already wasted most of your inheritance in a way that would have appalled even your father. Now you've got another chance. *We've* got another chance, darling. You can do better with this one. You can be part of your *real* family again. Isn't that what you really want?'

Owen watched Saskia, wondering what was going through her head at this moment. Was she tempted, he wondered, after all the struggles, all the heartache and hardship, to agree to her mother's suggestion? It would be easier, wouldn't it? And he remembered what she'd said, as they had sat side by side in the Gair Oak, his arm around her shoulders. That she was alone. He'd understood then that she didn't want to be. She wasn't Tim, a hermit whose only wish was to escape the world of people. In coming to Gair, she'd been searching for the family she'd lost. But that was Elsa, wasn't it? Every family had its faults. He couldn't blame Saskia for wanting the sense of connection that came with her own family, despite their flaws. Anyway, who was he to want her to tell this woman to piss off? He'd left her too, hadn't he? Saskia had needed him to be a solution, but he'd ended up being another problem. He had no right to want her to choose the difficult, lonely path that would see her here at Gair, alone.

But after a moment, Saskia shook her head. 'Do you know what's really offensive about all this?' she asked, quietly. 'It's that Richard couldn't even be bothered to come and ask for my help himself.'

'What?' Elsa whispered, her face paling.

'I really wanted to believe you yesterday,' Saskia said. 'I really did. Everything you said, about us having another chance to repair our relationship. About me having a home and a family with you, the twins and Richard. But the thing is, I know the truth now. I should have known all along that none of this was ever about me, about *us*. It was always only ever about you. I know what a hole he's dug for you, Mother,' she added. 'And you're not digging yourself out of it with my money. You're not getting any of it. I'll think about putting some in trust for the twins, but that's it. The Prick can deal with his own problems.'

'Don't call him—'

'As you pointed out,' Saskia said, her voice an infinity of ice. 'This is my land, and I'll call him anything I like while I stand on it. It's time for you to go. Owen, this is a building site and Mrs Cavendish isn't wearing a hard hat. She needs to leave. If she refuses, feel free to call the police.'

Thirty-Five

Julie asked if she could join Saskia when she went to visit Tim Burney, but Saskia thought it would probably be better to go alone. She knew from Christopher that his brother had been released from police custody without charge, and Tim was now staying with him in his apartment in Glasgow. Saskia didn't know quite what she was going to find when she went to see him, but she was fairly sure it wouldn't include a warm welcome.

Christopher himself wasn't there when Saskia arrived. She half wondered whether Tim would let her in at all. It took a long time for the concierge to get him to answer, but eventually she was told she could go up. The journey in the lift seemed to take longer this time, and Saskia was struck by how very divorced from nature the tower block was. The air was recycled, the enclosed lift letting in no sense of what was beyond. She could have been sealed inside a rocket, hurtling through the endless emptiness of space.

The door to Christopher's apartment was already open a

crack when she got to his floor. 'Hello?' she called, as she peered around it. 'Anyone home?'

'That depends on your definition of home really, doesn't it?' Tim's deep voice cut to her across the silence of the pristine space. 'Either way, I suppose you'd better come in.'

He was sitting on the sofa with his hands clasped between his knees, staring out of the floor-to-ceiling window at the city. As she got nearer, Saskia was struck by his appearance. Tim was far more unkempt now than she had ever seen him in his forest home, as if here, enclosed in this perfectly constructed modern space, he himself was beginning to unravel.

'Hi,' she said, when she stood beside him. 'Thanks for letting me come up.'

He grunted, but didn't move or look up at her. Saskia perched on the other end of the sofa. He didn't offer her a drink, but then she hadn't expected that he would.

'What do you want?' Tim asked. 'Come to make sure I'm safely distant while you get back to destroying – oh, I'm sorry, I mean *preserving* – Gair?'

Saskia let the bitter jibe go. 'I just wanted to see how you're getting on and bring you a few things I thought you might want.' She pushed the holdall she'd brought with her towards him a little. It contained the whittled chess set, among other things. 'And also to ask you about this.' From her pocket, Saskia took a small velvet pouch, which she opened and then upended onto her palm. One of the Roman coins fell out and lay there, as polished and golden as the day it had first been minted more than two thousand years before.

Tim gave his trademark twisted smile and reached for it. He held it up, rolling it between thumb and forefinger so that the precious metal caught the sterile light of his brother's apartment. 'I wondered how long it'd take you to find these. Pretty, aren't they?'

'That's one word for them,' Saskia agreed. 'Spectacular would be another.'

He nodded and dropped the coin back into her hand. 'What do you want to know?'

'Well, to be honest it's not me so much as the archaeologists,' Saskia told him. 'You've got quite a lot of people very excited. Actually, it'd be great if you'd be willing to talk to them yourself. I know they'd prefer that than getting it second-hand from me.'

Tim stared out of the window again, his expression dark. 'That's it then, is it? You've got the dirt devils in to winkle everything out?'

'Not quite yet, no,' she said. 'They're due to come in from next week.' She didn't tell him that there had already been an initial visit: a team of students and their professor from Lancaster University, so excited by the discovery that they had been almost overwhelmed. That had been one of her stipulations when she'd confirmed the existence of the ruins to the judicial review board: that there would be an entirely new team, independent of either her or the local LPA, allowed to access the ruins. Neither Nathan nor anyone else with any connection to the Historical Society would be part of the dig.

Tim nodded, but didn't look at her. She realized he was depressed. Deeply so, and probably sliding deeper by the day. Her sense of guilt was renewed, twisting in her gut as she looked at him, surrounded by material comfort and yet finding none. She knew how that felt. She'd been there herself.

'Look,' she said, taking the coin back and returning it to the pouch. 'You must know the gold alone is worth a fortune. I want you to know that once it's sold, I'm going to split the portion coming to me as landowner with you. It was your find, after all. Or maybe it was more than one find? That's one of the details the professor wants to know.'

He glanced at her. 'I'm not interested in money.'

'I know that,' she agreed. 'But think about what it could do for you, Tim. That forest you always wanted to buy for yourself? Maybe that's not so out of your reach after all. Or at least, some house on a plot somewhere so remote you never have to see anyone ever again if you don't want to.'

Tim frowned. 'That sounds good.'

She stood up to go. 'I thought it might.'

He nodded, gaze fixed on some non-existent place beyond the tower block's window. 'Still. It wouldn't be Gair.'

'No, it wouldn't,' she agreed. Saskia reached out and squeezed his shoulder. 'But it could be close, don't you think? Hang in there. And if you decide you're up for talking about what you found at Gair – about your whole experience, actually – let me know.'

*

When she got back to Gair, Saskia saw Ziggy's van coming in the other direction along the track. They stopped beside each other, winding down their windows.

'Hey,' the postman said, with his usual cheerful grin. 'Good timing. You need a post box.' He passed her a thin sheaf of letters that sat beside him on the empty passenger seat.

'Thanks.'

'Fingers crossed you've got some good news among that lot,' he said.

'We can but hope, eh?' she said, with a smile.

They said their goodbyes and he pulled past her, flashing his rear lights in a final farewell as he disappeared between the trees. Saskia dropped the letters onto the passenger seat and pulled up to the gates, glancing at her watch as she hopped out to open it. It was just after three.

She opened the door to her quiet little cabin to find Brodie on the other side, wagging his tail vigorously and huffing with excitement. She had left him with Julie, who had been due to take more photos of Tim's place anyway. The journalist had been happy to look after the dog for a few hours while Saskia went up to Glasgow, though she'd had to leave Brodie in the cabin before his owner got back.

'Sorry, boy,' Saskia said, rubbing behind his ears, feeling guilty that her faithful hound had been cooped up, even if only for a couple of hours. 'Come on, let's go for a big walk, shall we?'

He bounded past her and she went to place the sheaf of

letters on the counter, but one caught her eye. She removed it from the bundle, seeing the official council seal beside the postmark, and tore it open.

UPDATE TO JUDICIAL REVIEW, the bold letters read in the centre of the letter-headed page. They were followed beneath by lines so brief they barely took up half the space.

Ms Tilbury-Martin,

This is to inform you that the Judicial Review into the granting of planning permission at Gair Castle Estate in Cumbria has been dismissed.

There will be no adjustment of the original planning. You are free to continue work.

Yours sincerely,
Agnes Drayton, Secretary

Saskia's heart thumped painfully as she stared at the words before her. That was it, then. All that time wasted, all that *money* wasted, all those men lost from her workforce, and this was what it all came down to. A resumption of the status quo, with no explanation, apology or compensation.

She looked out through her open door at Gair, the ruins and the partial reconstruction spread out below her like an unfinished song. She waited for the joy to kick in, to flood out the anxiety and guilt. But it didn't come. She thought instead of what her mother had said.

Your father would be appalled.

Saskia wondered if those words would ever lose their

potency, if she would ever be able to dismiss them as simply more of her mother's biting selfishness. She walked down towards the castle with the letter still in her hand and for the first time, Saskia found the work that Owen's team had managed to complete uncomfortable. The steel baseplates, for a floor that had yet to be poured, glared in the afternoon sunlight, making her squint in a way that the soft-grey stone of the old castle walls did not. She went to the oak and laid her cheek against its rough bark, shutting her eyes. She saw Tim, staring out of his brother's window, desolate in his dubious comfort.

You're destroying it.

Was it true? She'd thought she was doing the right thing. She'd thought she had found a way to preserve both the castle and the oak, the quest that had kept her going her whole life, that had put her back on a path somewhere instead of the nowhere she had been headed after her spiral into that deep darkness. But had she missed the point? The important thing, she was now beginning to realize, was not preserving things as they were but finding a way to respect them as they would become. Again, another thing she'd thought she'd been doing. But had she, really? Her quest to rebuild Gair had been more about her than it had about this place. She'd wanted to prove herself: to her father, to her mother. To herself. She'd wanted to prove that she could do something that no one else had managed to do. She'd ignored the possibility that perhaps the whole point was that no one was supposed to do it in the first place.

Tim had the right idea, she thought, helplessly. *That's how you live with nature. Not . . . like this. Not by bending it around your will.*

But what, then? What was she to do now? This failure was deeper than the rest – wasn't it? – because it was so deep-rooted, so wrong-headed. Saskia found herself wishing she'd never come here, that she'd never known about her family's connection to this place, that she'd never been born with her father's talent.

She turned, despondent, to call for Brodie, and saw her little home standing among the trees on the edge of the clearing above them. It looked elegant in the mid-afternoon light, the soft-grey paint of its wooden cladding blending well into its surroundings. If she had chosen a green colour instead, it would be even more camouflaged. It did not tower over the trees but melded with them. It sat happily amid the landscape, and if she were inside it now, so would she. Her life would continue; she would potter about inside its minimal walls, leaving no mark outside them.

She leaned back against the enduring oak and contemplated this for a while.

Thirty-Six

Owen was on his way back from picking Hannah up from school when he received the text from Saskia, so it sat unopened while he dropped his daughter off at her after-school ballet class and let Tasha know she'd arrived safely. This wasn't usually a school run day for him, but Hannah's mother was poorly – some summer flu thing – and though Owen had now formally accepted the job in Collaton he had yet to start, so it was easy enough for him to fill in. He got back in his car after he'd seen Hannah in at the door, with an hour to kill before she'd be ready to come out again. He pulled out his phone, saw that the text was from Saskia and opened it to find a photograph of a letter. The judicial review had been dismissed. The note with the picture read: *Thought you'd like to know. No explanation, but still. It's over. Hope all is well with you. Sas x*

He read through the letter again, mystified by the lack of detail in a communication that was so monumental for the recipient. He thought about calling her, but decided that he'd simply visit, instead.

'I wonder how she'll manage?' Tasha had mused, when Owen had told her that he had confirmed the job at Collaton. 'Without you, I mean, and the rest of the team? What will she do now?'

It was a question that was stuck in his mind, too, and Owen continued to ponder it as he drove up to the castle. Now Saskia's mother and those machinations had been removed, would she want to get back to the build? Owen still felt as if he'd abandoned her. But he'd committed to Collaton now. There was no way he could work on both sites. He'd been trying hard to find her a replacement from further afield and had passed on a few of the more promising contacts in case she'd wanted to get in touch. Adrian had mentioned a Norwegian crew he was thinking of bringing in if they fell short of workers, for example.

Owen drove through Gair's main gates and parked beside Saskia's Land Rover, pausing with his forearms on the steering wheel to look down at the site. It felt wrong to think of someone else completing the build he had only just begun. He loved it here, Owen realized. It felt peculiarly like home in a way that nowhere had for a very long time. When had that happened? When had this place moved from being a necessity, or a burden, to somewhere he missed when he had to be elsewhere? He had a sneaking suspicion that it could all be connected back to that night he had found Saskia camping out amid the ruins, and he'd asked her a simple question.

Why is Gair so important to you?

That night had been a turning point in so many ways.

Not only in how he saw Gair and this project, but in how he saw Saskia herself. Now he was confronted by the reality of not seeing her every day, he realized how much her face was in his thoughts when he was not in her presence. He remembered that afternoon he'd spent with her at the 'swimming pool' with Hannah, seeing how good she was with his daughter and those tell-tale scars on her arms, realizing what they meant. How, when Hannah had fallen into that hole, she had not hesitated to go in head-first after her where he could not follow.

He didn't really want to leave, he finally admitted to himself, and that had less to do with Gair and more to do with Saskia herself. He didn't want this to be the last time he saw her, spoke to her, spent time with her.

Owen got out of the car, retrieved the gift he'd picked up on the way through town and walked into sunlight. Below him the castle ruins stood resplendent, the great oak at their centre. He was struck by the peace of the place and paused for a moment, eyes closed, to listen to a silence broken only by breeze and birdsong. He saw that the archaeologists' trenches had been backfilled and the grass was already beginning to grow back over them. Soon it would be hard to tell anything had happened there at all.

The door to Saskia's cabin was open, Brodie lounging in a late-summer sunbeam that fell through the door and onto the floor beyond. The dog leapt up when he saw Owen coming, huffing and puffing in hello. Owen scratched the creature behind the ears, leaning through the door. He couldn't see

Saskia anywhere, but since Brodie was here, she couldn't be far away. Was it possible she was taking a nap? He hesitated, not wanting to walk in without invitation. Owen raised a hand and knocked on the open door, calling out at the same time.

'Hello? Anyone home?'

He heard a creak from within and then she appeared, leaning back on the stool that stood in front of her drawing board in the tiny office at the other end of the tiny house. She had her glasses on, and he could see, in one hand, a pencil.

'Owen!' she said, sounding genuinely pleased to see him. 'Come in! Did you get my text?'

'I did,' he said, stepping through the door and holding up the chocolate cake he'd brought with him as a celebration. 'I thought I'd come and congratulate you in person.'

She stood, smiling, pencil still clutched in one hand, as if she'd forgotten it was there. 'That's kind of you. Coffee?'

'Sure, that'd be great. Although,' he added, glancing past her to where the stool now stood away from her drawing board, 'I don't want to interrupt if you're working.'

She smiled again and something about the expression surprised him. It was warm, perhaps even a little excited, and Owen realized that he hadn't expected her to be so unreservedly happy, if only because of the worries he'd had. Who would take his place to carry on with the rebuilding of Gair, if that's what she had decided to do? Had she forgotten that he was now committed elsewhere? Or – and this thought put an unexpectedly strong pang of regret through his heart – had it been easier to replace him than she'd thought, and she'd already gone ahead and done just that? Somehow the thought that she might have filled his slot already was upsetting, though he tried to hide it.

'You're not interrupting,' she said. 'Come and look at what I've been doing. I'd like your opinion on it, anyway.'

He ducked his head to enter the tiny room. It was only the second time he'd been inside it, the first being that night he'd realized, among so many other things, that there was more to her ideas for Gair than a rich girl's whim. Saskia spun the stool back around to face her drawing board, and he saw how comfortable she was, as if this was a natural position for her, as if this was her natural place. In front of her, on the board, was an A1 sheet of paper. On it he recognized the outline of Gair – not only the castle, but the clearing in which it stood, as well as the edges of the forest, right up to the river. What Saskia had mapped out in clear, minimalist lines was almost the entirety of her domain. The oak stood, as ever, at its centre, the walls of the castle spindling from it like the partial passage of a spirograph. There was no sign of her grand design for the rebuilding of the castle. This was the land as it had stood before their work had even started.

'It's . . . Gair,' he said, unsure what he was supposed to be seeing.

'Look closer,' she said, shifting on her stool.

He did, although that meant leaning right over her shoulder, so close that he could smell the familiar almond scent of her shampoo. Studying the lines he saw that there were small structures sketched amid the trees, rectangular but with pitched angles. He thought for a moment they were a series of sheds. Then, when he searched for Saskia's tiny home and found it, Owen realized that these other structures were identical.

He looked from the drawing board to her, trying to work out the meaning of what was in front of them. 'I'm not sure I understand,' he said. 'What is this?'

'I've been going about this in completely the wrong way since the start,' she said. '*This* is what I should have been doing. This is how you really live with nature. You blend with it. You slot yourself into it. You take up as little room and resources as possible. You live small. The way I've already been doing for years.'

Owen tried to take this in. 'But your dad—'

'I was wrong,' she said. 'And for all her faults, I think my mother is telling me the truth, or part of it, anyway. Dad's "problem" was never meant to be solved, at least not beyond theory. I would have found that out if he'd lived. I probably would have realized it myself if I hadn't been so single-minded. It was an exercise, that's all. It was supposed to open his students' minds to possibility and to make them think closely about the environments in which they were building. About not destroying in order to create.' She put down her pencil as Owen leaned back, and then she turned to face him with her hands clasped in her lap.

'I went to see Tim Burney again,' she said. 'It was awful, Owen. He's so unhappy, and it's my fault.' Owen began to protest at this, but she raised a hand. 'It *is*. It doesn't matter if it was the right thing to do, it doesn't matter if it was the only thing I could do. *This* is where he wants to be. It's where he's always going to want to be – like me.'

'Wait . . .' Owen said, looking at her sketch again. Those little houses, hidden among the trees. 'Are you thinking of bringing him back here?'

She turned, looked at the sketch with him. 'I can design a tiny home that'll suit his requirements exactly. It would be safe, warm and *here*. At Gair, among the trees. This is where he wants to be, Owen. This where he'll be happy. Close enough to civilization to be reachable, but far enough away that he can pretend he's still the only person in the forest, if that's what he wants.'

Owen tried to take in this new idea of hers. There were more than two dwellings sketched among the trees. 'But . . . what about the castle? What about preserving it?'

She turned her head; looked back to her new idea for Gair. 'Tim and I can't be the only people who would like the idea of living here. Part of that would mean becoming a caretaker of the castle, the oak, the forest, the river, the ruins . . . Living here would mean being willing to take that on, as a community. It'd be part of the lease conditions. But to be honest I would imagine anyone interested in living this far off the beaten track would already be the kind of person who'd be up for that.'

'Not Vivian, then?' he hazarded, and she laughed.

'No . . . probably not Vivian. Although she'd always be here to help if I asked. I know that much.'

Owen contemplated the sketch again. 'This would mean taking up the foundations we've already laid?'

'Yes,' she said. 'Don't worry, I know you won't be able to take that on. I'm going to look into ways I can reuse or recycle the steel sheeting.' She looked up at him. 'You think I'm mad, don't you?'

He rested a hand on her shoulder. 'No, I don't. Of course I don't. Why don't we go out and take a look at where you're thinking of putting these units?'

Together they went back out into the sun, Brodie at their heels. They slowly toured the site together, first going to the patch of ground deep in the forest that Saskia thought would work well for the first cabin: her proposed new home for Tim.

'It's far enough into the tree canopy to feel very isolated, and as you can see there's a natural clearing, so we wouldn't need to log out any trees,' she pointed out, as they both turned in place, surveying the site.

Owen nodded, his hands on his hips as he looked around. 'I think it's perfect.'

She smiled. 'You do?'

'Well, for Tim,' he amended. 'What about his neighbours, though? From what I can tell he won't want any at all. How many homes are you thinking?'

'There'll only be two, maybe three cabins, besides his . . . and mine. Which I'd probably leave exactly where it is, to be honest. Although I might paint it,' she added as they began to walk to the suggested site of the next dwelling. 'I'd like them all to blend in to the forest and mine could do that better. I thought that perhaps one of the archaeologists working in the ruins would like to live on site at least some of the time.'

They walked on, listening to the birds sing around them as Saskia showed him the areas she thought would work. Owen agreed with all of them. Each already had reasonable access and wouldn't require a lot of clearing of full-grown trees; the ground was level and far enough from the main ruins at Gair for privacy without being too isolated.

'You know this place well,' Owen observed. 'I mean, I already knew that you had the castle ruins and the oak mapped in your head, but since you've been here that seems to have expanded to the whole forest.'

'Not the whole forest,' she countered. 'But Brodie and I have spent so much time walking here together. It feels like home. It *is* home.'

He stopped beneath a sycamore tree. She walked on for a few paces and then turned back to him.

'Then how will you feel about having strangers moving into your home?' he asked. 'Sure you won't hate it once they're here?'

He watched as Saskia thought about what he'd said. The afternoon was warm; the dappled sunlight glanced off Saskia's cheekbones. She was wearing a white tank top, and it was only as Owen took in how the sunlight glowed against the freckled skin of her shoulders that he realized she wasn't wearing her usual long-sleeved shirt. She'd been comfortable enough with him not to cover her arms as soon as he'd arrived. The shirt was tied around her waist instead, a soft apple-green that blended with the olive drab of her ubiquitous work trousers. Her long dark hair was loose across her shoulders and Brodie sat at her heels, a shaggy golden sentinel at the feet of a forest guardian. She fit so well into this landscape that she seemed to him then to be a part of it – a true part, as essential as the great Gair Oak or the river, and as irremovable, too.

'I think,' she said, 'that as long as I choose carefully and they are here for the right reasons; as long as they feel about Gair the same way that I do and that Tim does . . . it'll be fine. Good, even, maybe. It can get lonely up here, even for someone who likes their own company. I know that from experience.'

He smiled. 'Very important to choose the right people, then.'

'Yes.' She took a step back towards him as Brodie went snuffling off into the brush. 'It would need to be the kind of person who would immerse themselves in living at Gair. They would probably need to be part of the build process for the homes, too. I can't build them all myself, not alone.'

'It would be a lot of work for one person,' he agreed.

'Which means,' she spread her hands, 'someone with building experience would be good.'

'Hmm,' he said, watching her as she moved closer. 'All that in one person? Sounds like quite a tall order.'

'I know. That's why I was hoping you might have some suggestions on that score.'

'I might have one, yeah.'

Saskia tilted her head to one side, her dark eyes sparkling. 'You do?'

They looked at each other for a moment. 'Well,' Owen said, slowly, feeling oddly light-headed. 'I was thinking that Hannah would really, really love the idea of visiting her dad every weekend and holiday she could if he lived at a castle.'

He was unprepared for the strength of her smile. Wide, genuine. Dazzling. 'You?'

Owen found himself smiling back. 'Why not? You need help building these cabins – I can do that, even if I'm employed at Collaton. Actually, I've already got some suggestions for ways you could incorporate some of the innovations I've seen down there into this development. They could work really well and it's the perfect environment. In fact, you should probably come down and meet the folks there anyway. With all your ideas, you'd be a great part of the team. Tasha might want to take on the house I've put in for down there; it'll give her a chance to get out of that poky flat.'

She was still smiling when she said, 'But would you really want to be my neighbour? You hated me when we first met.'

'Hate is a strong word,' he said.

'You did, though.'

'I didn't *hate* you,' he told her. 'I . . . had strong reservations about you.'

'I didn't think much of you, either,' she said, teasing. 'For the record.'

'I remember. That was a long time ago now though. Or at least, it feels like it.'

'It does,' Saskia admitted. Then there was a pause, in which she looked away, though her smile remained in place. 'What about now?'

'Now?'

Saskia looked back at him. In her eyes he saw shadows, but behind them was the soft light of hope, too.

'I'm not sure that what I think matters,' Owen said, then. 'But what I *know* is this. I know that you are the kind of person who will give someone like me a chance on the biggest project of their career despite a lack of track record and the huge chip on my shoulder. I know that you spent a lifetime and a fortune thinking about a single tree. I know that you are willing to set aside the only thing you ever wanted and everything you ever worked for because going a different route is the better thing to do. I know I want to help you achieve anything you want to achieve. And,' he added, his voice softer now, 'I know I want to get to know you – really *know* you, Saskia – while we accomplish it.'

Saskia took a small breath and looked away. When she spoke, her voice was very quiet. 'You know, relationships are something else that traditionally I've been *very* bad at.'

He nodded. 'I understand that feeling. But how about we just start with this?'

Owen reached out and took her hand, tugging her towards him until she was pressed up against him and he was backed up against the tree. He held her against him and could feel her heart, hammering in time with his as her hands rested at his hips.

'I've been thinking about what this would feel like for a lot longer than I should have,' Owen confessed, quietly, as he ran his fingers through her loose hair.

Saskia laughed a little, the movement of her against him shivering through his ribcage. 'Yeah,' she sighed. 'Me too. It's probably a terrible idea, though, isn't it?'

'No,' he said, leaning in. 'Actually, I think it's probably one of the best ideas I've had for about six years.'

Their lips met in a kiss that began softly but quickly gained momentum. It was hot and long, as if both of them might have thought about this quite a lot and equally thought it would never actually happen. Her hands found their way beneath his shirt, and Owen sucked in a breath as they moved up his back. He turned their bodies around, pushed her gently up against the tree and, somewhere amid the tumult and joy, he thought that this could never have happened anywhere but here, in an ancient forest surrounding a ruined castle in the last wild borderland between England and Scotland.

Later, they walked slowly back towards the ruins of Gair, hand in hand. The sun was setting earlier now that September was approaching, the shadows around them lengthening as they threaded through the trees. At the edge of the forest, Saskia came to a stop, surveying the landscape that rolled away from them into the falling dusk.

'This is going to work this time, isn't it?' she asked, quietly. 'We'll make it work.'

Owen let go of her hand, but only so that he could loop his arm over her shoulders and pull her closer. Saskia crooked her head into his chest and wrapped both arms around him.

'It's already working,' he said. 'Because you're here.'

Owen let go of her hand, but only so that he could loop his arm over her shoulders and pull her closer. Saskia crooked her head into his chest and wrapped both arms around him.

'It's already working,' he said. 'Because you're here.'

Acknowledgements

The idea of a woman trying to rebuild a castle and the builder who was willing to help her do it has been in my head for quite a while. I first wrote an early iteration of the story of as a very short tale for *The People's Friend* quite a few years ago. It changed a lot to reach this final form, but it was the then-editor of the *Friend*, Shirley Blair, who showed an enthusiasm for the story and convinced me that there might be something there that I should hold on to. Actually, Shirley was one of the earliest editors to show interest in my writing for adults (I'd already written a lot for children and young adults), so huge thanks to her for the encouragement. I've always had a love for trees, and especially old grandfather oaks. As I was looking for a way to turn the idea for what became *The Forest Hideaway* into a longform novel, I came across *The Oak Papers* by James Canton. A beautifully personal account of his relationship with an ancient oak and the transformative nature of the connection he had with the tree, it was a great influence on how I formed Saskia's love for the Gair oak. It's also where I came across the folk saying that prefaces this book, which I love. The original title for this book was 'What Will Survive', which is taken from the last line of the Philip Larkin poem 'From an Arundel Tomb', about the monuments we erect and what messages they unintentionally convey, when really the only important thing we can ever leave behind is love, whatever we might have actually intended. I hope Saskia's story encapsulates this sentiment. I hope we can find a way of saving more trees. I can't think of a better way of showing love for the next generation than making sure there are still forests for them to walk in. Except, of course, for making sure they have somewhere safe and affordable to live . . .

As always, I have to thank my invaluable editors at Simon & Schuster, Louise Davies and Clare Hey, for their brilliant guidance, expertise and patience in the development and execution of this book. Thank you to my agent, Ella Kahn, for so very many things but especially for patiently talking me through the inevitable mid-first-draft meltdown. Thank you to brand manager Sara-Jade Virtue, who is brilliant in all ways, and has been doing such amazing work with her 'Respect Rom Fic' mission. Because where are we going, if we are not going to love? Thank you to Pip Watkins for the most vibrant, amazing cover. And, as always, thank you to my husband, Adam Newell, for always being my oak.